# Rainbows Are Better

Carol Marie Lowe

ISBN 978-1-68526-075-0 (Paperback)
ISBN 978-1-68526-076-7 (Digital)

Copyright © 2023 Carol Marie Lowe
All rights reserved
First Edition

All rights reserved. No part of this publication may be reproduced, distributed, or transmitted in any form or by any means, including photocopying, recording, or other electronic or mechanical methods without the prior written permission of the publisher. For permission requests, solicit the publisher via the address below.

Covenant Books
11661 Hwy 707
Murrells Inlet, SC 29576
www.covenantbooks.com

# Contents

Introduction ..................................................................... v

Chapter 1: Sidney Davis ............................................... 1
Chapter 2: Life at the Orphanage ................................ 4
Chapter 3: Starting a New Life .................................... 9
Chapter 4: Another New Beginning .......................... 16
Chapter 5: When Love Walks In ................................ 23
Chapter 6: A New Little Friend ................................. 39
Chapter 7: Home, Sweet Home ................................. 51
Chapter 8: Servants and All ....................................... 54
Chapter 9: Sidney's First Houseguest ........................ 65
Chapter 10: The Woes of Being the Boss .................. 70
Chapter 11: Clothing Galore ..................................... 77
Chapter 12: Let the Building Begin .......................... 82
Chapter 13: Dating Is the Good Life ...................... 103
Chapter 14: Moving in Begins ................................. 117
Chapter 15: Those Strange Feelings Again ............. 122
Chapter 16: Happy Days Are Here at Last ............. 137
Chapter 17: Things Are Changing ........................... 142
Chapter 18: The Worst Was Yet to Come ............... 152
Chapter 19: There Has to Be a Way to Heal .......... 160
Chapter 20: There Has to Be Some Other Way ..... 169
Chapter 21: Hiring a Helper .................................... 172
Chapter 22: Life Is Getting Rosie ............................ 181

Chapter 23: Searching for a Family ............................................. 190
Chapter 24: Can't Hide from Love .............................................. 218
Chapter 25: Wedding Bells Will Finally Ring ........................... 232
Chapter 26: Let the Honeymoons Begin .................................. 238
Chapter 27: The Trip to Tibet ..................................................... 243
Chapter 28: Time to Visit Denver .............................................. 251
Chapter 29: The Family Grows .................................................. 261
Chapter 30: Her Life's Work Begins .......................................... 277
Chapter 31: What's in a Color? .................................................. 279

# Introduction

It was a cold and dreary night in New York City as a young professional couple were driving home. Their names were Martha and Leander Davis. They had just enjoyed a magnificent dinner and a soul-inspiring evening at the ballet. They were celebrating their tenth wedding anniversary. Happily they were headed home to their wonderful little girl, whom they loved so much. As they were driving along, Martha expressed to Leander how much she would like to take Sidney (their little girl) to the ballet. He totally agreed with her. They both knew Sidney loved dancing, and the ballet would be right up her alley. Suddenly, out of nowhere, a pickup truck came streaking across the median strip at high speed and hit them head-on. The man driving the pickup truck was so drunk, he didn't even know what happened. The truth is, even if he had known that he just killed two wonderful, innocent people, he could not have comprehended the true damage he had done. He had not only robbed Martha and Leander of their very lives but had also forever altered their daughter's life. He affected Sidney's life in ways he couldn't imagine. He had also drastically changed the lives of all the people their lives had touched.

    Few people who drink and drive realize the far-reaching damage they may cause. They damage not only their own lives in ways they never imagined but also the many lives their bad judgment will change. The chain of events they set in motion is more far-reaching than anyone can comprehend. All this as a result of their careless disregard for the lives and the safety of others on the road. For some unknown reason, they always tell themselves, and everyone else, drinking doesn't affect them that way. It isn't until after the fact that some of them, not all, are willing to admit they should never drink and drive. Sadly, this man could not admit what a terrible mistake he had made.

This is the story of how that fateful night transformed Sydney's life from that day forward.

# Chapter 1

## *Sidney Davis*

Sidney Marie Davis was the daughter of Martha and Leander Davis. She was an only child, who was always happy, witty, intuitive, and extremely intelligent. Her parents were so proud of her. Martha and Leander were upper middle class, and they enjoyed a very comfortable lifestyle. Their Black heritage was very important to them, so they passed this on to Sidney.

Sidney and her parents enjoyed living in an upper-class neighborhood in Manhattan, New York. They had a lovely and rather large two-story English Tudor brick home. When you entered their house, you could feel the warmth and love that filled every square inch. There was a tremendous amount of love and caring shared there. Martha was a very talented, self-employed interior decorator who earned a considerable income. Martha liked her work because it enabled her to be home with Sidney most of the time.

Leander and his partner, Sam Stiener, owned a very successful stock-brokerage firm. Leander and Sam had been good friends since college. When they graduated, starting a business together seemed only natural. Leander and Martha felt they were on top of the world, with good friends, a great marriage, the most wonderful little girl, and a lovely home. It seemed as though nothing could be more perfect than the life they had. They were extremely happy. On weekends, twice a month, they did charity work. They took Sidney with them so she would never take her blessings for granted. They wanted her to understand the plight of those who were not so fortunate.

Sidney loved these times with her parents. It made her very proud to know what kind and loving people her parents were. They were good not just to her, but to everyone.

Every Sunday, they attended the church a few blocks from their home. This always made Sidney happy because she could always feel God's presence there. She always said she took the angels home to guard her. Once, she asked her mother if there were real angels or if she was just imagining they were all around her. Martha took Sidney in her arms and said, "Of course there are angels. They are all around you every minute of every day of your life." Sidney said, "I'm glad I have angels to watch over me. I'm really happy to have you and Daddy to love me and take care of me." Martha (hugging her little darling even tighter now) said to Sidney, "Your father and I will always be close by to watch over you, no matter what happens." Sidney thought about that for a while. Then she asked, "Even if you and Daddy are out of town on a long trip?" Martha assured Sidney there was no trip so far away they wouldn't be there for her. She told Sidney, all she had to do was call them, and they would be there for her. Sidney felt very comforted by this and snuggled into bed for a peaceful night's sleep.

Unfortunately, good things don't always last forever. On that cold and rainy night, when Sidney was only eight years old, her parents were both killed by a drunk driver. At that very moment, Sidney's happy, secure life turned upside down. Sidney had never known any relatives. Leander was an only child, and his parents had both passed on. Martha's parents and only sister were killed in a tragic fire while Martha was away at college. As far as Sidney knew, she had no family without her parents. What a terrible, frightening, and lonely time for any child to endure. Sidney felt as though her heart would surely break. She wanted desperately for someone, anyone, to come to her rescue and make everything all right. Unfortunately, this was not to be the case.

Martha and Leander thought they had prepared for their daughter's future if anything should happen to them. In their will, they even made arrangements for Leander's friend, Sam, to be their little girl's guardian. Sam was going to take care of everything, or so they thought. Well, he took care of everything, all right, or perhaps I should say he just took everything. It seems good old Sam wasn't as good a friend as Martha and Leander had thought. Sam had pretended to be Leander's friend in college because Leander was smart and he helped Sam get through school. Sam went into business with Leander because he knew he couldn't make it on his own. Sam had been embezzling money for years. He had been making rather-substantial deposits in a Swiss bank account in his name only.

When Leander died, it was the perfect time for Sam to announce the company insolvent and declare bankruptcy. He had no intention of taking care of Sidney. He made arrangements to have Sidney put in a Harlem orphanage. After all, that was where he felt she belonged. Not Manhattan! Sam delivered Sidney, her clothing, a few toys, and a pillow her mother had made for her to the social workers. He took care of this the very next day after the accident. He then let the IRS sell the house and all the belongings to cover the back taxes he had not been paying on the business. Then, good old Sam left the country and never looked back or felt any remorse.

# Chapter 2

# *Life at the Orphanage*

Sidney was taken to the orphanage, which she would have to call home for the next few years. She had all her clothes and toys taken away from her. No one at the orphanage was allowed to own anything. They felt it would make the other children feel bad that they had nothing while she had such nice things. Everything became community property. They did let her keep the pillow. This was all right with Sidney; she was just happy to have the pillow her mother had made for her.

The day of the funeral, a social worker came to pick her up and take her to the church where the funeral would be held. This was so hard. Sidney looked around and saw there were a lot of people her parents had helped there. They all felt sorry for Sidney, but they were people who needed help and weren't able to help her. She noticed none of her parents' rich friends were there. They didn't go to the funeral, because they didn't want to feel bad about deserting little Sidney in her time of need. After the funeral, Sidney was returned to the orphanage, where she was left to grieve alone.

At the orphanage, she was treated like any other child they knew would not be adopted. To them, she was just another mouth to feed and take care of. On the day of the funeral, they excused Sidney from her chores and allowed her to spend the day alone in her room. A room that also belonged to nine other children. Sidney was fond of this room because it had a large window with a ledge she could sit on. She was happy she could sit there and see the stars at night. This and her faith were to be Sidney's only salvation during her time at the orphanage. That day, she was totally numb from grief and sadness. She had never been so alone and frightened in her young life. That night, she said her prayers, curled up with her pillow, and cried herself to sleep, just as she had done every night since the accident. She decided this would be her last time to cry like that. Crying only made her feel worse, and it didn't change anything.

Sidney soon learned the orphanage was a harsh place to live in. They had to get up early to do their chores before breakfast. After breakfast (usually oatmeal), they dressed in whatever they could find to wear and went to school. Sidney did exceptionally well in school. It gave her the opportunity to escape the unpleasant things going on in her life. She never forgot her parents telling her, if she worked hard, she could do anything she wanted to. Nothing would be impossible to her. Her dad always said, "If your mind can conceive it and your heart can believe it, then you can achieve it."

Although the people at the orphanage were usually grumpy and sometimes downright hateful, Sidney always smiled and tried to remember the happier times in her life. She did miss getting a hug once in a while and being tucked into bed at night. To make things better, she would hug the smaller children and tuck them into bed. This made the little ones happy. Somehow, this made Sidney feel closer to her parents and to the angels she knew were with her. After the evening chores and studying were done and the little ones were tucked into bed, Sidney would curl up on the windowsill, hugging her pillow, to say her prayers. She looked to the stars to find comfort and feel closer to her parents before going to bed. She knew it was good that they worked her so hard at the orphanage. That way, when it was bedtime, she was so exhausted, she fell asleep as soon as she laid her head on the pillow.

The days came and went at the orphanage, but nothing ever really got better. It was harsh, cold, and dreary there. Sure, there was an occasional caring person who would start working there. Sidney soon learned this wasn't something you could count on. If the people were nice, they didn't usually stay very long. They couldn't stand to see the children being so mistreated. They either left or were fired if they dared say anything in the children's defense. What can I say other than things were really bad in this place?

Sidney never let things overpower her or get her down. She knew this was only temporary. She also knew she was destined to have a better life than this. When things started getting her down, she worked that much harder toward the life she wanted. She made sure her grades were straight A's. To stay out of trouble at the orphanage; she worked extra hard.

Sidney accepted the other children as the little brothers and sisters she never had. This was the only thing that concerned her. She knew she would leave this place as soon as possible. She would miss them and worried about what would happen to them without her there to care for them. As the years rolled by, she began to distance herself from everyone. She knew, when the time came for her to leave, it wouldn't be so hard that way for her or the others.

As Sidney grew older, she began to develop into a very attractive young lady, although she was never aware of it. It's hard to know you're attractive when no one ever tells you you're pretty. There wasn't anyone to teach her things like wearing makeup, how to fix her hair, or how to wear her clothes. Luckily, she had some natural fashion sense. This was a real feat, what with having to wear whatever she could find. She just had a knack for putting odd things together and, somehow, making them look stylish. There were even times when she looked very elegant. Sidney had silky long black hair with just a little curl, you know, just enough to make it look perfect. She was light-skinned and very slender, with shapely long legs. She had soft large brown eyes and a smile to rival the sun itself. When the boys at school began to pay attention to her, she didn't know how to relate to them. She had no one to talk to about things like that, so she ignored them and went about her business. Sidney decided there would be plenty of time for boys later on, after she acquired an education.

Once, she was asked to go to a school dance. She had to say no because she had nothing to wear. Besides, she knew the custodians at the orphanage would never allow her to go. Sidney put her faith in God and remembered the words of her parents: "You can do anything you want to do, if you just want to bad enough." She worked even harder in school, doing extra work, even though she didn't need to. She was well aware, the more she learned, the better off she would be later on.

One day, in early spring, there was an incident at the orphanage. Someone stole some money from one of the workers' purse. Sidney, being the last one seen in the area, was accused of stealing it. She told them repeatedly that she would never do such a thing. They called her a liar and beat her with a strap they had for such occasions. This was an extremely bad beating. They wanted to make an example of her. That way, no one else would dare do that sort of thing again. Sidney went to her room and cried for the first time since her parents were buried. She wasn't crying just because the whelps were stinging and starting to swell and bruise, but because they believed she would do such a thing. She had never been dishonest or done anything wrong in her life. She knew, from now on, anything that happened there would be blamed on her. In their minds, she was now considered a bad seed.

She decided it was time to move on and find her own way. She was only fifteen years old at that time. She felt so frightened, she was sick at her stomach. Even though the orphanage was a terrible place to be, at least she had a bed, food, and somewhere to go to get out of the weather. What would be waiting for her out on the streets? At fifteen, she was too young to get a job. Lucky for Sidney, she looked older and, at five feet, seven inches, could easily pass for seventeen or eighteen years old. Scary or not, there was no other decision to make at this point.

She began to make plans to leave as safely as possible. Nothing worked like a good plan. Sidney never did anything without thinking it through and working out as many details as possible. That was just one of the good things about her. She never did anything without planning it carefully before taking action. After devising a plan, she visualized it over and over so as not to leave room for error. After a plan came into place, she worked tirelessly to make sure it would go smoothly. No detail was too small. She knew the most important thing would be getting a job. Then she could afford to rent an apartment and buy food. Living on the streets was not an option. Sidney knew it was too dangerous to be on the streets alone. She had to be able to support herself.

It wasn't going to be easy to find a job. First, she went to the post office and applied for a Social Security card. She had to sneak into her file at the orphanage to find her birth certificate. She had to do this without the workers catching her. While she was waiting for her card, she voluntarily cleaned tables at a diner for free. She knew they would see what a hard worker she was. She hoped that would get her a job there when her card arrived.

While she was helping out one day, she met the owner of the diner. A wonderful lady named Angel. Actually, her name was Angelica, but her husband had always called her Angel. Therefore, that was the name she had gone by for the past thirty-five years. Angel was a jovial widow who never had children of her own. She had salt-and-pepper hair and a round face, and you could say she was pleasingly plump. When you looked at her face, you could tell she laughed a lot. Something about Sidney made Angel love her from the day they first met.

When Sidney's Social Security card arrived, she went to Angel and asked for a job. Angel asked her what hours she could work. Sidney told her she could work from open until close. Angel asked her, "What about school?" Sidney lied (which she hated doing) and said she had already finished school last year. She told Angel she left home and was starting out on her own. Angel agreed to hire her and inquired where she would be staying. Sidney told her she hadn't found a place to stay yet. Angel offered to let Sidney rent a room from her. She told Sidney it would be close to work because she lived over the restaurant.

Sidney was thrilled to know she would have a place to stay, and she wouldn't have to be alone. She accepted with great delight. Angel and Sidney were about to become the best of friends. That night, after everyone had turned in at the orphanage, Sidney gathered what few things she had and snuck out. She was hoping no one would see her and try to stop her. It was her good fortune that no one noticed. The next day, when they noticed she was gone, they figured she had run away. They didn't really care. It was just one less kid to worry about.

# Chapter 3

# *Starting a New Life*

This was a new beginning for Sidney. She could scarcely believe she had escaped the horrible life at the orphanage. For the first time since her mom and dad died, she felt secure and cared about, not frightened. When she saw her room, she was so happy, she could have danced. It had a large window seat, like the one she had as a child. It was much nicer than the windowsill at the orphanage. How lucky could she get? Always being so grateful was a great thing about Sidney. She was always grateful for everything she ever got or anything good that ever happened to her. She loved the quiet, peaceful feeling of her room. Angel had decorated it in soft pink and cream, with burgundy accents. She had pastel pictures on the walls. This was amazing to Sidney. These were the same colors Sidney's mother had decorated Sidney's bedroom in. Sidney's little pillow, which was burgundy with pink stitching, fit right in.

Truly, God had guided Sidney to this place. With her landlord and employer having a name like Angel, how could she think otherwise? That night, after Sidney said her prayers, she sat in her window and looked to the heavens. She knew her parents had to be watching and feeling pleased to see her so happy again. She quietly asked God to bless her parents and Angel too. After sitting there for a while, she went to bed. She could have sworn, when she climbed into bed and pulled up the covers, she was being hugged by the bed and the covers. It was so comfortable and warm. It brought back warm and pleasant memories of her childhood, before the orphanage.

As soon as Sidney figured her monthly wages, she made up a budget. This budget included all of her expenses and money to set aside to buy stocks. After a few months, Angel told Sidney, since she was such a hard worker and kept the whole apartment so clean, she didn't need to pay rent anymore. Sidney insisted, if she was going to live there, she would pay rent. Angel argued it should at least be cut in half. After haggling for most of the day, they agreed on half the rent. Sidney took the extra money and invested it in stocks.

Sidney never spent her money on frivolous things. She never even spent money on things like getting her haircut. She cut it herself and did a good job too. She felt lucky, having uniforms to wear for work. That way, she only needed a few sweats since she worked all the time. She never wore makeup or perfume. That saved her even more money, which she promptly invested. One day, when Sidney was at the investment firm, she overheard some employees talking. They were saying how badly they needed someone to clean the office at night. Sidney thought this would be a great way to keep an eye on her money. After talking it over with Angel, Sidney took the job. She worked days at the diner and nights at the investment firm. Sidney was amazed at how much information you could get from the trash cans in the office. She studied everything she could get her hands on. This wasn't as easy as it might have seemed. Sidney only had six hours of sleep every night and three hours to clean up and eat her meals. The rest of the time was spent working. On Sundays, she had five hours to herself to do laundry, clean, shop, and study. She cherished this time because she understood how important learning was. Other than Sidney being tired most of the time, everything was going along pretty smoothly. This was definitely the happiest time in Sidney's life since her parents' death, but things would not go smoothly much longer.

One morning, Sidney got up and noticed Angel hadn't gotten up yet. She went in Angel's room to awaken her, only to find out Angel wasn't feeling well. First, Sidney took care of the breakfast crowd at the restaurant, like Angel had requested. Then, she took the rest of the day off and took Angel to the doctor. The doctor seemed very concerned and began running some tests. After a thorough examination, he told Angel, they were going to put her in the hospital and do some more tests. At first, Angel was reluctant to go. That was the last place she had seen her husband alive.

She knew the news wouldn't be good. She had been having problems with her health for a long time. She just never took the time to check it out. Now, she was out of time, and going to the hospital was the only thing she could do. Sidney read the worried look in Angel's eyes and knew her best friend in the world was in serious trouble. There was no sense waiting, so Sidney took Angel to the hospital and checked her in. After admitting her, Sidney went home to get Angel's personal belongings. When Sidney returned, she found Angel in tears. Sidney wrapped her arms around Angel and asked what was wrong. Angel replied, "I have always wanted a daughter, exactly like you. Now that I've found you, this had to happen." Sidney assured her she was going to be all right. She told Angel not to worry about anything. Even though these words were honestly meant to reassure Angel, neither one of them felt comforted. Sidney asked Angel if there was anything she could get for her. Before Angel could answer, a nurse came to take Angel down and start her tests.

Sidney was going back to work, promising to return after the dinner rush to spend the evening with her. When Sidney returned, Angel was back in her room. Sidney asked her how it went. Angel told her she didn't know yet. A few days and a lot of tests later, Sidney was visiting her dear friend, when the doctor walked in. He had a grim look on his face as he told Angel the news wasn't good. The tests were back, and she had liver cancer. He told her no one could say, for sure, how long she had, but her time was definitely limited. Angel asked if there were any treatments she could take. He told her it wouldn't do any good; it had already spread too far. The treatments would put her through a lot of pain and discomfort for no good reason. He told her, if it were him, he would make the best of the time he had left and get his affairs in order.

Angel and Sidney sat in shock as the doctor walked out of the room. This was far more than either one of them had bargained for. For what seemed like the longest time, they held hands and sat quietly, not knowing what to say to each other. Finally, Angel told

Sidney she should go home and get some sleep. They would discuss this the next day, after they both had time to think about it. Sidney was reluctant to leave her dear friend alone at a time like this. Angel insisted she needed time alone to think things through. That night, both Angel and Sidney cried themselves to sleep.

The next morning, Sidney was up bright and early to get the morning breakfast crowd taken care of. She knew Angel would be concerned about the diner. She wanted to do all she could to make things easier for her dear, sweet friend. As soon as Sidney had things under control, she left and hurried to the hospital. When she walked into Angel's room, she found her sitting up and smiling, with an absolute glow about her. This was not at all what Sidney had expected to find. Sidney felt so excited. Obviously, they had made a colossal mistake, and Angel was going to be fine. She hurried to Angel's side and asked, "Is everything, going to be all right?" Angel replied, "Yes, it is." Sidney said, "They made a mistake on your tests, right?" Angel answered, "No, there was no mistake." However, Angel felt God had given her a special gift. The gift of knowing ahead of time what was going to happen. Angel was thankful she would have the time to do all the things she had always wanted to do. Things she hadn't taken the time to do. Angel told Sidney she was going to sell the diner. She said a gentleman who wanted to buy it had come in a couple of weeks earlier. At that time, she told him she didn't think so. Now, things had changed, and she was going to give him a call. If his offer was still good, she was selling. Then, she told Sidney she would like for her to quit her jobs and do some traveling with her. She said that she had saved plenty of money for both of them. That way, Angel wouldn't be alone in case something happened to her. She told Sidney it would be fun and give her and Sidney the chance to see things they might otherwise never get to see.

She, also told Sidney that whatever money was left, when Angel's time came, would go to her. Then, Angel could rest in peace. Angel said, "You will come with me, won't you?" Sidney said, "Of course I will. I love you, and I'll do whatever I can to help." So they set about making arrangements for their big adventure. Angel called the gentleman who wanted her diner. He told her he was most definitely still interested. He agreed to keep the people who worked for Angel at their present salary. That made Angel feel so much better.

Next, they made arrangements to go to Italy. That was where Angel's family came from. She had always wanted to go there. They got their passports, shots, and tickets. Then, they went shopping for some new clothes. This was something Sidney felt strange about. She had never done anything so extravagant before. Angel insisted, so that was just what they did. Angel had all her belongings put into storage and gave Sidney the key. Angel told Sidney, "All these things will belong to you when I die."

Angel took a day to herself. Sidney wanted to go with her to keep an eye on her. Sidney didn't want Angel to get out of her sight, for fear something might happen to her. Angel refused and said it was something she had to do alone. She went to the funeral home and made her own funeral arrangements. She visited her lawyer to put in her will that everything she had would go to Sidney when Angel passed on. She signed papers, giving Sidney her power of attorney in case she needed her to take care of things. With all her affairs now in order, Angel could concentrate on having the time of her life. When Angel returned home, Sidney was very relieved to have her back. Angel told her that was the last time she would take off like that. She explained to Sidney what she had done. Now she was ready for some real fun times.

The next day, they started packing and prepared to leave the following day. On the way to the airport, Sidney asked Angel if she was sure she wanted to go through with this in her condition. Angel replied, "I've never been more sure of anything in my life." She told Sidney they were going to travel for as long as she was able to and then they would return home. Meanwhile, life was going to be one long party. Sidney could see the excitement in her eyes. Angel told her this was the right thing to do. Sidney decided there would be no more lecturing or fussing over Angel. Sidney would wait for her to call the shots. After all, it was her life.

For the next six months, they would travel to places most people only dream of. They went to Italy, France, England, Spain, Egypt, Africa, Australia, Tahiti, Hawaii, Japan, and Alaska and were about to go to Costa Rica, when Angel announced she was ready to call it quits. She told Sidney she was tired and wanted to go to Los Angeles. She had heard there were some really good doctors at the UCLA Medical Center. She remarked she thought she would check them out.

Without a word, Sidney got on the phone and made all the necessary arrangements. The next day, Sidney and her good friend left for Los Angeles. They checked into a hotel suite close to the UCLA campus. Two days later, Angel went for her appointment. After, checking her records and running a few new tests, the doctor advised her to go home and get plenty of rest. There was nothing more anyone could do but pray.

Angel told Sidney she wanted to go to Florida and sit in the sun, on the beach, and rest. That was what they did the very next day. Sidney rented a condo on the beach. Angel and Sidney spent their days sunning on the beach. They rented all the funny movies they could find (those were Angel's favorites). They laughed until they thought their ribs would collapse. They played cards and games, and on Angel's good days, they even went to play bingo. They were having such a good time they almost forgot about the problem that was facing them. Angel figured, why dwell on the bad things when there was so much fun to be had?

The cancer began to take its toll. Angel became so weak Sidney had to get her a wheelchair. At first, Angel didn't want to give in. Then Angel decided she was darn lucky there were such things to make her life more livable. She knew this was no time to be so stubborn.

Then one morning, Sidney went to help Angel get up for breakfast and realized Angel had passed away in her sleep. It happened just the way Angel had hoped it would. Sidney knelt next to the bed and thanked God for the time she had spent with Angel and for allowing Angel to die such a peaceful death. Sidney called an ambulance to take Angel to the hospital, where they could pronounce her dead. She made arrangements to take Angel back to New York, where her funeral arrangements had been made. There, Angel would be buried next to her beloved husband.

## RAINBOWS ARE BETTER

At first, Sidney was so busy, making all the arrangements to take Angel home and making sure everything was done just the way Angel had requested. She didn't realize her own loss. After the funeral, it hit her like a ton of bricks. Now, she was truly alone again. It reminded her of how lonely she felt that first night after the death of her parents. Before, she had wondered why such a bad thing had happened. Now, she knew how lucky she was to have had such loving people in her life. Although she felt physically alone, she knew, spiritually, she would never be alone. She knew the spirits of her parents and of Angel would always be with her.

That night, when she said her prayers, she thanked God for allowing her to be loved by such wonderful people. She also prayed for his continued guidance and help. Just as before, she decided to bury herself in work. Angel had left her about fifty thousand dollars and all her belongings. She rented a small one-room apartment. She made sure it had a windowsill big enough to sit on, of course. She furnished it with Angel's things. This made her feel closer to Angel somehow. That first night in her apartment, when she snuggled down in her bed (which Angel had been kind enough to give her), she felt the comfort she had been longing for.

## Chapter 4

## *Another New Beginning*

Sidney went back to work at the investment firm, cleaning at night. She also found a day job at a nursing home. Working at the nursing home made her feel useful and needed. She knew she would be too tired at night to worry about anything. She promptly invested the remainder of the money Angel had left her. She felt at the ripe old age of eighteen years old that she was starting her life all over, and in a sense, she was.

Sidney's first day at the nursing home was just what she had hoped. She was so busy she had no time to think about anything. She didn't once think about how she wished things could be. She met the other employees, and perhaps more importantly, she met the residents there. The wonderful people she would be caring for. She knew this was the right place for her to be at this point in time. She couldn't help but love these people. They were so kind and overjoyed to have someone to talk to. Everything you did for them was so appreciated. Sidney actually hated leaving them at night when she left for her other job.

Her job at the nursing home was more like having fun than working. Her job at the investment firm was more like going to school. At the investment firm, she met an elderly gentleman named Sal Goldstein. They almost immediately became the best of friends. Sal would stay late at night and teach her how to read and interpret the money section of the newspapers and magazines. Sal was about to retire and call it quits, when he met Sidney. When he saw what a hunger for knowledge she had, it gave him a renewed interest in living. Sal was amazed at how fast Sidney learned and what great instincts she had for understanding the stock market. At first, they just played on paper to see how things would go. It didn't take Sal long to decide to play for real.

One night, when Sal and Sidney were picking their stocks, she told Sal about her father. She told him her dad had owned a stock brokerage firm. She explained she thought that might be why she had an understanding of the stock market. Sal didn't know how you could inherit a talent like that. Sidney was eight, when her father died, Sal didn't think she could have picked up that much from him. But he had lived a long time and knew stranger things have happened, so why not. Whatever it was, it was still a great gift he had only wished for. Sal didn't really need the money. He already had more than enough for his retirement and then some. However, with the new enthusiasm Sidney brought to him, he couldn't help feeling excited about making more money. This time, for the sheer pleasure of teaching Sidney and watching her learn.

Sal enjoyed teaching Sidney so much he started working half a day, in the afternoons, at the investment firm. That allowed him time to teach at the local junior college in the mornings. What a thrill it was, to feel so useful again. He was actually working harder now than he was in the past twenty years. It felt great. As we all know, when we're doing the things we love, it brings us great pleasure and an exhilarated kind of exhaustion.

Sidney met and loved many people at the nursing home. One was an elderly gentleman named Mactavich O'Doul (very Irish, as you may have guessed). She was especially fond of Mac (which was what everyone called him). He spoke with a heavy Irish brogue. Sidney loved to hear him speak, and Mac loved to talk. This was a match made in heaven. I mean, really, made in heaven. Mac filled a void in Sidney's life like no other could. She never knew her grandfathers, but she hoped they would have been just like Mac. He had so many stories to tell, it was hard for Sidney to get her work done. She decided to set up a story time at the home. That way, she could take all the patients able to be moved out to the meeting room for story time each week. She later rigged up a speaker system to carry the stories to the patients who couldn't be moved.

Mac was a real ham, and everyone at the nursing home, employees and patients alike, enjoyed his jokes and stories. Sidney made this time even more enjoyable by baking cookies, popping popcorn, and making lemonade. Everyone looked forward to story time. They began planning for it all week. Some of the employees and residents got in on making the desserts. They even started dressing up for the occasion. Sidney found out some of them had other talents, such as playing piano, singing, and playing other instruments. It soon became known as talent day. The whole place started coming alive. Everyone who worked there felt happier, as well. Everyone started coming up with new ideas about how to make the home a more pleasant place to be.

Mac and Sidney were very close, and when she had time, they would sit and talk. He told her she worked too hard and wasn't taking the time to enjoy life before it passed her by. Sidney told him how hard it had been since her parents died. She wanted to stay busy and make enough money so she would never have to worry again. Mac told her, "You can't work away your troubles, and there isn't enough money in the world to buy real security. You can always lose your money, but good memories last forever. Money is only worth the pleasure it can buy for you or for someone else. Sometimes, the pleasure you give to someone else is the greatest treasure in the world for you." Sidney told him, "That's easy for you to say. You have enough money to live comfortably." Mac said, "While that's true, the happiest times in my life didn't come from having money. It came from loving and being loved. Giving money is more fun for me than having it." Sidney told him, "You can't give money if you don't have it now, can you?" Mac laughed, and he said, "Point well taken. You still need to spend more time enjoying life. Life never last long enough to do everything you would like to do. I don't want you to end up my age and discover you've let life pass you by while you were busy trying to make it easy. You need to have a young man in your life, go see a movie, eat out once in a while. You shouldn't always worry about hurrying to your next job. Take a walk in the park with a friend.

Look around, and see what's there. You need to know what's going on in the world. There's a lot out there to know about."

Sidney told Mac she was still very young and had plenty of time to do all those things. Mac still insisted, "You don't always have as much time as you think. The only things you can count on are the moment and God." He asked Sidney what she planned on doing when she had all the money she thought she needed. He also asked, "How much money do you think you need?" Sidney told him she didn't know yet how much money would be enough. She couldn't think about what to do until she had enough money to do it. Mac laughed and told her it didn't sound like much of a plan to him. Sidney told him not to worry. Right now, she just wanted to stay busy. That way, she didn't have time to worry about anything. She assured him she was perfectly happy with her life just the way it was. At least for now.

Sidney told him about Sal at her other job. She told him Sal was teaching her how to invest in the stock market. Mac said he was sorry he didn't know she was learning new things. That, at least, made more sense to him. Sidney giggled and told him how much she loved him and the fact he was so concerned about her future. He told Sidney he was still concerned that she had no social life. She rolled her big brown eyes at him and said, "I've got all of you, don't I?" Mac decided to give up; he wasn't winning any battles here. Sidney did listen to him. She just didn't feel the time was right for her to do anything differently in her life. It was almost Thanksgiving, and she had a lot on her mind.

Sidney rarely ever took money out of her account, except on holidays. On those days, she took out enough to pay for a large dinner at the orphanage, with all the trimmings. She had the dinners at the orphanage catered. She also had the caterer stay to serve the meal and oversee the activities. That way, she was sure the children would benefit from what she did. She just couldn't go back to the orphanage herself. Still, she cared deeply for the children there. Not only did she take care of the holidays, but once a year, she also had a big birthday party. She had one big party for all the children. Since she didn't know when their individual birthdays were, she decided to have one party each year, on August 20th, which was her birthday. That way, she would never forget. Besides, she felt she could only afford one birthday party a year, although she never understood why, right after she withdrew the money for their parties, her stocks always did well. She would end up with more money than she had before taking the money out. She knew these parties were better than the nothing she had endured while she was there. She, on the other hand, had dinner at the nursing home with all her friends.

She worked all the holidays so the other employees could be home with their families. She invited Sal over for dinner. He was so pleased she had asked him. He readily agreed to be there. For Sidney, these were the happiest holidays since her parents were still alive. She and Angel always shared a quiet meal together. That was great, but this was more fun. It was wonderful to be with all these people who were just as lonely as she was.

For the next couple of years, things went along great. Then one day, several of her stocks, with the most money in them, split and doubled. She was so excited. She felt her life had truly been blessed. She couldn't wait to see Sal and tell him the good news. When she got off work, she rushed to her next job, feeling as if her heart could sing.

When she arrived at the investment firm, Sal wasn't there. One of the secretaries said Sal had a heart attack and was rushed to the hospital. Sidney hurried through her chores at lightning speed. As soon as she was finished, she rushed to the hospital to see her dear friend. At first, they weren't going to allow her to see him. She explained to them he didn't have any family and she was his closest friend. She just knew he would be expecting her. The head nurse came out and told them to let her see him. She said no one else had come to the hospital to even check on him.

When Sidney went into his cubicle in the ICU, a chill went through her body. She had never seen anyone with all those wires and tubes attached to them. This whole thing was really scary for her. She felt so much sympathy for Sal. She knew, if she was feeling this frightened, how frightened he must feel. Sal was sleeping, when she walked in. She just sat on a chair beside the bed to wait until he woke up. As she was picking up a magazine, he awoke. He smiled at her and said, "I knew you would come when you got off work." He was curious how she got there so early. Sidney said, "I bet you didn't know I could work so fast, did you?" Sal laughed, and he said, "Oh yes, I did. You're one of the best workers I've ever seen."

Sidney asked Sal if he was in much pain. He said he was in a little pain but they kept him fairly drugged most of the time. Sidney held his hand and told him she was going to stay the night. He told her to go home, that he would be all right. Sidney told him not to argue; the nurse had already brought her a pillow and a blanket. The nurse said she could sleep on the sofa in the waiting room right outside the ICU. If he needed her, she would be right there. He thanked Sidney for being so considerate. The nurse came in with a needle in her hand. "Time for your night-night shot," she said. Sidney kissed Sal on the cheek and told him to call her if he needed anything. The nurse said she would go out and get her if there was any change. Sal told the nurse he wanted Sidney to be in charge if anything went wrong. The nurse informed him, unless Sidney was a family member, he would have to take that up with his lawyer. She told him not to worry, that nothing was going to happen on her shift. He could get that idea right out of his head.

When morning came, Sidney woke up early and called the nursing home. She asked for a week of vacation time. They agreed, of course, since Sidney had never even taken so much as a sick day since she started working there. Her supervisor asked her if there was a problem. Sidney explained about Sal having a heart attack and not having any family or friends to look after him. Her supervisor asked her to let them know if there was anything they could do. They all loved her and would do whatever they could. Sidney thanked her and said she didn't even know if there was anything she could do aside from being there for him.

When Sidney got off the phone, she went in to see Sal. He was awake and surprised to see her still there. Sal asked her if she shouldn't be at work. She told him she had a few days off and decided to spend them with him. He didn't say anything, but he knew what a kind gesture this was. He knew Sidney never missed going to work and was always on time. Most of the time, she was early. The nurse went in and told Sidney she might as well go have some breakfast because Sal was going for some tests.

# Chapter 5

# *When Love Walks In*

While she was having breakfast, she heard someone from over her shoulder ask her (in the sexiest voice she had ever heard) if the seat next to her was taken. She looked up and saw the most gorgeous man she had ever laid eyes on standing there. He was tall and well built, wearing a white hospital jacket, and he smelled wonderful. He smiled, and he repeated, "Is this seat taken?" Sidney could hardly find her voice to say no. She asked him to please be seated. He introduced himself as Shade Domingo and asked her name. She told him, "Sidney Davis." He said he was happy to meet her. He said he wasn't looking forward to breakfast alone. Sidney said, "I understand, I don't like eating alone, either."

Shade asked her what brought her to the hospital. He knew he hadn't seen her there before. If he had, he would have remembered. She told him about Sal having a heart attack. Then, she asked him what he did at the hospital. He told her he was an intern serving his residency there. She asked what kind of doctor he was. He told her he was doing his residency as a cardiologist. Sidney laughed, and she said, "We've barely met, and already, we have two things in common." Shade said, "What's that?" Sidney answered, "We don't like to eat alone, my friend is a heart patient, and you're a heart specialist." They both laughed, and then they started eating breakfast. They continued laughing as they chatted for about an hour. How quickly the time had gone by.

They both hated that breakfast was over. Shade saw the clock on the wall and had to excuse himself to go back to work. As he was leaving, he told Sidney he would go by the ICU to see her friend when he made his rounds. He was hoping to see her too.

Sidney had the strangest feeling, as she watched him walk away, she had ever had. It felt like she had butterflies in her stomach, and she felt strangely light-headed. Moreover, she felt exhilarated and just plain giddy. She didn't seem to have any control over these feelings either. It was wonderful. When she got back to Sal's room, he had already returned from his tests. He was waiting for the doctor to come in and tell him what they found out. To help him pass the time (and because she couldn't wait to tell him), Sidney told Sal about the young doctor she had just met. She told him the whole story. Sal told her he couldn't believe it had taken this long for her to meet someone. He told her, not only was she a beautiful young lady but she also had a beautiful spirituality about her. He joked he wasn't sure there would ever be anyone good enough for her. Sidney giggled and felt a little flushed, having someone say all those nice things about her. It was hard to take a compliment when she wasn't accustomed to receiving them. Sidney was squirming in her chair. She was so excited, waiting to see Shade again. She managed to keep herself composed though it was hard. She asked Sal about the tests they had run and how he was feeling.

Finally, after what seemed like forever, Sal's doctor came in with the test results. He told Sal the news wasn't so good. He said he'd had a massive heart attack and only a third of his heart was still alive. Sal wanted to know what that meant to him. The doctor replied, "You won't be able to do much of anything without putting too much strain on your heart. You really have to take it easy, and I do mean easy, not just easier. You may have to be bedfast from now on." Sal looked pale and said, "I can't do that. Can't you do surgery or something?" The doctor replied, "I'm afraid not, you would never survive the surgery. I'm talking serious here." Sidney asked, "Is there any chance he'll get better if he takes good care of himself?" Again the doctor said no, adding, "That's the way it is from now on just to keep him alive." Sal's next question was when he could go home. The doctor told him he wouldn't be going home. First, he would be under close supervision while they got his medication regulated. Then he would be going to a nursing home, where he would be cared for and monitored twenty-four hours a day.

Sidney could see the disappointment written all over Sal's face. He had never had to depend on anyone since he was a child. Sidney hugged him tenderly and told him not to worry, that he could live at the nursing home where she worked. That way, she would be able to take care of him herself. That would be easier than working two jobs, and she had been thinking about quitting her job at the investment firm anyway. Sal said, "You'd do that for me?" Sidney said, "I'm doing it for both of us. I'd like to have a little time off once in a while." So it was agreed, as soon as Sal was able, he would live at the nursing home. Sidney told Sal, if he wanted her to, she would help him sell his house and any belongings he no longer needed. The rest could be put into storage. She said she would take care of all the arrangements so he could just rest his mind. He could just lie back and take care of the business of getting well.

Shade walked in, and Sidney smiled and got that flushed feeling again. She introduced Shade to Sal, and she felt as though her voice even quivered a bit. They talked for a while and even had a few laughs together. It was as though they had always been good friends. Sal told Sidney that she and Shade should go get a cup of coffee or something. He said he was feeling tired and needed to rest. Sidney knew he was just trying to get the two of them to spend time alone. She also knew he did need to rest, so she agreed. Shade was only too eager to get her alone. This time, they went to a lounge area to sit and talk.

Sidney's first question was what the origin of his accent was. Shade asked her if it was that bad. She said it was quite the contrary; she loved to hear him speak. He told her he was born in Jamaica. He and his family had moved to America when he was about ten years old. She wanted to know about his family. He told her there was his mother, his father, and his two brothers. He said they all became American citizens eight years ago. He told her his family had just recently moved back to Jamaica but they kept their American citizenship. She asked where he had gone to college. He answered, "University of California, Los Angeles, or better known as UCLA."

Shade said, "Enough about me, what about you?" Sidney felt a strange sense of sadness when he asked her this question. She told him there wasn't much to tell (even though that wasn't really true). She simply didn't know how to share her life story. She was afraid he might not like her if he knew about her orphanage days. How could she tell him about running away when she was only fifteen years old and dropping out of school? She really wanted him to like her and didn't know what to say. How she hoped he would let it go without asking any more questions. About that time, Shade was paged over the intercom and had to excuse himself. Sidney assured him she understood, and she breathed a deep sigh of relief.

Sidney sat there alone, thinking how much she liked this young man. She really wanted to pursue a relationship with him. She knew eventually she would have to tell him the truth about her life. For some reason, Sidney had a dim view of her life, so far. She couldn't seem to concentrate on all the positive things that had happened to her. This was the first time she had thought about her own life and what it had meant so far. She needed time to sort things out in her own mind. Maybe then, she could share her story with him. She went back to Sal's room to check on him. The nurse told her he was resting and she should go home and do the same. The nurse assured Sidney, if anything unexpected happened, she would call her right away. Sidney decided to listen to her and go home. She was tired and knew she needed some time alone right now. She gave the nurse her phone number and once again, asked her to call, even if Sal just asked for her. She didn't want him to feel alone at a time like this.

On her way home, Sidney stopped at the grocery store and bought a few things she needed. When Sidney got home, she was so exhausted, she showered, put on her pajamas, and cleaned her apartment. She fixed some dinner and called Sal to make sure he was doing all right. She curled up on her windowsill and thought about her life. After that, she said her prayers and went directly to bed. She had experienced a lot in the past twenty-four hours.

It felt so good to curl up in her comfy bed. It felt as though Angel was right there hugging her.

Sidney truly loved that bed. Not only was it the most comfortable piece of furniture she had, but the feather bed was also so soft, you could snuggle right down in it. It felt like snuggling in her mother's arms, as near as she could remember. She always slept like a baby when she was in her bed. She thought to herself it was strange to feel this way about a piece of furniture. Still, she had very little in her life that gave her the complete comfort and peace that this bed did. As she lay there, enjoying the sheer bliss of her bed, she slipped off into a deep and restful sleep.

The next morning, when she awoke, she felt completely refreshed and renewed. She felt so good that she thanked God and the bed for a wonderful night's sleep. She thanked God for allowing her to have such a wonderful bed. As she sat at her small table, near the window, she saw a bird sitting on top of a sign, singing its little heart out. Somehow, she felt that it was singing just for her. It certainly made her feel as happy, as if it were. She thought, *Wow, what a great morning this is.* She got ready, then she called into work to check on things. She wasn't used to missing work and felt strange about it. They told her everyone and everything was just fine, so she did not need to worry. They informed her they knew she had enough on her mind right now, so she should relax; they would be fine. Sidney asked if Mac was all right. They told her he was fine, but he missed her.

After she hung up the phone, she slipped on her coat and started out the door. She hesitated and went back in the bathroom and checked in the mirror. She brushed her hair again and fluffed it up a little. She also put on a little lipstick, which she hardly ever did. Yes, she was thinking about Shade all morning, and this was the proof of it.

When she arrived at the hospital, she was very happy to see Sal in such good spirits. He was smiling and having some breakfast. The nurse said, "Can you believe this man?" Sidney answered, "Of course I can, I wouldn't expect any less from him." Sal laughed, and he said, "That's my girl, you tell her."

When the doctor came in a little later, he, too, was amazed at Sal's quick recovery. The doctor gave the order to move Sal to a semi-critical care unit. He also gave the okay to remove some of the tubes and wires. Not all of them, though. The doctor told Sal he wasn't out of the woods yet. He told Sidney he was counting on Sal to take this seriously. He told Sal he wanted him to cooperate with him and the nurses. It would be vital to do as he was told, if he wanted to survive this. The better Sal followed his instructions, the sooner he would get out of the hospital. Sal was so relieved to have some of the tubes removed and to know he was getting better, that he gladly agreed. Sidney asked the doctor how long he thought it would be before Sal could move to the nursing home. The doctor told her that depended on Sal and how willing he was to cooperate. Sal laughed, and he said, "How about today?" As the doctor was leaving the room, he told Sal, "It's going to take more patience than that."

Sal looked over at Sidney and said, "You look especially nice today. Are you hoping to see that young doctor, by any chance?" Sidney blushed, and she said, "Am I being that obvious?" Sal said, "No, I just know you that well."

Sal asked Sidney while he was being moved into his new room why she didn't go shopping and buy herself a new dress. She argued that she was there to see Sal, not to go shopping. Sal told her it would do his heart good if she would let him buy her a new dress. He told her he knew she rarely ever did that sort of thing but that, once in a while, she should. He also said there wasn't anything she could do while they were moving him anyway. The nurse said, "Take him up on his offer, it's not every day someone is willing to buy you a new dress." Sidney finally gave in. She agreed to go shopping, only to make Sal feel better. Sal said, "Make sure it's a red dress. I think red would be the perfect color for you. Besides, you could use a little color in your life." He told her she looked good in whatever she wore but that a red dress would be just the ticket. Sidney kissed him on the cheek and said, "Thanks, Sal, I'll be back in a little while." Sal told her to take her time and enjoy the trip; she deserved it.

When Sidney went in the store, she meant to look for a red dress, but she kept looking at beige, brown, gray, and black dresses.

# RAINBOWS ARE BETTER

She told herself, "No, I'm going to get a red dress just for Sal." She selected three red dresses to take to the dressing room. When she tried them on, she decided the first one was just too flashy for her. She finally decided on one even though she still didn't know how she felt about it. The saleslady assured her that red was definitely the best color for her.

She bought the dress and told the saleslady she would like to wear it, if that was all right. The saleslady said, "Of course, it is." Sidney left the store, feeling a little bit like a clown all dressed in red. She had never owned a red dress before, as far as she could remember. She stopped and bought Sal some magazines and newspapers about money, stocks, and businesses. She knew he would like that.

As Sidney was walking back to the hospital, she passed a little pawnshop. She wasn't sure why, but she stopped to look in the window. Much to her surprise, there was a beautiful gold locket in the window. It was just like the one her mother used to wear. She went inside and asked the shopkeeper how much he wanted for it. He told her he'd had that locket for a very long time and that she was the first person, to ask him about it. He asked her what she thought it was worth. Sidney told him she didn't know but that it looked just like the locket her mother always wore. He asked her if she would pay fifty dollars for it. She offered him thirty dollars. He agreed, and she gave him the money. He handed her the locket and her receipt. When she opened it, much to her surprise, there was a picture of her when she was a baby. On the other side was a picture of her mom and her dad. Tears came to her eyes as she realized this was her mother's locket. She turned it over and saw the engraving her father had put on the back. It said, "To Martha, with all my love, Leander." She thought to herself as she put the locket around her neck, what were the chances she would ever have found her mother's locket? Indeed, this was her lucky day. She felt a warm closeness to her parents, which she hadn't felt for a long time. She thanked the shopkeeper, then she scurried back to the hospital. She couldn't wait to see Sal and tell him what had happened. In the back of her mind, she was also hoping to see Shade.

When she arrived at the hospital, she met Shade on his way in. Shade wolf-whistled, and Sidney felt as red as the dress she was wearing. Shade told her she looked beautiful in that red dress. Sidney knew she was turning red from the heat she felt in her face. She shyly said "Thank you" but was clearly embarrassed by the whole thing. Shade, noticing this, apologized if he had embarrassed her, but he couldn't resist. He asked her if he could see her later. She told him she would love that, if he was sure he would have the time. He said, "For you, I'll make the time." He wanted to know if she would be in Sal's room later. She told him, "Yes, but Sal has been moved, and I don't know his new room number." He told her as he walked down the hall, "Don't worry, I'll find you."

Sidney went to the information desk to get Sal's new room number. They told her he was in room 202, bed A. As she was walking to his new room, she couldn't help noticing that people were watching her. She hoped it was because they thought she looked nice, not because they thought she looked like a clown. She was very insecure about her looks. If you could see her, you would have to wonder why she felt that way. She was beautiful and just naturally so.

When she walked into Sal's room, he smiled a smile that let her know he really approved of her new dress. Sal told her, he just knew red was going to be the right color for her, and he was right. She hugged him and thanked him not only for the dress but also for sending her out. She told him about the pawnshop and her mother's locket. She said, "It's a miracle that I found my mother's locket after all these years." Sal looked at it and told her it was beautiful and her parents were very attractive people. He told her he knew they would both be very proud of her. If only they could see what a wonderful person she had become. Sidney said, "Thanks, Sal, that means a lot to me." She told Sal it had been a magical day for her. He was doing better; she got a new dress, which made the young doctor whistle; and she found her mother's long-lost locket. Sal said, "If anyone deserves a magical day, it's you, kid." After that, she couldn't speak, so she gave him another big hug.

Sidney asked Sal how he was doing after the move. He confessed he was a little bit tired. Sidney told him, she would go to lunch while he took a nap, and she'd be back. Sal agreed that sounded like a good idea to him. When she arrived at the lunchroom, there was Shade. He appeared to be waiting for her. Sure enough, he was doing just that. He told her he thought she would never arrive. Sidney asked him what he would have done if she had just gone home. He told her he wasn't worried; he knew she would come. Shade said he had taken an extra hour for lunch so they could get to know each other. He said, "Since you're dressed in that lovely red dress, let's leave here and go somewhere special." Sidney felt flushed again. This would be her first date. She informed the nurses where she would be. She wanted them to know, if anything should happen, they could reach her there. Shade took her to a quiet little Italian restaurant and asked for a secluded table for two. Because of her life with Angel, this restaurant made Sidney feel right at home. When they were seated, Shade told her it was time for him to know more about her.

Before Sidney found her mother's locket, she didn't think she could tell him about herself. She didn't feel her life was special enough to share with anyone. Finding the locket like she did made her think her life had been somewhat interesting, maybe even special. She looked at Shade and said, "I don't really know where to start. I don't talk about myself that often." He said, "See? That wasn't so hard, was it?" Sidney, looking puzzled, said, "I don't know what you mean." He said, "You just told me, you don't like talking about yourself." They both laughed, and the mood instantly became more relaxed. Shade said, "I want you to start at the very beginning." He wanted to know everything there was to know about her. Sidney decided to tell him the absolute truth about her life. If he was no longer interested in her, she would be better off to know it now. She started by showing him her mother's locket with the pictures inside. He smiled and said, "What a beautiful baby you were and still are." Sidney told him not to start that stuff. She didn't want to be embarrassed. She knew, if she felt embarrassed, she wouldn't be able to tell him anything. He agreed he would try to contain himself but made no promises. She told him about her parents and the accident that took their lives. He told her how sorry he was and asked who raised her after their death. She told him she had no family other than her parents. She explained how her legal guardian, who was her father's best friend and partner, had put her in an orphanage, how he took all the money and left the country. Shade said, "Some best friend he was. I don't know how he could do such a terrible thing." Sidney said, "The way I saw it, since he was that kind of person, I was glad to be in an orphanage rather than be with him." Shade said, "I would never have thought of it that way, but you're right."

Sidney told him a little about the orphanage. She hesitated a moment before telling him about running away. Shade could feel the pain she was experiencing, trying to tell him about herself. He told her, "If it is too painful to talk about, I understand." He never meant to make her feel ill at ease. He explained he simply liked her so much, he wanted to know everything about her. He assured her, nothing she told him could make him feel any differently about her. She said, "I know you mean that. It's just hard for me to think about my orphanage days, much less talk about them." She told Shade she would try to go into greater detail later on. For now, she could only tell him she ran away when she was fifteen. She felt it was the only thing she could do under the circumstances.

She told him of her good fortune when she met her darling Angel. She told him how Angel took her in and gave her a much-better life than she had hoped for. She also told him how Angel had died of cancer and how much she missed her. Shade said, "No wonder you're so concerned about Sal and how he's getting along." Sidney told him she would be that concerned about Sal, anyway. He had been a special friend to her since right after Angel's passing. He had helped her learn important lessons for her life and well-being.

She told Shade that she worked two jobs, one at the investment firm and one at the nursing home. He said, "I don't like the sound of that. It sounds like you're going to be too busy to see me anymore when you go back to work." She laughed and said, "You still want to see me knowing what I've told you about my life?" He answered, "Of course, why wouldn't I?" Sidney said, "You're so well educated, and my education has been rather limited, so far." She told Shade she was going to quit her job at the investment firm. When Sal was able to leave the hospital he would be living at the nursing home where she worked. Therefore, she would rather be there to care for him.

She explained she wanted to have enough time to take a few college courses a couple of nights a week. She told him she was sure she would be able to work him into her schedule. Shade told her not to worry; he would help her do her homework so they could spend more time together. When they ordered their food, they had to laugh because they both picked spaghetti marinara. They shared it being their all-time-favorite food. The lunch went great; they laughed, talked, and discovered they shared a lot of things in common. Both their mothers were interior decorators, they had both traveled abroad to many of the same countries, and of course, they both liked Italian food.

All too soon, the lunch was over, and they both hated for it to end. Sidney knew this was the happiest day of her life, as far as she could remember. Shade said, "I'm not ready for the lunch to end, so how about walking back to the hospital through the park?" Sidney was elated, not just because she desperately wanted to spend more time with Shade but also because walking in the park was just what Mac had ordered.

They hadn't gone far when they came across a street vendor selling flowers. Shade stopped and bought Sidney two dozen long-stemmed red roses. Sidney almost cried. No one had ever bought her flowers before. She couldn't help herself; she threw her arms around his neck and thanked him with all her heart. Shade said, "You make me feel as if no one has ever bought you flowers before." Sidney told him no one ever had. He said she should have flowers every day. He told her he was glad he had been the first. He whispered, "Every woman deserves flowers once in a while." Sidney felt weak in the knees. She knew this guy had to be the most wonderful man in the world. Shade took her hand in his as they walked back to the hospital hand in hand. All felt right with the world.

When they arrived back at the hospital, it was very difficult for both of them when they had to say goodbye. Oh, they knew it wasn't going to be forever, but suddenly, anytime spent apart from each other felt like forever. Shade went back to work, and Sidney went to Sal's room. There she found Sal with the head of his bed raised and him reading some magazines and newspapers. Sal looked up and smiled a big smile and said, "Thanks for the reading material. I didn't know how much I would miss reading this, until now." He laughed and asked Sidney if she had a good time at lunch. Before she could answer, he said, "Never mind, I can see it written all over your face. Why, my dear, you're positively glowing." Sidney smiled and said, "Is it that obvious?" Sal said, "It sure is, and it's very nice to see."

She showed Sal, the flowers Shade had given her. Sal said, "You act as though you've never gotten flowers before." Sidney answered, "That's because I haven't." Sal said, "You have got to be kidding me."

"No, I'm not kidding anyone," replied Sidney. "I've never even been on a date before." Sal looked at her with a sympathetic look. He said, "That's a shame, you're way too special to have been overlooked this long."

"Thanks, Sal," said Sidney. "You're a good friend. It makes me feel good to hear you say things like that."

Sal said, "Enough of this mush, are you ready for your lesson about the stock market?"

"Sure," said Sidney, "but are you sure you're up to that?" Sal replied, "This is a piece of cake." He opened some stock reviews, and they began going over the stock together. With pen in hand, they began to map out their market strategy for the next day. Sal told Sidney she was, by far, the best student he had ever taught. He gave her instructions on what to do before coming to the hospital the next day. Just as they finished their business for the day, the nurse came in with a shot and some medications. She told Sidney Sal needed to rest for a while. Sal told Sidney she should go on home and get some rest. He knew she would need to get an early start the next day. Besides, he knew she liked to call work and check on things. Sal said, "Maybe if you leave now you could go by the nursing home and check on your other friends." Sidney agreed she had been concerned about them and decided to go. She kissed Sal goodbye and told him to rest and she would see him in the morning.

She left the hospital and went to the nursing home. When she arrived, everyone was so happy to see her. They wanted to know how her friend was doing. She told them Sal was doing much better and that if he continued to improve, she should be back to work in a few days. She explained he would be moving to the nursing home when he was released.

When she looked around the room, she noticed Mac wasn't there. She asked where Mac was. They told her he had been feeling a little under the weather lately. One of the nurses told Sidney she thought he was just homesick to see her. Sidney said she was going to check on him before she went home. She excused herself and went to his room.

When she knocked on his door, he answered, "Who is it?" When she answered "Sidney," he called out, "Come in, come on in here." When Sidney walked in, he was sitting there with a big smile and said, "I wondered if you were coming back." Sidney said, "Of course, I'm coming back. Didn't the nurses tell you what happened?" He said, "Oh sure, but I didn't know if that was the truth or if they were just telling me that. They would do that to keep me from feeling bad about you being gone." Sidney told Mac she would never leave without telling him herself in person. Mac said knowing that made him feel better. He told her she was more than just his nurse; she was the only family he had.

Sidney hugged him and told him how dear he was to her. She couldn't wait to have him and Sal there together. She just knew the two of them would be the best of friends. Mac asked if Sal was getting along all right and if he would be visiting there when he was well. Sidney said, "Better than that, he'll be living here, and yes, he is doing much better." Mac told her it would be fun showing him the ropes, so to speak. Sidney told Mac she was on her way home. She explained she wanted to check on him before going home. She told him not to worry; she would be back at work as soon as possible. She told him she missed him dearly. She hugged him and said goodbye. Mac said, as she was leaving, "By the way, kid, that's a real sharp dress you're wearing there, and a lovely locket too. I don't think I've ever seen you wear either one before." Sidney sat down and told him all the incredible things that had happened to her that day, including the walk in the park. She said, "Thanks for noticing, Mac. You're a dear, but tomorrow I have a busy day scheduled, and I think I'd better get some rest tonight."

All the way home, she was basking in the warmth of a very special day. When she entered her apartment, as soon as she closed the door, she thanked God for giving her such a comfortable place to live. She also thanked God for such a wonderful day, for helping Sal do so well, and for the lovely people in her life. She hesitated for a moment and said a great, big thanks for letting her meet someone like Shade. He made her feel so happy, her heart could sing. As she prepared for bed that night, she sat on the window seat and checked her phone messages. What a perfect day. The real estate salesman called to say he thought he had a buyer for Sal's house and asked if she could meet him at eleven o'clock in his office to discuss it further. She decided to call him in the morning before going to the investment firm.

She said her prayers; climbed into her nice, soft bed; and almost instantly fell asleep. When she awoke the next morning, she felt so rested, and energized, she danced around the room. She felt so happy, it was almost as if she had a tickle inside (for lack of a better description). She called the real estate broker and confirmed their appointment. As she was leaving the apartment, she stopped for a moment and gave thanks for such a wonderful day and this tremendously happy feeling.

On her way to the investment firm, she held a baby for a lady on the bus. As she looked down at the baby, she thought to herself for the first time, *I'd like to have a baby of my own someday.* Then she almost giggled, which she wasn't prone to do, at the idea of wishing for a baby. She decided to stop this and gave the baby back to the mother. Sidney had a lot of plans for her life, and having a baby just wasn't a part of those plans, at least not now.

She took care of the stocks and headed for the real estate office. She hoped they wouldn't mind that she was running ahead of schedule. When she arrived, the real estate broker was happy to see her arriving early. He explained he had another appointment come up and this was working out perfectly for him. Sidney said, "Great, now what about the buyer for Sal's house?" He said, "These people need a house right away, and they can pay cash. They've already sold their home, and Sal's place is just what they want." He added, "You might want to run this by Sal. If it's all right with him, we can probably get this finalized in two weeks. Do you think you can handle things that quickly?" Sidney said, "If it's all right with Sal, I can get things done by then." She thanked him and headed for the hospital. On the way, she stopped at the newsstand and picked up a newspaper and a joke book. She knew, Sal would like that.

When she arrived, he was sitting up and smiling. He greeted her with "Good morning, sunshine. How's my girl today?" Sidney gave him a hug and answered, "I'm fine, but I'm not the one in the hospital, so how are you?" He replied, "The only way I could be better is if I could resume my life the way it was, before." Sidney said, "I'm sorry about that, Sal, but I do have what I think is good news." He said, "Don't make me guess, what is it? I could use some good news." Sidney exclaimed, "Not only did the real estate broker find a buyer for your house, but while I was at the investment firm, one of our stocks split and doubled. How is that for a good morning?" Sal was thrilled and wanted to know how long the real estate deal would take to go through. Sidney told him it would take about two weeks. He said, "You've got to be kidding." He asked her if that would be too much for her to do. That was such a short amount of time. She told him not to worry; she could handle this with her eyes closed and one hand tied behind her back. He said, "There's a lot to do, Sidney. Are you sure?" She answered, "All right, maybe not with one hand tied behind my back." They both had a good laugh.

Sidney said, "I take it this is all right with you then?" Sal said, "What's not to be all right? All I have to do is lay here in this bed while you do everything for me. I'm not crazy, you know. How many people get a deal like that?" Sidney said, "I was concerned how you might feel about actually selling your home." Sal told her he had already come to grips with this situation. He understood this was what he had to do. "Besides, now I'll be with my girl every day, right?" Sidney said, "That's for sure." Sal teased, "If you can handle this whole thing and you're sure you don't mind, it's just fine with me. That house was kind of lonesome, anyway, since my wife, Mona, died." Sidney told him, as soon as the papers were drawn up, she would bring them in for him to sign. Sal said, "That won't be necessary," reaching over to his nightstand. "This morning, I had my lawyer bring over my power of attorney papers, naming you my power of attorney. Now you have the power to act on my behalf regarding everything that needs to be done." Sidney said, "Are you sure, Sal? That's a lot of authority to give someone else." He said, "I'm not giving it to someone else. I'm giving it to you, and you're my girl, aren't you?"

"Sure, I am," said Sidney, "and I won't let you down. You can count on it." Sal said, "I know that. That's why I picked you, my little friend."

"Hey," said Sal, "is that newspaper for me?"

"Well," said Sidney, "it's for you to read and give me my lesson for the day." Without further ado, they opened the paper and started. After they had mapped out their strategies for the next day, Sal was feeling tired, and the nurse went in with his shot. She told Sidney he would have to rest now. Sidney said, "I was just getting ready to go to lunch. Is there anything I can get you, Sal, while I'm out?" Sal answered, "A new butt for them to put these shots in." Sidney and the nurse laughed as Sidney left.

Sidney was going out the door, when she heard someone calling to her, "Wait, wait up." She knew right away who was calling her. It was Shade. Suddenly she had that ticklish, happy feeling again. That feeling only he could give her. She stopped and turned around to see his smiling face. "Are you going to lunch?" Shade asked. Sidney said, "As a matter of fact, I am." Shade asked if she would mind waiting a few minutes while he finished his rounds, so he could go with her. She told him she would love to. He said he would hurry so she wouldn't have to wait that long. She told him to take his time. She was sure his patients deserved no less than his full attention. She said she would go to the cafeteria and have a soda while she waited for him.

## Chapter 6

# *A New Little Friend*

Sidney went into the cafeteria and sat across the table from a little girl. This little girl was about eight or nine years old. Sidney smiled and said hello. They started talking like they had always known each other. The little girl said her name was Larkyn Saunders. She told Sidney her mom was in the hospital, with cancer. Sidney told her how sorry she was to hear that. Sidney asked her if her mom was there for a treatment. Larkyn said her mom was dying, and the doctors said there was nothing anyone could do. Sidney took her little hand and said, "You can still pray." Larkyn said she didn't know how to pray. Sidney thought to herself how strange it was that someone wouldn't know how to pray. Sidney didn't know how anyone could get through a day, much less a life, without praying. She knew she couldn't and wouldn't want to try.

She asked Larkyn if her parents were agnostic or if they belonged to any certain religion. Larkyn said, "We're not anything. We've just never had time to go to church." Sidney asked her, "Do you want to learn to pray?" She said she could teach her, if she wanted. Larkyn said, "Oh yes, please do." Sidney went to the cash register and asked the cashier if she would tell Dr. Domingo she would be in the chapel for a little while with a friend and she would be back shortly. The cashier said she would be happy to. Sidney also asked her to watch for Larkyn's father and that if he was looking for her, that was where she would be too. The cashier agreed, so Sidney and Larkyn left for the chapel.

Sidney took Larkyn's hand and said, "This is the simplest thing you will ever do. When you pray, you're simply talking to God. You just tell him what's in your heart." Sidney told her she would leave her alone if she would like some privacy or she could stay with her if she wanted the company. Larkyn said, "Maybe you should stay and make sure I'm doing it right." Sidney told her, "You can't do it wrong, as long as you're sincere and say what's really in your heart. All your prayers should come directly from your heart. That way, God knows you're being sincere and truthful with him." Larkyn asked Sidney, "How do you get started?" Sidney said, "I like to start with the Lord's Prayer, or you can start by saying 'Dear God,' just like you're writing a letter. Just say 'God, I need to talk to you about the things I need help with.' The nicest thing about praying is there isn't just one way to do it. Just talk to God, and tell him, 'This is my first time, so please be patient with me while I learn.' Tell him you really need to talk to him, then tell him why." Larkyn said, "I think I understand now. I can take it from here." Sidney said, "Okay, I'll be standing right outside the doors. If you need me, just call, and I'll be right there."

When Larkyn came out, she seemed more at peace and more collected. She thanked Sidney for her help and said, "Praying really does help." Sidney said, "I know. I do it all the time. It's the greatest tool we have to deal with life and the problems we encounter. You should remember, though, we don't always get the things we pray for, but we always get the things we need. Even when we don't think so. I know sometimes I've felt God wasn't answering my prayers. That was when the answer was no. Believe me, he always listens and answers our prayers. He gives us the best answer for all concerned, not just the one who's praying. So if God makes a decision and it's not what you asked for, remember, it's the way God knew things had to be. When that happens, you pray for the strength to get through the things you must. He will always give you that. The best way to help yourself get through bad times is to help others. It works like magic. I know because when I was living in an orphanage after my parents died, I couldn't have made it if I hadn't spent my time helping the other kids." Larkyn said, "Thanks, Sidney, for talking to me and helping me deal with all this sad stuff." Then, she wrapped her arms around Sidney's waist and gave her a big hug. Sidney hugged her, too, and said, "No problem. I'm glad I could help."

Sidney looked up and saw Shade walking down the hall toward them. There was another man coming down the hall behind him. Sidney asked Larkyn if that was her father. Larkyn said, "Yes. Can you wait just a minute so my dad can meet you?"

"Sure, I can," answered Sidney. Larkyn introduced her dad, John Saunders, to Sidney, and Sidney introduced them both to Shade. Sidney told Larkyn she would check on her when she got back from lunch, if that would be okay. Mr. Saunders assured her that would be not only all right but also very much appreciated. He told Sidney he was very happy that Larkyn had found someone she could talk to. Sidney told him it was her pleasure.

Sidney and Shade left to go to lunch. While they were at lunch, they discussed Larkyn and her family's problems. Shade promised Sidney he would check on Larkyn's mother and see if there was anything, medically, that could be done. Sidney told him how wonderful she thought he was to do such a nice thing for people he didn't even know. Shade told her she was rather special herself. After all, she didn't know them either. Sidney said, "Okay, that's enough patting each other on the back, let's dwell on happy things the rest of our time together." Shade agreed. He asked her how Sal was doing. She told him Sal was doing remarkably well.

Sidney said, "After we finish lunch, I'm going over to the real estate office and sign the papers to sell his house." Shade asked her what she would do with his furnishing and such. She explained she had called an estate consignment store and talked to them about selling his furnishings. She said she needed to make a list, with Sal's help, of the things he wanted to keep and get those things put into storage. Shade said, "I'm impressed that you're so well organized."

"Actually," Sidney said, "I've been through something very similar to this when my best friend, Angel, died. She knew she was dying, so I helped her sell her home and business. We put the rest of her belongings in storage. After her passing, she left everything to me, so I've used the estate consignment store before.

Shade said to Sidney, "For such a young person, you've certainly been through a lot."

"I've never really thought about it before," said Sidney, "but I guess you're right. I was so busy living my life, it felt normal to me. At the time, I had nothing to compare it to, so it seemed normal." Shade said, "I didn't mean it wasn't right or normal, I just meant it was interesting. You've done a lot of living most people haven't done at such a young age." Sidney laughed and said, "The life I've lived isn't what I would wish for anyone. Not that it's been all bad, but at times, it's certainly been scary." Shade said, "Whatever happened to you in the past only made you the very special person you are today." This time, Sidney just said "Thank you" instead of getting all flustered and embarrassed. Could it be she was getting used to having nice things said about her?

Shade and Sidney talked and laughed all through lunch. Too soon, it was time for Shade to go back to work. He took Sidney's hand and told her he would miss their walk through the park after lunch. He understood she needed to take care of Sal's affairs. Sidney told him she, too, would miss their walk in the park. Maybe another time. Shade said, "Absolutely, without a doubt, we will do it another time and, hopefully, many, many, other times. Maybe tomorrow, if you'll let me take you to lunch." Sidney said she would love to, and she was so happy he wanted her to go to lunch with him again. She knew soon she would have to return to work and these happy outings would have to come to an end. They walked arm in arm outside the restaurant.

As Sidney was about to say goodbye, Shade leaned over and kissed her very gently on the lips. Sidney felt herself swoon. Suddenly she felt warmly flushed all over. She dearly hoped he couldn't tell how excited she felt. Then again, maybe she did want him to know. She wasn't sure what she wanted. He said he would see her back at the hospital. He added, "Please be careful, I don't want anything to happen to you." She laughed and said, "Take care of yourself, I would hate to have lunch all alone from now on." He waved down a cab and helped her get in. He stepped back as he waved goodbye. Sidney sat

# RAINBOWS ARE BETTER

quietly in the cab, thinking how happy she was to have met Shade. She said a quiet thanks to God for her good fortune.

Sidney arrived at the real estate office, and it was back to business. She told the broker she had discussed the sale with Sal and he was totally in favor of the deal. She relayed Sal's message, "The sooner, the better." She explained she had Sal's power of attorney to take care of everything. She pulled the papers out of her purse and asked him if he needed a copy of the power of attorney. He said yes, and he would get the paperwork for her to sign while his secretary made the copy. When he brought the papers in, she asked if he had a quiet place where she could be alone to read the papers over before signing. He assured her everything was in order and all she had to do was sign. She explained to him, "While that may be true, I never sign anything without reading it first." He told her she could read it right there in his office. She refused, saying, "No offense, but I'd like to take my time and read it alone." He took her to an empty office and said, she could use this office and take all the time she needed.

As Sidney was reading it over, she saw the broker was asking 10 percent for the selling fee. That was the only thing she saw wrong with it, but that was not acceptable. She knew the going rate for real estate dealers, and that was too much. She went back into his office and told him she felt his commission was too high. He said that was the amount he always received. Sidney looked at him sternly and said, "Why do you get so much when everyone else in town gets only 6 percent?" He answered, "Yeah, but do they have a buyer ready to buy right now?" She retorted, "No, but do you have a house they want you to sell them right now?"

"Touché," he quipped. "Okay, just for you, this one time, I'll do it for 6 percent." She said, "Thank you," as she marked through the 10 percent and wrote in "6 percent." She then asked him to initial it. He laughed as he initialed it and said, "Boy, you don't miss a trick, do you?" She said, "Sal taught me a lot about finances, and I wouldn't dream of letting him down." The broker said he would call her as soon as he had the check and the title search was complete. Sidney thanked him and left.

Sidney had to hurry to her next appointment, at the estate consignment store. Ms. Jones was the lady she had spoken to. It was Ms. Jones who met her at the door. Sidney explained she would like to meet her at Sal's house the next day at about two o'clock. That way, she could show her the items she was going to sell. Sidney asked if that was agreeable with her. Ms. Jones agreed and said she would bring a couple of guys and a truck when she came. With all this done, Sidney headed back to the hospital, feeling like things were going very well.

When Sidney returned to the hospital, Sal wasn't doing very well. He's had a slight setback, the nurse told her. She took Sidney outside and explained to her this was not unusual. She said, "This kind of thing happens all the time. Sal needs to understand he has to really take it easy from now on. When he's tired, he will have to rest, or it could kill him. That's a hard thing for most people to understand. His heart is extremely bad, and only he can determine when he needs to rest. He'll just have to pay attention and do what needs to be done." The nurse said, "For now, I've given him a shot, which should make him sleep for a while. If you've got something to do, this would be a good time to do it." Sidney said she wanted to check on a little friend of hers. Then, she would go back and read quietly until he woke up. The nurse said she would page her if there was any problem.

Sidney went down the hall to the elevators. She went to Larkyn's mother's room. She found Larkyn sitting outside in the hallway. Sidney asked Larkyn if she was all right. Larkyn said, "Yes, I guess. They're in there giving my mom a shot for pain. The nurse said it would make her sleep for a while." Sidney said, "They must be giving everyone a nap." She told Larkyn they had just given her friend, Sal, a shot to make him rest too. Larkyn's dad stepped out and told Larkyn, if she wanted to have dinner in the cafeteria, this would probably be a good time. Sidney said, "Why don't you let me take Larkyn to dinner in the cafeteria? You're welcome to join us, if you like." He said he would like that but he didn't want to leave his wife. Sidney told him they would bring him something back and he could eat it in her room.

# RAINBOWS ARE BETTER

First, Larkyn and Sidney went down and got a tray of food for Larkyn's dad. On the way back to the cafeteria, they laughed and talked about some of the funny things they had seen people do while they had been at the hospital. Sidney was trying to take Larkyn's mind off the situation she was in. At dinner, Larkyn and Sidney talked about Larkyn's school, friends, and her little dog, Toby. Larkyn missed all these things, and it felt good to talk to someone about them. She told Sidney she thought Toby was the smartest dog in the whole world. She explained he knew something was wrong with her mom long before the rest of them did. They discussed everything, from the type of clothes they liked to their favorite color, favorite foods, and television shows. They laughed about the worst haircut they ever had and the silliest thing they ever did.

When dinner was over, Sidney walked Larkyn back to her mother's room. Larkyn and her dad thanked Sidney for taking Larkyn to dinner. Mr. Saunders told Sidney it meant a great deal to him that she was being so kind to Larkyn. Sidney told him it was truly her pleasure. She told him Larkyn was a special little girl and she loved spending time with her. Sidney hugged Larkyn and told her she would see her later.

Sidney went back to Sal's room to check on him. She went in, and he was still sleeping. She sat down and began reading a book about the stock market and money management. She read for about an hour before Sal woke up. He wanted to know why she was still there, instead of going home. She told him it was because she couldn't have rested without knowing he was going to be all right. Sal assured her he was all right and that he had learned his lesson. From now on, he would rest more often.

Sidney told Sal she had taken care of the house and furnishings. All she needed now was to go over the things he wanted to keep so she could get those things removed. She told him, when she arrived the next morning, they would make the list together if he was up to it. If not, it could wait until he was. Sal thanked her as she bent forward to kiss him goodbye. She told him she would be back in the morning, so he should get lots of rest. Sal assured her that was all he felt like doing. He said, "Whatever was in that shot was really powerful."

Sidney left and went straight home. She felt exhausted. She thought to herself, if she had worked fourteen hours (a usual day for her), she wouldn't feel this tired. She couldn't fully understand why this was the case. She knew this was definitely wearing her down. She also knew it was making her appreciate her small apartment more and more. She said her prayers and went straight to bed.

When morning came, she felt a little better. On her way, she stopped again to pick up some magazines about stocks for Sal. While she was there, she saw a magazine about women's business opportunities, so she picked it up for herself. Then, it was straight to the hospital.

When she arrived, Sal seemed much better. His color was better, and he was sitting up in bed, eating his breakfast. Sidney asked him how he felt. Sal said, "I'm feeling fine, but I'm not going to overdo it again like I did yesterday." Sidney said, "Good, I intend to hold you to your word. That gave me quite a scare." Sal told her he was ready to quote a list of things he wanted to keep, as soon as he finished his breakfast. After he finished eating, Sidney took a pencil and paper and started writing the things he listed. She asked him if he was sure that was all he wanted to keep. He said, "I don't have a lot longer to live in this world, so what good are things to me now?" Sidney said, "Now don't start talking to me like that, Sal." He said, "It's true, Sidney. I'm not a young man, so even if I didn't have this heart problem, I can't live forever. Maybe it takes something like this to make you realize the things you work so hard to accumulate in life are not the important things in life at all. The people you love and those who love you, plus any good deeds you've done, are the only things that matter. It's too bad I had to live most of my life before I figured that out."

He told Sidney, while he was lying there, he had time to think about the things he wished he had done differently. Things like adopting a child since he and his wife couldn't have children. He had been too stubborn and set in his ways. He was always telling his wife, "If God had wanted us to have children, he would have given us our own." He looked at Sidney and said, "If only I had known about you, we could have adopted you and made all our lives better." Sidney said, "That's water under the bridge. You can't worry about the past. It's over." Sal said, "I know it's too late for all that now. I'm just glad I have you now. I don't know what I'd do without you." Sidney said, "Don't waste time beating yourself up for the things you didn't do or might have done. I think everything happens for a reason, and who knows what those reasons are. The important thing is we found each other before it was too late."

"That's right," said Sal. "I might not have appreciated you nearly as much then as I do now."

Sal said, "I don't mean to give you the bum's rush, kid, but I'm exhausted. Cleansing your soul is a taxing experience." Sidney giggled and said, "I have a meeting with Ms. Jones from the estate consignment shop in about an hour. I'll go on over to the house and check out what I'll have her take, to sell." Sal said, "If you see anything, anything at all, that you might like to have, please help yourself to it. I would like you to have whatever you want. That way, I'll feel like you really are my child." Sidney told Sal he was too funny for words. Sal said, "I'm not joking. I'd really love it if you could use or just like to have something from my home." Sidney said, "Fine, I'll try to find something that reminds me of you." Sal said he had a better idea. Why didn't she just take the house, with everything in it? That way, it wouldn't be gone. He told her, it wasn't as if he needed the money or anything. He told her he really did hate the idea of everything being sold to strangers. Sidney told him she couldn't do that; she just couldn't. Sal said, "Why not? Don't you like the place or the stuff inside?" Sidney said, "It's not that, it's just that I can't accept such a huge gift."

"All right," said Sal, "you can be my house sitter until I'm well enough to move home again. How about that? I'm telling you, Sidney, you'd be doing me a huge favor, bigger than you know."

Sidney said, "Okay, if I'm going to live there, and I'm not saying I will, I have to pay rent." Sal said, "If you just keep the place up, that's rent enough. Now, please do an old man a favor and just say yes." Sidney said, "What about the real estate dealer and the people who want to buy the house?"

Sal said, "Don't worry about them. Those people can find another place, and the broker will get a fair fee for his work. I don't have to sell if I don't want to, and I don't want to. So, my dear, do we have a deal?" She said, "But what about when you get well enough to move home? I'll just have to move again." He said, "No, you won't, unless you want to. Besides, what are the real chances of me getting well enough to move home again? I just want to know it's there, if I ever did. More importantly, I'll know you're there, and nothing could make me happier. I just can't believe I didn't think of this before. It would have saved everyone a lot of time and trouble. So what do you say, kid, yay or nay?" Sidney said, "Okay for now, but if I change my mind or you change yours, we'll go ahead and sell it, with no more arguments?"

"It's a deal," said Sal. Sidney told him she would have to sell a few of the things in one of the bedrooms so she could put her things in there, if he didn't mind. "Mind," said Sal, "I insist that you do whatever you have to, to make yourself comfortable. My dear Sidney, I want you to make this your home and feel completely comfortable in it. You can redecorate, knock out a wall, repaint, or wallpaper, even add a new room. I don't care, as long as you're happy."

Sidney hugged him and told him to rest now and she would see him later. She went to the courtesy phone and called the real estate broker. She explained to him the house was no longer for sale and why. Then she called Ms. Jones and told her there would only be one room of furniture, she would be selling. Ms. Jones said that would be fine but asked if it would be all right if she met her at about three o'clock, instead of two o'clock. Sidney said, "That would be great." That would give her more time to sort through things.

Sidney went upstairs to check on Larkyn. She found her out in the hall, sobbing deeply. Sidney asked what was wrong. Larkyn said her mother had gone into a coma, and the doctor told them she might never wake up. Sidney took Larkyn in her arms, and said, "Don't be so sad, sweetheart. God has probably decided she was in too much pain. This way, he can give her relief. You wouldn't want her to suffer more than God would allow, would you?" Larkyn said, "No, but I need her, and I don't want her to die." Sidney said, "Sometimes, we have to be brave and let our loved ones go back to God so they will never have to suffer again. It's very hard to do because we want them to be with us forever. Just remember, her spirit will be with you, as long as you need it. Even if it's the rest of your life." Larkyn looked up at Sidney and asked, "Is your mother's spirit still with you?" Sidney hugged her and said, "Of course it is because I still need her." Larkyn said she thought she understood, but what would happen to her dad if her mom died? Sidney told her not to worry; he would be sad, but as long as they had each other, they would never be alone. She told her they would have to help each other get through the sad times and go on with their lives. Sidney felt sure that was what Larkyn's mom would want for them. Larkyn told Sidney she hoped she was right and her dad would be able to get through this whole terrible nightmare. "Trust me, Larkyn," said Sidney. "You'll get through this because you have to. You can't just jump off the earth if you don't like the way things are going. You ask God for the strength to get through it." Larkyn's dad came to the door and called Larkyn into her mom's room. He asked Sidney to excuse them; his parents were on the phone and wanted to speak to Larkyn. Sidney told him she needed to check on Sal, but if they needed her, they should let her know. He thanked her, and Sidney left feeling very concerned about all three of them.

When she got back to Sal's room, he was sleeping. She picked up her magazine and read a few articles about how to run your own business. Sidney began to think what type of business she would like to own someday. She just wasn't sure what she wanted to do. She had always been concerned about making money, but she never thought about what she would do to earn that money. She couldn't believe that she hadn't planned for the future better than this. She felt that this had been a huge oversight on her part.

Just as she was getting deep into thought over this, Sal woke up. He asked her what time it was. Sidney said, "I don't know, but I can go to the nurses' station and find out." Sal laughed and said, "I just meant is it time to eat?" Sidney told him it was, if he was hungry. She asked him if he wanted something from the kitchen or if he would rather have her get him something. Sal said something from the kitchen would be fine. He told Sidney he liked the food there. Sidney agreed they did have good food for a hospital. She said she always heard hospital food was awful. Sal said he was glad that wasn't the case here. Sidney asked the nurse if she could call the kitchen to send Sal his lunch. The nurse said she was way ahead this time. She knew Sal would be waking up anytime, so she had already called, and lunch was on its way up. Sidney said, "Boy, aren't you the efficient one?" The nurse laughed and said, "We aim to please."

Sidney went back to Sal's room and told him how thoughtful his nurse had been. Sal said, "I have to admit, they take good care of me here." Sidney said, "I think I'm going home early today. I have an appointment with Ms. Jones at three o'clock, and then I need to start packing if I'm going to move." Sal said, "I'm fine and in good hands." He wanted Sidney to do her packing and get moved in right away. Sidney kissed him on the cheek and said, "Call if you need me."

# Chapter 7

## *Home, Sweet Home*

When Sidney arrived at Sal's house to meet Ms. Jones, she looked the place over, this time in a new light. After all, this was to be her new home. She thought to herself, *This is a really nice house.* The furnishings were contemporary, which made it look very clean and uncluttered. This was a very different look from that of Angel's home, but it was nice, and Sidney liked it. She had to admit, she liked the warm look and feeling of Angel's home, but this was nice, for a change. She decided to leave things the way they were, for now. She went upstairs and picked the room of furniture she would sell, and that was hard since all the furnishings were so beautiful. She knew her furniture wouldn't go very well with the furnishings here, but she loved her things and knew she couldn't part with them. She needed the comfort they afforded her. When Ms. Jones arrived, Sidney had her take the furniture from one of the guest bedrooms. Yes, one of the guest bedrooms. The house had four guest bedrooms and a master bedroom suite. It also had six and a half bathrooms, a huge kitchen, a breakfast nook, a formal dining room, a large library, a huge recreation room, a family room, and a living room.

    Ms. Jones couldn't help but comment on what a large and beautiful home this was. Sidney said, "I know, it's hard to believe that only two people lived here." Ms. Jones told Sidney she would call her as soon as the furniture sold. Sidney thanked her as she left. When Sidney turned around and went back into the house, she thought, if this house was too big for two people, what was she going to do as only one person living there? She decided to worry about that later.

She went upstairs to move the furniture around so she could put her bedroom set in the master bedroom. It was too freaky that it happened to have a large bay window with a padded window seat. She sat on the window seat and looked out. The view was breathtaking. It over looked a flower garden, a fishpond, a weeping willow tree, and a gazebo. She knew, right then, she would definitely be happy in this house. You'd have to be crazy not to be happy.

She went downstairs and checked out the library, and what a library it was. One whole wall and a third of another, from floor to ceiling, was a built-in bookcase. It was full of books, every kind you could imagine. This room was destined to be Sidney's favorite, second only to the bedroom, of course. They both had a warm and cozy feeling about them. There was a fireplace and two black leather overstuffed chairs with ottomans along with a matching sofa. In the corner was a very large mahogany desk with a glass overlay on top to protect the wood. It was beautiful. The pictures on the wall were Native American modern art.

The whole house had an elegant feel to it. Sidney thought there must have been great love in this house for it to feel this way. Even as elegant and as beautiful as this house was, she could see how Sal would feel lonely in it without his wife. It was huge. Unless you went into the library and closed the huge double sliding doors, you felt like you were rattling around the place. She loved the house, though, with its three sleek large black marble fireplaces, one in the den, one in the family room, and one in the master bedroom. Next, Sidney went down to the basement. Down there was a gym with every kind of exercise equipment. It even had racks of free weights along the wall. It had a game room, with a billiard table, a fully stocked bar, and a soda machine full of pop. She also found the laundry room and utility room.

When she went back upstairs, she went out to the garage. In the garage were two cars (a Cadillac and a Lincoln town car), a riding lawn mower, and a workshop with a lot of tools. She couldn't help thinking, *What am I going to do with all this stuff? I can't even drive.*

## RAINBOWS ARE BETTER

She walked the grounds and couldn't believe how beautifully landscaped the place was. The fishpond had some large fish swimming in it. They seemed to be hungry, so she found some fish food in the garage and fed them. She thought, *How am I ever going to take care of such a large place?* She locked up the place and headed home to her little apartment.

When she arrived home, she knew she would miss this little apartment. She had been quite happy living here. She also knew a promise was a promise. She began to pack what few things she had. She decided to take Angel's good crystal and bone china out of storage to put in her new home. She called her landlord to tell him she would be moving. Then she called the nursing home to tell them how Sal was doing and that she would be moving. She told them she would call them when she was finished moving. It didn't take long to pack the few things she would be taking with her. There were some things Sidney knew she wouldn't need anymore. She decided to check with the young mother down the hall from her place. Sidney knew she was having a hard time. Sidney asked her if she could use any of her stuff. The young woman was thrilled to death. She thanked Sidney for being kind enough to give her the pots, pans, dishes, utensils, appliances, and TV she had.

Sidney called a moving company to move her belongings. They told her they could do it right then, if she was ready. They had a cancellation and were available immediately. Sidney agreed, and they said they would be there in about an hour. By seven o'clock that night, Sidney was all settled in her new home. She called Sal and told him she was already moved in. He could hardly believe his ears. Sal told her, "You're a miracle worker. I can't believe how fast you can get things done." Sidney said, "In all fairness, Sal, I didn't have that much to move." He told her that was still quick. Knowing she was there made him feel much better about everything. He asked if she would mind feeding the fish in the pond. She told him she already had.

# Chapter 8

# *Servants and All*

Sal said, "There's one other thing you should know so you don't get spooked in the morning. Su Yen is my housekeeper, and she will be there in the morning to clean house. I hope you don't mind if I keep her on. I know she depends on this job to care for her two small children. If it's going to be a problem, I'll call some people I know to see if they will hire her." Sidney said, "I don't mind at all." She was wondering how she was going to take care of such a huge house while she worked and went to school. Sal said, "Then it's a deal. I know Su Yen will be happy." He said, "I'll call her and let her know you'll be living there now. I wouldn't want her to be shocked in the morning, when she gets there." Sidney asked, "When does Su Yen usually arrive?" Sal said, "At about six thirty or seven in the morning." He told Sidney, "Don't worry, Su Yen has her own key. You won't have to get up to let her in." He told Sidney she should sleep in and let Su Yen do the cleaning while she slept. Sidney didn't think she could sleep through someone being in the house, cleaning.

Sidney went upstairs to decide which room she would sleep in that first night. She decided she needed to sleep in her own bed, so she started putting it together. Once it was all assembled, she put on the sheets and comforter. She thought, *This doesn't look bad at all. It'll look even better when I get my own curtains put up.* When she opened the closet to hang her clothes, she was shocked to see a closet that large. It was like a whole room by itself. It was filled with Sal's clothes and what she assumed were his wife's clothes. Sidney made room for her few things and closed the door.

She decided that was enough for now. She went downstairs to check out the food situation. Boy, was she surprised to find such a well-stocked kitchen. She thought the refrigerator might have a few things that needed to be thrown out. She was surprised to find everything was just fine. There was a large side-by-side refrigerator. The freezer was stocked full of frozen dinners. There was also a subzero freezer. It was built into the wall and had every kind of frozen food you could imagine. She couldn't help thinking, why would one person have so much food in their house? She took out one of the frozen dinners and heated it in the microwave oven. While it was cooking, she made a salad and set the table in the kitchen nook. As she sat there, eating her dinner, she thought to herself how surreal this whole thing suddenly felt. Just this morning, she was living in a small one-room apartment, and this evening, she was living in a lovely huge estate. Sidney finished her dinner and cleaned the kitchen.

She went into the library to read for a while before going to bed. When she looked around the library for something to read, she saw a Bible on the end table, next to one of the chairs by the fireplace. She thought, *Sal must have left that there when he was here last.* She found that to be strange because she knew Sal was Jewish. She might have expected to see a Torah instead. She felt very sad for Sal not being able to go home to this place. Here where he and his wife had lived their life together. She wished, with all her heart, things could be different for him. Sidney knelt down and prayed for Sal and thanked God for putting him in her life. She sat down in Sal's soft, cushy chair and picked up the Bible to read.

She read for about an hour then decided to go upstairs and get ready for bed. The wall at the foot of her bed had some built-in cabinets. She went over and opened the center doors. Inside, there was a fifty-five-inch television set with a remote control. This was much nicer than the thirteen-inch set she had. Of course, she never had much time for watching television before. She went to the window seat and sat there to say her prayers. She asked God to bless this house and her living in it, along with all her usual prayers. Then, she climbed into to her wonderful bed and turned on the television to watch the evening news before going to sleep. When she turned off the TV, she went right to sleep. She'd had a full day and needed to rest. She'd been concerned earlier that she might have trouble sleeping in her new surroundings, but that was not the case at all.

When she woke up the next morning, she smelled coffee and something wonderful coming from downstairs. She looked at the clock, and it was eight o'clock in the morning. She couldn't believe that she had slept so long. She thought, that must be Su Yen downstairs, having breakfast before starting work. She got up, showered, and got ready to go to the hospital. When she was ready, she went down to find something to eat before leaving. When she entered the kitchen, she saw someone who must be Su Yen, taking something out of the oven.

Su Yen was a small person, about five feet tall, and probably weighed about ninety pounds, soaking wet. She had straight, shiny shoulder-length black hair and a sweet smile. Sidney introduced herself to Su Yen and told her how happy she was to meet her. Su Yen told Sidney her breakfast was ready, if she was ready to eat now. Sidney said, "You didn't have to fix breakfast for me, but thank you very much." Su Yen had prepared a place at the table in the kitchen nook, for Sidney. Sidney asked if she was going to join her for breakfast. Su Yen said no, she had already eaten with her children before coming to work. Sidney asked her where her children were. Su Yen said, "Outside, playing." Sidney said, "Don't you at least want to sit down and have a cup of coffee with me?" Su Yen seemed embarrassed and said, "I must clean now." Sidney ate her breakfast of bacon, scrambled eggs, and homemade cinnamon rolls. Everything was so good. She told Su Yen she was a very good cook. Sidney told her, from now on, it wouldn't be necessary to fix so much food. She explained, she never ate that much for breakfast. She and Su Yen discussed Sidney's eating habits. Su Yen said, "I do better next time." Sidney said, "You didn't do anything wrong. The meal was wonderful, but if I ate like that every day, I'd weigh a ton in no time." Su Yen giggled, and Sidney returned to the kitchen to clean up. Su Yen was right behind her, saying, "I clean, that my job." Sidney, not wanting to make any more waves, backed off and said, "Okay."

Suddenly Sidney felt a strange sense of urgency to get to the hospital. She didn't understand what she was feeling, but she knew she had to get there right away. Sidney usually took the bus wherever she was going. Today, however, she wished she could drive one of those cars. Since she couldn't, she called a taxi to pick her up. She told them to hurry; it was an emergency. She didn't really know it was an emergency, but she felt strongly that it was. The cab arrived in about two minutes; still, Sidney had been pacing the floor. It seemed much longer than two minutes. She sat very stiff in the seat of the cab, all the way to the hospital, which was only three miles away. It seemed much longer, though. When they arrived, she jumped out of the cab and hurriedly paid the driver.

She practically ran into the hospital, and she was all but sprinting to Sal's room. That sense of urgency was getting stronger and stronger. Just as she entered Sal's room, she saw him struggling to breathe. She rang for help and ran into the hall, yelling, "Sal needs help!" The nurses went running. Sal's monitor sounded the alert that his heart had stopped. The code-blue alarm sounded, and everyone went running into Sal's room. They worked on Sal for about fifteen minutes before they declared him dead. Sidney went into Sal's room and threw herself across Sal's chest. She began to weep with a deep sadness she hadn't felt in a long time.

All of a sudden, she thought she felt Sal's hand move. Then she felt him touch her arm. She raised up, and Sal asked her, "What's wrong?" Sidney said, "I thought I had lost you." Sal said, "I'm not ready to go yet, so I came back." Sidney called the nurse back to Sal's room. You could only imagine the shocked look on her face to see Sal alive and talking. The nurse called the doctor back to the room, and he, too, was startled to see Sal alive. The doctor thought to himself, *This is impossible.* But obviously, it wasn't impossible, if he was alive, and he certainly was alive. When the doctor finished checking Sal over, they let Sidney back in his room. He told Sidney it was a good thing for Sal that she happened to arrive in his room when she did. It probably saved his life. Sidney said, "I didn't save his life. There was a power much higher than mine at work here today." When the doctor and the nurse left, Sal told Sidney he had something he needed to tell her. He said he didn't want her to think he was crazy. He knew, if someone told him what he was going to tell her, he would probably have thought they were crazy. Sidney said, "I know you're not crazy, no matter what you tell me." Sal said, "Good, because I need you to believe me. This experience was so wonderful, I just have to share it with you. When you came in this morning, I saw you ring for the nurse. I also saw you run about half way down the hall, yelling for help. I saw the doctor and nurses in my room working on me. The strange part was that I was watching, from above, everything. Then, I went into a dark place that went all around me. It wasn't scary, just quiet and comforting. It felt like I was floating through this darkness. Then, I saw a very bright blue light at the end of this darkness. I knew instantly this was the light of God. As I got closer to the light, it began to penetrate my soul. It filled me with such warmth, love, and great joy like I have never known. I wondered why I was there and what was going to happen to me. Then, I knew instantly all the answers, without a word being spoken. It was just a knowing without words. I guess the closest way I can describe it is speaking telepathically. It was much more than that, though. It was purely knowing, without even trying, all the answers I had questions for. I didn't have to think about it. I knew, completely, with absolute comprehension and no doubt whatsoever, everything I desired to know. I knew I was in the presence of God. I learned God doesn't really pass judgment on us. Instead, he lets us see, feel, and experience all the good and bad things we've done and what the repercussions of those deeds were. I guess you could say he lets us judge ourselves. He lets us experience all the pain or happiness we have created during our time on earth. Then, God informed me it wasn't time for me to come home. He relayed to me I had other things to do while I was here. He let me know, when the time was right, I could come back. At first, I didn't want to leave, but I knew he was right, so I agreed to come back. I told him I hoped it wouldn't be long before I could come home again. After all, it was more perfect and wonderful there than anyone could ever imagine. The next thing I knew, I was back in my body.

I've got to tell you, this earthly body felt very heavy compared to my spirit self. Then, I saw you, and you were crying. Sidney, I know I have some things to finish before I can go back home. But please, don't ever cry for me again. Where I'm going, there is nothing to cry about." Sidney said, "I know, Sal, but I wasn't crying for you. I was crying for me because I would be without you. I think, when people cry over someone that's passed on, it's really for themselves. They're sad that they've been left without that person in their lives ever again. They know that's the way it'll be until it's their time to go home."

Sal said, "So you do believe me?" Sidney replied, "Of course I believe you. I've heard about other people experiencing the same thing you did. It happens quite often, when they are declared dead and come back." Sal said, "Thanks, kid. I needed to hear you say that. I wanted you to know how wonderful life will be when this life is over." Sidney told Sal she already believed what he told her, but it made her feel better about her parents and Angel hearing him say it was true. Sal hugged her for a long time, because he knew she was one of the reasons he had come back. He really did love her like his own daughter.

Sidney asked Sal if he needed to rest after all that. He answered, "No way, I have never felt better." Sidney said, "Good, because all that's happened this morning has me excited too." She explained to him why she happened to be in his room at just the right moment. Moreover, until he told her his story about what happened, her part of the story didn't make too much sense. She told him all about how she had felt a real urgency to get to his room. He knew it was true, because he knew Sidney never used a cab. She was much too frugal for that. Sal told her he would never doubt that kind of thing again.

He told Sidney he was deeply concerned about this experience. It was forcing him to rethink some of his beliefs and what God wanted us to do while we were here on earth. Sidney explained to him that her dear Angel would call this a gift. She would say, "You were allowed to know the truth while you're still able to do something about it." Sidney said, "Sal, you shouldn't be confused about this. You already know, in your heart, why you were shown this and what God wants of you." Sal smiled and said, "I guess you're right. I do. It truly is the most wonderful gift a person could possibly get." The two of them talked a long time about all the events that had taken place that morning. They both knew it was one morning they would never forget. Finally, Sal said he was tired and needed to rest for a while. Sidney agreed and told him she would check on Larkyn and her mom. She said she would be back later.

When Sidney approached Larkyn's mom's room, she felt sick at her stomach. She seemed to know that something was wrong. When she looked in the room, the bed was empty. She knew Larkyn's mom had passed away. She went to the nurse's station and asked what had happened to the lady in room 406. The nurse wanted to know who Sidney was. She answered, "Sidney Davis." The nurse said, "The patient's family left a letter for you."

Sidney went down to the chapel and sat down in the back to read the letter. The letter was from Larkyn. She thanked Sidney for being such a good friend during the past few days. She said her mom had died while in the coma. The doctor told them she felt no pain. Then, she told Sidney not to worry about her and her dad; they were going to be all right. She finished the letter, saying, "Thanks to you, I've learned to pray, and I know my mom is better off now." At the bottom of the letter, she put her address and phone number, in case Sidney wanted to call or come by.

Sidney did call right away. She told Larkyn how sorry she was about her mother. Sidney also expressed how proud she was that Larkyn was being so strong and brave. Larkyn told Sidney she was doing what she told her to. She was helping her dad get through this, and it really did help to stay busy. Sidney told Larkyn where she lived, her phone number there, and her number at work. Sidney let her know, if she needed a friend, she could call her day or night. Larkyn thanked her and asked if she called her with the funeral arrangements would she come. Sidney told her she would definitely be there. She told Larkyn she loved her and they would talk again soon.

When Sidney got off the phone, she turned around, and there stood Shade. He said he had been looking for her. He had heard about the strange happenings in Sal's room that morning. Sidney told him this had been the strangest day of her life, so far. Shade asked

# RAINBOWS ARE BETTER

her if Sal had talked about a near-death experience. Sidney asked him how he knew about that. He said, "I wouldn't be a very good doctor if I hadn't listened to several of my patients tell me about their near-death experiences." Sidney asked him if he believed what they told him. He answered, "I don't know, but I do know they believed it. I only hope they're right."

Shade asked Sidney if she wanted to have lunch with him in about an hour. Sidney said, "I don't know, I hate to leave Sal right now." Shade said, "That's okay, we'll have lunch here in the cafeteria. Maybe your little friend, Larkyn, would like to join us." Sidney told Shade that Larkyn's mother died and Larkyn and her father had gone home. Shade took Sidney in his arms and said, "You've had a tough morning, haven't you?" Sidney said it had been unusual, at the very least. Shade said he hated to leave her, knowing how she must feel. Sidney insisted she was fine and she would see him in an hour in the cafeteria.

Sidney headed back to Sal's room. When she arrived, Sal was sleeping, so she pulled out her magazine and started reading. It was about half an hour before Sal woke up. He asked her how little Larkyn was doing. Sidney said, "I'm afraid Larkyn's mom wasn't as lucky as you were." Sal said, "You're wrong, Sidney. She was the lucky one." Sidney said, "I know you're right. I just feel so sorry for Larkyn and her dad." Sal said, "Just be there for her if she ever needs you. That's all anyone can do now."

Sal asked Sidney why she didn't drive one of the cars to the hospital instead of taking a cab. Sidney said, "Because I don't know how to drive." Sal said, "You have got to be kidding. We're going to get you some driving lessons." Sidney said, "I don't mind taking the bus." Sal said, "Sometimes, like this morning, you need to be able to drive. I know of a driving school that's supposed to be a good one. We'll get you signed up as soon as I'm out of the hospital." Sidney said, "I don't think I could drive such big cars." Sal said, "That's not a problem, we'll trade one in on a smaller car. After all, you own those cars as of this afternoon, when my lawyer gets here with the papers for me to sign. I meant it when I said everything I have is yours." Sidney said, "I feel so strange about all this."

Sal asked her how she slept her first night in the house. Sidney said, "Like a baby. I didn't even wake up until eight o'clock this morning." She told him it was so peaceful and quiet, even Su Yen didn't wake her up when she came in. Sal said, "By the way, Sidney, there's someone else you should know about. I have a gardener named Joe Banks, who comes on Thursdays each week to do the gardening. He's very good, and I'd like him to stay on, if you don't mind." Sidney said, "You really have me well taken care of, don't you?" Sal said, "I hope so, you are my girl." Sidney said, "Well, when you put it that way, whatever you want is okay."

Sal looked over and said, "Here comes the nurse, with my lunch, I hope." The nurse said, "If that's what you want, that's what you shall have, Mr. Miracle Man." Sidney and Sal both laughed. Sal said, "and don't you forget it, either." The nurse left to get Sal's lunch. Sidney said she, too, was going to lunch. She was having lunch in the cafeteria. Sal said, "Take your time, I know you'll be meeting the young doctor down there. Am I right?" Sidney said, "You couldn't be more right. What did that experience this morning do, make you a psychic?" Sal said, "Of course it did."

Sidney proceeded to the cafeteria, where Shade was waiting. He said he finished his rounds early. He couldn't wait to spend time with his favorite girl. Sidney asked him if there were many girls. He laughed and said, "That was just a figure of speech. There's only one girl, and you're it." As they ate their lunch together, the cares of the day seemed to melt away. Sidney was lost in the warmth and happiness she felt just being near him. When lunch was over, Shade and Sidney walked hand in hand back to Sal's room.

Shade told Sidney he wanted to see her again after he got off work. He asked if she thought that would be all right. Sidney said she wanted to wait and see how Sal was doing. Shade said, "Of course, how thoughtless of me. I'm having trouble thinking about anything but you these days." Sidney blushed and said, "You're not thoughtless. I know exactly how you feel. I feel the same way. If you could check back with me in a couple of hours, I should know how things are going." Shade said, "You can count on it."

When Sidney entered Sal's room, she was surprised to see him wide-awake and smiling, the biggest smile, especially for someone who, just a short time ago, was pronounced dead. She told Sal, "You certainly look chipper." He said, "That's because I'm feeling chipper. I somehow feel renewed and revitalized. Maybe it's because I know I'm going to be all right. After all, it's not my time to go."

Sal told Sidney his lawyer was on his way over with the papers to sign. Sidney said, "Are you sure you don't want to change your mind?" Sal said, "I have never been more certain of anything in my life. After all, he who gives while he lives knows where it goes. I want things put in order. I've also called a car dealer about getting you a smaller car so you can learn to drive. Do you have any preference as to which of the two cars you like best?" Sidney said, "I don't know anything about cars." Sal said, "Then I think you should keep the town car. It's newer and hasn't had any problems." Sidney said, "That's fine." Sal said, "I know that will make Joe, the gardener, happy. He likes driving the town car when he fills in as the chauffeur. Keep that in mind, Sidney. He'll be happy to take you anywhere you need to go."

Sidney asked Sal how often Su Yen and Joe went to the house. Sal told her, "Su Yen comes every day but Sunday, while Joe comes once a week. From time to time, Joe will show up just to check on things. He likes to see if anything needs to be repaired or if I needed him for anything. They're both real good people, and I know they'll take good care of you." Sidney said, "I'm not really used to someone taking care of me." Sal said, "Look at it this way. They need the job, and you deserve to be taken care of. This way, I don't have to worry about any of you, because you'll have each other. It works out well, don't you think?"

"Okay," said Sidney, "we'll see how things go."

As they were discussing the things Sal felt Sidney needed to know, the lawyer arrived. When he went in the room, he introduced himself as Samuel Epstein. He said, "You must be Sidney. I think I would have known you anywhere. Sal has done nothing for the past year but talk about you." Sidney said, "Thank you, Mr. Epstein. Can I get you anything before you get started?" He said, "No, thanks, this won't take long. Sal, I drew up the paperwork you requested, and all I need is your signature. I'm going to leave this with you. You can read it overnight. I'll be back tomorrow with a notary for your signature, if that's okay?" Sal said, "That would be great." That way, he and Sidney would have time to go over everything together. Mr. Epstein told Sidney it was nice to finally meet her, and then he left.

Sal told Sidney, "He's a nice guy, but he's all business." Sidney asked Sal if he needed a nap before going over the papers. Sal said no; he never felt better. He wanted to get things taken care of as soon as possible. As they went over the paperwork together, Sal explained everything to Sidney. That way, in the future, she would know the things she needed to know. When they were done, Sidney said, "This was a fun lesson for today." Sal said, "You are such a good student. I'll never get over how fast you learn things." Sidney said, "I love you, Sal, but I know you need to rest." He said, "You're right, kid. I do need to rest. I think I can now."

He told her to go on home, and if he needed her, he would call her at home. He laughed as he told her he knew that telephone number very well. She said, "That's another thing I need to ask you. What about having the utilities put in my name?" Sal said, "I'm going to let you make up your own mind about that. There's no big hurry. I've got to admit, I hope you'll leave the phone number the same. I've always liked that number." Sidney said, "Don't worry, I won't change it. I like that phone number myself. It's very easy to remember." She asked him if he was sure he didn't need her to stay. He told her to go on home; he was fine. He said, "I think I'll ask that nurse for one of those knock-out shots and go to sleep for the night." Sidney kissed him goodbye and told him to rest well.

# Chapter 9

## *Sidney's First Houseguest*

Going down the hall, Sidney met Shade. He asked her how Sal was doing. She answered, "Remarkably well. I'm going home for the evening. Sal said he would call if he needs me. How would you like to come over to my new home for dinner?" Shade said, "You bet, what time do you want me there?" Sidney said, "How about seven thirty?" Shade said, "I'll be there with bells on. Is there anything you would like me to bring?" Sidney said, "Just you, your appetite, and that great smile of yours." Sidney gave him her address and phone number then left to go home.

When Sidney got home, Su Yen was still there. Sidney sat down and talked to her for a while. She told Su Yen she was having company for dinner. Su Yen wanted to know if she could prepare dinner for them before going home. Sidney was shocked that she actually wanted to prepare their dinner. Sidney said, "Are you sure that won't be too big an imposition?" Su Yen said she would like to do something to thank Sidney for letting her keep her job. Sidney told her that wasn't necessary. Nevertheless, Su Yen insisted it would make her feel better. So Sidney thanked her and said she would be very grateful if she would fix dinner.

Sidney heard children giggling in the background. She knew it had to be Su Yen's children. She turned around, and there were two of the most adorable children. They were both such beautiful little cherubs. She told Su Yen her children were very beautiful. Su Yen smiled at the mere mention of her children. She said, "Thank you."

Sidney asked their names and ages. Su Yen said Brian was four years old and Blake was two years old. She told Sidney she thought they looked like their father, James Johnson. Su Yen went on to say he was Black and that was why the children had such beautiful big brown eyes like he did.

Sidney asked, "What happened to him?" Su Yen said, "He killed, in line of duty right before I give birth to Blake." Sidney asked if he was a police officer. Su Yen told her he was a fireman. She explained how he died trying to save the lives of two small children in a burning building. How he saved one child. When he went back in, the ceiling collapsed. He wasn't able to get out with the second child. It killed both of them. She said, "He such a good man. He love so many people so much, he give life for them." Sidney told Su Yen how very sorry she was to hear this. Su Yen said, "He give me two beautiful children, so I not alone. I very grateful, but sometime, I so lonely for him." Sidney hugged her and said, "I know how you feel, and I know we're going to be the best of friends." Su Yen said, "Yes, I, too, think so. Now, I fix dinner." Sidney followed her into the kitchen, and the two of them planned the dinner. While they talked, Sidney found some cookies. She asked Su Yen if the children could have one. Su Yen agreed. So did the boys. Su Yen prepared the dinner while Sidney sat the table. Sidney broke out the good china, crystal, and silverware. Then, she found some white linen place mats and napkins. She put white candles in the beautiful crystal candlestick holders she found. She placed the flower arrangement that Su Yen brought that morning on the black lacquer table. The table was so shiny, you could see yourself in it. When she was done, she stood back and thought, *What a beautiful table setting*. She didn't even know she had it in her to set such a fine table. When Su Yen saw it, she said, "Very beautiful, Ms. Sidney. Your young man be very pleased." Sidney said, "I hope so. He's so wonderful."

Sidney went upstairs to get ready. She remembered seeing a soft and silky silvery-gray lounge dress. She had moved it out of Sal's closet when she moved in. She went to the guest room, where she had put it, and tried it on. It fit as if it had been made for her. She was somewhat surprised that it fit so well. However, this had been another magical day in her life. She decided to wear it. She looked in a jewelry box and found the most beautiful earrings she had ever seen. She wasn't sure, but they looked like real diamonds. They were far more gorgeous than any she had ever seen. She had never worn dangling earrings, but there was a first time for everything. She put them on, then she put on her mother's locket. She put on a little lipstick. Then she pulled her hair up and let it cascade in loose curls. She couldn't help but think she looked better this evening than she ever had. It was almost like looking in the mirror at someone else. When Su Yen saw her, she said, "Ms. Sidney, you so elegant, just like fashion model." Sidney felt embarrassed but managed to say "Thank you." She didn't want to make a fuss about getting such a nice compliment.

Everything was ready, and it was almost time for Shade to arrive. Su Yen asked if Sidney wanted her to stay and serve. Sidney said, "No, you've done more than enough. I know the children are ready to go home. They already have their coats on." Su Yen laughed and said, "If you sure, we leave now. You have nice evening." Sidney thanked her for all she had done, and Su Yen left. Sidney checked the food, and Su Yen had done a great job. Everything smelled wonderful and looked great.

When the doorbell rang, Sidney got butterflies in her stomach, the size of B-2 bombers. She rushed to the door, and there he was. Shade couldn't believe his eyes. He said, "You look ravishing." Sidney couldn't help it; she began to blush all over. Sidney asked him to come in. Shade said, "This is quite a house you have here. I had no idea you were so rich." Sidney said, "I'm not, and it's a long story that I'll tell you later." Shade said, "Boy, something smells incredible in here." Sidney told him her housekeeper had prepared a terrific dinner for them. Shade said, "Did I hear you right, your housekeeper?" Sidney said, "I told you, it's a long story. First we'll eat, and then I promise to tell you, the whole story." Shade asked if he could help. Sidney said, "Sure, you can light the candles while I bring in the food." Shade lit the candles and then helped carry in the food. Sidney dimmed the lights, and they sat down to enjoy the wonderful meal Su Yen had prepared. As the meal progressed, Sidney explained to Shade how she had come to live in Sal's house. She explained she had moved in only the day before. When the meal was over, they got up and cleaned the table together. When they finished, Sidney asked Shade where he would like to have their coffee and dessert. He said, "Wherever you want." She told him, "There are so many rooms around here, it's hard to know which one would be best."

Shade said, "Before we have our dessert, why don't you give me the grand tour of the palace? Then I'll help you decide." Sidney took him from room to room. He was overwhelmed by it all. Then, Sidney took him downstairs to the game room. He said, "We can stop right here. I love to play billiards, don't you?" Sidney said, "I don't know, I've never played billiards." Shade said, "You have lived a sheltered life, my love. I'll be happy to teach you." Sidney said, "I'll get the coffee and dessert." Shade said, "Are you kidding, when we have a soda machine right here? That's my favorite drink." Sidney said, "I must confess, I like it, too, once in a while." So it was decided they would spend the rest of the evening right where they were.

Shade said, before they started a game, he needed to call the hospital and check in. He asked if would be all right to give them her phone number in case they needed to call him. Sidney said, "Of course, you can." She asked him if he could check on Sal while he had them on the phone. Shade replied, "No problem." With that done and Sal resting peacefully, they set up the table.

They began Sidney's first lesson in the game of billiards. Like everything else, she picked it up very quickly. Shade asked her, "Are you sure you've never played this game before?" Sidney said, "I'm positive. I've never done much of anything for recreation. All I've done is work, study, and travel. I rarely even watch television." Shade said, "Well, you have some nice television sets to watch now." Sidney said, "I know, I never dreamed of having so many television sets, much less such big ones, all with remote controls." Shade shook his head and said, "You have lived a lot of life in some areas, and in others, you've not lived at all. I'm going to make it my life's work to fill in the fun part of your life that's been missing."

It was getting late, and Shade said he'd better go. He had a busy day scheduled the next day. Sidney walked him to the front door, where Shade kissed her rather passionately before thanking her for such a wonderful evening. Then, Sidney kissed him and said he was entirely welcome. She told him, now that he knew where she lived, maybe he could come again. Shade kissed her again and again to let her know she could count on it. He asked, "If all went well the next day, can we have lunch together?" Sidney answered, "I thought you would never ask." They kissed again, and Shade said, "Goodbye," and went to his car. Sidney waved to him and watched him go down the driveway and through the gate. She pushed the button to close and lock the gate. She closed the door and stood there for a while, savoring the evening and the kisses. Then checked all the locks and prepared to go to bed. She sat on her window seat to say her prayers. She had a lot to be thankful for tonight. She was so full of love and thankfulness, it was hard for her to fall asleep. Somehow, the soft hug of her bed only made her think of Shade and how wonderful it felt to be in his arms. Finally, she fell asleep.

CHAPTER 10

## *The Woes of Being the Boss*

When she woke up the next morning, it was six o'clock. She thought to herself, *That's more like it.* She got up and jumped in the shower. By the time Sidney was dressed and ready for the day, Su Yen was coming in the front door. Sidney went downstairs, noticing it was seven o'clock. She said "Good morning" to Su Yen and hugged the little boys. Su Yen asked her what she would like for breakfast. Sidney said, "I will only eat breakfast if you and the boys join me." Su Yen said, "We already eat. Boys, play outside now." Sidney said, "All right, but maybe you could have a cup of coffee with me." Su Yen reluctantly agreed. She put the coffee on, and Sidney got out a box of cereal. She told Su Yen, "Cereal will be fine this morning." Su Yen said (speaking in her cute, slightly broken English), "You need good breakfast, it most important." She fixed a few strips of bacon and some toast, cut up a cantaloupe, and poured a glass of orange juice to go with her cereal. She asked Sidney if she would like some eggs. Sidney said, "No, thanks, this is more than enough." Su Yen started her cleaning while Sidney ate her breakfast.

When Sidney had finished eating, Su Yen went in and poured them both a cup of coffee and sat at the table. She wanted to know how dinner went the night before. Sidney said, "It was wonderful. Thank you so much." Su Yen smiled and said, "I happy you enjoy." Su Yen told Sidney she saw Joe outside when she came in. Su Yen asked Sidney if there was anything she would like for him to do while he was there. Sidney said, "I don't think so. I haven't been here long enough to know what needs to be done." Su Yen said, "I handle for you till you ready." Sidney thanked her and expressed how much she would appreciate that.

Sidney asked Su Yen where she lived. Su Yen told her she lived in an apartment about ten miles from there. Sidney said, "You mean you get up, get yourself and two kids ready, have breakfast, and drive over here by seven o'clock every morning?" Su Yen said, "Not come Sunday." Sidney said, "From now on, you can have Saturday and Sunday off. I can take care of myself, and your salary won't change, I promise." Su Yen said, "You most kind. I not mind come here Saturday. Children like play here. You have big yard, high fence. They like play outside. Neighborhood where we live not so nice, there no place for play. Apartment have one bedroom, very small. If you not mind, we like come Saturday. You not want us to?" Sidney said, "I'm sorry, I didn't know. Of course, you are more than welcome to come whenever you want to. I was just trying to do something nice for you, but I will really appreciate the company. Listen, I have to get to the hospital." Su Yen said, "Tell Mr. Sal I say hello, he please get better soon." Sidney said she would.

Sidney went out to catch the bus. When she went out, she saw Joe puttering around in the garage. She stepped inside and asked if he was Joe. Joe was a large man, about six foot two or three inches tall, and weighed about 220 pounds. He wasn't heavy, just very muscular, and looked extremely strong. He had brownish-blond hair and large sky-blue eyes that had a childlike innocence about them. She couldn't help but think maybe the accident helped give him this warm and kind demeanor. Joe asked, "Who might you be?" She answered, "I'm Sidney Davis, and I live here now. "It's nice to meet you, Ms. Sidney. Su Yen told me all about you. She thinks you're a very special person." Sidney said, "Thanks, Joe. It's very nice to meet you too."

She told Joe she was on her way to the hospital. She was just waiting for the bus. Joe said, "You don't need to wait for the bus, let me take you. The car hasn't been driven for a while. I'll be happy to take you." Sidney replied, "Thank you, Joe. That would be very nice." They got in the car, and Joe took her to the hospital. When they arrived, Joe asked Sidney if she wanted him to pick her up later.

She said, "No, thanks, Joe. I don't know when I'll be going home." Joe asked her to tell Sal they were all rooting for him. "We hope he'll be out of here real soon." Sidney assured him she'd be glad to tell Sal. She knew he'd be happy they were thinking of him.

Sidney entered the hospital and was headed for Sal's room, when Shade came up behind her. He said, "You're just the person I wanted to see." Sidney asked, "Why do you want to see me?" Shade said, "I just wanted to see you, that's all." Sidney smiled and asked if they were still on for lunch. Shade said, "You better believe it. I can hardly wait." Then he excused himself to do his rounds so he wouldn't get behind.

Sidney went on to Sal's room. When she arrived, Sal was looking so much better than he had since his heart attack. She told Sal that Su Yen and Joe both wished him well and hoped he'd be out of the hospital soon. Sal said, "That's really nice of them. Do they understand I won't be coming home?" Sidney said, "Yes, I explained everything to them." Sal said, "Thanks, kid. I didn't want to be the one to tell them."

Sidney said, "I have a question for you, Sal. Maybe I have several questions for you. First, why didn't you leave your house to Su Yen or even Joe?" Sal said, "Sidney, I know you don't think you deserve anything from anyone, but you do. You're the one I love like my own daughter. I want you to have everything that means anything to me. I helped Su Yen and Joe when they needed it. I don't feel as though I owe them any more than I've already given them. When Joe had a car accident and injured his head, it left him a little slow. No one else would hire him after that. I knew he was good at fixing things, and he loved gardening and taking care of the landscaping. He needed work, so I gave him a job with decent pay and benefits. When Su Yen lost her husband, I read in the papers about his death and how the city refused her any benefits or pension. According to the city, James hadn't been with them long enough to qualify for anything. I thought that was really stinky, so I hired Su Yen and basically gave her the same deal as Joe. That way, she had insurance on her and the kids."

## RAINBOWS ARE BETTER

Sidney said, "I know you've been more than kind. But did you know Su Yen lives in a one-bedroom apartment with no place for her children to play?"

"Yes," said Sal, "and I also know they get to play in my yard while Su Yen works, so she doesn't have to pay a babysitter. You probably wouldn't like knowing that Joe lives in a small one-room shack down by the train tracks, either. I know I can't save the world. I just try to help as much as possible when I can." Sidney asked Sal if it would be all right if she asked Su Yen and the children to move into the spare bedrooms. At least then, they would have a decent place to live. Sal said, "Don't let your heart overrule your head. You're going to need some privacy, and you'll never have any if they're living there too." Sidney said, "It just hurts me to know I have everything and they have so little." Sal said, "It's your house now. You can do anything you want. Just give me a few days to consider other options, okay?" Sidney said, "Of course, I shouldn't be bothering you with all this." Sal said, "I wouldn't love you so much if you weren't the kind of person you are. Don't worry, kid. We'll work this out."

About that time, the lawyer arrived with a notary to get the papers signed. He said, "No offense to Ms. Davis, but are you absolutely sure this is what you want to do, Sal?" Sal said (with more than a little disdain in his voice), "Sidney had nothing to do with this decision, and yes, I'm absolutely certain." The papers were signed, and Sal gave Sidney the original and told her to put the papers in a safe deposit box. The lawyer and the notary left. Sal told Sidney she should never use that lawyer if she ever needed an attorney. She should find someone else. Sidney said, "Don't worry, Sal. He was just trying to look after your best interest. I can understand that." Sal said, "Well, I didn't like his attitude and innuendos."

Sal and Sidney looked over the newspaper and mapped out their strategies for the next day. Sal asked Sidney if she had any special feelings about the stocks. Sidney picked two she felt needed to be sold and one she thought they should buy. Sal agreed. He asked her if she was going to the investment firm in the morning. Sidney thought she would run over right now and take care of it. She felt the next day might be too late. Sal asked if she was sure. She said she felt very strongly about it. He said, "Then by all means, go for it." She called a cab and went right over. When she returned, she told Sal it was all taken care of.

Sidney told Sal she hoped he didn't mind that she had Shade over for dinner the night before and she wore one of the dresses she found in his closet. She said, "I know it must have been your wife's dress, and I also wore a pair of her earrings. I hope that was all right." Sal said, "All of that stuff belongs to you now." He said he was happy she was getting some good out of it. He asked her how the dinner with the young doctor went. Sidney said, "It was wonderful." She continued, telling him, after dinner, they spent the evening playing pool or, as Shade informed her, it was billiards. Sal laughed and said, "You know, of course, the good doctor, is right. It is billiards." Sidney said, "I honestly don't know the difference. I hadn't played either one before last night." Sal said, "You're kidding." Sidney said, "No, I've never done anything other than sightseeing, swimming, and playing bingo for recreation." Sal said, "So do you like to swim?" Sidney answered, "Oh yes, I truly love swimming, but I don't have time to do that much of it." Sal said, "You've got to learn to have fun once in a while. God only knows you deserve it, if anyone does." Sidney said, "Thanks, Sal, but I have a lot of things to get done in my life, and having fun takes too much time. You'll be happy to know I do have lots of fun when I see Shade. He makes me laugh, and I can't stop smiling when he's around." Sal said, "That makes me happy too. So are you and the good doctor going to lunch today?" Sidney said, "As a matter of fact, we are. Is there anything you would like me to get you while I'm out?"

"No," replied Sal, "but if you could bring me a Bible tomorrow when you come over, I would really like that. I'm going to be reading it with a new understanding now."

The nurse went in and asked Sal if he was ready to eat his lunch. Sal said, "Do ducks quack? Of course I am. My friend here was just leaving to go to lunch." Sidney asked, "Are you giving me the bum's rush?" Sal said, "I'd never do that. I just want you to go out and have enough fun for both of us." Sidney was turning around to leave, as Shade walked in behind her. He asked Sal how he was feeling. Sal

## RAINBOWS ARE BETTER

said he was doing much better. He told Shade he understood he was courting his girl. Shade said, "You have that right. By the way, that's a great house you have. I love that billiards room." Sal said, "Thanks, but you have it all wrong. That's Sidney's home. Now, you kids get out of here so I can eat my lunch." Shade said, "I'll be happy to do just that." Sal laughed and said, "I'll bet you will."

When lunch was over, Sidney and Shade took their walk through the park. Walking hand in hand, it felt so right. When they got back, Shade kissed her and wanted to know when he could see her again. Sidney said, "I'll be back tomorrow, how about lunch?" Shade said, "I can't wait until tomorrow. You're all I think about these days." Sidney said, "I know how you feel. I feel the same way." He kissed her and went back to work.

When Sidney returned to Sal's room, the nurse was there to give Sal a shot. She said she thought Sal had a full day and needed to rest. Sal said, "Sidney, you can use the rest of this day to take care of the things I know you've been neglecting since I've been in here." Sidney said, "Are you sure?" Sal said, "Yes, I'm sure. You can go home and try on the rest of those clothes. Let me know in the morning if they fit all right." Sidney said she did have some laundry she needed to do. Sal said, "I'll bet not." Sidney said, "Yes, I do. It needed to be done, when you had your heart attack, and I haven't had time, to get it done." Sal said, "You don't understand. Su Yen has more than likely washed everything, ironed it, and hung it in the closet or put it in the drawers. Su Yen stays right on top of anything that needs to be done. She's the best there is." Sidney said, "What am I going to do if she does everything for me?" Sal said, "Don't worry, now is the time to do some of that fun stuff you've never done." Sidney said, "But I don't even know any fun stuff to do." Sal said, "Go home, and brush up on your billiards, or find a good book and read it just for the pleasure of reading. You could even watch a movie on TV. If you'd rather, there's a lot of movies you could watch." Sidney said, "Okay, I get the message. I'll go home and see if there's something I can waste my time on."

When Sidney arrived home, she went upstairs. Sure enough, Su Yen had washed her clothes. They were neatly pressed and hung in the closet or folded in the drawers. Sidney went downstairs to see what Su Yen was doing. There she was, fixing a casserole for Sidney's dinner. Sidney said, "You don't have to do all these things for me." Su Yen said, "I like do for you, beside, it my job." Sidney said, "Thank you, I'm just not used to people doing things for me." Su Yen said, "Maybe it time someone do for you." Sidney asked Su Yen who did things for her. Su Yen, giggled and said, "You do. You let me keep job. I need job." Sidney said, "Bear with me, Su Yen. I'll have to get used to all this. For me, it's all too new." Su Yen said, "I happy I help you."

Sidney went out back to check on Joe. She found him out there planting some flowers. She asked him if she should be feeding the fish. He said, "It's all right to feed them once a day, but only give them one scoop of food." He asked Sidney if she would like a light installed out back. Then, she could look out back in the evening, or she could use the gazebo in the evenings. Sidney asked, "Will that be very expensive or too much trouble?" Joe said, "I've already got the things I need to do the job. I just wanted to clear it with you first." Sidney said, "Thanks, Joe. I would love that." Joe asked if she needed to go anywhere. Sidney said, "No, thanks. I think I'll go inside and try to relax." He said, "If you change your mind, just say the word, and I'll drive you there."

"Thanks, Joe. I'll keep that in mind," Sidney said as she walked back in the house. She asked Su Yen where the children were. Su Yen said, "They upstairs, take nap."

# Chapter 11

# *Clothing Galore*

Sidney went upstairs to the guest room with the clothes in it and started trying on everything. They all fit like a glove, and they were beautiful designer clothes. Sidney felt like she was dreaming. This whole thing was too surreal. She looked around and found some shoeboxes. When she opened them, they had what looked like brand-new shoes in them. There were many boxes. She could tell a few pairs had been worn but just barely. She tried them on. They also fit, and what comfort they gave. Sidney was shocked that everything fit so well. What were the odds of that happening?

Sal's wife had very good taste in clothing, shoes, and jewelry. She obviously enjoyed shopping and home decorating. The amazing thing about these clothes, shoes, and jewelry was she bought them at least five years ago. Yet they were not only still in very good shape but also timelessly fashionable. As Sidney was marveling at all there was, Su Yen went in. She told Sidney that Larkyn had called earlier and left a message. Su Yen gave Sidney the message, which was about the funeral. Sidney said, "I'd better find something to wear to the funeral, if it's tomorrow afternoon." Su Yen said, "You have lot to choose from." Sidney said, "I know. I've never had so much in my life, at least not that I can remember. This feels so strange." Su Yen said, "You deserve all, Ms. Sidney." Sidney thanked her for being so kind.

Sidney started going through the clothing, stopping at a black silk suit. She asked Su Yen what she thought of this one. Su Yen answered, "That one be very good." Su Yen heard the children waking up, so she went to check on them. Meanwhile, Sidney searched for a pair of shoes to go with the suit. Su Yen went back in and told her, "Closet in room where boys sleep, have many box." Sidney went in and was amazed. It was as if the lady had bought something in every color and style. The boxes were filled with hats and purses. She found a black hat with a white stripe around the brim and a white hat band. She also Found a black purse to match the shoes. She checked the jewelry box and spotted a pair of black onyx and diamond earrings. She tried on the whole outfit and looked in the mirror. It looked like someone she didn't even know looking back at her. The person in the mirror looked elegant and rich. Sidney couldn't believe it was really her. Su Yen knocked on the door to tell her she would be leaving now if Sidney didn't need anything. Sidney opened the door, and Su Yen said, "You most elegant, beautiful lady I ever see." Sidney said, "You don't think it's too much?" Su Yen said, "No, you look like model." Sidney hugged the children and told them goodbye and told Su Yen she would see her in the morning.

Su Yen told her, on her way out, that Joe was still out back, working on that lighting thing. Sidney changed her clothes. She put on her sweats and went out back to check on Joe. She asked him if he wanted to have dinner with her. Joe was so happy she asked him, he immediately replied he would like that a lot. He asked her if she needed any help. Sidney told him no, that Su Yen had made everything. She added, as soon as she set the table, she would call him in to wash up. As Sidney set the table, she thought this was nice, having someone to eat dinner with. When Joe had washed up, he thanked Sidney for asking him to dinner. She said, "Don't thank me, Joe. I should be thanking you. It's nice to have company for dinner." They ate their dinner, chatting about Sal and how Joe had come to work for him.

When dinner was over, Joe got up to help Sidney clean up. She told him, "No, you can go back to what you are doing, while there is still daylight." Joe asked her if there was any place she would like to go. Sidney knew he wanted to drive the big car (as he called it), so she said, "Maybe in a few minutes, when I'm finished in the kitchen." She decided she would let Joe drive her to the nursing home so she could check on everyone there. When she was finished in the kitchen, she went outside and called to Joe. She told him she was ready whenever he was. Joe said he was ready. He knew he could finish the light project in the morning. They got in the car and headed out. Joe seemed happy as a clam to be driving. It was definitely something he enjoyed.

When they arrived at the nursing home, Joe told Sidney he would wait outside for her. But Sidney insisted that he go in with her and meet her friends. He actually felt very pleased as he got out of the car and went inside with her. Everyone was glad to see Sidney and wanted to know who her friend was. She told them this was her chauffeur and groundskeeper. Joe felt so proud of Sidney's new titles for him. It made him feel important. It also made him feel good when the people there treated him like a long-lost friend. Joe was the life of the party. He couldn't remember having so much fun.

It gave Sidney a chance to sit down and visit with Mac for a while. She had a ton of things to tell him since they had talked last. Mac was so happy that Sidney was finally having a life. He thought it was real nice that Sal had been a part of it. The one thing that made Mac feel best was that she finally had a boyfriend. He knew she needed to be around people her own age. There was nothing wrong with her being around people older than herself, but sometimes she needed to be with people her own age, as well. He told her he couldn't be happier for her. They talked and talked, until Sidney realized it was time to go home. She hugged Mac and told him how good it felt to talk to him one-on-one again. She had really missed him and their talks. She went to round up Joe so they could leave. Joe was still having a good time. He hated to say goodbye to everyone. He told them he would be back. Then, he looked at Sidney and said, "If that's all right with you, Ms. Sidney?" Sidney laughed and said, "That's absolutely all right, Joe. But now, we need to go home." On the way home, Joe thanked Sidney for letting him go in with her. He told her he had so much fun. Sidney said, "You were wonderful. You helped all those people have so much fun." He smiled a very satisfied smile that lasted the rest of the way home. When they got home, Joe went in with Sidney and checked the house over. He wanted to make sure it was safe for her. Then, without further ado, he said, "Good night, Ms. Sidney, I'll see you tomorrow." Sidney told him "Good night" and locked up as he left.

Sidney checked her messages. Shade had left her a message to call him when she got home. She couldn't believe just his voice on the answering machine made her feel giddy, but it certainly did. She went into the library, and since there was a slight nip in the air, she turned on the gas log in the fireplace. She curled up in her favorite chair to call Shade back. When he answered the phone, she said, "I got your message, what did you want?" He said, "Just to hear your voice and make sure we're still on for lunch tomorrow." Sidney said, "I'm sorry, but I can't go with you tomorrow." He said, "Why not? I really look forward to our lunches together." Sidney said, "Me, too, but tomorrow is the funeral for Larkyn's mother. I promised her I would be there." He asked, "What time is the funeral going to be?" Sidney replied, "Two o'clock." He said, "Well, you have to eat lunch, don't you?" She said, "Yes, but I have to allow myself enough time to get across town. I wouldn't want to be late." He explained to her that he had a good idea: why didn't he take her to lunch, and they could go to the funeral together? She asked, "Are you sure you don't have to work?" He assured her that he didn't have anything special on his agenda and he would like to go with her. So it was agreed. When they finished their conversation, Shade told her to have sweet dreams, and he would see her tomorrow.

Sidney sat there in her chair for a few minutes, just enjoying the glow she was feeling. It was great knowing he wanted to spend so much time with her. Then, she took down a book and started reading, just for the fun of reading. She felt more relaxed than she ever knew was possible. After a while, she shut off the lights and the fireplace. She went upstairs and laid out everything she was going to wear to the funeral. Then she went to her room and sat by the window, looking at the stars, wishing her parents and Angel could meet this wonderful man she was dating. Suddenly she felt they had seen him and they approved. She said her prayers and a special prayer for Larkyn and her father. She prayed they would get through the funeral and be all right. She also included a prayer for Sal, that he would be much improved by tomorrow. Then, she climbed into that wonderful bed and snuggled down into the soft warmth that always lulled her to sleep.

CHAPTER 12

# *Let the Building Begin*

When Sidney awoke the next morning, she showered and started getting ready. While she was putting her clothes on, she turned on the television to watch the morning news. She saw something about the stocks she had sold the night before. Since she was only half watching, she didn't hear what happened. She decided to eat breakfast before putting on her suit. She slipped on a robe and headed downstairs.

As usual, Su Yen was in the kitchen, and she had prepared a wonderful breakfast for Sidney. Su Yen asked Sidney if there was anything really special she liked for breakfast. Sidney said, "I've never really thought about it. I'm used to eating something simple, something I can fix in a hurry." Su Yen said, "You eat better now I cook for you." Sidney said, "Thanks, Su Yen, you're a doll. I haven't had anyone take such good care of me since my mother died when I was only eight."

Sidney excused herself for a moment to make a quick phone call before eating breakfast. She tried to call the investment firm, but no one was there yet. She went back in the kitchen and asked Su Yen if they received a newspaper. Su Yen said, "Yes, I put paper in library." Sidney went in the library to retrieve it. She took it with her to the breakfast nook. She looked up the stock section. There wasn't any new information yet on those stocks. She called the television station and asked about the stock report that she missed. They told her about the stocks in question. The stocks she sold had crashed, and the stock she had purchased had split and doubled. Sidney thanked them and hung up the phone. After a deep breath, she yelled, "Yahoo!" Su Yen asked, "Ms. Sidney, why you so happy?" Sidney said, "You can't imagine how happy I am. I just made a lot of money. I can't wait to get to the hospital this morning and tell Sal the good news." Su Yen insisted she eat a good breakfast first. Sidney said, "All right, I wouldn't dream of arguing with anyone this morning."

Sidney ate her breakfast and hurried upstairs to get dressed. She pulled her hair back in a twist and put the hat on. *I hope this isn't too much*, she thought, as she looked in the mirror. She was always worried about looking overdressed. Before stepping out of the room, she walked back over to the mirror and looked again. She thought she didn't look too bad, or at least she hoped not. When she went downstairs, Joe was waiting on her and asked if he could drive her to the hospital. She said, "I would love that, Joe." Su Yen said, "You very pretty, Ms. Sidney." Joe said, "Yeah, double that." She thanked them both and hurried out to the car Joe had waiting right outside the door.

When Sidney arrived at the hospital, she hurried to Sal's room. She found him taking his morning medications. He said, "You're here kind of early this morning, aren't you, kid?" Then, Sal leaned back and said, "Wow, look at you, you're absolutely beautiful. What's the occasion?" Sidney said, "I'm going to the funeral for Larkyn's mother this afternoon. You don't think it's too much, do you?" Sal said, "You're a vision of loveliness, and that's never too much." Sidney said, "Thanks, Sal, but I never know if you mean it or you're just being kind. In either case, that's enough about me." Sal said, "Look, kid, I know you have trouble taking a compliment. Trust me, I know class when I see it, and you're all class." Sidney said, "Thanks, Sal, but we have more important things to talk about. First, how are you feeling this morning?" Sal said, "I'm feeling better than I have since this whole thing began."

"Okay," said Sidney, "I have some good news for you. This morning, I called the television news channel to get the stock report. They told me the companies we sold the stocks from went belly up and the stock we bought split and doubled. We just made a whole lot of money." Sal said, "Let's call the investment firm and see exactly how much." Sidney was right. They had made a lot of money, even more than she thought they had.

Sidney said, "Sal, I know what I would like to do with part of my money. That is, if you don't mind." Sal asked her, "What would that be?" She replied, "I'd like to build a maid's quarters behind the garage, for Su Yen and her boys. If it doesn't cost too much, I'd also like to put an apartment above the garage, for Joe." Sal said, "That's just like you to think of others." Sidney said, "Look who's talking. You gave me much more than I could ever give them." Sal said, "Whatever you want to do to that place is your business, Sidney. That's your home, lock, stock, and barrel." Sidney said, "I suppose I'll need to get a building permit. I'll also need a contractor to give me an estimate." Sal said, "I know a good contractor that will do right by you." Sidney said, "Thanks, Sal. I know I can always count on you to help me." Sal laughed and asked, "Now that we've spent all your money, what do you want to do next?" Sidney said, "I'm not worried about spending my money. As long as I do something good with it, God will always take care of me." Sal said, "When you're right, you're right."

Sidney said, "In all the excitement, I almost forgot your Bible, but here it is." Sal said, "Thanks. I think I'll be busy this afternoon, reading and reevaluating my life." Sidney said, "Sal, God knows you're a good man who did the best he could with what he knew."

"Sidney, how did you get so wise at such a young age?" asked Sal. Sidney said, "I just know God is a loving and forgiving god." She asked Sal if he would like for her to read to him for a while. He said, "I'd like that more than anything." She read for a while until she could see Sal was getting tired. She said, "Why don't I leave you alone so you can take a nap. I'll be back before I leave for lunch." Sal said, "As usual, you're right." Sidney leaned forward and kissed him on the forehead before leaving the room.

Sidney was on her way to the cafeteria for a glass of juice, when she heard a now-familiar wolf whistle. Yes, it was Shade. As he caught up to her, he asked where she was going. She said she was on her way to the cafeteria to get some juice. He wanted to know if she would like some company. Of course, she would always like his company. They went to the cafeteria together. He asked her what time she thought they needed to leave for lunch. He needed to tell his service. She didn't know how long it would take to get there. He decided they should leave by eleven thirty. He thought that should give them plenty of time. That sounded good to Sidney. Shade left so he could get back to work.

Sidney took her juice and went to a courtesy phone. She called City Hall about a building permit. The lady told her there shouldn't be any problem getting a permit. She explained the necessary steps to take. Sidney went back to Sal's room and sat there reading the newspaper. She happened across an article about laptop computers and the stock market. She decided this would be much more convenient than running to the investment firm every time she needed to conduct some business. She knew this was the only way she would be able to keep up with everything. Sal would be able to watch the stock movements while she was working.

Suddenly she had the urgent feeling there were going to be more stock changes the next day. She felt sure she needed to sell some stocks and buy two others. She looked over the stocks and marked the ones they needed to sell. Then, she carefully looked over the ones they should buy and marked those with a *B*. It was like her father was speaking to her mind, telling her what to do, which stocks to buy and which ones to sell. He always seemed to be doing this for her. She thought, if she told anyone, they might try to lock her up in a padded room. Still, it had been working for her since she started investing. When Sal woke up, she showed him the stocks she was concerned about. She explained how she felt about those stocks. She asked Sal if he thought she should act on it right away. Sal said, "You haven't missed one yet, kid, so you do what you think is right." Sal asked Sidney how she always knew these things. Was she psychic or something? Sidney said, "You really don't want to know." Sal said, "Yes, I do. I've never known anyone to be right all the time like you are." Sidney told him not to think her crazy, but she felt it was her father telling her, not in words, but letting her know just the same. Sal said, "And why would you think I'd find that to be crazy? I'm the guy that just told you I died, went to heaven, and came back. You didn't question that, so why would I question you? If it works, it works. There has to be some kind of explanation for that kind of accuracy. After what I've been through these last few days, I can believe a lot of things I wouldn't have believed before."

"So," said Sidney, "do you want me to take care of it?" Sal said, "You bet."

Sidney told him what she thought about using a computer to keep up with things. Sal said he didn't know very much about using a computer. The only things he knew about them were what he learned at work. That was just enough to get his work done. Sidney told him she didn't, either, but they could learn together. She said, "You'll see, it'll be a great new way of doing business." Sal said, "I'm willing, if you are." He said, "I'll buy the computer, and you can teach me how to use it." Sidney said, "It's my idea, so I'll buy it and teach you how to use it." Sal said, "No, you don't. You just spent all your money on the hired help. I'll buy the computer. That way, if I break it, it's mine."

"Okay, Sal," Sidney conceded. "I'll pick one up after the funeral today. By the way, I had better find Shade and ask if we can leave early enough to take care of the stocks before lunch." Sal said, "You're getting awful thick with the young doctor, aren't you?" Sidney said, "I think so, or maybe I should say I hope so. I'll see you later."

Sidney went to the nurse's station and was about to have the nurse page Shade. She looked up to see Shade coming down the hall. Sidney asked him if he was busy now. He said no. He had been visiting with some of the other doctors until it was time to go to lunch. Sidney said, "Then you wouldn't mind if we leave early? I need to go by the investment firm, on the way to lunch." He quipped, "Investment firm?" She answered yes. She explained that she and Sal had been playing the stock market for some time now. Shade said, "I learn something new about you all the time. Sure, we can leave early. I'd much rather spend time with you than the other doctors."

On their way to the investment firm, Sidney asked Shade if he knew anything about computers. He said, "Yeah, why?" She told him that she had decided to purchase a laptop. She wasn't sure, how

## RAINBOWS ARE BETTER

to check them out or what was a good buy, that sort of thing. Shade said, "We'll pick up a magazine about shopping for computers and check that out first. Then, we'll go from there. Do you know how to operate one?" Sidney said, "No, but I know how to read, so I'm sure I can learn." Shade said, "I didn't mean you couldn't learn how. I just meant I'd like to help you, if you need it." They laughed and discussed it until they arrived at the investment firm.

When they arrived at the funeral home and walked inside, Larkyn was waiting. She ran to Sidney and threw her arms around Sidney's waist and hung on for dear life. After a while, she told Sidney she was so glad she had come. She really needed her to be there. Sidney held Larkyn in her arms and told her to be strong. Her mother was in a better place where there's beauty, peace, and love beyond compare. Sidney continued, saying, "The love there is so great, it's unimaginable what it will be like. There's no pain or suffering. God left you with a wonderful dad who loves you very much. Even though that can't replace your mother, in time, things will get better. You keep saying your prayers and asking God to help you, and he will. The main thing to remember is take one day at a time, that's all you can live, anyway. I promise, it will get much easier with time." Larkyn said, "My dad wants us to move to Australia. Then, I won't even have my friends." Sidney told her, "Never be afraid of change. Change can be a very good thing. You're a sweet little person, and you'll make new friends in no time. Your dad may need to get away to deal with the loss of your mother. Look at this as a great new adventure, and try to have fun." Larkyn asked if Sidney would be able to visit her there. Sidney said, "I don't know. We'll see what time brings. I'll write to you, and we'll talk on the phone whenever you need to." Larkyn said, "I love you, Sidney, and I'll write you, every week." She learned Larkyn was leaving in just a few days. After the funeral, Sidney hugged Larkyn and said goodbye to both of them. Sidney told Shade as they were leaving, "I hope Larkyn will be okay. I love her so much." Shade said, "I know, she's going to be fine. How could she miss with all that good advice?"

When Sidney got home that evening, she called Sal to tell him about getting the magazine about shopping for computers. She told him she was going to study up on computers for the rest of the evening. He told her he had contacted his friend Alan Solomon in the construction business. Alan had agreed to do an estimate on what it would cost to build on the rooms. Sal told her Alan would be at the house the next day, early in the morning. Sidney asked Sal if he wanted her to wait until he left before going to the hospital. Sal said, "Yeah, and have him put everything in writing." Sidney said, "Got it. If I'm not coming in until later, it'll give me more time to make a decision about these computers and what we'll need." Sal said, "Just buy the best one you can get. Those things are outdated before you can get them out of the carton." Sidney laughed and told Sal she would see him in the afternoon, so he should get a good night's rest.

Sidney curled up in her favorite chair in the library. She began reading and made a few calls to do some price comparisons. She soon found out she had to know exactly what she wanted on the computer to get a price quote. She started making a list of the options she would like to have on the computer. She hadn't realized how many things there were to know about a computer. Fortunately, in the magazine, they had a good article about the novice computer buyer. It explained all these things to her. She read until she was exhausted. She thought she was going to fall asleep before she could get up the stairs. She went upstairs, said her prayers, and went straight to bed. She hardly felt the bed beneath her before she was asleep.

Morning came, and she was up bright and early. She knew she had a full day scheduled for herself. She went downstairs as Su Yen was arriving, and asked if Joe was there yet. Su Yen answered he was driving in just as she was getting out of her car. Sidney went out and caught Joe. She told him about the contractor coming. She showed Joe where she thought the living quarters should be built. He told her he thought that would be a good place. She told Joe she was also having an apartment built over the garage. She asked him how he would feel about living over the garage. He almost cried, and he said, "Me, Ms. Sidney? You want me to live over the garage?" She said, "Yes, but only if you would like to." He said, "I would love to, and that's about the nicest thing anyone has ever done for me. Thank you, Ms. Sidney." Sidney said, "No, Joe, thank you for being such a

# RAINBOWS ARE BETTER

good worker. I'll feel better knowing you're around." Joe assured her he would always be around and he would work really hard for her. Sidney told him she knew he would. He already did, and she didn't expect any more than what he was already doing.

Sidney went back in the house, where she found Su Yen preparing breakfast. She asked Su Yen how she would feel about living there in the new servants' quarters she was having built. Su Yen was just as surprised as Joe. Tears came to her eyes, and she said, "You not need do this, Ms. Sidney." Sidney said, "I know that, but I want to. So is it a deal? The contractor will be here in about an hour." Su Yen said she would be grateful and happy to live there. She told Sidney she would work extrahard for her. Sidney said, "You already work hard. I just want you and the children to have a nice place to live, a place where they can play whenever they want to." Su Yen hugged Sidney and said, "Thank you, thank you."

After breakfast (now that Sidney had her computer list), she made several calls about a computer. Ultimately, she found one she felt was a good deal. She called the local community college and found out when they would be giving classes on computers and drivers' education. She also asked when their next GED test was scheduled. They told her the GED test would be given in a week. Sidney asked if they could sign her up, and they did. Then, Sidney called the computer company she liked best and ordered the computer. She had just hung up the phone, when Su Yen announced the contractor was there.

Sidney went into the living room and introduced herself. He introduced himself as Alan Solomon. Sidney took him out back. She explained to him what she wanted him to build. She asked him what he thought. He made a few suggestions, and they both agreed. Then, she took him in the garage and told him what she would like to do there. After looking the garage over, Alan said, "That'll be a piece of cake." She asked him to put his estimates in writing for her. She explained she needed to take them to City Hall to get the building permit. He said it would take him a while to get everything written up. Sidney responded, "Take your time, Joe is working out back, and I feel sure he will help you as much as he can." She went outside and asked Joe if he would mind helping Mr. Solomon if he needed it. She explained he was going to be adding on the new rooms. Joe was overjoyed that she trusted him to do this.

Sidney went in the house to wait. While she was waiting, she went upstairs to find something to wear to the hospital. However, once upstairs, she decided to wear the pink sweats she had on. She turned on the TV to the stock market channel Sal told her about. You couldn't imagine her surprise or delight when she heard the stock market had repeated the history of yesterday. The stocks she had sold dropped drastically, and the new stocks had split and doubled. At this rate, she was going to be a very wealthy young woman in no time.

Sidney called a local discount store and ordered the biggest swing set they had, to be delivered immediately. They asked her if she needed someone to set it up. She said, "No, thanks, I already have someone." She knew Joe would love putting it together for the children. Then, she told Su Yen what she had done. Su Yen said, "No, Ms. Sidney, you do too much." Sidney said, "Nonsense, you can never do too much for others, especially the people you love." Su Yen said, "Boys not old enough for swing set. Brian be all right, Blake get hurt." Sidney told Su Yen she was sorry, and from now on, she would check with her first. Then, she called the store and canceled the order.

Joe asked Sidney when she wanted him to take her to the hospital. She said, "As soon as Mr. Solomon finishes looking things over." Joe said, "Things are busy around here since you came, Ms. Sidney." Sidney said, "I'm sorry, Joe. Am I asking you to do too much?" Joe said, "No, Ms. Sidney, you make things more fun. I like it when things are busy and exciting. I love Sal, he's been very good to me, but you're more fun." Sidney said, "Thanks, Joe, but if I do start asking too much, will you promise to tell me so I'll know to slow down?"

"Okay, Ms. Sidney, but I don't think that will happen."

Sidney told Su Yen she would be in the study, reading, and asked that when Mr. Solomon finished, she would let her know. Su Yen said, "I make sure you know." Sidney picked up the book she had been reading earlier. She read it until Mr. Solomon had finished outside. When he went in, he gave her the paperwork and told her to go over it with Sal and let him know what they thought. Sidney thanked him for his time and effort, as he left.

Sidney called Joe in and asked him if he was ready to take her to the hospital. Su Yen said, "You wait, it time for lunch." Sidney said, "Only if you, Joe, and the children will join me." Joe said, "Come on, Su Yen, that's not so bad, is it?" Su Yen agreed this was a celebration, so they could all eat together. While they were eating, Sidney told Su Yen, Joe, Brian, and Blake that she had no family of her own, so she was adopting them as her make-believe family. She added, "I hope you don't mind. After all, we're going to be spending a lot of time together." Su Yen said they would be her family but she would still be their boss. Sidney said, "Okay, I think I understand. It's a deal."

When lunch was over, Sidney and Joe went to the hospital. Sidney asked Joe if he would like to go in and see Sal. Joe answered, "Not today, I have that lighting to work on." Sidney could see the excitement in his eyes. She asked, "Do you want to pick me up here at about five thirty? We'll go shopping for Su Yen's children." She told him she would call Su Yen and okay it with her first. Joe said, "I'd like that." He liked going shopping. Sidney told him they would have to find some safe toys for the boys to play with outside.

Sidney went inside the hospital. She had the newspaper in her bag, so she gave it to Sal. She asked him if he had heard the news about their stocks. He said, "Oh yeah! You did it again, kid, and this time, it was really big." She giggled and said she was amazed at how much money they made. She told him Alan Solomon had been at the house already and she had the estimate he gave her. Sal looked it over and said, "This is a pretty good deal. I see he even threw in an enclosed porch from the main house to the servants' quarters." Sidney said, "Actually, I asked him to do that. I thought it would be nice to sit out there even when the weather is bad. I enjoy the view, plus Su Yen won't have to wade in the snow in the winter." Sal said, "It looks like you've got the whole thing covered." Then he said, "I have a better idea, why don't we have Alan expand that porch into an indoor swimming pool? Su Yen can have her entrance through the garage. Her place is going to be built on the back of the garage, anyway. We wouldn't want the children to accidentally drown in the pool." Sidney said, "Whoa, Sal. I can't afford all that." Sal said, "I'll pay for the extra expense. After all, I'm richer than I've ever been. I insist. After all, you said the other day that you like to swim." Sidney responded, "Sal, I'm not going to be home that often." He said, "But when you are, it will be there, and you can enjoy it year-round." Sidney said, "But Mr. Solomon has already written up his estimate."

"Trust me," said Sal. "He'll be glad to write up another one."

No matter how much Sidney objected, Sal would not be dissuaded. "Okay," said Sidney, "if you insist."

"I do insist," declared Sal. "It'll be great, you'll see." Sal called Alan and explained the changes he would like to make to Sidney's plans. He asked him if he would mind writing up a new estimate. Alan assured him he would be happy to and he would get right on it. He asked Sal where he would like for him to deliver the estimate when it was ready. Alan explained it would take him a couple of hours to get it done. Sal said, "Bring it over to the hospital. I'm in room 202, and Sidney is here with me."

Sidney and Sal went over the stocks for the next day. Sal said, "Do you have any great ideas for tomorrow?" Sidney said, "No, I think we should let things ride tomorrow." Sal said, "Good, I'm not sure the old ticker is up to as much excitement as we've had in the past two days." Sidney laughed and said, "I know what you mean. I'm not sure mine is, either." She explained to Sal what she had done about the computer. She told him it would arrive sometime the next week. She told Sal that Shade was going to help her learn how to use it. Sal told her he wasn't worried for a minute about her learning to use that computer. He knew how quick she picked up on everything.

Sal said, "By the way, I have some good news today. The doctor told me, as soon as they get my medication regulated, they're going to let me out of this place." Sidney anxiously asked, "Do they know how long that might be?" Sal told her the doctor had estimated maybe it would be two or three more days. Sidney said, "I'll go to the nursing home this evening and make sure your room is ready. Mac will be happy to have you there. He's also waiting for me to come back to work. To tell you the truth, I need to get back to work before

I get used to this life of leisure." Sal said, "You've been running yourself like crazy since I came in here. I don't think you even know what a life of leisure is."

"Maybe not," said Sidney, "but I like to stay busy. I always have." Sal said, "One other thing you might want to think about is furniture. I don't know about Su Yen, but I'm pretty sure that Joe doesn't have any furniture of his own. Sidney said, "Is that why you thought moving them to the house was a bad idea?" Sal said, "No, I actually think it's a good idea. I was just concerned about your privacy. With them having their own living quarters, it's a very good idea. If they live there, you won't be alone." Sal told her she should go to the Salvation Army and purchase some used furniture for them. "Thanks, Sal, I'll put that on my list of things to do." Sidney and Sal visited the whole afternoon, and the time just flew by.

The nurse went in and told Sal his dinner would be coming soon, so he needed to take his medicine. Sidney said, "Look at the time, Joe will be here in about ten minutes." Sal asked, "Is Joe picking you up today?" Sidney said, "Yes, and we're going shopping. I think he's very excited about that." Sal said, "I'm sure he is. He loves to do things and feel useful." Sidney said, "I'm glad he feels that way, because I've been keeping him really busy."

"Gee," said Sal, "he probably doesn't even miss me then." Sidney told Sal no one would be able to take his place with Joe and Su Yen. After all, he was the one who helped them when no one else would.

Sidney started getting her things together. As she was about to leave, Alan walked in with the estimate on the construction project. He apologized for taking so long, but he had to find out how much it would cost to dig the pool and have it finished. Sal said, "That's all right, Alan. I understand. Sidney, what do you think?" Sidney answered, "I don't know much about things like this." Sal said, "Well, look it over, my dear. These are things you will need to know." Alan said, "You can call me in the morning if you want to make any changes. I have to get going. It was good to see you again, Sal. I hope you get better soon." Sal said, "Thanks, Alan, and take good care of my girl, okay?" Alan said, "For you, Sal, anything."

Sidney said, "I really have to go. I love you, Sal," she said as she kissed him on the forehead.

Sidney hurried outside, and there sat Joe, waiting for her. She asked him if he had been waiting long. Joe said, "No, ma'am, I got here at five twenty-nine."

"Okay, Joe." Sidney giggled. "Let's go shopping." They picked out a sandbox with a cover and a little picnic table. Both Joe and Sidney felt sure Brian and Blake would love them. Joe couldn't wait to get home and put them together. When they got home, Su Yen was on her way out. Sidney didn't say anything about the toys. She decided to let Joe put them together first and have them ready the next day. Sidney and Joe went out back to assemble the toys. Sidney sat on a lawn chair and handed the tools to Joe while he did the work. This made Joe very happy. He had never had anyone help him like that before. When he was done, he asked Sidney if there was anything else she wanted him to do before he went home. She said, "No, Joe, you go on home. I'll see you in the morning." Sidney went into the house and watched Joe drive out the gate. She pushed the button, locking them up for the night. She went into the kitchen to find something to eat. Su Yen had baked lasagna for her dinner. There was a note, which read, "Thank you for being an angel." Sidney had tears in her eyes. She knew she was no angel, but that was still very sweet for Su Yen to say.

She was getting out a plate, when someone buzzed the gate. She went to the intercom and asked who was there. She thought Joe had probably forgotten something. A voice answered, "It's Shade, and I miss you, so open the gate, okay?" Sidney pushed the gate opener as a smile lit up her face. She opened the door to let Shade in. He could not have known how much she wanted to see him, but there he was. As he walked through the door, he stopped and gave her a kiss. It felt as if it could last forever and still not be long enough. It was definitely a "weak in the knees and make your head reel" kind of kiss. After she regained her composure, she told Shade she was just getting ready to have some lasagna for dinner. She asked him if he would join her. Shade kissed her again and said, "Lead the way."

## RAINBOWS ARE BETTER

They went into the kitchen and set the table in the kitchen nook, at Shade's insistence. He thought it was cozier than the dining room. As they ate, Shade said he was sorry he came over unannounced. He added, he just couldn't go home without seeing her all day. She said, "I was at the hospital, but I didn't see you." He said, "That's because I was in surgery all day long." When they had eaten, they cleaned the kitchen together. Then, Sidney took him out back and showed him the toys for Su Yen's little boys. She told him all about the events of the day. She asked if he would like to play some billiards. He answered, "But of course, that's the real reason I came over." Sidney looked at him, and he said, "Just kidding, I needed to eat too. Just kidding, just kidding." Sidney said, "I knew you were kidding, because you didn't have to kiss me to get fed or play billiards." After they played billiards for a while, they went into the library. Sidney started a fire in the fireplace. They curled up on the sofa and talked, and kissed, all the while nestled in each other's arms. Shade said, "It's getting late, and I have surgery again in the morning. I'd better go, or I won't want to." Sidney said, "Then you had better go." They said their goodbyes at the door, and Sidney watched him drive through the gate. She then locked up for the night.

When she went to bed, her prayers were so full of thanksgiving, it took much longer than usual. When she snuggled into her wonderful bed, she couldn't help thinking how blessed her life was. Then she closed her eyes and was asleep in barely a minute.

The next morning, she was up early, as usual. She was showered and dressed before Su Yen and the children arrived. She wanted to see their faces when they saw the new toys. She heard their car coming up the drive. She stepped outside to greet them. Su Yen was surprised to see Sidney come outside to greet them. Sidney said, "Before you go into the house, I have something I want you to see." She took them around back, and before she could say anything, the boys started squealing in delight. They ran to the picnic table and then to the sandbox. They didn't know what the sandbox was, with the cover on it. Sidney opened it up, and they jumped right in. Su Yen cried and, with tears still in her eyes, said, "Thank you, Ms. Sidney. You such a good person." The boys ran over and started hugging Sidney, saying, "Thank you, thank you!" Sidney said, "That's all the thanks I'll ever need." Sidney and Su Yen went into the house, and the boys stayed outside, enjoying the new toys.

Joe arrived just a few minutes later. Sidney took him out back to see the children playing in the sandbox. This was destined to become their favorite toy. They loved the buckets, shovels, and sand sifters that came with it. Sidney told the boys it was Joe who helped her pick out the toys. She explained how he was the one who put them together. They ran to Joe, hugging him and saying, "Thank you, Joe. We love you." Joe was grinning from ear to ear. Sidney smiled and thought, *What a wonderful day this is already.*

After breakfast, Sidney explained to Joe they needed to go to City Hall, the nursing home, and then to the hospital. Joe asked her when she wanted to go. She answered, "In a couple of hours, okay?" Joe replied, "It's okay with me. I love to drive you places." Sidney called Mr. Solomon to tell him everything appeared to be in order. She told him she would be submitting the plans to City Hall in a few hours. She was hoping to get her permit. He told her they would probably let them do the apartment over the garage right away because it was part of the existing structure. She said, "That's good. The sooner the better." Alan said, "If they okay it, we can get started on Monday." Sidney told him she would call him as soon as she knew something for sure.

Sidney sat down with Su Yen and asked her if she had any furniture of her own. Su Yen said she had a few things but not a refrigerator, stove, or anything like that. "So you do have a table and chairs, living room furniture, and bedroom furniture?" Su Yen said, "Yes, we have those things and television set, but only one bed."

"Good," said Sidney. "That tells me what we'll need to get." She called Ms. Jones at the estate consignment shop and asked if she had sold the furniture she had placed with her yet. Ms. Jones said, "No, not yet." Sidney said, "Good, I don't want you to sell it. I'll just pay you for the expense of moving it to your shop, because I'll be needing it, after all." Ms. Jones responded that would be fine and twenty-five dollars should cover the expense, if Sidney could pick it up. Sidney explained she had someone who could do that.

## RAINBOWS ARE BETTER

Sidney went upstairs and finished getting ready. When she was finished, she told Joe she was ready to go. First, they went to City Hall, and Mr. Solomon had been right about the apartment. She could go ahead with it right away. They said they would get the other permit for her sometime next week. Next, they went to the nursing home to check on Sal's room. Sidney told the nursing-home supervisor Sal would be moving in sometime the next week, and she would be returning to work the same day.

On the way to the hospital, she asked Joe if he had any furniture. He said no; his small house came furnished. Sidney told him she had a bedroom set, if he could pick it up. He said, "You did that for me?" Sidney answered, "I can't have my chauffeur and number one assistant tired all the time from not getting a good night's rest." Joe said, "Thanks, Ms. Sidney. You're the best person in the whole wide world." Sidney said, "No, Joe, I think you're much too kind. We just have to watch out for one another. You're my make-believe family, right?"

"Right, Ms. Sidney," Joe replied with a big smile. The rest of the ride was in silence. Joe asked if Sidney wanted him to pick her up later. She said, "No, thanks, Joe. I don't know when I'll be leaving, so I'll take the bus." Joe told her, if she changed her mind, to call him.

Sidney went to Sal's room and found him sitting up in bed and taking his morning medications. Sal said, "There's my girl, and don't she look great today?" Sidney was wearing a soft, silky white blouse and a pair of black gabardine slacks. Her hair was piled on top of her head, with loose curls hanging down, and she had on a pair of diamond stud earrings. She said, "I'm just wearing a shirt and a pair of slacks, Sal." He replied, "Yeah, but oh, what you do for them." He was right; she was the kind of person who could wear a gunnysack and make it look great. She was blushing a little as she summoned all her strength to say a simple "Thank you." It was still hard for her to take a compliment especially if it caught her off guard.

She told Sal she had gone to City Hall and applied for a building permit. She told him they gave her permission to go ahead with the rooms over the garage since it was an existing structure. Sal said, "That's great, now you need to tell Alan so he can get started." She asked if she could use his phone to call Alan. Sal said, "Sidney, when will you learn? What's mine is yours, and you don't have to ask." Sidney said, "It's a force of habit, and it makes me feel better."

"Okay, you may use the phone," joked Sal.

Sidney called Alan and told him he was right; the city gave the go-ahead on the rooms over the garage. He said, "Great, we'll get started Monday morning. It probably won't take us more than a week before it's finished." She exclaimed, "You could be finished that quick?" He answered, "Oh sure, and by that time, they should have the permit ready for the rest of the building. Of course, the rest of the project will take more time."

"This is great news," said Sidney. "I'll see you on Monday." Sal queried, "They'll be able to start work on Monday?"

"Yes," said Sidney, "and they'll be finished and ready to start construction on the rest of it in about a week." Sal said, "That's great, kid. It seems everything is coming up roses."

Sal told Sidney the doctor said he should be ready to be discharged on Monday. Sidney told him she had gone by the nursing home and checked his room on the way over. She assured him it was all ready for him. She further explained she planned on going back to work Monday, as well. Sal said, "I bet you'll be glad to get things back to normal." Sidney said, "I don't think I know what normal is anymore. Whatever I'm doing feels normal to me. I don't think I've ever had so much going on in my life all at once. I must admit, I like some of it. Not that I like what's happened to you or to Larkyn. Staying this busy, though, has been great. Not to mention meeting Shade."

Sal wanted to know how things were going at home. She told him how much help Joe had been. Sal asked, "Has Joe been there every day since you've been there?" She responded, "Every day but one, and that was the first day I was there." Sal said, "He must be pretty fond of you, because when I lived there, he only came once or twice a week." She said, "Joe has been driving me everywhere. He even wants me to call him so he can pick me up when I'm ready to go home." Sal told her how pleased he was to hear that Joe was taking such good care of her. He agreed that she should call Joe to drive her home. Sal said, "I don't like the idea of you riding the bus." Sidney

# RAINBOWS ARE BETTER

said, "We'll see. I know Joe loves thinking he's my chauffeur. He also loves driving that car, just like you said. He never wants to drive the Cadillac."

Sal said, "By the way, have you had time to think about what kind of car you would like to replace the Cadillac?" Sidney said, "Not really, that's been the least of my concerns right now." Sal conceded, "There's plenty of time later to think about it." Just then, Sidney heard a familiar voice saying hello. It was Shade. Sidney turned around and smiled a smile that would make anyone feel welcome. Shade told Sal, word had it he would be leaving them soon. Sal said, "That's right, not that I don't like your company, but it's about time." Shade laughed and asked if he could borrow his company for a while. Sal said, "You can if she's willing, and I think she is." Sidney said, "I'll be back in a minute, Sal."

Shade and Sidney walked down the hall and sat in the visitors' lounge, which happened to be empty. Shade asked if she would be able to go to lunch with him today, especially since their time was now limited. Sidney said, "I'd love to have lunch with you. I hope we don't have to quit seeing each other when Sal leaves the hospital." Shade answered that no power on earth could keep him from seeing her, even if he had to take the same college courses so he could be with her. Sidney said, "I don't think that will be necessary." Shade told her he'd go to Sal's room as soon as he finished rounds, to pick her up for lunch.

Sidney and Shade enjoyed a nice, leisurely lunch and walk in the park, neither one wanting their time together to end. Shade said, "How about doing something this weekend?" Sidney answered, "I'd love to." Shade suggested they could go to a movie or do whatever she would like to do. Sidney said, "I don't know what's fun to do, so I'll leave that up to you." When they arrived back at the hospital, Shade asked if he could come over to her house later that evening. Sidney said, "I'd love that, and I'll check with Su Yen about dinner. Maybe she can fix something that will keep until you get there." Shade said, "I'll be there at seven with bells on."

Sidney went to Sal's room and visited with him the rest of the afternoon. When it was time to go home, Sidney kissed Sal goodbye.

She said she would be there the next day, but she didn't know what time. She told him Shade was taking her out on an actual date. She didn't know yet what time. Sal said, "Don't worry about me. I'll still be here whenever you arrive." Sidney said, "If you're a good boy, I might bring you a surprise." Sal said, "Don't waste your money on me." Sidney said, "It's not going to be that big a surprise. Just a little something to let you know how much I love you." Sal said, "I already know. Now, how about calling Joe to pick you up?" Sidney said, "That's not necessary. The bus lets me out about half a block from the house." Sal said, "I insist, and you're not supposed to be worrying me, remember?" Sidney laughed and said, "Okay, just for you, Sal. I'll call Joe, but I have to get over being so spoiled." Sal said, "I hope you never do."

When Joe arrived, he went up to get Sidney and visited with Sal for a few minutes. He told Sal all that had been going on since his heart attack. Sal said, "So are you excited about your new apartment being built?" Joe smiled from ear to ear, saying, "Yes, sir, I'm so happy, I could burst." Sidney giggled and told Joe they were going to start work on it on Monday. Joe said, "Shouldn't they do Su Yen's place first?" Sidney explained, "They can do yours while we wait for the building permit for the rest of it." Sal said to Joe, "Take good care of my girl." Joe answered, "Don't worry, Sal. Me and Su Yen will take good care of Ms. Sidney. You can count on it. She's a good person." Sidney said, "Enough of this. Let's go home, Joe." She kissed Sal and said, "I'll see you tomorrow."

On their way home, Sidney asked Joe to stop at the little bookstore down the street. Sidney went in and bought Sal a book she knew he would enjoy. When she got home, she asked Su Yen if she could bake up something heart healthy for Sal. Su Yen answered, "Oh yes." She asked, "Mr. Sal do better now?" Sidney said, "If everything goes right, he'll be moved to the nursing home on Monday." She told Su Yen she would be going back to work on Monday, as well. She explained that the construction workers would be starting construction on Joe's apartment too. She said, "It's going to be a busy day." Su Yen said, "I fix supper, you warm up when you ready." Sidney asked, "Is there enough for two in case Dr. Domingo comes by?" Su Yen giggled and said, "I sure so. I make banana cream pie for you." Sidney said, "That's my all-time-favorite dessert. How did you know?" Su Yen giggled and said, "I know that most people favorite. I know, if not favorite, you still like." Su Yen said, "I go home now, I see you in morning." Joe went in the house and told Sidney to look out the back window. Sidney looked out, and it took her breath away. Joe had put a couple of spotlights shining on the weeping willow tree. He had two gorgeous, old-fashioned streetlamps with the round globes, at both ends of the fishpond. There were two spotlights shining on the gazebo. For an added touch, he had little walk lights all along the walkway and all the way around the pond and the gazebo. He had also strung white Christmas lights all over the gazebo and the bridge across the fishpond. She told Joe that was the most beautiful thing she had ever seen.

He told her he had put a switch to turn them off and on, not only by the back door but upstairs, as well. He put one of the switches beside her window seat so she could sit in her window and turn them on or off when she looked out at night. Sidney said, "How did you know I like to sit in that window?" Joe explained that Su Yen had told him. Sidney thanked him so much. She said, "That's the most exquisite sight I've ever seen." Sidney gave Joe a big hug. He told her he had to go home now, but he would be there early on Monday. He told her, if she needed him, to just call, and he would come right over. Sidney said, "You enjoy the weekend, I'll be all right."

It was about 6:55 p.m. when Shade arrived. He announced, "I'm never late for dinner." Sidney laughed and told him to come in and eat then. After they finished their meal, Sidney said, "I have a surprise. Su Yen made us a banana cream pie." Shade said, "That's my favorite pie. In this whole world, it's my absolute favorite." Sidney said, "Mine too." They really enjoyed that pie. Then, you guessed it; they played a few games of billiards. Sidney quipped that she didn't know if Shade came to see her or her billiards table. Shade said, "Let's put it this way: I'm glad you're both here." As Shade was leaving, he asked Sidney if she wanted to visit Sal in the morning or in the evening. She answered, "I'd like to go late morning." Shade said, "That's fine, then we'll have the rest of the day and night together." Sidney asked him what they would be doing. He said, "That's a surprise, my dear." Sidney said, "That's fine, but what should I wear?" He said, "Do you have a pair of jeans?" She said yes. "Then that's what you should wear." With that, he kissed her goodbye and left.

    The next morning, Shade was there by ten o'clock and raring to go. Sidney told him, as soon as Su Yen finished wrapping a little surprise for Sal, she'd be ready. Shade went into the kitchen to thank Su Yen for the great meals he'd been eating, but mostly for that wonderful banana cream pie. She smiled and said, "I glad you like." Sidney got her things together while Su Yen finished wrapping the homemade energy bars. She told Sidney, "Tell Mr. Sal get well soon, energy bar good for his heart." Sidney said she would and thanked Su Yen for baking the bars.

# Chapter 13

## *Dating Is the Good Life*

When Sidney and Shade arrived at the hospital, Sal was waiting for them. He wanted to know what they had planned for the day. Shade said, "It's a surprise for Sidney, so I can't tell you, but I'm sure she'll tell you tomorrow. Meanwhile, if you need her, you can have the hospital page me." Sidney said, "I told you I would have a surprise for you today. First, Su Yen baked these health bars for you, and she said they won't hurt your heart. She also hopes you get well soon." Then, Sidney gave him the gift from her. Sal ripped it open. It was a book about meditating. He said, "Thanks, kid. I've always wanted to know more about meditating. How did you know what I would like to read?" She said, "Sal, your bookshelves are full of books. Between what was there and what I know about you, it was easy to pick a book." Sal looked at Shade and said, "Isn't she the clever one?" They visited for a while, then Sal ran them out and told them to have a good time. Sidney said, "I'll see you tomorrow morning."

Shade said on the way to the car, "Now the day really begins." Sidney said, "Now, will you tell me where we're going?"

"Okay," said Shade. "First we're going to ride the ferry over to Staten Island and visit the Statue of Liberty. After we do those things, I'll tell you where we're going next." Sidney was so excited. These were things she had never done and always wanted to do. She told Shade she couldn't be happier. He said, "Judging from what you've told me, I didn't think you had done anything like this." They also had a wonderful lunch on Staten Island. After lunch, Shade asked her if she was ready to go home. Sidney looked stunned, because she thought they were going to spend the entire day together. She answered, "I guess so." Shade said, "I want you to have plenty of time to get ready for the Broadway play I have tickets for tonight. We have dinner reservations before the play starts." Sidney said, "That's so expensive." Shade said, "You let me worry about that." Sidney said, "I don't even know what a person wears to something like that." Shade said, "It's semiformal, but I don't care what you wear, you're always beautiful." When they arrived at Sidney's house, Shade let her out and told her he would be back in about two and half hours. She kissed him goodbye and said, "Okay."

Sidney went upstairs and started looking for just the right thing to wear. She was really glad that Sal's wife had so many beautiful clothes that fit her so well. She knew now why she never bought a lot of clothes. She felt like the donkey that stood between two bales of hay and starved to death because he couldn't decide which one to eat first. There were so many choices, she couldn't decide. She decided to shower first and then pick something. She put her hair on top of her head, with loose curls hanging down. She put on a little eye shadow, lipstick, and a little blush. This was the most makeup she had ever worn. When she looked in the mirror, she worried that it might be too much. After looking in the mirror again, she didn't really think it looked bad. Now it was time to make that decision.

As she was trying on different clothes, she felt like a little girl playing dress-up. Then she laughed at herself because it was about time she had the opportunity to do this. Therefore, she decided to just enjoy this whole experience. She found several very nice things she could have worn. Then, she tried on a pretty little black dress. The bodice was covered with black sequins. It had spaghetti straps, and the skirt was full with several layers of knee-length black chiffon. She really liked this dress, and it was really comfortable. She put on her silky long black stockings, which she rarely ever used. Then, she checked out the shoes and found a pair of black patent leather heels. She slipped them on and thought they were a little bit high. She looked on the box and saw they were three-inch heels, which was high for her (never having worn heels more than two inches before).

She practiced walking up and down the hall to see if she could pull this off. In no time, it seemed much easier than she thought it would be. She found a sequined black handbag and a black velvet swing coat. Now all she needed was a pair of earrings. For the first time, she went through all the jewelry and found a pair of dangling diamond and onyx earrings. When she put them on, it made her feel even more extravagant than they were. She never understood before why people bought such expensive things. She had to admit they did make her feel good. Then she picked up the necklace that matched them and put it on. She loved it, too, but she wasn't sure if this was too much. She decided to skip the necklace.

She hadn't had a mother to tell her how to dress. No one to say when it was enough or too much. Still, she felt good about the way she looked. She turned on some music and began to dance around the room, in front of the mirror. If she was called upon to dance, she wanted to be sure she could dance in those shoes without looking silly. She was actually having a good time. She had never danced around like that before. It felt so good.

She was so excited when she heard the buzzer at the front gate. It was Shade, so she opened the gate to let him in. Now, her heart was quickening, for fear she didn't look right. She could hardly breathe by the time he rang the doorbell. What if he thought she looked silly and he didn't want to hurt her feelings by saying so? She took a deep breath and opened the door. He just stood there, staring at her. Her heart dropped to her feet; she just knew something was wrong with the way she looked. Then he said, "You're the most beautiful woman I've ever seen. I knew you were beautiful before, but you're absolutely breathtaking tonight." Sidney said, "You don't think it's too much?" He said, "Oh no, it's just perfect. I'll be the envy of every man who sees us tonight."

It wasn't just the dress, shoes, jewelry, hairdo, and makeup that made Sidney look so beautiful. She was radiant because she was a wonderful, spiritual person and she was in love. These were the things that could make anyone shine. In all fairness, though, she really did look exquisite. Shade helped her, with her coat and out to the car. As she got in the car, he bent down and kissed her with what felt to Sidney like all the passion in the world. She felt light-headed when he finished, and so did he. Shade said, "Wow! You're dynamite tonight." Sidney said, "There you go again, embarrassing me." Shade said, "Sorry, I just can't help myself."

The evening went so well. They ate the most wonderfully delicious dinner Sidney had ever tasted. They danced to the most divine music she had ever heard. She felt as though she were melting in his arms as they glided across the floor. It felt like the most natural thing in the world. After dinner, they went to the play. It was a comedy. It made them both laugh until they had tears rolling down their cheeks and their ribs were sore. It was the most wonderful evening in Sidney's entire life and in Shade's too.

When it was time to go home, they both hated to see the evening end. Sidney said, "Thank you for the most wonderful day of my life. I have never had so much fun. I didn't even know it was possible to have that much fun." Shade said, "You should have this much fun every day of your life." He told her she was the most deserving person he had ever known. Sidney kissed him and said, "We had better go home now." Shade said, "I don't want to go home yet." Sidney said, "I think we've run out of places to go." Shade laughed and said, "No way, not even close. There are hundreds of places to go or maybe even thousands. This is New York, the city that never sleeps. This is the happening place." Sidney said, "I've heard that, but until now, I never thought of anything but working and getting by."

When they arrived at Sidney's house, she asked him, if he wanted to come in for a quick game of nine-ball. He said, "No, thanks. If I come in tonight, I wouldn't want to go home." Sidney blushed and said, "I don't think I'm ready for anything like that." Shade said, "I know, and that's why I'm going home. I will come in and check the house before I leave."

"Thanks," Sidney replied. "I don't like going into such a big old house alone at night." Shade checked out the house then kissed Sidney goodbye. He told her he would see her in the morning. She said, "Come early, and I'll fix breakfast for you." Shade quipped, "Without Su Yen?" Sidney answered, "I don't cook much, but that doesn't mean I don't know how."

## RAINBOWS ARE BETTER

"Okay, you've convinced me. I'll be here early, with a huge appetite." Sidney asked him if he liked pancakes or omelets. He answered, "Pancakes are fine, but I like both." She said, "Bacon or ham?" He replied, "Why don't you surprise me? I like almost anything." She added, "Could you be here by nine o'clock?" He kissed her goodbye and said, "I'll see you then." She could hardly wait to get upstairs and say her prayers. She had so much to be thankful for. When she went to bed, she dreamed of dancing all night long. Only, in her dreams, she was dancing on a cloud.

When morning came, she could hardly wait to start breakfast. Shade buzzed the gate at exactly nine o'clock. She couldn't believe he was so punctual. When he walked in the house, he noticed it was full of wonderful smells. He kissed her and said, "I hope one of those great smells is coffee." She said, "Oh yeah, I need my coffee in the morning." Shade said, "There's just one more thing we have in common." He asked if he could help her. She said, "Sure, you can pour the orange juice, and we're ready to eat." To tell the truth, he was amazed at how good everything was. Somehow, he couldn't imagine her being a good cook too. When they finished eating, they cleaned the kitchen together.

Sidney asked him what he had planned for the day and for him not to tell her it was a surprise. She needed to know what to wear. At first, he jokingly said, "The little black dress you wore last night." Then he laughed and said, "Slacks and a shirt will be fine. We're going to Atlantic City and do a little gambling." He wanted to know if she had ever been there. She said, "I meant it when I said I have never done anything that's considered recreational." She explained that the only gambling she had done was playing bingo. He said, "Well, I haven't been there in a very long time, but it's lots of fun." She asked if she could check on Sal before they went. He told her he knew she would want to do that, so he had already planned on it. "Thanks," said Sidney. "I'll be ready in a jiffy." Shade told her he'd go down and play a little billiards while he waited. Sidney said, "I won't take but a few minutes." Shade answered, "Take your time, I love playing billiards." Sidney put on a pair of pearl-gray cashmere slacks and a light-pink silk blouse. She put on a pair of comfortable tennis shoes and a little gray leather handbag that matched her gray leather jacket. She looked in the mirror and thought the shoes were all wrong. She went through the shoes and found a pair of soft gray leather flats that had a soft rubber sole. She slipped them on, and they felt like heaven. She knew, right then, Mona had been a professional and thoughtful shopper, leaving nothing to chance. Then, Sidney put on a pair of diamond-cut silver hoop earrings. She looked in the mirror again. She wondered if she should wear makeup. She decided, not today. Her skin was just the right shade of tan. She had large brown eyes, with a double row of thick, curly long black eyelashes. You couldn't even buy such beautiful eyelashes. It was very rare to have such good fortune. However, she didn't even realize that she had it.

    She went downstairs to get Shade. He was just finishing his game. He looked up and said, "Do you ever have a bad day? A day when you don't look like you just stepped out of a magazine?" Sidney blushed and said, "I'm glad you think so, but you've got to stop embarrassing me." Shade laughed and said, "Not a chance, so get used to it. I think you're beautiful, and I can't help saying so." He shot the last ball and said, "Okay, let's go. I'll bet Sal is waiting." Sidney laughed and said, "I'm sure he is."

    When they arrived at the hospital, one of the nurses caught Shade in the hall. She told him Dr. Young was looking for him. Sidney said, "I'll see you later. I'll wait for you in Sal's room." Sidney thought Sal was sleeping, when she went in his room. When she sat down, he said, "What, no hug?" Sidney laughed and said, "I thought you were sleeping." He explained he thought she was the nurse going in to give him a shot, so he was playing possum. Sidney said, "I think you're feeling much better. Are you ready for the move tomorrow?"

    "You better believe it," said Sal. "I've been here all I want to be, and more."

    Sal asked her if she had a good time the day before. She told him she had the most wonderful time of her life. She said, "I brought you a little something." She opened her bag and pulled out a small Statue of Liberty. Sal said, "You shouldn't have done this, but thanks. I've always wanted one, but I never got around to buying one for myself. This brings back happy memories of my beloved Mona. Mona and

## RAINBOWS ARE BETTER

I went to the Statue of Liberty the night I asked her to marry me. It was so wonderful. We couldn't imagine how big and beautiful it was, until we were there in person." Sidney said, "I'd never been there before. You're right. It's one of the most magnificent things I've ever seen. I've traveled all over the world and seen a lot of things. I think the only things I liked better were the pyramids." Sal said, "You've seen the pyramids?" Sidney said, "Yeah, when I was traveling with Angel. She called it her farewell tour. It's funny, but I've seen more from around the world than I have right here in the United States."

Sal told her he had read half of the book she gave him, and he thought it was working. She said, "I know that meditation is good for almost everything, heart attacks included. I felt sure you would like it." He said, "That's what I was doing when you came in. It works on the nurses every time. They think I'm sleeping and don't bother me." Sidney laughed at him playing games with the nurses. After Sidney and Sal had talked for a while, Shade came in. He asked Sal how he was doing. Sal answered, "I'm doing fine, but you kids get out of here and go have some fun." Sidney asked, "Is there anything we can get you before we leave or while we're out?" Sal said, "Just come back tomorrow with the same smile you had today."

When Sidney and Shade arrived in Atlantic City, Sidney didn't feel right about gambling money. Shade said, "You do it all the time when you play the stock market. You have to know how much you're prepared to lose. When you get to that amount, you stop. You have to know how much you're willing to pay to have a good time, then quit when it's gone." When they went inside and started playing, Sidney really liked it. It really was a lot like playing the stock market. She had the same kind of intuition about this that she had about stocks. Shade said, "I think I'm going to quit work and just gamble with you every day." That day, they won twenty thousand dollars. After a while, Sidney didn't like gambling that much. She told Shade gambling wasn't something she'd do very often. It was fun for a while, then she felt like she was cheating, even though she would never do that.

Shade said, "Okay, but let's take some of the money to go dancing and dining, okay?" Sidney said, "Now that sounds like fun."

Shade said, "Why don't we put this money in a joint account? We'll call it our let's-have-fun account." She responded, "Okay, I can really go for that. When it starts getting low, we'll come back and win some more."

"Now, you're talking," said Shade. They had a lovely dinner and went dancing. Sidney had so much fun, she felt light-headed. It was getting late, and she knew they both had a big day tomorrow. She told Shade she thought they should go home. Shade agreed, and they left.

When they arrived at her house, Shade went inside to make sure it was safe. Before leaving, he kissed her goodbye over and over. Sidney said, "I don't know if I'll see you tomorrow. I may not come to the hospital. I've already made arrangements to have Sal moved to the nursing home. If all goes well, I'm going back to work." Shade said, "But you've got to come home sometime tomorrow, don't you?" Sidney said, "Yes, but it will be late. I intend to work late and make sure everything goes smoothly." Shade asked, "Am I getting the old heave-ho?" Sidney said, "Not at all. I'll miss you, but you understand, don't you?" Shade said, "I guess so, but when will I see you again?" Sidney said, "I'll call you tomorrow night, when I get home, and let you know how things went. Then, we can talk about when I can see you next, okay?" Shade said, "I guess that's why I love you so much. I'll be waiting for your call tomorrow night, so don't forget me." Sidney kissed him and sighed. "I could never forget you." With that kind of assurance, he smiled and left.

The next day went just as Sidney had predicted. She got up and went to work early. First, she stopped by the hospital to make sure Sal was feeling well enough for the transfer. He was awake and excited to be getting out of the hospital or, as he put it, making the great escape. Sidney told him she would see him next when he arrived at the nursing home. She then went to work.

Everyone was happy to have her back at work. It felt good to be back. Mac wanted to know when Sal would arrive. Sidney told him he should be there any minute. About an hour later, when Sal still hadn't arrived, she called the hospital to see what was wrong. They told her they would check with the ambulance service to see why he hadn't been picked up yet. Sidney replied she would call them herself. When she called them, they explained they had a bad accident working. They weren't sure when they would be able to transport Sal. Sidney called the hospital to explain what had happened. She asked if they could please tell Sal what was going on. She didn't want him to worry. The nurse said, "We might be able to transport Sal ourselves. We have a van we use for transport when someone needs a ride for a doctor appointment. We use it even if they're bedfast, in wheelchairs, or unable to get here on their own due to health problems. If the ambulance isn't able to pick him up by, say, one o'clock this afternoon, I'll see what I can do." Sidney thanked her and assured her, if she heard anything, she would call them.

Sidney had just hung up the phone, when the switchboard operator told her there was a call for her on line 1. Sidney answered the phone, and it was a very worried Su Yen on the other end. Su Yen was scared to death when she got to the house that morning. The workers arrived, but Sidney was nowhere to be found. Sidney said, "I apologize, Su Yen. I decided to come in early this morning. I'm not used to anyone watching out for me. I promise, from now on, if I leave before you get there, I'll leave a note, okay?" Su Yen told her she would feel better if she would do that. Then, she wouldn't worry so much. Sidney asked if Joe had arrived yet to let the workers know where to start working. Joe had agreed to keep an eye on things. Su Yen assured her Joe was already there when she arrived. Sidney said, "Good, I'm glad something is going right."

Su Yen asked what she would like for supper. Sidney explained she wouldn't be home until late and she would eat there with Sal. Su Yen said she would wait until Sidney got home. Sidney said, "No, don't do that. I don't know when I'll be home." Su Yen informed her that she and her boys would spend the night. That way she wouldn't go home to an empty house. Sidney thanked her for being so thoughtful and said she would see her later then.

Noon came and went, but no Sal. At about one fifteen, the hospital called and said Sal was on his way. Sidney thanked them and said, "I'm so relieved." The nurse laughed and said, "You can rest easier now." A few minutes later, Sal arrived and was taken to his new room.

Sal was so pleased when he saw that Sidney had gone to great lengths to make this room look like his bedroom at home. She had even put his Bible next to his bed and bought a smaller version of the bedspread that had been on his bed. She took the pictures that had been on his bedroom walls and added them to his room, as well. She even put a large screen television in his room because she knew he was used to it. Sal was exhausted after the move. He kissed Sidney and thanked her for all she had done. Sidney said, "Sal, it's you that has done so much for me, not the other way around. Don't you forget it, because I won't."

Sal had to rest most of the afternoon. When dinnertime rolled around, he was awake and ready to visit. Sidney went to his room and had dinner with him. They discussed what he could expect that night and the next morning. Sidney suggested maybe she should stay with him his first night there. Sal refused. He told her to go home and get some rest. He assured her he would be fine, and if he needed her, they could call her at home. Sidney quizzed, "Do you promise to call if you need me or even think you need me?" Sal agreed but assured her he would be fine.

Sidney was getting ready to go home, when Joe walked in. He asked if she was ready to go home yet. She asked Joe what he was doing there. He replied he was there to drive her home. She asked how he knew she was about ready to go home. He replied Sal had called him and asked him to come over and pick her up. Sidney said, "That Sal. I don't know what I'm going to do with him. He's got to stop worrying about me." Joe asked again, "So are you ready to go home now?" Sidney said, "I guess so since you're here."

On their way home, Sidney asked Joe how the construction was going. He informed her things were going well. He was amazed at how much they had accomplished in only one day. He said, "At this rate, I may be moved in by this weekend." Sidney said, "I wouldn't count on it, Joe. The plumbing and electricity will probably take some time." Joe replied, "But, Ms. Sidney, that's what they did today." She said, "You mean the plumbing and electrical wiring are completed?"

# RAINBOWS ARE BETTER

"Yes, ma'am," Joe replied. Sidney laughed and said, "Maybe you will be moved in by the weekend." Joe said, "I hope so, then they can start work on Su Yen's place. I know she's worried about you coming home late at night with nobody there." Sidney said, "You're both so sweet to me. I can never thank you enough. I don't know how I got along without the two of you all this time. You spoil me rotten." Joe said, "Ms. Sidney, you could never be rotten. You deserve to have somebody take care of you." Sidney said, "Nonetheless, I'm very grateful." Joe said, "You gave us a job and a place to live, I think that's enough."

When Joe and Sidney arrived home, Su Yen was waiting up for them. Sidney said, "Su Yen, you didn't have to wait up for me. You need your rest." Joe asked Sidney if she wanted to see what the workers had done. She told him she would look at it in the morning. Joe said, "Okay, I'll just be going home now. I'll see you in the morning." Sidney saw Joe to the door and locked up when he went out the gate. She turned to Su Yen and said, "I don't know about you, but I'm ready for bed." Su Yen agreed.

The next morning, while Sidney was getting ready, she heard the little boys giggling and running about. She loved this pleasant sound. When she went downstairs, Su Yen had her breakfast ready and waiting. Sidney told Su Yen she was planning to be home at about six o'clock. If she was going to be late, she would call her to let her know. Su Yen asked her if she would be eating dinner at home. Sidney told her yes and Shade might be having dinner with her. Su Yen said, "You two get serious, yes?" Sidney said, "I think I've felt serious about him from the first day I met him." Joe came in and asked Sidney if she wanted to see his apartment now. She said, "Sure, Joe, let's take a look at it." Sidney was amazed to see how much they had accomplished in just one day. Joe told her he would like to take her to work now, if she was ready to go. She told Joe she could take the bus. He said, "No way, Sal said to drive you wherever you need to go."

"Okay, Joe," said Sidney. "I'm ready to go, just let me get my purse."

At the nursing home, everything started settling into a normal pattern. Sidney called Shade and invited him to dinner. Shade told her he couldn't wait to see her. She told him dinner would be ready by six thirty but it could wait until he got there. She said, "Su Yen knows you're coming. She'll make something that I can reheat, if you're late." Shade answered, "I won't be late. I'm getting off early this afternoon, so I'll be on time." He told Sidney, the next time, he was taking her out. He explained he didn't feel right eating there all the time. Sidney said, "Okay, I don't care where we eat. All I care about is spending time with you." He said, "Okay, I'll see you tonight." The rest of the day, Sidney couldn't wait to see Shade.

Sidney felt Sal was a little lonely or maybe just disoriented being in a strange place. She tried to comfort him. He wasn't complaining; it was just something she sensed. She asked Sal if there was anything she could do or get for him that would make him feel better. His answer was no; he was doing fine. He explained it would take some time to get used to his new life and surroundings. Sidney said, "I wish I could do something to make things easier for you." He told her not to worry; he'd be all right. She said, "If you think of something, please let me know, and I'll take care of it."

Sidney called home and told Su Yen that she would be home around five thirty and Shade would be there by six o'clock. Su Yen assured her she would have dinner ready by six o'clock. She asked Sidney if there was anything special she would like for dinner. Sidney said, "You've done an exceptional job, so far, so I'll leave it up to you. There are a couple of things that I don't like, liver or seafood." Su Yen said, "You not like seafood?" Sidney said, "No, I really don't." Su Yen said, "Seafood very good for you. You need seafood." Sidney said, "I don't think so." She asked Su Yen how the construction workers were doing. Su Yen related she didn't know but that they had been busy all day.

When they were finished talking, Sidney went to Sal's room and asked him if the food was okay. He said it was fine; he didn't really know what he was feeling, but he was sure he would be fine in a few days. Sidney called the doctor and asked if Sal's medicine might be causing him to feel blue. The doctor told her he'd come by the next day and check on him. Sidney thanked him because she felt very concerned. As she hung up the phone, Joe walked in. She asked him what he was doing there. He answered he was there to pick her up and take her home. She said, "I'm not quite ready to go yet." Joe said, "That's all right, I'll visit with Sal for a while." Sidney said, "Okay, I'll come get you when I'm ready."

Joe visited with Sal, telling him all that was being done to the house. He told him how excited he was that it was going so fast. Sal said, "That's great, soon you'll be able to move in. I'm going to feel much better knowing there's someone on the grounds, in case Sidney needs help." Joe said, "Don't worry, Sal. I'll take good care of her." He told Sal about the lighting he had done in the backyard. He told him he was thinking about building a waterfall on the north side of the fishpond, for Sidney's birthday. He explained he had a friend who had some large rocks he needed hauled off. He figured he could use those to make a real nice waterfall. Sal told him, if he needed any money to complete it, to just let him know. Joe said, "I'm pretty sure I already have everything I need, and her birthday isn't until August 20th. I'll have plenty of time to get it done." Sal said, "I know she'll love that. You're a good man, Joe." Joe smiled about as big a smile as he was able to. Sidney went in and asked Joe if he was ready to go. They both said goodbye to Sal.

When they got home, Sidney ran upstairs to get ready. When she came down, Su Yen was getting ready to leave. She thanked Su Yen and told her she would see them tomorrow. Su Yen had even set the table, but Sidney wanted to add a few personal touches, like adding flowers and candles. She exchanged the glasses for the good crystal. She had just finished the table, when she heard Shade buzz the front gate. She ran to let him in and went back to light the candles. When he got to the door, she was waiting with open arms. He walked in and gave her a big kiss. Then, he gave her some pink roses and a box of chocolates. She said, "I can't believe you did this. Thank you." Shade said, "I've missed you so much." Sidney said, "It's only been one day." Shade said, "I don't know about you, but it's been the longest day I've ever spent." Sidney said, "I know exactly what you're talking about, I've missed you too."

After dinner, they went in the library to have their dessert. Shade lit a fire in the fireplace. Then, he checked the stereo to see if it had a CD player. He was very impressed to see such a nice stereo system. It had a nice CD player. He went into the hallway and retrieved a CD from his coat pocket. He went back into the library and put in the CD. Sidney brought in the dessert. When she heard the music, she asked what kind of music was playing. Shade told her it was Jamaican music. Sidney asked, rather surprised, "Sal had Jamaican music?" Shade said, "I brought it with me to see if you would like it." She told him she had never heard it before but she loved it. Shade couldn't believe she had never heard Jamaican music before. She told him that was one corner of the world she and Angel hadn't traveled to. He asked her what type of music she liked. She said, "I like jazz and easy listening. Quite honestly, I don't listen to music that often." Shade said, "I can't believe that. Music is the rhythm of life." Sidney said, "I hardly have time for anything. I've been working two jobs and taking care of the business of living. When I have any spare time, I spend it meditating and praying. I haven't even watched television enough to know what shows are on." Shade said, "This is one area of your life we need to work on. I don't believe a person can live life without music." He told her anyone with a fantastic stereo like the one she had should have music all the time. Sidney said, "Until you turned on that stereo tonight, I hadn't even thought about having one." Shade said, "I have another CD in the car. I know you're going to love it." He said he'd be right back. When he got back, he put on a CD of love songs. When Shade and Sidney finished eating their dessert, they slow-danced until late that night. Finally, Shade said he had to go home. He explained the hospital had a busy day scheduled for him the next day. Sidney said, "I understand completely. I have a busy schedule, as well." He told her he was giving her the compact discs he brought with him. He wanted her to listen to them once in a while. She responded, "That's an easy assignment." They laughed and kissed good night.

# Chapter 14

## *Moving in Begins*

Things were going very smoothly. The doctor changed Sal's medicine, and he was much better. Sidney was so happy, she felt like singing all the time. When Friday rolled around, Joe's apartment was ready for him to move in. On Saturday, Su Yen, Joe, and Sidney got up early and started moving Joe in. While Joe was setting up the bed, Su Yen and Sidney went to buy curtains and blinds. On the way home, Sidney and Su Yen stopped at the thrift shop. Sidney bought Joe a recliner chair, an end table, a chest of drawers, and a small dinette set. When they returned, Joe had finished setting up the bedroom. Sidney sent him to the thrift store to pick up his furniture. Meanwhile, she and Su Yen hung the blinds and curtains. By the time Joe arrived with the furniture, it was late afternoon. He went to his old place to pick up his personal belongings. Su Yen and Sidney made the bed and hung the shower curtain. Sidney took some towels and throw rugs from the main house, and they put them in his new bathroom. Everything was ready for him to spend the night in his new home. When he returned with his belongings, tears came to his eyes when he saw how nice everything was. Sidney said, "None of that. We're all happy you're moving in."

Sidney told him he could take her shopping the next day to get a stove and refrigerator. She suggested they might even find a microwave oven. She told him to sit in his chair and see if it was comfortable enough. He sat down and said, "It's great." Sidney said, "Now push back and put your feet up." He did then said, "This is the most comfortable chair I've ever sat in. It feels like it was made for me." Sidney said, "It was Joe. I'm sure of it." Joe, Su Yen, and Sidney carried up his meager belongings. Sidney suggested, when they finished, they should leave him alone and let him get acquainted with his new surroundings.

Su Yen said, "Supper be ready in forty-five minute." Sidney said, "Tonight we'll all eat together to celebrate." Sidney and Su Yen went into the house to start the evening meal. Su Yen told Sidney to get some rest while she prepared the meal. Sidney responded, "Not a chance. You've worked as hard as anyone today, so I'm helping you." Su Yen argued that Sidney was the boss and she should not be working so hard. "Okay," said Sidney, "if you're going to insist that I rest, we're calling and ordering a pizza. That way, we can both sit down and rest." That was exactly what they did, and the little boys were so excited. They loved cheese pizza. Sidney ordered a small cheese pizza for the boys and an extralarge combo pizza for Su Yen, Joe, and herself. When Joe came in, Sidney asked if a combo pizza was all right with him. He said, "Next to pepperoni, that's my favorite." She laughed, went to the phone, and ordered a medium pepperoni pizza.

While they waited for the pizza to arrive, Sidney asked them if they would like to hear her new CD, which Shade had given her. They answered with a resounding yes. The little boys loved the Jamaican music. They began dancing around the house, having a wonderful time. When the pizza arrived, they sat down together, held hands, and said a prayer of thanks. Then they shared not only the pizza but also conversation and laughter. Joe told them he couldn't wait until Monday, when they would start Su Yen's new place. Sidney said, "I think we all feel that way. I'll be so happy when I have you all living here."

It was getting late, and Joe excused himself to go home and enjoy his new apartment. Su Yen said, "Boys getting tired, we go home too." Sidney said, "You can spend the night here tonight. I don't want you to drive home this late." Su Yen said, "You sure it all right?" Sidney said, "Of course, it's all right. I'd rather have you stay here than have you out driving around this late at night on a Saturday night." It was agreed Su Yen and the boys would stay the night. Su Yen bathed the children and put them to bed. Su Yen and Sidney sat in the library and talked for hours.

When Sidney went in her bedroom, the phone rang. She answered the phone, and it was Shade.

He said, "I hope I'm not calling too late. I needed to hear your voice before I went to bed." Sidney said, "I'm glad you called." He asked her how the big move was going. She told him they were almost finished. She explained they still had to get Joe's large appliances. Joe still had to unpack his personal belongings. Shade said, "Perfect, now we can do something tomorrow, right?" Sidney said, "After we get his appliances, I don't know, why not? What did you have in mind?" He asked her if she liked basketball. She told him she didn't know but it might be fun finding out. He said he would pick her up at noon and they could have lunch before the game.

When Shade arrived, Sidney asked him if he had time to see Joe's new home. He said he had as much time as they needed. Sidney took him around to the side of the garage, where there was now a double carport and a staircase that led upstairs to Joe's apartment. They knocked on Joe's door. When Joe answered the door, he had a smile that nearly covered his whole face. Sidney said, "Joe, I want you to meet Shade." Joe said, "I'm glad to meet you, Shade." Shade said, "I'm glad to meet you, too, Joe." Joe asked them to come in and see his new home. Shade told him he had a very nice place there. Joe said, "I know. Thanks to Ms. Sidney. Ms. Sidney is very good to me and Su Yen." Sidney said, "Enough of that, Joe. You and Su Yen are very good to me, as well." Sidney said, "Joe, I've got to go now, but I thought you might like to show off your home." Joe said, "I just wish Sal could see it."

"I know," said Sidney. "Me too." She told him they would take some pictures and show him.

Shade and Sidney left for another fun-filled day. They went to a basketball game. Sidney told Shade that was the most exciting thing she had ever seen. "Happy days, you're going to be a sports fan!" exclaimed Shade. She replied, "It looks that way. If the other sports are that much fun, I definitely will be."

When they got back to Sidney's place, Shade went in, and they played a few games of billiards. Shade said, "I better go home." Sidney said, "Why don't you stay for supper?" Shade said, "I don't want to wear out my welcome." Sidney said, "Trust me, you could never do that." She added, "Let's go to the kitchen and see what we can find." Shade said, "The TV dinners look fine to me." Sidney said, "Are you sure? I can cook, you know." He said, "Why bother when that's so easy?" Sidney said, "A man after my own heart." While the dinners were heating, Sidney cut up a salad, and Shade set the table. Sidney told him she loved doing things with him around. Everything was fun, as long as she had him to do it with. Shade said, "I'm happy to be of service." Sidney said, "You know, even these TV dinners taste better when you're here." Shade said, "I think they taste pretty good too. I thought it was just the way you cooked them." Sidney laughed and said, "I don't think so." She asked him, "What sounds good for dessert, cheesecake or ice cream?" Shade said, "Ice cream." She said, "It's toffee crunch, is that all right?" He answered, "That's my favorite kind." Sidney said, "It's mine, too, imagine that." He said, "We were made for each other." Sidney said, "I have to agree with that."

Shade told her he was glad to hear the music he gave her playing in all the rooms. Sidney explained Joe had wired speakers in every room so she could listen to it wherever she was. Shade told her he had to leave after dessert. He had a heavy schedule for the next day. After he left, Sidney went upstairs and got ready for bed. She turned on the lights outside while she said her prayers. Then she turned out the lights and went to bed.

For the next month, everything was busy at work and at home. One night, when Sidney went home, Su Yen told her she had a surprise for her. She took her out back, and not only was Su Yen's new home finished, but with Joe's help, she had also already moved in. Sidney asked why they hadn't told her it was finished. She told Su Yen she could have helped them with the moving. Joe said, "We knew you would. That's why we did it while you were at work. We think you already work too hard." Sidney said, "No matter, I'm just happy you're moved in now." She told Su Yen everything looked very nice. Blake and Brian were running around the house, giggling and dancing. They really loved their new home. Sidney felt very satisfied, knowing these four people she loved so much now had a good place to live.

It seemed as though everything in Sidney's life was better now than she had ever hoped for. She had Shade, the love of her life. She had Mac and Sal, who were like her fathers and mentors. She also had Joe and Su Yen, who loved her and took good care of her. She also had Su Yen's children, Brian and Blake, who brought her so much joy. Considering everything she had been through, this was a life heaven-sent. This was the kind of life we would all like to have.

# Chapter 15

## *Those Strange Feelings Again*

One day, shortly before Sidney's birthday, she was on the phone, ordering the orphanage birthday party. She suddenly just hung up the phone. She felt such a strong sense of urgency; she felt as though it were consuming her body. No matter what she did, she couldn't turn off this feeling of impending doom. She hastily ran outside and hailed a passing cab to take her home. She kept saying to the cabdriver, "Hurry, faster." She didn't know what was wrong, but she knew, for sure, time was of the essence. As they approached the house, she knew something was wrong with Blake in the backyard. She opened the gate and ran as fast as she could around to the backyard. There she found him floating facedown, in the fishpond. She pulled him out and started CPR. Su Yen went running out of the house, screaming, and Brian was crying. The cabdriver went back around to get his money. Sidney shouted, "Go inside, call 911, and hurry!" Su Yen ran inside, tears streaming down her face. She dialed 911 and told them what happened. They told her the ambulance was on its way. Sidney continued CPR until they arrived. By the time the paramedics got to Blake, he was breathing on his own. They told Su Yen she should be thankful Sidney got to him when she did. Otherwise, he would probably have died. Su Yen said, "I thankful, I very thankful." Sidney told Su Yen to go to the hospital with Blake. She would follow in a few minutes with Brian. Sidney was searching for Joe, when the cabdriver said, "Hey, lady, I need my money." She asked him not to leave until she found Joe. Brian said, "Joe went to the hardware store and might not be back for a while." Sidney asked the cabdriver to take them to the hospital. She left Joe a note, and they left for the hospital.

While traveling to the hospital, Sidney asked Brian how Blake fell in the fishpond. Brian said, "He squatted down at the edge of the water and bent over to watch the fish. He just lost his balance and fell in. I tried to reach him, but I couldn't, so I ran inside to tell Mom." He asked Sidney why she was home so early. Sidney said, "I just had a feeling something was wrong."

When they arrived at the hospital, they went to the emergency room. There, they found a very distraught Su Yen still in tears. She hugged Brian and told Sidney they were still working on Blake, and the doctor hadn't come out yet. Su Yen quizzed Sidney as to why she was home so early. Sidney laughed and replied, "Brian just asked me the same thing on the way over here. I was at work when suddenly I just knew there was something wrong at home. I didn't even tell anyone I was leaving. I ran out, caught a cab, and rushed home. When I arrived, I knew Blake was in trouble in the backyard. I jumped out of the cab and ran around back. That's when I found Blake floating facedown in the fishpond. I've had this kind of feeling once before. It was when Sal went code blue in the hospital." Su Yen hugged Sidney, saying, "I so grateful you come in time. You save Blake's life." Su Yen said, "When this over, I take CPR class. This teach me all mother need know CPR." Sidney agreed, "If anyone needs to learn CPR, it's mothers. They're the ones most likely to be there when it's needed the most. Unfortunately, most people don't think about it until after the fact."

When the doctor came out, he reassured them Blake was going to be fine. He explained they were going to keep Blake overnight for observation, just to be on the safe side. They were concerned about a possible lung infection, due to the fact he fell into a fishpond. He told Su Yen they were starting an IV of antibiotics as a precautionary measure. Su Yen asked, "That necessary?" The doctor responded he believed it was the best course of action. Sidney knew Su Yen was also concerned about Brian. She told Su Yen that Brian could stay with her until Blake was able to go home, so she did not have to worry about that. Su Yen said, "Thank you, Ms. Sidney. You angel for us."

Sidney called work and explained what happened. She related how sorry she was that she took off like that without telling anyone, but she really felt she had to. She asked if she could take the next day off, since it was a Friday, so she'd have a three-day weekend to watch Brian. They fully understood and told her that was not a problem; they would see her on Monday. When Sidney hung up, she called Joe and told him what happened. She asked him if he would come to the hospital and take them home. Joe told her he would be right over and he would meet her in the lobby.

When Joe arrived, he wanted to see Blake before they went home. He found Blake sleeping. Su Yen told Joe they had given Blake a shot to make him rest. She assured Joe, "I tell Blake you come see him when he wake up." Sidney asked Su Yen if she wanted to eat dinner while they were there. She could stay with Blake. Su Yen agreed that would be a good idea. She knew it might be a long time before she would have another chance. Sidney asked Joe if he would like to take Su Yen and Brian to dinner. Joe was all smiles as he answered "Sure." Su Yen said, "What about you, Ms. Sidney?" Sidney told them she would stay with Blake and eat something at home later. She said, "You never know Shade might come over for dinner tonight. You go ahead and don't worry about me."

When they returned from dinner, Sidney asked Su Yen if there was anything she could do for her before she left. Su Yen couldn't think of anything. She expressed concern that if she stayed for more than one day, she would need clean clothes. Sidney said, "I think we can take care of that, just give me a call in the morning." Su Yen gave Sidney instructions on where to find their clothes. They all hugged Blake and Su Yen before going home.

When they arrived home, Sidney had a message from Shade on the answering machine. She called him to tell him what had happened. She asked if he would like to come over for dinner. Shade answered he was hoping she would ask and that she need not fix anything. He would bring Chinese food. He asked if Brian would like that. When Sidney asked Brian, he exclaimed, "I love crab puffs!"

# RAINBOWS ARE BETTER

Sidney told Shade that Brian had already eaten supper, so he only wanted crab puffs. Shade said, "Consider it done. I'll be over in less than an hour." Sidney took Brian upstairs and gave him a bath while they waited for Shade to get there. He put on his pajamas and went downstairs to play while Sidney slipped into her sweats.

When Shade arrived, they were all ready to eat. Brian ran to the door, when Shade came in. He said, "Did you know Sidney saved my brother's life today?" Shade said, "Sidney saved his life?" Brian responded, "Yes, she did. She came home early and found Blake face-down in the fishpond. She pulled him out and did CPR on him, until the ambulance got here. The ambulance took Blake and Mom to the hospital." Sidney said, "Okay, let's eat our dinner now." While they were eating, Brian filled Shade in on all the details.

When they were finished eating, Sidney told Brian it would be a good idea to brush his teeth before going to bed. He asked, "Aren't you going to help me?" Sidney said, "Sure, if you need help." He said, "My mom always helps me." Shade said, "You help him while I clean up down here." When Brian was ready for bed, he ran downstairs to tell Shade "Good night." Sidney tucked him into bed and kissed him good night. She asked him if he needed a night-light on. He told her no but asked if she could leave the door open a little bit. She replied "Of course" and left the door slightly ajar.

Shade and Sidney settled down in the library and talked about the events of the day. Sidney hoped Shade didn't think she was crazy. This thing of knowing something was about to happen, might sound a little bit crazy. Shade told her he would believe anything she told him because he knew she would never lie. She said, "I have to confess, I thought I was going crazy both times." She told him, if it hadn't happened to her, she didn't know if she could have believed it. Shade said, "I've heard of people knowing things before it happens. I don't think I've ever known anyone personally, until now." He asked if it would be all right if he took her and Brian to the hospital the next day. Sidney said, "I'd love for you to go with us. You'll have to ride with our chauffeur, though. Joe likes to drive, and I know he wants to see Blake too." Shade said, "That's even better." He kissed Sidney good night and went home.

The next day, they all went to the hospital to see Blake and Su Yen. Sidney took them enough clean clothes to last a couple of days. She stopped on the way to pick up a teddy bear for both Blake and Brian and flowers for Su Yen. She also bought a couple of books for Blake. She thought it would keep him entertained while he was recovering. When they arrived at the hospital, Su Yen was very excited to see them. Sidney asked her if she wanted get cleaned up while they watched Blake. Su Yen was very happy to take her up on her offer. Sidney asked Blake how he was feeling. He said, "Okay, but I was awake coughing most of the night." Sidney said, "You must be tired. It's good that you're coughing to get all that yucky water out of your lungs." She hugged little Blake and asked, "Why don't you try to get some sleep, and I will stay with you." It didn't take long for him to doze off. Brian asked Sidney if his little brother was going to be all right. Sidney said, "Sure, he will. He's just very tired from all he's been through. In a few days, he'll be up running around and playing, just like before."

When Su Yen got back, she felt much better. She hugged Brian and asked him if he had been a good boy for Ms. Sidney. Sidney assured her he had been wonderful. Sidney asked Su Yen if she had eaten her breakfast yet. She said, "No, not yet." Joe volunteered to take her downstairs and make sure she ate something. Brian wanted to go with her. Sidney said, "Why don't all of you go? Shade and I will stay here with Blake while you're gone." Sidney and Shade sat on the sofa in the room and discussed what they would do the rest of the day. Shade wanted to take Brian to an amusement park or maybe play some miniature golf. Sidney said, "We should ask Su Yen first. Then we'll ask Brian what he would like to do." She said, "You know, of course, Joe would enjoy going along also." Shade said, "I don't have a problem with that. It's actually a good idea." When Su Yen returned, Sidney took her out in the hall. She asked if it would be okay to take Brian on an outing. Su Yen answered, "That be very nice." She knew Brian would have a good time.

They stayed for a while and visited with Blake when he woke up. Just before they left, the doctor went in to check on Blake. He checked him over and explained he would need to spend at least one more night. He wanted to make sure those little lungs were clear. If all went well, they would release him the next day. He told them Blake's lungs sounded clear, but he was still concerned about an infection. He thought one more day of intravenous antibiotics would be the safest bet. Sidney asked if Blake would need any special care when he went home. He told her, "We may want him to come in once a day for about a week to take breath treatments." Sidney said, "Is that something we could do at home?"

"Sure," said the doctor, "but you would have to rent the equipment to do it." She told him she was a nurse's aide and she routinely gave the treatments to some of their patients at the nursing home. He said, "Great, that would be easier on Blake." He told Sidney he would get her set up with the necessary equipment when they released Blake. Su Yen thanked Sidney for volunteering to help Blake. She said, "You save his life, now you nurse him to health." Sidney hugged her and said, "No thanks are needed. I can't take credit for saving his life. If God hadn't spoke to me in a voice I couldn't ignore, I wouldn't have been there." Sidney looked at the door, thinking they should go now, when the nurse entered with Blake's lunch. Sidney asked Su Yen, if she would like to go to lunch while they were still there. Joe quickly offered to take her to lunch. Su Yen asked Brian if he wanted to go to lunch with her. He said, "No, I want to go to lunch with Shade and Sidney." Sidney explained they had already made plans for lunch and she would help Blake while they were gone.

Shade made a call while they were gone and arranged for Su Yen to have her meals sent to Blake's room until he was released. He told Sidney she wouldn't have to wait until someone was there, to eat her meals. Sidney said, "I think you're wonderful." Blake wanted some ice cream, so Shade asked the nurse if he could have some ice cream. She said, "I'm afraid not. He has a congestion problem." Shade said, "How about a popsicle?" The nurse said, "That should be okay. I'll bring one right in." Shade told Blake they couldn't let him have ice cream but they were going to bring him a popsicle. Blake said, "Okay, I like popsicles too." Shade told him, as soon as he could have ice cream, he would bring him a big bucket of ice cream. Blake smiled and said, "Yeah!" Shade said, "You won't mind sharing with

Brian and your mom, will you?" He said, "Not me, I like to share." When Su Yen and Joe returned, they said goodbye to Blake and Su Yen. Sidney said, "I'll be back in the morning to stay with Blake while you get cleaned up." They waved goodbye and left.

Joe said, "Okay, where to now?" Sidney said, "First, we'll go for pizza, right, Brian?" He was smiling from ear to ear. Pizza was his absolute favorite food. When they finished the pizza, they went to the amusement park. They all had a good time there. First, they drove the bumper cars. Brian and Joe had so much fun, they rode them five times. Finally, Sidney talked them into trying something else. Once they tried the other rides, they were running from one ride to the next. After they had tried all the rides, Brian and Joe agreed they liked the bumper cars best. Shade said, "Bumper cars it is then." They rode the bumper cars three more times. Sidney could tell Brian was getting tired and it was time to feed him supper. This time, they went to an Italian restaurant and had spaghetti for dinner. Brian liked the spaghetti and breadsticks, but most of all, he liked the Italian ice.

It was getting late, so Sidney said, "We better go home now, don't you think?" Brian admitted he was getting tired. Joe said, "Me, too, Brian." When they got home, Sidney bathed Brian, and he brushed his teeth. She let him go downstairs to say "Good night" to Shade and Joe. He hugged them both and thanked everybody for a very happy day. Joe said, "I'd like to thank everybody for a great day too." It was agreed by all they had a very good time. Shade added they would have to do it again, when Blake and Su Yen could join them. Sidney asked Brian if he would like to call his mother and tell her "Good night." He answered, "Could I?" Sidney said, "Sure, you can. You can call her anytime you want to." Brian was so excited when he spoke to his mom. He was having trouble remembering everything he wanted to tell her, but she got the message. Then, Brian hopped in bed and asked Sidney if he could have his new bear to sleep with. She said, "Sure, you can. I'll have Joe get it out of the car and bring it up so he can say 'Good night' again." Joe got the bear and took it upstairs. You could hear them giggling all the way downstairs as they recounted the events of the day. Sidney looked at Shade and said, "That was a wonderful thing you did today. As a matter of fact, I had

## RAINBOWS ARE BETTER

a fabulous time too." Shade said, "So did I," and he gave her a kiss that expressed his thanks to her.

They were both so happy to finally spend some quiet time together. It had been a busy day, and tomorrow promised to be more of the same. Sidney told Shade he didn't have to go with her the next day unless he wanted to. She would understand. He said, "Are you kidding? I want to spend as much time with you as possible. I don't care what we're doing as long as we're doing it together. How early do we need to leave in the morning?" Sidney said, "Thanks to you having Su Yen's food delivered to Blake's room, we won't have to leave as early in the morning. I'd say about ten o'clock will be fine." Shade joked, "I'd better leave and throw a load of underwear in the washer before going to bed. Give me a kiss that will last until tomorrow, and I'll go home." Sidney was happy to oblige. She watched as Shade drove out the gate. She then decided she would call the nursing home before going to bed to tell Sal how Blake was doing.

The next day, they were on their way by 10:00 a.m. Brian was excited to go see his mother. Sidney could tell he was getting a little homesick to be with her. He had never spent any time away from his mother before. Needless to say, he missed her and his brother. Sidney stopped at the toy store, on the way to the hospital, and let Brian pick out a toy for Blake. Brian picked the game Operation. He knew Blake liked playing games. Joe got Blake a present too. He bought Blake a karaoke machine. Joe knew both the boys liked to sing. Shade bought some children's sing-along disc to go with it. Sidney bought Su Yen a deck of cards and some magazines to keep her busy while Blake was sleeping. Sidney was hoping the whole time that Blake would get to go home today. When they arrived at the hospital, Sidney asked Su Yen if the doctor had been in yet. Su Yen said, "No, not yet." She thanked Shade for having her meals delivered to the room. That was so much better. Sidney told Su Yen she could get cleaned up while they visited with Blake. They gave Blake his new toys, and he was so excited. He asked if it was his birthday. They all laughed and said, "No. We just wanted you to have something to do until you come home." Brian and Blake tried out the disk first and then the game. They were laughing and giggling as if nothing was wrong. Sidney hoped that would be the case, for his sake, as well as Brian's.

When Su Yen came back, Sidney gave her the cards and magazines. Su Yen said, "I hope we coming home today. He seem much better." They all visited until the doctor came in. When he finished Blake's examination, he said, "Not today. More than likely, tomorrow morning, this young man can go home. He still has a slight raspy sound in his lungs. I don't want to take any chances. We'll keep him on the IV one more day. We'll see what he sounds like in the morning."

Sidney asked Su Yen if she wanted to go shopping or do something to get away for a while. Sidney volunteered to stay with Blake. Su Yen wanted to take Brian to lunch. She needed to spend a little time with him and maybe run home for a few minutes. She needed to pick up some clothes for her and Blake to wear home tomorrow. Joe said, "I'll take her, if that's all right." Sidney said, "Thanks, Joe, that would be great." When they got back, Brian seemed much happier having spent some time with his mom. Sidney said, "We need to get out of here so Blake can get some rest." She told Su Yen they had been playing Operation the whole time she was gone. Su Yen said, "I hope I be home tomorrow." Sidney said, "If they release him before we get here, just call, and Joe will come to pick you up." Su Yen hugged Sidney and thanked her for everything.

When they left the hospital, Sidney and Shade were ready to eat lunch. Sidney asked Joe and Brian if they were ready for some dessert. Brian said, "You bet." While Sidney and Shade were ordering, Shade had them bring the dessert cart over to let Brian and Joe check it out. There were so many good things on it, they were having trouble deciding what they wanted. Sidney said, "Take your time, and pick your absolute favorite." Sidney and Shade were halfway through their lunch before Joe and Brian knew what they wanted. Brian had caramel-ice-cream brownies. Joe had strawberry shortcake. Sidney said, "Excellent choice, guys." Shade said, "While they're ordering, what would you like, Sidney?" Sidney quickly answered, "The German chocolate cake." Shade ordered the pumpkin pie. When the desserts arrived, they all sampled one another's tasty treat and couldn't believe how good everything was. When they finished eating, it was on to play miniature golf. Brian and Joe had so much fun, they played five rounds of golf. Sidney felt sure Joe could have played all night. Brian, on the other hand, was showing signs of being tired. They had Chinese for dinner and went home. What a wonderful day it had been. Sidney couldn't remember ever having so much fun in her whole life.

She knew she wanted to have children of her own someday. Now, she was sure she wanted them to belong to her and Shade. She thought to herself that Joe would make a great father for some lucky kids too. She hoped someday he would find someone and have some kids.

The next morning Su Yen called and told Sidney they were ready to go home. Brian wanted to go with Joe to pick up his mom and Blake. Sidney said, "I think we'll all go to pick them up." They loaded everyone in the car, and Joe drove them to the hospital. When they arrived, Blake and Su Yen were ready to go home. The doctor had made the equipment available for them to take with them. He had included written instructions. Joe loaded everything in the car while Su Yen and Sidney went around and thanked all the nurses for their help and kindness.

They were finally on their way home. When they arrived, Su Yen said, "I almost forget how wonderful my new home is." They were all glad to have everyone home again. Sidney and Joe left to let them get settled in.

Sidney went in the house and started making some phone calls. She called around until she found a dog who had been trained in search and rescue. The man she spoke with told her he had a dog who was trained as a watchdog and very good with children. Sidney went out back and asked Joe if he could take her to the dog training center. Joe said, "Okay, but we don't have a dog." Sidney had to laugh and said, "We may have, before the day is out." When they arrived, the man took them out back and introduced them to a bright-eyed golden retriever named Peaches. The dog ran right to Sidney and Joe. It was love at first sight. Sidney asked the man if she had been trained to rescue children from water. He answered, "Most definitely. She's been well trained to do all sorts of rescue, and she's one of the smartest dogs we've ever had." Sidney said, "Okay, we'll take her." Joe said, "I just love her, Ms. Sidney." She said, "I just hope Brian and Blake will like her." Joe said, "Oh, I know they will." Sidney paid the man, and they loaded Peaches into the car.

When they got home, Peaches acted as if she had always lived there, and made herself right at home. Sidney said, "Don't get too comfortable. I want you to meet the little boys you'll be taking care of." Sidney took Peaches out to Su Yen's house. When Su Yen went to the door, she was shocked to see a large dog standing there. Sidney, noticing her reaction, said, "I should have asked you first if this would be okay. I bought Peaches to watch after the boys. She's been trained in search and rescue." Before Su Yen could say anything, the boys ran to the dog and wrapped their little arms around her neck. The dog walked right in and lay on a rug in the living room. The boys were lying next to her, hugging and kissing her. It was for sure; the boys wanted a dog. Su Yen said, "Okay, but dog not stay in house." Sidney said, "That's okay, she can stay in my house with me." But Peaches had plans of her own. When they went outside, she ran up to Joe's place. She stood there and whined at the door so he would let her in. There was no doubt, from that day on, who her favorite person was. Peaches loved everybody, but her heart belonged to Joe. Sidney asked Joe if he would mind letting Peaches spend her nights with him. His answer was "Could she?" That said it all. The boys were disappointed that their mom wouldn't let them keep Peaches in their house. Su Yen told them the dog was too big to stay in their house. Sidney felt bad that she had caused trouble.

Sidney asked Joe if he could put a fence around the fishpond, then she wouldn't worry so much that the boys might fall in again. He told her he'd be glad to. He told Sidney not to feel bad about the dog. Su Yen would learn to like her when she got used to her. Sidney said, "I know she won't be able to resist Peaches once she gets to know her. She's a lovely dog, and I think anyone with a heart would love her."

Sidney told Joe she was going back to work the following day. He happily responded, "I'll be ready to drive you, okay?" She said,

# RAINBOWS ARE BETTER

"I'd like that. I'll be ready to leave at seven thirty." Sidney went into the house and called the nursing home. She told them she was going back to work the next day. Then, she called Shade and talked to him for a few minutes. She looked at the time and realized it was time for Blake's breathing treatment. She went back to Su Yen's house and set up the equipment. She told Blake she was going to give him a breathing treatment just like they did at the hospital. She asked Su Yen if she wanted to watch, explaining if he needed an extra treatment while she was at work, Su Yen might be able to do it. Su Yen took notes so she wouldn't forget what to do. Sidney told her not to be nervous; it was really quite simple. Sidney said, "I'm going back to work in the morning, but I'll give Blake his morning and evening treatments. The doctor ordered two treatments a day, morning and night. I'll be here at seven in the morning and seven at night." Su Yen said, "What time you want breakfast?" Sidney said, "You've got the next few days off. You'll have your hands full taking care of Blake. Besides, Brian could use some of your time too."

Su Yen told Sidney she was sorry about her reaction to Peaches. She explained, "When I little girl, big dog attack me. I afraid ever since." She told Sidney, "I not mind little dog, just big one scare me." Sidney said, "When you get to know Peaches, you'll feel differently, she's a wonderful dog and well trained." Su Yen said, "I like her, but I not sleep if big dog in house." Sidney asked, "Would you feel better if I got the boys a small dog? They have a lot of small dogs at the dog pound. They all need good homes." Su Yen said, "That be better, not so big." Sidney said, "If Blake's up to it, this weekend, we'll all go pick one out. You can come along to make sure it's the right one." Sidney told them "Good night" and went to the main house. She was ready for bed herself. She needed a good night's rest so she could get up early and get things done.

When Sidney arrived at work, she found Sal and Mac together, as usual. She told them all about what had happened during the past four days. Sal was worried about the children falling in the pond again. Sidney assured him she had taken every precaution she could think of to make sure it wouldn't happen again. She told them about the dog and the fence around the fishpond and putting a new rail on the bridge. "I'm making sure they can't get their bodies through the rail." Sal had an idea; he wanted to have something done to the bridge so they could watch the fish without getting hurt. He wanted to put two Plexiglas panels on the floor of the bridge. That way, they could lie on the bridge and look at the fish as much as they wanted without getting hurt. Sidney thought that was a wonderful idea. She assured Sal she would call Joe and see if he could do that while he was putting in the new fence and rails. Sal said, "It's my idea, so I'll pay for it." They argued about that for a little while, but Sal won, as usual. Sidney couldn't upset him in his condition, and he knew it.

Sal and Sidney looked over the stock market. Sidney had another strong feeling about three of their stocks. She felt it was time to sell. Sal quizzed her about what they should do with the money from their sale. She suggested putting the money in some stocks they already had. Sal said, "I hear, and I obey. You have my blessings. After all, you've made us a fortune, so far." Sidney said, "Only because I had a very good teacher. Also, I feel my dad is giving me clues about what to do." Mac said, "Put me down for a hundred thousand, and we'll see how good you are." Sidney asked, "Are you sure? It's always a gamble." Mac said, "I've got enough money to gamble with the best of them." Sidney said, "Okay, but you asked for it." Mac went to his room to get a check. On her lunch hour she went to the investment firm to take care of business. Sidney went by the house, on her way over, to check on Blake. While Sidney was home, they delivered her new desktop computer. Then, she went to the investment firm and bought the stocks for Mac and did the transfers for her and Sal.

Since Sidney had a new computer at home, she took the laptop to Sal. She told him and Mac it would be easier to watch the market with the laptop there. Sal said, "I don't know how this little thing works." Sidney said, "It works just like the one you used at work, and I'll help you get started." Sal said, "What about you, kid?" She told him her new desktop arrived while she was home, checking on Blake. She showed Sal and Mac both how to operate the computer so if one forgot, the other one could help out. The next morning, Sidney checked the stock market, and they had made out like bandits again. When she arrived at the nursing home, Sal and Mac started singing

# RAINBOWS ARE BETTER

"We're in the Money." She had to laugh. Sal quipped, "You're a natural at this, kid." Mac told her he had never made so much money overnight in his life. The stocks Sidney put their money in had split and doubled. Sal said, "It seems like she always knows when a stock is about to do that." The rest of the week went great. Mac took some of his money and threw a party for everyone in honor of Sidney and his good luck. That was the kind of person Mac was. He and Sal gave a ten-thousand-dollar donation to cancer research. Sidney thought that was great. She wanted to know why they didn't count her in. Mac said, "Oh no, we don't have a long time to live, but you do."

"You're always giving your money away," added Sal. He told her he knew about the orphanage and what she did for the kids there. She asked, "How do you know so much?" He answered, "I have my sources, and that's all I'm going to tell you."

That weekend, Sidney, Shade, Joe, Su Yen, Blake, and Brian all went to pick out a smaller dog for the boys to play with, one their mom would let them keep in the house. The boys loved most of the dogs they saw, but Su Yen had other ideas. She told the boys they needed a dog who would stay small. She said, "If dog small now, not mean it small later." They all saw the same little dog at once. He was a little beagle puppy. The man showing the dogs to them said the puppy had all his shots and he had already been neutered. Sidney asked why they did that while he was so young. His answer was it was to keep them from developing bad habits and to ensure it gets done. Sidney asked him if that did any damage to them. The man laughed and said, "You could say that. It damaged him, all right, but he's okay, and he'll be okay. We have to do something, about animal control. There's already more animals than there are homes for them. That's why we make sure it gets done. People are really bad about dumping their animals if they have too many." The man told the boys the dog's name was Poncho but they could name him whatever they wanted to. Brian liked Poncho, and Blake could say "Poncho." Sidney asked, "Su Yen, what do you think?" Su Yen asked the man how big the dog would get. He took her to a cage where they had a full-grown beagle. He told her Poncho was a purebred beagle, so he wouldn't get any bigger than this dog. Su Yen was sold. She told her boys, "This dog all right." The boys started jumping up and down, saying, "Thank you, Sidney. Thank you." They could hardly wait for the man to open the door on Poncho's cage. When he did, they knelt down and started hugging their new dog. Poncho's little tail was about to fall off from all that wagging. He kept licking the boys' faces, first one and then the other. It was obviously a perfect match. Sidney felt so happy, she had tears come to her eyes.

Sidney knew, at that very moment, there was some happiness that a little money could buy. This little puppy cost no more than a donation to help the facility stay in business. Yet it was the most valuable thing she could have given these little boys. That puppy gave the boys love, and they gave it right back to him. Sidney told the man he was doing a great service, so she wrote him a check for five hundred dollars. She told him, if they ever had trouble buying dog food, to contact her and she would see what she could do. He gave them a sample bag of the dog food they had been feeding him. They also had a list of things to do to make him healthy and happy.

On the way home, they stopped to get more dog food, chew bones, toys, dishes, and beds for both of the dogs. You would have thought it was Christmas. The boys were so excited, they could hardly sit still going home. When they arrived home, the boys jumped out of the car, and so did Poncho. They were running and playing the way all children should be able to. If only every child could be this happy. Su Yen fixed lunch for everyone, and they had a picnic in the backyard. Peaches checked out the new puppy while they ate. She obviously decided he was all right, so they curled up and took a nap together. Joe said, "Isn't that the cutest thing? I think they really like each other." When lunch was over, Su Yen told the boys it was time for their naps too. After their naps, the boys and the dogs had a good time playing. Su Yen and Sidney were trying to keep Blake calmed down, but to no avail. Finally, Shade said, "Obviously, Blake was doing much better." Shade suggested running and playing like that was probably the best thing for him. The adults sat around and watched the children play. What a great day this had been.

# Chapter 16

## *Happy Days Are Here at Last*

Brian overheard Sidney talking on the phone, ordering things for the orphanage birthday party. He asked his mom, who was having a birthday. Su Yen said, "What you mean?" He told her he heard Sidney on the phone, ordering stuff for a birthday party. Su Yen didn't know about a birthday party, so she asked Sidney if they were having a birthday party. Sidney chuckled as she explained, "It's a party for the kids at the orphanage I once lived in." Su Yen inquired if she could help. Sidney answered, "That won't be necessary. I always hire a firm that just takes care of it." Su Yen quizzed if she had a birthday party for each one of the children there. Sidney told her, "Actually, I only have one big birthday party a year. I don't really know when their birthdays are." Su Yen further questioned why she picked the day she did to have the birthday party. Sidney replied, "I picked my birthday so I would always remember." Su Yen said, "That nice, Ms. Sidney. You need help, I help you."

Su Yen called Sal and asked him if he knew the date of Sidney's birthday. He answered he didn't know but he would find out and call her back. When the nurse came in, Sal asked her if she knew when Sidney's birthday was. The nurse had no idea. Sal asked her if she could check Sidney's records and see when her birthday was. She said she could, but they frowned on that. Sal told her, "Sidney is like my own daughter, but I've never asked her when her birthday is." She asked why he didn't ask Sidney herself. He told her they would like to have a small birthday party for her and they wanted it to be a surprise. She agreed to check the records and let him know. When she told him Sidney's birthday was on August 20$^{th}$, he picked up the phone and called Su Yen to tell her. Su Yen said, "We not have much time, but I plan party." Sal said, "Just make sure you plan this party at the nursing home so Mac and I can be present." Su Yen started making plans right away. She told Joe when Sidney's birthday was and what she was planning. He told her he knew Ms. Sidney's birthday was the twentieth. He added, "Sal must have forgotten." He told Su Yen he was building the waterfall by the fishpond for her birthday. He explained he and Sal had discussed it several months ago. Su Yen said, "He not well, that why he forget." Su Yen and Joe began to make plans for the birthday party. She told Joe not to tell anyone because it was going to be a surprise. Joe asked if he could tell Shade. Su Yen agreed they should tell him.

The next two weeks went by, and Sidney never noticed a thing. She was so busy, she wasn't paying attention. Sidney felt relieved knowing the birthday party for the children was all taken care of. She gave thanks to God that she was able to do this small thing for the children at the orphanage. She prayed that each one of them would find a good home and have a wonderful life.

The next day was the day of the party or, should I say, both of the parties. When Sidney was ready for work, Joe took her outside and showed her the gorgeous waterfall he had made for her.

She hugged him and thanked him so much. She told Joe he couldn't know how much this meant to her. She told him that was the first birthday present she'd had since her parents' death. Joe told her he was sorry to hear that. He said, "You're always doing nice things for everybody else. Now it's your turn to have something nice done for you." Sidney laughed and told him that people did nice things for her every day. She also told him she absolutely loved the waterfall and he had done a beautiful job on it.

Su Yen had prepared her a special breakfast before she left for work. They all wished her a happy birthday. She felt as though she was going to cry. When she arrived at work, it was business as usual, or so she thought. She went into Sal's room, where they had their morning meeting to discuss the stock market. Sidney did notice the lunchroom was closed all morning. They explained there was some work being done in there and it should be finished by noon. At noon, Su Yen, Brian, Blake, and Joe showed up with a present. Sidney said, "You guys have got to stop this. I don't need anything. I already have you." They told her they were also there to visit Sal. Then, Shade showed up. Sidney asked what he was doing there. He said, "Can't a guy visit his girl and ask her to lunch?" Shade took her out to the car. He said, "Why don't you ask Sal if he would like anything while we're out?"

When she reentered the building, the lunchroom door was open. Everyone yelled "Happy birthday!" There were balloons, flowers, candles, and a huge birthday cake. There was also a big sign on the back wall. It read, "We love you, Sidney. Happy birthday." This was too much; her eyes were filled with tears now streaming down her lovely face. She said, "This is the most wonderful thing I could ever imagine." Shade said, "Why don't we just eat here today?" Sidney responded, "You. You knew all the time, didn't you?" He answered, "I did my part well, don't you think?" Sidney said, "You all did. Thank you, all, from the bottom of my heart." Sal even hired a clown to go in after lunch. What a magnificent day it was.

That night, Shade took Sidney out to dinner. He wanted to celebrate with her in private. He took her to a very elegant restaurant. He knew she didn't drink liquor, so he ordered their best bottle of sparkling grape juice. Sidney had to giggle when she saw the waiter's face. Shade took her hand in his, and asked her if she would marry him. He reached in his pocket and pulled out a small box that opened to reveal a beautiful diamond ring. Sidney sat there in shock. He said, "So will you marry me?" Sidney answered, "Of course I'll marry you." There was a lot of hugging and kissing going on the rest of the evening. When Shade went home that evening, Sidney had a lot of trouble going to sleep. She lay in her bed, looking at her dazzling diamond ring. She kept thinking how very lucky she was. Maybe she was the luckiest person alive, because she certainly felt like it.

The next morning, when she went downstairs, she couldn't wait to show Su Yen the ring and tell her the good news. Then, she ran outside and found Joe to tell him. They both congratulated her and wished her well. She hurried to work that morning to tell Sal, Mac, and everyone else the great news. She felt all day as though her feet never hit the floor. She knew for sure her life just kept getting better, and better. That night, Sidney and Shade discussed their wedding plans. Shade wanted to get married right away, but Sidney had other ideas. She wanted to have the kind of wedding her mother and her father would have given her. She wanted a large church wedding, with candles, flowers, and beautiful music. She also wanted to wear a long white bridal gown. After all, she felt she had earned the privilege. She didn't think she had to earn it, but since she had, that was what she wanted. Shade said, "Could we get married first and then have a big wedding?" Sidney just laughed and told him they had waited this long, so they could wait a few more months. He told her she was right, because he knew he could wait forever if he had to. After all, they would have the rest of their lives together. They decided on a November wedding. Shade asked her, "What are our colors are going to be, red?" She told him she wanted to use pink, white, burgundy, and gray. He asked, "Why those colors?" She said, "Pink and burgundy were my mother's favorite colors, and gray was my dad's favorite." Shade told her it sounded good to him. He didn't really care what the colors were, as long as she showed up and said "I do." Sidney assured him she would be there and he could count on it. Shade said, "I'll leave all the details up to you, and if you need any help, all you have to do is ask." He suggested considering a Latin rhythm band for the reception. Sidney told him that was a wonderful idea. She wanted him to tell her about their Jamaican customs so she could work them into their wedding. Sidney asked Su Yen to be her maid of honor. Shade asked his brother Javier to be his best man. Brian and Blake were to be their ring bearers. Shade's niece Luann was asked to be the flower girl. Shade's sisters-in-law, Joan and Iris, were to be the candlelighters. Sidney was having the time of her life making all these plans. She spent hours going through bridal magazines, looking for the perfect dress. She found the best photographer, caterer, and florist and the perfect music to be played.

 The next few months went by in a blur. She was so busy, she could hardly think of anything else. Still, she never forgot to keep her

## RAINBOWS ARE BETTER

finger on the pulse of the stock market. Having the computers made it much simpler to take care of business. She noticed that Sal was a little under the weather. She asked what was wrong. Sal expressed how much he would like to walk her down the aisle. "As it is, I won't even be able to attend the wedding." Sidney replied, "Nonsense, of course you'll be there. I'll have an ambulance pick you up and deliver you there. Mac can ride over with you. I wouldn't think of getting married without you and Mac being there. After all, you're the only family I have."

"Thanks," said Sal. "I needed to hear that." Sidney said, "Sal, I love you. You're the only father figure I've known since my parents died. If necessary, we'll have the wedding right here in your room."

# Chapter 17

## *Things Are Changing*

Sidney knew she still didn't like the way he was looking. She was calling the doctor to come over, just to be on the safe side. Sal thought his medicine might need adjusting. When Sidney called the doctor, he sounded concerned and said, "I'll be right over." By the time the doctor arrived, Sal was feeling much worse. Sidney asked the doctor what was wrong. The doctor took her out in the hallway and told her it didn't look good. Sidney told him to do something. He said there was nothing he could do. He had told her and Sal, from the very beginning, that he was living on borrowed time. He was surprised that Sal had lasted this long. He told her to make him as comfortable as possible. She asked the doctor if it might be a good idea to take him home for what little time he had left. The doctor said, if he lasted through the night, she could make arrangements tomorrow. If that was what Sal wanted to do, it might be the best thing for him. She thanked the doctor for coming. Sidney called Su Yen and told her she would be spending the night at the nursing home. Su Yen asked why. Sidney told her it was because Sal was extremely ill. She asked Su Yen to tell Joe so he wouldn't come to pick her up. Then, she called Shade, and he told her he would come over to help stand watch through the night.

Sidney went back to Sal's room. She asked him why he didn't tell her he was having a hard time. He explained that he knew the time was near and he didn't want her to worry. She responded by telling him how much she loved him. She offered to get married right there in his room that night. He told her he wanted her to have the kind of wedding her mother and her father would want for her. She said, "We can have a formal wedding later, just like we planned." Sal replied, "Sidney, that won't be necessary. I'll be there in spirit. I don't want you to worry about me dying, I've already had a preview of heaven, and I'm not afraid of dying. As a matter of fact, I'm ready to go home. I'll miss our times together here on earth, but we'll be together again, when the time is right. I know that God will let me be present at your wedding. You may not be able to see me, but I'll definitely see you. I don't want you to cry for me. Just be happy for the times we've shared." Sidney remembered something her mother had once said to her. "You should never ask a person to suffer more than God would allow. When God knows you're suffering more than you can bear, he takes you home and ends the suffering." Sidney knew not to argue with Sal about trying harder to live. Even though she desperately wanted to, she wouldn't. Sal added, "I know my wife, Mona, will be waiting for me, and I'm anxious to see her again. I told you, when I died before, that I was sent back for a reason, and you were a part of that reason. Well, a few months ago, I figured out the other part of the reason, and I took care of it right then. It will be completed in a few days, and I'll trust you to take care of the rest." Sidney queried what he was talking about. Sal told her, in honor of his wife, he was having a new orphanage built for the children in the orphanage where Sidney had grown up. He went on to say, "I had a trust fund set up when Mona died. It was the money she had inherited, and I couldn't bring myself to spend any of her money. I think I knew all along that money was for something special. I told you she always wanted to adopt a child, and I wouldn't let her. Now, she will have a lot of children to watch over." Sal continued, "I hope this will, somehow, make up for the terrible mistake I made so many years ago." He wanted to surprise Sidney with the orphanage when it was completed, but he couldn't wait any longer. He said, "I don't think I've ever been happier in my life." Sidney promised she would not cry if he really felt it was his time to go. "Sweet Sidney," Sal whispered, "I don't just think it. I know it." Sal told her he knew Mac would take good care of her, and so would Shade. Sal looked at Sidney, smiled, and said, "That's my girl." Then closed his eyes to all worldly things.

Sidney knew he was gone. She just sat there and held his hand, then she stood up, leaned forward, kissed him on the forehead. She whispered softly, "Goodbye, my dear friend." She knew this was how he wanted her to handle his death, so she did. When she walked out into the hall, she saw the nurse and said, "He's gone." The nurse went in and checked him. When she went out, she called the coroner to pronounce him dead. She asked Sidney if she was all right. Sidney said, "Yes, because I know he's all right from now on." Sidney went back to Sal's room to wait for the coroner. She called the funeral home to pick him up as soon as the coroner was finished. Shade arrived and asked Sidney if she was all right. She told him she was going to be fine, because that was the way Sal wanted it. She said, "I need to tell Mac. I wouldn't want him to come in tomorrow morning and find that Sal is gone." Shade said, "Let me come with you."

They went to Mac's room and told him what had happened. He said, "I knew Sal was going to die tonight, he told me earlier. He left this letter for you, Sidney. I think it's instructions on what needs to be done." Sidney smiled and said, "That Sal. He's still taking care of me." It was a personal letter, a list of things that needed to be done, and the necessary papers signing everything over to her. These included the trust fund for the orphanage.

Sal had a lot more money than Sidney realized. The trust fund for the orphanage had twenty-five million dollars in it, and the building was already paid for. It wasn't until later Sidney added up Sal's accounts, insurance, and safety deposit box, stocks, and bank accounts. These all amounted to about fifty million dollars, not counting the coin collection, stamp collection, the house, and the trust funds (which he also left in her name) for Su Yen and Joe. Sal had made a request that he have a traditional Christian funeral, in memory of his wife (who was Protestant). Sidney felt Sal was leaving out a big part of his life. She combined a Jewish and Christian funeral, and it came together beautifully.

A few days after the funeral, Mac asked Sidney if she thought she had enough money now to take life easy. She told him that was

Sal's money and that she didn't know yet what she would do with it. She hadn't earned it, so she didn't feel like it was hers. In other words, no. She had things she wanted to accomplish in life. Mac told her he thought she should get married and have a few kids. That would be the most important thing she could ever do in life. He said, "Ask me, I wish my wife and I could've had children. It's too darn bad some people wait until they're too old, to realize how important having children really is. I think you and Sal were right, people should be more willing to adopt children. Not just for the child's sake, but for their own, as well. If someone loses a child, they should try to adopt rather than give up." Mac told Sidney, if she needed any help, he would do all he could. Sidney hugged him and said, "Thanks, but you being here for me is what helps me most."

Sidney buried herself in work again. Shade didn't understand what she was doing. He asked her if he had done something to upset her. She told him she was sorry but that, when she lost someone she loved, all she could do to find peace was to work until she was too tired to think about it. Shade wanted Sidney to let him help her through all her tough times. He told her she was not alone anymore. That he would do anything to make her feel happy again. Sidney said, "It's not that I'm unhappy. I just miss Sal, and this has always been my way of coping." She kissed Shade and told him she would try to slow down. She assured him she wasn't trying to worry or upset anyone. Shade told her he loved her and couldn't stand to see her so sad. He worried she would work herself to death. She started laughing and said, "I hardly think I'm going to work myself to death. I'm used to hard work." She put her arms around his neck and said, "Starting tomorrow, we'll spend more time on the wedding and less time on other things, okay?" He agreed that was a great idea.

Sidney managed to get the orphanage open. She had it furnished, and the children moved in within two weeks of Sal's death. A month to the day after Sal's death, she dedicated the orphanage to Sal and Mona. She named it the Goldstein Home for Children. She had always hated the word *orphanage*. The children were so happy, they ran over and took turns hugging and thanking her. They couldn't wait to tell her how much they loved their new rooms. The home had only two children to each room, except in the nursery, where all the babies were kept together. They even had closets with their own clothes in them.

Sidney hired a cook who not only could cook great food but also had great patience with the children. The children liked helping her in the kitchen. Sidney arranged to have fresh fruit delivered to the home every day. The lady Sidney put in charge of the home loved children. She assured Sidney these children would never suffer any cruelty, as long as she was there. Sidney remodeled the old orphanage and converted it into a recreation center. It looked so nice, everyone in the area loved it. It wasn't hard to get volunteers to run it. Sidney was pleased everything went just the way Sal would have wanted it. She felt sure things would be much better now.

Again, it was not meant to be. Just a few days after Sidney had completed the recreation center, Mac died in his sleep. This time, Sidney could not hold back the tears. She needed him, and now he was gone. He had followed Sal's lead and left her a letter and some instructions. He told her he was so sorry he had to leave all this work to her. It read, "You're the only family I have." He, too, had left her everything he had. Mac had much, much more money than she ever suspected he had. He was even richer than Sal. When all was tallied up, he had left her around fifty-seven million dollars. His letter said, "I hope now you have enough money to slow down a little." Sidney decided she couldn't take it anymore. She quit work that day, and she cried almost continuously for the next two weeks. She loved Sal and Mac so much. What would she do now?

Shade assured her that dying was just a part of living. She said, "I know, but everyone I love dies." Shade said, "In all fairness, they were sick or old or both. I know your parents weren't, but that was a tragic accident, and those things happen. You're lucky you've had so many people who have loved you so much." Sidney said, "Just promise me you'll never leave me." Shade said, "If there is any earthly way I can be with you for the rest of your life, I will. You can count on it." Sidney promised she wouldn't cry anymore. Shade said, "You can cry all you need to. You should do whatever you need to, as long as it gets you through this without making yourself sick." He told her he loved her but please don't shut him out. He asked her to promise always to talk to him. If she would tell him what was going on, he wouldn't worry so much. "Who knows," he said, "I might be able to help. Even if that help is only to hold you in my arms until things don't hurt so bad." Sidney thanked him for being the most wonderful person she had ever known. She promised, from now on, he would be included in all her problems. They both laughed, hugged, and kissed the rest of the evening.

It was almost two o'clock in the morning before Shade realized he needed to go home and get some rest. Sidney thanked God so much that night in her prayers for helping her find such a perfect love. As she snuggled down in her bed, she thought about Angel and what she had told her. "You can't get caught up in the whys of things that happen, just enjoy the moment. Let tomorrow take care of itself." Angel was always grateful for everything. She really believed that saying "When one door closes, another one opens." Then she would add, "Besides, if you don't like what's happening, what are you going to do? You can't jump off the earth. You have to go on and make the best of things." Sidney decided it was time to quit wallowing in self-pity. She had to get on with life and make the best of it. She went to sleep that night feeling as though Angel was right there in her room, hugging her. That alone made her feel everything was all right.

The next day, Sidney was feeling much better. She took care of her stocks, especially since she had a lot of money invested now. She began setting up a wedding schedule in the computer. This was all well and good for the first few days after she quit work. It didn't take long before she was bored. She had always worked and stayed busy. She didn't know how to deal with having leisure time on her hands. Sidney had always taken care of other people since her parents died. First, it was the other children at the orphanage, then Angel, and most recently, the nursing home. Now, it was just herself, and she didn't know how to do that.

When Shade saw she was still struggling with her problems, he thought she was still depressed about Sal and Mac. She told him not being busy was the real problem. Shade suggested maybe she needed to get her job back and go back to work. She explained she couldn't put herself through that again. She needed to do something different. Shade asked her, "What?" She told him she didn't know yet. They sat down and began to discuss the possibilities. Shade thought the best thing she could do while she was deciding what she wanted to do was sign up for some college courses. Sidney said, "Of course, you're right. I had hoped to put that off until after the wedding, but I need something to occupy my time now. I'll check with the local college tomorrow."

When Shade went home that night, he, too, said his prayers. He asked God to help him think of something to get Sidney through this crisis. As he was falling asleep, it occurred to him that Sidney had never had a pet of her own. Maybe a lovable little kitten would fit the bill. The next day, Shade went on his lunch hour and found the most adorable Siamese kitten. It was not only lovable, but playful, as well. He told the salesman he would pick up the cat around five o'clock that evening. Shade asked him to put a red bow around the neck of the cat before he picked him up. When Shade got back to the hospital, he called Sidney and asked if he could come over for dinner that evening. Sidney was delighted and asked if there was anything special he would like for dinner. He told her one of Su Yen's banana cream pies sounded good. Sidney said, "I think you can consider it done."

That night, when Shade arrived, he told Sidney to go into the library and wait for him. He told her he had a surprise for her. She did as he asked. Shade went to the car and got the kitten. When he got to the library, he said, "Close your eyes and hold out your hands 'cause I've got a big surprise for you. When she did, he put the kitten in her hands. She immediately opened her eyes and squealed in delight. Shade had never seen her so excited. She asked if it was for her. He answered, "Of course, it's for you." She hugged Shade and told him that was the nicest thing anyone had ever done for her. Shade said, "You have got to be kidding. People have given you houses and huge sums of money. I can't believe you think this is the nicest thing you have ever received." She told him she had always wanted a kitten. When her parents were alive, her mom was allergic to cats, so she couldn't have one. The rest of her life, it was impossible to have one because of her circumstances. She asked if it was a he or a she kitten. Shade said, "It's a male." He explained how he had wanted a female kitten but they weren't as lovable as he was. Sidney said, "I'll need to get him a litter box and some cat food." Shade said, "Just a minute." He ran out to the car and packed in a bunch of things for the little fella. He had cat food, litter, litter box, a scratching pole, with a nap apartment on top of it, balls, a catnip mouse, and some other toys. Sidney said, "Wow! You've thought of everything." He said, "I hope so," and he reached in his pocket to pull out a brush and a collar. Sidney said, "All he needs now is a name." When Shade dropped the catnip mouse, the cat jumped off Sidney's lap and was on that mouse in a flash. Sidney was stunned at how fast this little kitten was. She said, "I think he has a name. His name should be Flash." Shade said, "This cat belongs to you. You can name him anything you like." When she called the kitten Flash, he responded to it. It was as though he had always had that name. Shade laughed. "I think he likes that name." Shade and Sidney went into the dining room to eat dinner, and Flash was right at her heels. When she sat at the table, he jumped on her lap. He sat there, sniffing at the table. Sidney said, "I think he likes the smell of the chicken." She took her saucer, put a few small pieces on it, and placed it on the floor, beside her chair. Flash sat on her lap, as if waiting for the okay to sample that wonderful-smelling dish on the floor. Sidney put him on the floor, beside the saucer. She said, "Go ahead, Flash, that's for you." With those words, he began to delicately eat the chicken while they ate their supper.

    Sidney looked down at Flash, and he was washing up after he finished his chicken. Shade said, "I won't have to be jealous of the cat, will I?" Sidney said, "You will never have to be jealous of anything or anyone for the rest of your life. My heart belongs to you. This little present tonight just clinched the deal." They took their pie into the library. Flash was right at Sidney's heels. When they sat on the sofa, Flash jumped up on the sofa too. He curled up right against Sidney and fell asleep. By the time, they finished their pie, Flash had finished his nap. He was wide-awake now and ready to play. Shade picked up one of his toys and started playing with him. Sidney had never laughed so much in her life. Shade knew he really had done the right thing when he got her the cat. He closed his eyes for a moment and quietly said, "Thank you, God." They laughed and played with Flash until he could play no more. They introduced him to his new litter box, and he wasted no time initiating it. Sidney went to the kitchen and got him a bowl of water. He lapped that right up. Then, he went to his scratching pole and climbed up to the nap apartment and went to sleep. Shade laughed and said, "I think we wore him out." They were glad to spend some quiet time together before Shade went home.

Sidney picked up Flash and headed upstairs. She placed him on her bed. Flash enjoyed that bed just as much as Sidney did. When she got in bed, he was still purring with delight. She stroked his fur and told him they would be the best of friends from this day forth. Flash had already figured that out. The next morning, Flash ran in a flash to find his litter box. Sidney woke up laughing. Flash would prove to be a constant source of amusement.

When they went downstairs, Su Yen wanted to know who Sidney's furry little friend was. Sidney giggled and said, "His name is Flash." Su Yen picked him up, and his little motor started running. Sidney opened his food, filled his dish, and gave him fresh water. She saw Joe out back and asked him to come in and see what Shade had given her. Joe loved animals, so he really took to Flash in a flash. Sidney asked Joe if he would take her shopping after breakfast. She told him she wanted to get a litter box for every level in the house, then Flash wouldn't have any trouble finding a place to go potty. Joe answered, "Good idea, he's just a baby." Joe asked if Peaches could come in and meet the newest member of the family. Sidney said, "Of course, she can." Sidney hoped they would get along. When Flash had finished breakfast and so had Sidney, Joe took Peaches in and introduced them to each other. Peaches and Flash hit it off wonderfully. Peaches gave Flash a good bath, and Flash liked it. It must have felt like his mother cleaning him, only with a much-larger tongue. When Peaches was finished, Flash curled up in her fur and went to sleep. Sidney laughed and said, "I guess I've found a babysitter for Flash if I have to leave the house." Joe responded, "That Peaches,

# RAINBOWS ARE BETTER

she's a good dog." Sidney had to agree; Peaches looked after everyone and loved everybody.

Su Yen told the boys about Sidney's new kitten, and they went running to see it. Poncho was right with them. The boys woke Flash up so they could play with him. Poncho, on the other hand, didn't care for the kitten. He didn't take to Flash like Peaches did. As far as he could tell, that darn cat was stealing his boys. The boys giggled and said they didn't think Poncho liked Flash. Sidney said, "It's making him feel bad that you want to play with Flash instead of him." They both hugged Poncho and took him outside to play. They liked Poncho much better than the cat.

Sidney went shopping and purchased three litter boxes for Flash: one box to put in the basement, one for upstairs, and one for Joe's apartment. Joe wanted to be the one to take care of Flash while Sidney was away on her honeymoon. She also bought more cat food and a book about caring for her cat. When she got home, she showed Flash where all his litter boxes were. She was hoping he would remember. It wasn't long before he let her know he did. She went into the library and curled up in her favorite chair to read her new book about cats. When she got comfortable, Flash jumped up on her lap and rubbed her hand. He was letting her know he wanted some petting. His little motor started running as soon as she touched him. She sat there stroking his fur and reading the book. This felt so soothing to both her and Flash.

That night, when Shade came over, he had made dinner reservations at Sidney's favorite restaurant. Sidney asked him if they could stay home since Flash was so new. She didn't want to leave him alone yet. Shade answered, "Sure." He called the restaurant and canceled the reservations. Shade hugged Sidney and reassured her she was right. She asked, "Right about what?" He said, "Right about not leaving the kitten alone so soon." He added, "I can tell from this that you're going to make a wonderful mother for our children." Sidney cooed, "That sounds so nice, having our own children." Shade asked her, "How many would you like to have, a dozen or so?" Sidney squealed. "No way. I wouldn't mind two or three, but that's enough for me." Shade agreed, whatever she wanted was fine with him.

# Chapter 18

## *The Worst Was Yet to Come*

Sidney was working hard getting all the last-minute details tended to as the wedding was now only a few days away. She was so busy, she hadn't been thinking so much about Mac and Sal. All of a sudden, she felt a strange feeling she couldn't explain. It felt almost like a presence around her. She had a sinking feeling, as if something was wrong. Just as suddenly, she realized something was wrong with Shade. She thought, *No, not Shade, please, God, not Shade.* She called Joe and told him she needed to go to the hospital quickly. He asked if something was wrong. She answered, "I'm not sure, but I think so." When they arrived at the hospital, Sidney jumped out of the car and ran to the emergency room. She wasn't sure what was drawing her there, but she went with the feeling. When she got there, a man ran past her and then the security guards. Her panicked feeling became intensified. She asked the nurse where she could find Dr Domingo. The nurse seemed in shock as she pointed to the door across the hall. Sidney ran inside to find the other doctors lifting Shade (who was bleeding) onto a gurney. Sidney screamed, "No, not you, Shade!" The nurses tried to pull her out the door, but Shade reached for her, and they turned her loose. She went to him, with tears streaming down her face. Shade looked up at her with a look in his eyes she knew she would never forget. He said, "I don't think I'll be able to make it to the wedding, but I'll always love you." Then he whispered, "I'll return to you someday, somehow." His last words were "I love

# RAINBOWS ARE BETTER

you." With those few words, he passed from this life to the next, leaving all worldly cares behind.

Sidney fell to her knees and started crying hysterically. When the nurses tried to help her to her feet, she fainted. They took her to another room for treatment. When Sidney didn't go back to the car right away, Joe went in to look for her. The nurse took him to see her and explained what had happened. Joe saw Sidney lying there so pale and lifeless. He sat beside her, holding her hand until she regained consciousness. She looked at Joe and started crying again. She told Joe she would never love anyone again. She sobbed. "Every time I do, they die." Joe said, "Ms. Sidney, it wasn't your fault. Sometimes, bad things just happen." Then, he told her about the crazy man who went in the hospital and just started firing a gun. He sadly explained, "Shade just happened to be in the wrong place at the wrong time." Sidney looked at Joe, with tears streaming down her face, and said, "Why him? Why can't I have someone to love and someone to love me?" Joe answered, "You still have me, Su Yen, and the boys, and we love you." She said, "Don't love me, it's not safe."

Sidney was so distraught, the doctor decided to keep her in the hospital overnight. He thought they should keep an eye on her. He told Joe they were going to keep her sedated until the next morning. Joe told the doctor he knew Su Yen would want to see her. The doctor agreed to give Sidney a mild sedative until Su Yen had a chance to visit her. He still felt, under the circumstances, it would be better to keep her completely sedated for the night. Joe responded, "I understand, and I'll be right back with Su Yen."

Joe went straight home. He told Su Yen what had happened. Joe told her he would watch the boys in the waiting room while she visited with Sidney. Su Yen was puzzled about what she could say to help Sidney at a time like this. Before, Shade had helped her, and she knew how much Sidney had relied on him. Now, with him gone, Su Yen had to wonder how Sidney would get through this tragedy. It didn't seem fair that Sidney had been through so much in her young life. Su Yen knew she would have to say something that would help her, but what? She walked in Sidney's room, only to find her sobbing her heart out. Su Yen hugged her and said, "Ms. Sidney, you not cry, it make you sick." Sidney said, "What difference does that make? You and I both know this is all my fault. If I had married Shade when he wanted me to, this might never have happened. At least I would have known him in the biblical sense. If only I hadn't been so sure we had to wait until after the wedding, maybe I would at least be pregnant with his child. At least then, I would have something left to live for."

Su Yen got stern with her and said, "This not, you fault. You do right thing. I tell you it not easy, raise children without father. I not know why this happen. I know God still let something special happen for you. If not, you arrive few second earlier, you be shot, same as Shade. I hear you say many time, must play card dealt you. I believe this true." Sidney threw her arms around Su Yen and said, "It just hurts more than I ever knew it could. He was my strength and happiness." Su Yen said, "Yes, he good man, but you strong before Shade. You not make it this far if you not." Su Yen said, "Tomorrow, Shade family be here." She asked if Sidney wanted to ask them to stay at her house. Sidney said, "They were coming for the wedding." With those words, Sidney began to cry again. Su Yen apologized. Sidney said, "It's not your fault, I just can't quit crying. The answer to your question is yes. I would like for them to stay at the house. They may want to stay at Shade's place, though. Whatever they want to do is fine with me. Ask Joe if he would pick them up at the airport." Su Yen called the doctor in and told him she was going home now and she thought he should give Sidney that shot.

The next morning, Sidney asked the nurse if Shade's family had arrived yet. The nurse said, "I don't think so, but they are on their way. They're going to call your chauffeur when they arrive. They were delighted you offered to let them stay with you until everything was settled." Sidney said, 'I have to get home right away. The nurse told her, "Not so fast, the doctor will be in shortly. You'll have to discuss that with him."

The doctor walked in the door as the nurse was leaving, and asked what she wanted to discuss with him. Sidney said, "I need to go home right now." The doctor checked her pulse and heart rate then her lungs. He said, "Sidney, I know how difficult this has been for you. It's been hard on all of us. The only way I'm going to allow you to go home now is to have a nurse go with you. She will stay with you for the next few days or a week. We're going to do whatever it takes to get you through this. We all knew how much you and Shade loved each other. Because of that, we're going to take care of you for him. I know he would have wanted it that way." Sidney saw he wasn't going to budge from his decision, so she agreed.

Sidney got showered and dressed. Then, she called Su Yen to let her know she was on her way home. She told Su Yen the doctor was sending a nurse home with her. The doctor came back by and told her she could go home as soon as she was ready. He added he would have the nurse take her home in a few minutes. He said there would be three nurses a day. That way, she would have twenty-four-hour nursing care. Sidney said, "That's really not necessary." The doctor said, "Yes, it is, or no dismissal." Sidney said, "Okay, so can I go home now." He said, "Yes, you may, and I'll be coming by to check on you myself, so don't get any funny ideas." When Sidney arrived home, Joe had already left to pick up Shades family. Flash ran to Sidney and rubbed her legs, wanting her to pick him up. Sidney picked him up and said, "My dear little Flash, you're all I have left of my love." Su Yen told her he hadn't gone out of her bedroom since she left the house. She said, "I feed in bedroom, or he not eat." Sidney gently rubbed his ears as he purred loudly. It was almost as if this tiny kitten understood what was wrong with her. It was as if he were trying to let her know everything would be all right. Su Yen tried to convince Sidney she should go lie down until Shade's family arrived. Sidney insisted she would wait in the library.

Su Yen said, "Not worry, Ms. Sidney. I fix lunch, I made rooms ready. If stay here, I ready." She told Sidney she took the liberty of moving all the clothes, shoes, purses, and hats into the master closet. Sidney said, "Thank you, I've been meaning to do that. Then I started thinking about putting Shade's clothes in the master closet and forgot about it." Her eyes began to well up with tears again. Before Su Yen could say anything, the doorbell rang. Su Yen answered it. The private nurse the doctor sent over was bringing in her supplies. Su Yen said, "Ms. Sidney feel sad again." The nurse tried to get Sidney to rest for a little while. Sidney explained she couldn't do that until she had met Shade's family and had lunch. The nurse agreed but still insisted she take a mild sedative. Sidney didn't want to take anything. The nurse told her it was doctor's orders. It was either a pill or her giving Sidney a shot, and that would put her to sleep. She asked Sidney, "Which would you prefer?" Sidney answered, "The pill, I guess." The nurse said, "That's more like it."

When Shade's family arrived, Sidney introduced herself to them. Shade's mother hugged Sidney and whispered, "Thank you for loving my son so much." Sidney's eyes started tearing up as she replied, "It was my pleasure." Then Shade's dad hugged her and told her he was sorry for her pain. They knew how much their son loved her. After they all hugged one another and introduced themselves, Sidney had Joe show them to their rooms to freshen up. Sidney explained, "Su Yen has prepared a bedroom in the basement, for someone. That is, if you would like to stay here." They assured her they would love to stay if she was sure it wouldn't be an imposition. Sidney told them it would be no imposition at all. Shade's youngest brother, Sam, said, "I'll take the basement room." As Sidney showed him the way downstairs, she told him, "This was Shade's favorite room. He loved playing billiards." Sam said, "What a room, I love billiards too." Sidney told him he might want to freshen up; lunch would be served shortly. Sidney went upstairs to make sure everyone had what they needed. She told them lunch was almost ready. When they joined Sidney in the living room, she introduced them to Su Yen. After the introductions, Su Yen announced, "Lunch ready." They had a lovely lunch. Sidney felt so close to these people. It was as though they had always known one another.

Shade's dad asked, "Who's the little furry guy? The guy that keeps following you around." She told them his name was Flash and how Shade had given him to her just two days before he was shot. Again, Sidney started to cry. She kept saying "I'm so sorry." She knew they were trying to deal with their own loss. Still, all she could do was cry. The nurse got up from the kitchen table, where Su Yen, the boys, Joe, and the nurse were eating their lunch. She said, "Sidney, I think it's time to rest now." Sidney felt so embarrassed, but she knew the nurse was right. She realized she was only making things harder for everyone. After Sidney went upstairs, Su Yen explained about the doctor insisting on Sidney having a private nurse for a few days. Su Yen also told them about all the tragic things that had happened in Sidney's life. The family understood.

Su Yen showed them the pool, if they would like take a swim. She showed them the big screen television in the family room, if they would like to watch TV. She added, if they would like to take a nap after their long trip, she would wake them in a couple of hours. She said Joe would take them to the funeral home to see Shade. Luann (Shade's little niece) wanted to go outside and play with the boys. Everyone else wanted to rest for a while. Su Yen told them she would watch Luann while they rested.

When the funeral was over, Shade's parents prepared to return to Jamaica. They told Sidney they wanted to take Shade's body back to Jamaica and have voodoo rights performed for him. Then he would be buried in the family cemetery. However, Sam decided to stay on in Shade's condo. He wanted to go to college and study law. His parents were all right with that and gave him the keys. They told him they would take part of Shade's insurance money and pay for his first year's tuition. They told him, if he made good grades and didn't mess up by partying all the time, they would continue paying his tuition. When they were gone, the house seemed so empty.

Sidney tried over and over to convince herself she should be celebrating Shade's life. She knew she should be happy she had any time with him. The time was so short, though. The man who shot Shade didn't just shoot Shade. He also shot all of Sidney and Shade's hopes, dreams, and unborn children. She couldn't help herself as she began to cry again. The nurse asked Sidney if she would like to rest for a while. Sidney said, "No, I think, I'll just have to cry this one out." She told the nurse she had always believed in being positive about everything. Now, she was having the hardest time ever being positive about anything. Shade was the love of her life. She didn't care if she was young. She loved him so much. She couldn't imagine she could ever love anyone else that much. The nurse told her she might never love anyone that much again. That didn't mean she would never love again. Time changes all things and heals all wounds. She told Sidney,

"Go ahead and have a good cry." The nurse knew, if Sidney didn't snap out of it, pretty soon, she was giving her a shot and putting her to bed.

About an hour later, Su Yen took Sidney a sandwich in the library. She found her still sobbing away. Sidney said she couldn't eat. The nurse said, "Okay, let's go upstairs and take that shot now. I'm going to pull you through this, no matter what it takes." The nurse called the doctor after giving Sidney her shot and told him how Sidney was doing. He told the nurse he would come by on his way home. When he arrived, Nadine (the nurse on duty) told him she wanted to stay with Sidney around-the-clock until she was better. The doctor refused, telling her she had to sleep sometime, and he needed someone to keep an eye on her all the time. Nadine asked him to at least let her work the first two shifts and someone else could work the night shift. He agreed to that because he could tell how much this meant to Nadine. He told Nadine maybe she shouldn't get so personally involved with a patient. Nadine laughed and said it was already too late for that. She told the doctor, 'Sidney is such a sweet kid, and I've been there myself, so I understand what she's going through. I honestly think I can help her make the necessary adjustments to her life so she can get on with living." He told the nurse she could call him at home if she needed him for anything. Nadine asked him if he wasn't getting too involved himself. He told her, "Shade was a very good friend of mine, and I feel like I owe him no less. After all Shade did for me, this is the only way I have of paying him back. There's no doubt, in my mind, how much he loved this young lady."

When the doctor left, Nadine went back upstairs to Sidney's room. She was sleeping like a baby, and Flash was curled up right against her. He looked up and saw it was just Nadine and went back to sleep. Nadine thought it was amazing how much that cat loved Sidney, considering she had gotten him such a short time ago. Then she realized, "Look at me, I haven't known her as long as that cat has, and I feel like she's a member of my family. As a matter of fact, I like Sidney better than most of my family."

The next morning, Flash was licking Sidney's eyelids to wake her up. He was starving and didn't want to eat until she got up.

## RAINBOWS ARE BETTER

When she woke up she couldn't believe it was morning already. She had slept for twelve hours straight. Flash was so excited, he kept running around on the bed. She said, "Okay, I'm up now. As soon as I go to the bathroom, I'll go downstairs and feed you." He stayed right at her feet until they went downstairs. Sidney fed Flash and said, "You know, Flash, I'm hungry this morning myself." Su Yen overheard her and went to the kitchen. She told Sidney she had made some french-toast batter and would have it cooked in a jiffy. Sidney said, "Thanks, Su Yen, you never forget my favorites, do you?"

Sidney and Su Yen talked and joked for a while. Then, out of the blue, Sidney got that sad look on her face. Sidney said she didn't know how to live the rest of her life never looking into Shade's big brown eyes and kissing his soft lips, to never feel his strong, loving arms around her or be able to lay her head on his chest and feel so safe and secure. She longed for him to hold her close and make her feel happy again. Su Yen asked her if she would like to know how she got through losing her husband. Sidney said, "Yes, I would, if you feel like telling me." Su Yen told her she had a hard time at first, but she knew, being pregnant, she couldn't continue to grieve. She pretended James wasn't really gone. She told herself he was away on a trip or he was at the fire station. She made believe she could see him anytime she needed to. She said, "In heart, I know truth. I play game with mind, it help me through first months. After time pass, I accept James gone." Sidney thought this sounded like a great idea. She told Su Yen she would try it. After several days had passed, it wasn't working anymore. Sidney didn't know how to get a grip on herself. She prayed to God, day and night, to help her heal. Then, she started praying for God to help her get through just one day at a time. She finally decided to go back to her old way of getting over things. She would work herself to exhaustion.

# Chapter 19

## *There Has to Be a Way to Heal*

She started her new college courses and took a full load of classes. When she got home at night, she studied the stock market and took care of business. It wasn't as much fun playing the stock market, now, not like it had been when Sal was alive. Nonetheless, it kept her busy. She had already managed to double the money she had received from Sal, Mac, and Angel, which she kept separate from the money she had earned on her own. She had made two and a half million dollars of her own. One night, while she was looking over the stock market, she felt distressed about having so much money that wasn't really her own. She decided to test herself. If it paid off, she would accept the money as being meant for her. If she lost it all, it wouldn't matter, because it wasn't really hers, anyway. She took the entire amount and bought a stock she felt really good about. The next morning, she was one very rich lady. She decided it was a sign, so she took the money and divided it up in stocks she considered to be a safe bet

She decided to take some of her money and take a trip. She would go as soon as the semester was over at school. She thought she might pay Larkyn a visit to see how she was doing. After thinking it over, she decided she might as well visit Shade's parents in Jamaica on the way. She asked Su Yen and Joe if they would like to go with her. They talked about it for a few days. Joe told Sidney he felt he should stay behind and take care of the property and the animals. She told Joe she had already taken care of all that stuff.

# RAINBOWS ARE BETTER

Joe said he had been troubled about something for a long time. Sidney asked him what that was. He said he didn't know if he should talk to her about it. Sidney said, "Joe, you're my family, you can talk to me about anything." He said, "I don't want to hurt your feelings." Sidney assured him she would be fine. So he told her he wanted to ask Su Yen if she would marry him. Sidney said, "You don't need my permission to ask her." He told her he had wanted to ask Su Yen for a long time. The time was never right. Sidney said, "The time is right now. Don't make my mistake and wait too long. You ask her and let me know. If she says yes, we'll have a wedding before we leave. You can make the trip your honeymoon." Joe said, "If she says no, I don't want to go okay?" Sidney said, "I understand completely." Sidney asked, "Why not ask Su Yen out to dinner? I'll watch the boys while you're out." Joe went to Su Yen's house and asked her if she would go to dinner with him. She said she couldn't because of the boys. Joe countered, "Ms. Sidney has already agreed to watch them." Su Yen said, "So Ms. Sidney fix everything. I be honored."

That night, while they were eating their dinner, Joe told Su Yen how he felt about her. He told her he had loved her for more than two years. Su Yen confessed she, too, had been interested in him. Joe shuddered a bit as he asked, "Will you marry me?" She told him they couldn't do that now. He asked, "Why not?" She told him it might be too upsetting for Sidney. Joe explained he had already discussed it with Sidney, and she thought it was a great idea. He said, "Ms. Sidney even told me, if we got married before the trip, we could use the trip for our honeymoon." Su Yen said, "Yes, on condition Brian and Blake agree." Joe said, "Let's go pick out a ring." Su Yen said, "Wait, first talk to boys."

Joe was so excited, he couldn't wait to get home and ask the boys what they thought. As soon as dinner was over, they hurried home. When they walked in, Joe asked Sidney if they could talk to the boys alone. Sidney replied, "Sure, you can." Sidney sent them into the living room. Su Yen asked the boys what they would think if Joe married her. They wanted to know if that meant he would be their dad. Su Yen answered yes. They both ran to Joe and hugged him. For Joe and Su Yen, that was enough said.

The boys didn't remember their real dad. Joe was the only father figure they had ever known. They ran out into the hall, yelling, "Sidney, Joe is going to be our dad!" Sidney was so happy. This was just the situation she had hoped would happen for all of them. They all shared hugs and tears of joy. Sidney asked, "Where and when will you be married?" Su Yen looked at Joe. He said, "I'm ready tomorrow. We can go to City Hall." Su Yen agreed that would be fine. Sidney asked, "How about right here in the living room?" Su Yen questioned if she was sure she wanted to do that. Sidney said, "Absolutely. If you'll let me, I'll take care of everything. I can have everything done by tomorrow afternoon." She quizzed if they had a preference about who would perform the ceremony. Joe laughed and said, "We were going to use the justice of the peace, so anyone will do." Sidney wrote down everyone's sizes and Su Yen's favorite colors. Then Sidney said, "Wait, what about the marriage license?" Joe seemed shocked when he said "You need a license to get married?" Sidney said, "Yes, and I think there's a three-day waiting period." Su Yen said, "We get marriage license. We have more time for wedding." Joe said, "Yeah, we still need to buy a ring." Sidney said, "It sounds like we're all going to have a busy day tomorrow. All of us should try to get a good night's sleep."

When Sidney got up the next day, she heard Su Yen downstairs, fixing breakfast, as usual. She got ready and went downstairs to find Su Yen putting breakfast on the table. Sidney told her that wasn't necessary. Su Yen replied, "It my job." Sidney offered to take care of Brian and Blake while they were out. Su Yen told her how much she appreciated her offer, but they wanted the boys to feel a big part of all this. She asked if she could have a rain check if things started getting too hectic. Sidney told her she was there to help her as much as possible. While everyone was out, Sidney called a catering service, a photographer, a florist, and a minister. When she was finished calling, she sat down, read the newspapers, and took care of her stocks. She called Shade's brother Sam and asked if he would be Joe's best man at the wedding. Sam was very pleased she had thought of him. He thanked her for asking him. He told her he'd be honored to be a part of their wedding.

## RAINBOWS ARE BETTER

The next day, Sidney, Su Yen, Joe, Brian, Blake, and Sam all went shopping for new suits and dresses for the wedding. The guys all got charcoal-gray suits and white shirts. Su Yen was so tiny, they were having trouble finding a wedding dress small enough to fit her. Sidney told her, "Just pick out something you like close to your size." She added, "We'll just have it altered." Su Yen didn't think it could be done in only two days. Sidney said, "It can, if you hire the right person." Sidney's dress was burgundy taffeta. Su Yen loved the dress she picked for Sidney. Su Yen found a beautiful ivory lace dress she liked for herself. Sidney told the store manager she wanted Su Yen's dress fitted and ready for the wedding in two days. He argued they couldn't get it done that quickly. Sidney said, "There's an extra hundred dollars in it if you do." She added, "I don't care what you have to do, I just want it done and done right." He decided, for a hundred dollars, it could be done, after all.

Sidney asked Su Yen if she or Joe had friends or relatives they would like to invite. Su Yen responded, her family had all been killed and she didn't know anyone well enough to invite them. When Sidney asked Joe, it was pretty much the same answer except for the family part. He told Sidney his family had washed their hands of him after his accident. They wanted to put him in an institution. If it hadn't been for Sal, that was what would have happened. Joe knew they would never approve of him getting married. They all agreed it would be just the six of them and the minister to perform the ceremony. Sidney laughed as she included the photographer and the caterers. Su Yen quizzed, "You do all that for us?" Sidney answered, "I'd do much more for you if I could."

On the day of the wedding, the dress was delivered, and it fit like it had been made for Su Yen. I guess you could say it practically was. The house was filled with burgundy and yellow roses. The cake was as beautiful as it was delicious. Everything seemed to be perfect, so why was Sidney feeling like she was about to have a panic attack? She knew it was because of what happened before her own wedding. She wanted to get this wedding over so nothing could go wrong. She was feeling so strange, she took a tranquilizer to calm herself down. That was something she hated to do. Under any other circumstance, she wouldn't have done it. She wasn't about to spoil this wedding. Sidney was so happy to see she was wrong and everything went as smooth as silk. It was a glorious day and a perfect wedding.

After the wedding, Sidney told Su Yen and Joe she had reserved the bridal suite at an elegant hotel for them. Su Yen hugged her, and so did Joe. It made Sidney extremely happy to see them so happy and so in love. Sidney told them she would watch the children. She told them she and the boys would have their own celebration. Su Yen was going to clean the house before they left. Sidney exclaimed, "No way, that's why I hired all those people." She told them to go on and she didn't want to see them for two days. Two days later, Su Yen and Joe were back. They were wearing the biggest smiles Sidney had ever seen on either one of them. She said, "I take it the honeymoon went well." Su Yen said, "Oh yes, it fantastic."

The next few days, they were busy packing and getting passports and shots (which Brian and Blake hated). Sidney hired a private jet to fly them wherever they wanted to go. That way, she could take Flash with her. The boys wanted to take Poncho and Peaches with them too. Su Yen explained that Sam was going to be there to take care of the dogs. She continued explaining that people didn't like dogs barking in hotels and cats didn't bark. Sidney told them they could play with Flash and that, when they got home, the dogs would be waiting for them. Sidney felt bad about this because she knew she couldn't bear to leave Flash behind. Sidney told them to let her make some telephone calls and see what she could do. She rented a house, with maid service, in Jamaica and Australia. That way, the boys could take the dogs. Sidney knew they would have a much-better time that way. Now, everything was set. A limousine came to the house and picked them up to go to the airport. The plane was waiting when they arrived, and off they went on a marvelous vacation.

When they arrived in Jamaica, Shade's parents were at the airport, waiting for them. They took them to the house Sidney had rented, to drop off their luggage. Then, they took them all to their home, where they had a scrumptious meal waiting. Shade's family made them feel as though they were a part of their family. The next few days, Shade's parents took them sightseeing. They did some boating, snorkeling, and swimming and made a few sandcastles. The atmosphere there, was so calm, and relaxed. The people were very friendly and helpful. Sidney felt as though she was in paradise. All too soon, for Sidney, it was time to continue on to Australia. They said their goodbyes, and off they went.

When they arrived in Australia, Larkyn and her dad, were waiting at the airport. Joe, Su Yen, Brian, Blake, Poncho, and Peaches took the rental car. They followed Larkyn, her dad, Sidney, and Flash to the house Sidney had rented. The house in Jamaica was great, but this house was nothing short of fabulous. Everybody was tired from the long trip. Sidney asked Larkyn and her dad if it would be all right if they took a nap before going anywhere. Larkyn's dad replied they fully understood and that they would be back about six thirty that evening to take them to dinner. Sidney asked what they should wear. Larkyn said, "T-shirts and shorts will be fine."

When they got up from their naps, they took showers and got dressed. The little boys were complaining they were hungry. Su Yen told them they could eat when they went to dinner with Mr. Saunders and Larkyn. Sidney whispered to Su Yen, "The kitchen is full of fresh fruit." Su Yen agreed to let them have a piece of fruit to tide them over until dinner. They fed and watered the dogs and the cat. Sidney and the boys took them for a walk before they left for the evening. When they returned, the maid had arrived and apologized for arriving so late. She introduced herself as Josey James. She explained she had car trouble. Sidney assured her it was okay. Josey inquired what they would like for dinner. Sidney told her they had made arrangements to go out for dinner. Josey told them she would get their clothes unpacked and put away while they were out. Sidney assured her they wouldn't need her for anything until morning. She promised Sidney she would not be late again.

As Josey was leaving, Larkyn and her dad drove up. Right behind them, a limousine drove up and stopped. Sidney told Larkyn and Mr. Saunders she hoped they didn't mind that she ordered a limousine for the evening. She explained she thought that would give them all ample room.

Larkyn said, "Are you kidding? This is cool." Sidney asked Larkyn where they were going. Larkyn told her, "It's a surprise." Mr. Saunders instructed the driver where to take them. When they arrived, they were near the beach. There were a lot of people there. Larkyn said, "You wouldn't want to come to Australia without attending an Aussie barbecue." Mr. Saunders said, "You haven't lived until you've been to an Aussie barbecue. It's the best food you'll ever eat."

They proceeded to introduce them to the people who were having the barbecue. One of the guys yelled out, "Throw another shrimp on the barbie!" Sidney turned to Mr. Saunders and said, "I don't eat seafood." He laughed and said, "They have much more than shrimp. That's just an expression they use down under. Believe me, there will be more than enough food to choose from. Not only will there be a lot of food, but you're obligated to eat lots of it." Larkyn said, "Afterward, there will be a sing-along. That's my favorite part, next to the food." Larkyn took them around and showed them all the food being prepared. Then came the part where they ate until they were stuffed. There was singing and dancing until they were totally exhausted. What a wonderful time they all had. Sidney noticed the boys were getting very tired. She decided they needed to go home now. On the way back to the house, Sidney asked Larkyn and her dad if Larkyn could spend the night at her house. She told him they needed to catch up on all the latest happenings. Mr. Saunders agreed. Sidney thanked them both for a lovely evening. Mr. Saunders asked them if they would like to go out in a glass-bottom boat the next day. He told them they could see the Great Barrier Reef. They all agreed that was a great idea. Sidney said, "Let's make it in the afternoon." He told her he understood and would be there in time to take them to lunch. He told them they could go to his favorite restaurant.

Sidney and Larkyn sat up for several hours, talking about everything that had happened to Larkyn since she moved there. She told Sidney she loved it there. The people were so friendly and nice. Her dad had a supercool job. She told Sidney his boss was so nice, he gave him the whole week off so he could visit with his guests. Larkyn and Flash hit it off well together. Peaches loved her too. Poncho, on the other hand, went to bed with the boys. Sidney and Larkyn slept until ten o'clock the next morning. When they got up, they had a light breakfast of fruit and toast. By the time they all got ready, Larkyn's dad had arrived. He asked if they were ready for a fun-filled day. What a fun day they had. Sidney worried that they were wearing out Brian and Blake from doing so much. Su Yen told her they could handle it, and if not, they would take them back to the house and give them a nap. She said they had been napping in the car, between stops.

The boys couldn't wait to go to the zoo. They wanted to see the kangaroos and the koala bears. Mr. Saunders made sure they did, along with so many other animals they hadn't even heard of. This was their favorite place, so far. Su Yen decided they needed to take the boys back to the house after the zoo and let them rest awhile. She noticed they were getting fussy with each other. Mr. Saunders remarked they would pick them up later to go to dinner. Su Yen said, "Maybe next night, boys need quiet time this night." Sidney replied, "I'll see you later then." That left just the three of them. Larkyn and her dad took Sidney to their house to freshen up before dinner. Sidney told them what a lovely home they had. Larkyn took her out on the patio and showed her their pool and the garden. Their house sat on a hill, which gave them a great view of the ocean and the city below. Larkyn gave Sidney a sarong to wear to dinner. After dinner, they went to a musical play at the amphitheater.

What a marvelous day it had been, but now, the ever-energetic Sidney was feeling tired. Larkyn said to her dad, "I think we've managed to wear everybody out." Sidney laughed and said, "You certainly did." They took Sidney home. On the way, they asked her what she would like to do the next day. Sidney told them she would leave that up to them. After all, they were familiar with the area, and she wasn't. Sidney said, "Just let us know what we should wear."

When Sidney arrived home, Su Yen and Joe were relaxing and watching television. They asked what she had done, and she filled them in on everything. Su Yen said, "I think, rest of time here, we spend late afternoon and evening at house. Boys getting too tired. We need quiet time." She questioned if that would be all right with Sidney. Sidney told her this was her vacation too. Anything she wanted to do was just fine with her. Sidney asked if they would like for her to take the boys for a day to give the two of them some time alone. Su Yen and Joe told her they wanted to spend the time with the boys. Sidney told them, if there was something they would rather be doing, they can just take the car and do it. They weren't obligated to do what Mr. Saunders and Larkyn wanted to do. She knew Brian and Blake would like to do things that maybe Larkyn wouldn't and vice versa. She told them she never wanted them to feel obligated to do whatever she was doing. She didn't take them along to babysit her. She took them to enjoy themselves and have a good time.

Joe said, "Ms. Sidney, Su Yen made a chocolate cake for you." Sidney said, "That sounds wonderful, let's all have a piece." Joe told her the boys had already had a piece before they went to bed. Sidney told Su Yen the cake was wonderful but she didn't have to do any of the cooking while she was on vacation. Su Yen giggled and said, "I like cook. It relax me." The next day, Su Yen and Joe took the boys to the zoo again. Sidney, on the other hand, spent the entire day with Larkyn and her dad. That night, when Sidney got back, they exchanged stories about the events of the day. It was evident that everyone had a good time. The last day in Australia, they all went together for a day of boating. They had a clam bake that night on the beach. Even Sidney tried the baked clams. She decided she would rather eat the hot dogs. Still, their last night there couldn't have been better. When Larkyn realized this was the last time she would see Sidney for a long time. She clung to Sidney, telling her how much she would miss her. Sidney felt bad for her and tried to console her. Sidney explained they could keep in touch by computer. Larkyn said, "I don't have a computer." Sidney said, "You will have in a few days. I'll set everything up, then we can chat or email anytime we want to." Sidney told her she would call her when she got home and let her know when to expect her new computer. Sidney hugged and thanked Mr. Saunders and Larkyn for all they had done for them. She let them know they had made their stay extra special. She told Larkyn she would come visit again and that maybe they could come to visit her sometime. Mr. Saunders promised they would when he could get more time off, but it would be a while.

# Chapter 20

## *There Has to Be Some Other Way*

The next day, they flew home. When they arrived home, everyone but Sidney seemed relieved. Walking back in that house where Sal had lived and Shade had spent so much time with her made her feel sad again. She had always been able to overcome things like this before. This time, however, was worse than she could have imagined. The next morning, Su Yen was singing in the kitchen, and the children were giggling and playing with the dogs. Joe was working on the grounds and laughing at the boys playing with the dogs. It seemed everyone else was very happy to be home. She decided she would have to get over it for their sakes. She would never want to make them worry.

After breakfast, Sidney checked her stocks and couldn't believe her eyes. She now had more than three hundred million dollars. She thought to herself, *That's a lot of money, and I still don't know what I want to do with my life.* She thought having this much money would make her happier than she had ever been. While the money didn't make her unhappy, it didn't make her happy, either. She still had a broken heart, and no amount of money could fix that. It was at that moment she understood it was not what you had or having what you wanted that made you happy; it was how much you enjoyed what you had that truly brought you happiness.

Sidney sat in her favorite chair, reading the business section of the newspaper, when she saw there were several stocks that need to be sold and others she knew would surge. She decided, for some reason, to take care of it in person. She got dressed and called a cab to take her to the investment firm. When she arrived, the stock broker who was handling her account wasn't there. She asked if he was on vacation. One of the secretaries explained he had been fired. Sidney asked her if she knew why. She responded it was very hush-hush, the whole thing. Sidney inquired if she knew how she could contact him. The secretary explained she couldn't give out that information. She told Sidney she could speak to his supervisor if she wanted to. Sidney said, "That'll be fine."

When Sidney went into the supervisor's office, her intuition told her this man was a cold fish. She was right, as usual. The supervisor seemed confrontational when she asked if he knew how she could contact Mr. Worthington. He questioned what she could possibly want with anyone at their firm. Then he said, "If you're looking for a maid's position with Mr. Worthington, I don't think he'll need anyone for a while." She assured him she was not looking for a job. She informed him she did need to contact him right away. He said, "We don't give privileged information to hookers or whatever you are." With that remark, Sidney was so angry, she could no longer speak to this jerk. She turned around and walked out of his office. She marched right into the office of the owner of the firm. She explained what had just taken place and told him she would be closing her accounts with their firm effective immediately.

The owner took her back to the supervisor's office and asked him why he had made such off-color remarks to Ms. Davis. He responded he never made any off-color remarks to her. He said, "Ms. Davis came in here demanding that I give her privileged information." He added, "When I refused to give her that information, she stormed out of my office, and now she's telling a bunch of lies." Sidney said, "That does it. This man is not only a liar but a bigot, as well." She walked out of the office, saying, "Prepare to close my accounts now." The owner of the firm told the supervisor he was fired for his behavior and losing such a large account. The supervisor said, "Are you going to take the word of that Black bitch over mine?" The owner of the firm informed him that Ms. Davis was not only a wealthy client but also once had been a valued employee. He would definitely take her word over his. The owner told him to get out of the building immediately and there would be no severance pay.

# Chapter 21

## *Hiring a Helper*

As Sidney was leaving the building, she saw Brandon in the lobby. She stopped him and asked how he was doing. He answered, "Not too bad for someone who just lost his job and future." Sidney replied, "You may have lost your job, but not your future." He said, "When you get fired from a firm like this one, you can't get a job with another firm. They think you must have done something really bad to have been fired." Sidney inquired, "So did you?" He said, "No, but my stupid supervisor made it look as though I did. He made some big mistakes and lost a lot of money for a couple of our clients. Then, he set me up to take the fall. They wouldn't believe me over him, so they fired me." Sidney declared, "Well, I believe you over him. It may please you to know I just got him fired." Brandon uttered, "I could kiss you." Sidney said, "Why don't you save that part. A simple thank-you will be sufficient." Sidney started to walk out, then she turned around and asked Brandon how he would like to work for her. He questioned, "Are you kidding?" She answered, "Do I look like I'm kidding?" She explained to him she had just instructed the firm to close her accounts with them. She asked, "Why don't you come over to my house this afternoon. We'll have lunch and discuss all the details." He agreed to be there and asked if she wanted him to bring anything. Sidney laughed and said, "I don't think that will be necessary." He told her he would collect his last check and pick up the rest of his belongings while he was still there. Sidney said, "Be at this address"—she handed him her business card—"at about one o'clock, and bring your résumé. You do have a résumé, don't you?" Brandon said, "Yes, I do. Don't worry, I'll bring it and be on time."

When Sidney returned home, she told Su Yen she was having a young man over for lunch. Su Yen was so happy to hear this, she couldn't help but smile. Sidney said, "It's not that kind of lunch. It's strictly business. Besides, this young man is White." Su Yen said, "So he human, right?" Sidney said, "Yes, he's human, but I'm only thinking about hiring him to be my secretary, not my boyfriend." When Brandon arrived, he walked through the door, with his résumé in hand. Sidney said, "Lunch is ready, if you're ready to eat." He told her he was famished. She introduced him to Su Yen and told him she was the best cook around. Su Yen giggled and said, "Ms. Sidney, you embarrass me." Sidney added, "Well, it's true, as you'll see for yourself, Brandon."

As they ate lunch, Sidney explained to Brandon what the job would entail. She told him he would basically be her secretary and asked if that job title would bother him. He told her he needed the job and he didn't care what title she put on it. She asked him if he could handle everything on the sheet of paper she handed him. He looked at it and replied, "No problem." He asked her how much money the job paid. She questioned how much he made at the investment firm. When he told her, she responded she would pay him half again as much as they did, plus medical benefits. She instructed him he would have to save for his own retirement. He laughed and said, "With that much money, I can do that." He asked where they would be working. She answered, for now, they would work out of her home.

After lunch, she took him to the library and showed him the computers she had. He told her they would need to update her computers. She said, "Are you available to start work now?" He said, "I see no reason to wait." She told him she would have Joe drive them wherever they needed to go to get the equipment they needed. Brandon said, "You don't mess around, do you?" Sidney said, "I feel better when things get done as quickly as possible." Then, Sidney said, "By the way, I hope you like dogs and cats." He said, "They're all right, but I'm not exactly wild about them." She quipped, "That's too bad, because they'll probably be all over you. You might want to dress casual unless I ask you to do otherwise. Most of the time, sweats or jeans will be fine." Brandon explained he didn't have clothes like that. Sidney asked him what he wore to be comfortable. His answer was golf slacks and polo shirts. She asked him if he liked to swim or play billiards. He said, "Yes, but is that necessary to this job?" She answered, "No, silly, but you might want to leave a pair of swim trunks in the closet by the pool. You might like to take a swim and relax if things start getting intense."

Joe drove them to the computer store to get the necessary equipment. Brandon selected a computer and software necessary to connect to the stock market. Sidney informed the salesman she would take two of everything. She asked if they could deliver it right now. After checking, he said, "We have a technician that could go to your house in thirty minutes." She said, "Good, here's my address." She dropped Brandon off at the house to wait for the computers. Joe took her to an office furniture store. There, she bought a desk, an office chair, and filing cabinets. She instructed them it all had to be delivered within the hour. At first, they grumbled, but a little extra cash stopped the grumbling in a hurry. When they returned home, she asked Joe and the furniture movers to move the black leather sofa to the basement in the billiards room. Brandon asked if she wanted the chairs to go, as well. She said, "No way. That's where I do most of my relaxing." She did have them move the chairs around. That gave them more space.

When all was done, Sidney asked Brandon if he could make some changes for her. He told Sidney it was late and the stock market would close soon. He said, "I need one more day to do the necessary paperwork." Then he would be able do all her business from the house. He asked what was so urgent. She told him she had a gut feeling about some stocks and tomorrow would be too late. He told her he could tap into the investment firm's computers and do the transfer. He told her it would only work if they hadn't already closed her accounts. She asked him to give it a try. When he managed to get connected, he found they hadn't even started closing her accounts. He made the necessary changes in a matter of minutes. Sidney said, "Thanks, that was really important to me." He said, "I've been your representative for the last two years, and I know, when you need things done, it needs to be done in a hurry." Sidney told him, now that it was taken care of, he was free to go home. Brandon told her he would rather stay and get as much set up as he could. He said, "That way, it won't be long before we're up and running." Sidney said, "You are a good worker, aren't you?" She added, "The fact is I'm tired and ready to call it a day. Besides, I want you here in the morning by eight o'clock ready to work. I'd rather you kept your mind fresh. Too much work will make Brandon a dull boy." When Brandon left, Sidney said to Su Yen, "This is going to work out well, don't you think?"

The next morning, Brandon was there by seven thirty and ready to start work. Sidney asked him if he had eaten breakfast before coming to work. He said, "No, I rarely eat breakfast." Sidney said, "Su Yen, did you hear that? He doesn't eat breakfast." Su Yen began explaining to him how important it was to eat a good breakfast. She poured him a cup of coffee and instructed him his breakfast would be ready in a jiffy. Sidney laughed and said, "When she's right, she's right. By the way, that's another perk that goes along with the job. You'll feel sharper when you've had a good breakfast. Being sharp is very important, as you already know."

When Brandon finished eating breakfast and properly thanked Su Yen for such a great meal, he hurried into the library. There, he found Sidney already busy at work. He questioned what she was up to. She advised him she had already set up the computers and she was putting in some finishing touches. He said, "I wasn't aware you knew your way around computers. Why didn't you tell me that yesterday?" She laughed and said, "If I had, I couldn't have found out how much you knew." He laughed and said, "So, boss, did I pass?" She answered, "Yes, you did." He asked, "So are we ready to transfer the money from the investment firm this morning?" She told him not only that but also that she made a cool five hundred thousand dollars overnight by making the change that was so important the afternoon before. He couldn't believe his eyes when he saw the stock-market report. He said, "I know it's none of my business, but I have to ask, how do you do that?" Sidney said, "I don't really know, and I'd prefer not to discuss it just yet, if you don't mind. Maybe someday I'll feel comfortable enough to tell you." She could only hope he would understand. Brandon told her he didn't mean to pry. He added, he shouldn't have asked, anyway. Sidney said, "You can ask me anything you want to, and if I can give you an answer, I will."

When the day was over, everything was set up and ready to go. Now, they were in business. Sidney thought, *We're in business, all right, but what kind of business?* She asked Brandon what kind of business he thought it was. He laughed and said, "The business of making money." She said, "I'm serious here." She wanted to have some business cards made, and she didn't know what to put on them. He said to put on them "Sidney Davis, human dynamo and entrepreneur extraordinaire." She told him she was serious and that hardly sounded like a business. Brandon told her she was in the business of making money for herself, so it wasn't really a business. A business is usually a service you perform for someone else. Brandon added, "If I were you, I'd have some personal cards made up, with my name, address, and phone number on them. You could add *entrepreneur* below your name, if you like."

Brandon told her he could design the cards for her if she wanted him to. Sidney queried, "Would you do that for me?" He assured her he would do almost anything for her. After all, she gave him a job and turned his life around. He told her his family had always considered him a failure. If he had gone back to Iowa after losing his job, they would never have let him live it down. He said, "Now I have a job that pays more money than I've ever made. They can't laugh at me anymore." Sidney told him she was sorry his family felt that way. She assured him she considered him a very bright young man who obliviously had his head on straight. She didn't know how anyone could want more from another person. Brandon said, "Thanks, Sidney. You'll never know how much that means to me." "Okay, Brandon, let's not get all mushy here. Why don't you go home, get some rest, and be here in the morning in time for breakfast?" She told him she would wait and have breakfast with him. He thanked Sidney and told her he was looking forward to it. He promised her he would come up with some good ideas for those cards.

Sidney was fine during the day while they were working. At night, it was a different story. She missed Shade with a passion. This evening was no exception. She went for a swim, thinking it would tire her enough that she could sleep. Yet when she went to bed that night, sleep didn't come easy. She got up and turned on the lights in the backyard. She sat there, enjoying the beautiful masterpiece Joe had crafted. She looked at the sky and asked God what she could do that would help her get over this. She told God, if she only had some family left, it wouldn't be so hard to take. She knew, as she was saying this, it was ridiculous. She had no living family. She sat there thinking maybe she needed to help out at the children's home. After all, those kids were as close to family as she had. Maybe what she had been doing for them wasn't enough. She knew those kids needed love as much or more than a nice place to live. Then, she said, "Thanks, God, that's just what I'll do starting tomorrow." When she went back to bed, she had no more trouble falling asleep.

When Brandon arrived the next morning, she told him about the children's home. She thought it was a good idea if they started going there once in a while. She said, "I know this isn't in your job description. If you don't want to go, I'll understand." Brandon replied, "I don't mind. I like kids." Sidney added, "Since a friend of mine built this home, I'm in charge of the trust fund. I also contribute to it on a regular basis. You'll be dealing with all the paperwork. I thought it might be helpful if you know what you're dealing with." He asked, "How many surprises do you have up your sleeve? Should I ask or just wait and find out gradually?" Sidney giggled and responded, "I think it'll be better if you find out gradually. I don't want to overload your circuits. You might blow a fuse or something like that." Brandon said, "In that case, I'll try wading into the waters instead of jumping in."

When they went to the children's home that afternoon, Sidney had a strange feeling that she didn't understand come over her. She knew she looked a little pale, because Brandon asked her if she was okay. She told him she was fine. Evidently, a lot of old memories came rushing back and had a profound effect on her. They went inside, and once inside, Sidney was better than fine. She was so happy to see the children laughing and playing. They were all clean and dressed in nice, clean clothes. The home was comfortable and so much nicer than anything she had known as an orphan. She whispered a quiet thank-you to Sal and Mona for giving these children such a lovely environment to live in.

The supervisor of the home, Ms. Williams, came in. She said, "Ms. Davis, how nice to see you." Sidney introduced Brandon as her new employee. He said, "You could call me her secretary, that's what she told Su Yen I am." They all had a good laugh as they were seated. Ms. Williams asked Sidney what they could do for her. Sidney said, "It's more like what can I do for the children?" Ms. Williams, feeling a little surprised, responded, "You already do so much." Sidney said, "I mean things like help them with their homework, diaper the babies, or read to them. You know, that kind of thing." Ms. Williams answered, "The children love having someone read to them or play games with them." Brandon told Sidney she could help with the babies, and he would play games with the bigger ones. So that was what they did for the next four hours. Sidney loved feeding, changing, rocking, and singing to the babies. She could tell they loved it too. Brandon read story after story to the bigger children, and they played games. He kept them giggling all afternoon. When it was time for them to go home, the children wanted them to stay.

Sidney looked at Brandon and asked him if he had dinner plans. He answered, "It just so happens I'm free this evening." Sidney agreed to stay for dinner. Sidney knew being invited to dinner unexpectedly would allow her to see how the children were being fed. Sidney wanted to make sure the children were being fed properly and that the food tasted good. She was thrilled when the food not only tasted good but was also a balanced meal, complete with dessert. After dinner, they stayed long enough to tuck each and every child into bed. Sidney hadn't felt this good since she last felt Shade's arms around her. She was exhausted in a very satisfactory way. When they left, Ms. Williams told her how much they all appreciated what they had done for the children. She said, "You know, it really means a lot to them to know people care what happens to them." Sidney said, "I do know what that means." Ms. Williams asked her if she knew someone who had been an orphan. Sidney replied, "You could say that."

On their way home, Brandon thanked Sidney for taking him with her to the orphanage. He elaborated he couldn't remember ever having so much fun. She responded, "It was a lot of fun, wasn't it?" She went on to say "I'm the one who should be thanking you." He told her she could count on him whenever she wanted to go back. She said, "Good, because I think I'd like to do this at least once a week." She was even thinking about taking Peaches with them the next time. She was sure the children would like spending time with such a special dog. She knew Peaches loved children and everyone, for that matter. She thought that it would make the children happy. She asked Brandon what he thought. He thought it was a great idea. Sidney told Brandon she hoped his feelings weren't hurt when she introduced him as her employee. He told her she could call him her doorman and he wouldn't care. Sidney said, "Nevertheless, tomorrow we need to discuss what your job title should be."

When Sidney said her prayers that night, she gave many thanks to God for making her understand she should be more giving of her time and energy. She told God she didn't know when it happened, but she knew, now, she had been too caught up in worrying about her own happiness. She had forgotten you couldn't be truly happy unless you were making an effort to make others happy. There was nothing better than being needed by someone and being there for them during that time of need. Sidney looked down at Flash, who was purring on her lap, and said, "You knew that all the time, didn't you?" When Sidney went to bed that night, her bed seemed to give her an extra big hug. At least it felt that way to her. She even fell asleep smiling, something she hadn't done in a long time.

The next day, she told Su Yen what a wonderful experience it had been to go to the orphanage and work with the kids there. Su Yen told her it was nice to see her so happy for a change. Su Yen asked Sidney if she, Joe, and the boys could go with her sometime. Sidney said, "I think that's a splendid idea." Sidney explained her idea about taking Peaches the next time she went. "We could all go and take all three of the animals with us. It's really a lot of fun." Su Yen said, "I hold baby?" Sidney said, "Yes, you can. I love holding the babies too" Su Yen said, "That good, for I pregnant." Sidney said, "Already?" Su Yen said, "Sometime, it happen quick." Sidney questioned if she was sure about being pregnant. Su Yen answered, "For sure." Sidney hugged her and congratulated her. She asked Su Yen when the baby was due. She said, "Not for seven month." Sidney said, "I'll bet Joe is wild with happiness." Su Yen said, "He so happy, he smile all time." Sidney asked if they had told the boys yet. Su Yen said, "No, we tell tonight." She was hoping they would be happy about it. Sidney said, "They love babies. I've seen them around little ones before." Su Yen said, "It be different if it never go home." Sidney assured her she wouldn't worry about it; they were the sweetest little boys she had ever known. Sidney said, "When the time comes, I'll take you shopping for new maternity clothes, okay?" Su Yen said, "That be very nice." Sidney said, "I'm so excited, I don't know what to do with myself. I've never been around anyone having a baby. By the way, should you still be working?" Su Yen laughed and said, "Not worry, Ms. Sidney." She told Sidney she was doing fine and should be able to work up to a couple of weeks before the baby was due. The doctor told her she was healthy as a horse. She assured Sidney she was feeling great. She hadn't even experienced morning sickness this time. Sidney explained, "When things start getting to be too much, you have to promise to let me know." Sidney didn't want her to overdo it. Su Yen told her not to worry; she had no intention of doing anything that would harm the baby.

That night, Joe and Su Yen told Brian and Blake about the new baby coming. They were both so happy, they started dancing and singing. Adding to the excitement, Sidney told them they were all going to visit the children's home. She asked how they felt about that. Brian asked her if there were kids there to play with. Sidney told them there were lots of kids there and they even had babies there to play with. Blake said, "Mama, is that where we're going to get our new baby?" Su Yen hugged him and explained she was going to have their new baby just like she had him and Brian.

# Chapter 22

# *Life Is Getting Rosie*

The next few months went by very quickly, and it was almost time for Su Yen to give birth. The doctor told her, from then until after the baby was born, she would have to quit work and take it a little easier. Su Yen went home and told Sidney she wouldn't be able to work until after the baby was born. Sidney reassured her and told her not to worry; she would call the temp agency and have them send someone out. Sidney had grown accustomed to having a maid. The temp could take care of things until Su Yen was ready to resume her job. Sidney interviewed several people before she found someone. She felt this woman would do a good job and be good to Su Yen and the boys. Her name was Rosa.

Sidney liked Rosa from the moment she met her. She was a sweet, slightly plump Latina lady in her late forties. She had the most contagious laugh, and she laughed a lot. Brandon asked Sidney if Rosa ever quit smiling. Sidney said, "I hope not. I haven't seen her without a smile, so far." Sidney asked Rosa if she would like to move into the apartment above the garage. Rosa almost cried when she told Sidney that would be so kind of her. She told Sidney, for the time being, she was living with her daughter, her son-in-law, and her five grandchildren. She said that would certainly give them more room. Sidney said, "All right, it's settled then. We'll get you moved in this weekend." Su Yen didn't say anything, but she was afraid Sidney wouldn't be needing her anymore. Joe told Sidney how Su Yen felt. Sidney just laughed and said, "That's not it at all. I want Rosa here to help her out now and later after the baby is born." Joe said, "I told her you wouldn't fire her. You're too nice for that." He continued, saying, "Don't worry, I'll tell her it's okay and Rosa is going to help all of us." Sidney said, "That's right, and Rosa has already agreed to help with the children." Sidney added, "This weekend, she'll need us to help her move into your old apartment." Joe said, "You can count on me." Sidney thanked him. She told him he was a good person and she knew she could always count on him. When Sidney told Brandon about Rosa moving in, he said, "Count me in." He told her, if they needed any help, he would be glad to lend a hand. That weekend, they all got together (except Su Yen and the boys) and moved Rosa in. Su Yen ordered pizza for lunch. They were done with the moving by that time and ready for a celebration. Sidney did love being surrounded by the people who meant the most to her. After lunch, Brandon played the piano while Rosa sang, and the little boys danced and sang. Sidney couldn't help but think this was the way life should be for everyone, with everyone laughing, singing, dancing, and having fun.

 The next few weeks went by, with business as usual. One morning, Sidney woke up and felt something was different about this day. She wasn't sure what it was. It was just different. When she went down for breakfast, Rosa was singing and cooking, as usual. Then she saw Brian and Blake in the kitchen, waiting to eat breakfast. Sidney asked Rosa if everything was all right with Su Yen. She told Sidney Su Yen wasn't feeling very well. Rosa asked if Sidney would like to go check on her while she finished fixing breakfast. Sidney said, "That's what I was thinking." She went out to Su Yen's living quarters and knocked on the door. Su Yen called out for her to come in. Sidney walked in and found Su Yen curled up on the sofa. "Are you all right?" Sidney asked her. She thought she would be fine, but she was having a few pains. Sidney asked her if she had been timing them. She said she had, and they were about six minutes apart. Sidney asked, "Have you called the doctor?" Su Yen answered, "Not yet, maybe should now." Sidney called Su Yen's doctor and told him what was going on. He said not to rush, but they might want to get her things together and head for the hospital. She told Su Yen what

# RAINBOWS ARE BETTER

he said. Sidney asked her if she was ready to go. Su Yen told her to get Joe and tell him while she got ready. Joe came running when Sidney told him what was happening. Sidney asked him if he wanted her to go with them or take care of the boys. Joe answered, "I don't know." Su Yen came in, telling them her water had broken. Sidney asked her if she wanted her to go with them or take care of Brian and Blake. Su Yen asked if Rosa could take care of the boys. She wanted Sidney to go with them. Sidney ran in the house and told Rosa what was happening. She asked Rosa if she could take care of the boys while she went to the hospital with Joe and Su Yen. Rosa said, "Of course, you go ahead. We'll be fine."

"Thanks," said Sidney as she hurried out to the car.

By this time, Su Yen's pains were only one minute apart and five minutes long. Sidney said, "Are you sure you'll be all right?" Su Yen answered, "We need hurry now." They were hurrying to the hospital, when suddenly Joe stopped the car. Sidney said, "What's wrong?" Joe replied, "There's been an accident ahead, and I can't move the car." Sidney used her cell phone and called the doctor, who was on his way to the hospital. She told him about the accident. He knew what she was talking about. He was stopped in traffic, going the other direction. He said, "I called the hospital and had them dispatch an ambulance to the scene." He inquired how far apart Su Yen's pains were. Sidney answered, "They're constant now, and her water broke before we left the house." He told Sidney he was going to stay on the phone. From the look of things, she might have to deliver the baby. Sidney panicked. "I've never done anything like that. I'm not sure I can." The doctor assured Sidney he would talk her through it as best he could. He told her to stay calm. She knew she had to keep Joe and Su Yen as calm as possible.

Sidney gave the doctor her cell phone number in case they got disconnected. He started helping her prepare. She did everything he said to. She told Su Yen she was preparing to deliver the baby. She assured her the doctor was going to talk her though it. Su Yen said, "I trust you, Ms. Sidney." She knew that Sidney would do a good job. Sidney promised her she would do her best. Joe asked what he should do. Sidney said, "Watch the traffic, and as soon as we can move, get us to the hospital. If you see a policeman, stop him and tell him we need to get to the hospital in a hurry." Su Yen said quietly to Sidney, "Baby coming." She didn't want to scare Joe. Sidney delivered the baby without any further conversation.

Everything turned out fine. Sidney leaned over the seat and said to Joe, "The baby is here, and it's a beautiful little girl." Joe started to cry when he saw her. He asked Su Yen if she was okay. Su Yen said, "I fine, Joe. Policeman come, you ask him take to hospital. We need get baby to hospital, she need be checked." It was only about two minutes when a policeman went to their car. He informed them he would get them to the hospital. He told Joe to follow him. Sidney asked, "How did you know?" He told her the doctor had caught him and explained what was happening. He got to them as quickly as he could. When they arrived at the hospital, Sidney felt a great sense of relief. Su Yen thanked her for delivering the baby. Joe hugged Sidney then Su Yen. Sidney handed the baby to him so he could carry her in. Sidney had to giggle a little because he carried the baby, like it was a vial of nitroglycerine.

Finally, they were attending to Su Yen and the baby. Sidney went into the bathroom to clean up and splash some cold water on her face. Then, she called home to tell Rosa and the boys the baby was a girl and everything was wonderful. After that, Sidney went over and sat down because all of a sudden, her knees turned to rubber. The doctor went out and asked how she was doing. Sidney told him, except for two rubber legs, she was fine. He told her she did a great job delivering the baby. He knew he couldn't have done better himself. Sidney asked how Joe was doing. The doctor assured her he would survive, but right now, he was pretty emotional. "You can go in now and see them, if you think your rubber legs will carry you." Sidney got up, and her knees buckled again. She laughed and said, "I think I'll wait here for a few minutes and get a grip." The doctor had to laugh. He asked, "Does this mean you don't want to be a doctor?"

Sidney answered, "I think that's a real safe bet, and I never want to be a midwife, either."

"Now, Sidney, you know that was a very special experience. Wasn't it good to be able to help your friend bring that new little life

# RAINBOWS ARE BETTER

into the world?" She smiled and said, "Yes, it was special, but I don't want to do it ever again." She didn't think she was cut out for that kind of work. He said, "That's too bad. After the great job you did, I was thinking of asking you to be a midwife for the poor. You know, the ones who can't afford to go to the hospital." Sidney said, "I love to help people, but this time, how about a donation? You can use the money to train someone else to do it."

    Sidney tried standing up again, and this time, her knees held. She told the doctor she would like to see Su Yen now. He took her to Su Yen's room. She found Joe and the baby waiting for her. Su Yen asked them not to take the baby, until Sidney got there. Sidney took the infant in her arms, and when she looked down at her, tears of pure joy filled her eyes. She was a beautiful baby with large blue eyes, a lot of shiny black hair, and the most gorgeous, delicate little face. Sidney thought the baby looked so much like Joe. When she said so, Joe smiled from ear to ear. He was so proud. Su Yen told Sidney they hadn't picked a name for her. They wanted it to be something very special. Sidney said, "We'll have to work on that. We can't just leave her without a name." She agreed it should be a very special name. Sidney told them she was going home to talk to the boys. She would tell them what a pretty little sister they had. She gave the baby back to Su Yen and kissed her on the cheek. She hugged Joe and told them she would be back later. She was going to bring Rosa and the boys to see the baby. Sidney informed them she would get a book of names to help them decide. She said, "Joe, you could make a list of names you like." Su Yen thanked Sidney for everything. Then Su Yen told them she thought she needed to rest for a while.

    When Sidney arrived home, everyone wanted to know everything about Su Yen and the new baby. Sidney told them Su Yen, Joe, and the new baby were doing fine. She told them, after she cleaned up, and had a bite to eat, they were all going to the hospital together. Brandon volunteered to drive them over. Rosa asked Sidney what she would like to eat. Sidney, suddenly feeling very tired, answered, "I don't know, why don't you surprise me?" She then quietly climbed the stairs and started to get ready. Before she climbed in the shower, she went to her window seat and thanked God for the wonderful, new little life he had helped her deliver. When she had finished getting ready, she felt renewed and hungry. When she went downstairs, Rosa had prepared a wonderful meal for her. It smelled heavenly. After they ate, Sidney and Rosa cleaned up the boys before going to see their mother and their new little sister. On the way to the hospital, Sidney stopped at a gift shop and bought flowers and a book of baby names.

When they arrived at the hospital, Su Yen looked rested and glowing. The boys were overjoyed to see their mother and wanted to know where the baby was. Su Yen rang for the nurse and asked to have the baby brought in. Sidney gave her the flowers and the book. Su Yen thanked her for bringing them, but she had already decided on a name. She told Sidney, while she was sleeping, she kept hearing this name repeated to her. When she woke up, she decided to name the baby what she kept hearing. Sidney asked, "What is it?" Su Yen answered, "Lily Marie Banks." Brian looked at his mom and asked, "Why is her name going to be Banks instead of Johnson, like mine and Blake's?" Su Yen felt stunned; she hadn't thought about this. Brian said, "If your name is Banks and Joe's name is Banks, and now the baby's name is Banks, does that mean me and Blake aren't part of the family?" Su Yen said, "You, Blake, Lily, all three my children." She told him they just had a different daddy than Lily. Blake said, "Does that mean Joe isn't our daddy? Will he like the new baby instead of us now?" Joe said, "No way." Joe told them he had loved them since he first met them. "You're still not our dad if we have a different name," grumbled Brian. Joe asked, "Why don't you meet your new little sister now? We can talk about this later." That seemed to work temporarily.

When the nurse came in with Lily, the boys loved her instantly. They couldn't get over how small her hands and feet were. Su Yen told them they were little like that when they were born. Blake said, "No way, I'm bigger than that." Su Yen giggled and explained they were bigger now but that, when they were born, they weren't. Blake wanted to know if she was going to get as big as him. Su Yen assured him, in time she will, but by that time, he would be much bigger. She knew he wanted to make sure that he would still be bigger than

Lily would be. They all took turns holding Lily and admiring what a beautiful baby she was. Blake wanted to know why the baby didn't look like him and Brian. Su Yen answered that it was because they had different daddies. This answer only brought Brian back to being confused about the name thing. Su Yen began to show signs of fatigue. Sidney told the boys they needed to let their mom rest now. She told them they could see their mom tomorrow. With that, they gave Lily, their mom, and Joe a kiss goodbye.

After everyone left, Su Yen turned to Joe and asked him how he would feel about adopting the boys. She told him then they would all share the same name. Joe agreed it was a wonderful idea. He had wanted to do that since they first got married. He didn't say anything because he thought it might upset her to change their names. Su Yen said, "Then, it might. I want them carry on daddy's name. Now, that not important. James want them be happy. They need belong. It not like James have family they carry name for. This right thing. I keep James's picture, they know he real father. If when grow up they want name back, I let them." Joe said, "So it's decided then?" Su Yen said yes. He asked her if he could tell the boys when he went home, or if she wanted to be the one to tell them. She answered, she thought it would be a good idea if he told the boys first. That way, they would know he wanted to be their dad. Su Yen said, "I not know why I worry. A name only a name. It what you like that make you special." She knew what a kind and thoughtful man James was, and he would only want what was best for his sons.

When Joe went home that night, he took the boys home to have a talk with them. He asked them how they would feel if he adopted them and changed their name to Banks, just like Mommy's, Lily's, and his. At first they yelled "Yeah!" Then Brian expressed he wanted to have the same name they did. But he asked, "Does that mean you're our dad instead of our real dad?" Joe said, "No, it's more like you would have two dads. You'll always have your real dad, and I'll be your second dad. The only thing that will change is your last name." The boys started dancing around the room. They were singing "Blake and Brian Banks" over and over. Joe's heart soared to know how happy it made them to be his sons. What an incredible day this had been. He had become a father to three children.

Blake wanted go tell Sidney. Joe said, "Okay, let's all go tell her. First, let's call your mom and tell her." When the boys told Su Yen how happy they were, she asked to speak to their new dad. They gave the phone to Joe. Su Yen thanked him not only for being a wonderful husband but also for being a terrific father. Joe was a little embarrassed, but he said, "Thanks for making me both of those things." He knew, without her, neither one of those things would ever have happened.

When Joe hung up the phone, he felt more pride and happiness than he had ever felt in his life. He had a good reason for living and maybe a reason for everything that had happened to him. After all, that was what had taken him to this point in his life after his accident and his parents telling him he was damaged goods. Then they deserted him. He became so depressed, he didn't want to live. Then Sal came along. Now he knew for sure that all things did happen for the best even when we couldn't see it or believe it. The way he saw it, sometimes, you had to pay a big price for this much happiness. Luckily, the price wasn't as big as the reward. Joe and the boys went to tell Sidney the good news. When Sidney heard this, she was overjoyed. She hugged the boys and then Joe. She told Joe she always knew he would make a wonderful father and a good husband for someone. She was glad it turned out to be Su Yen and her boys.

Rosa stepped out of the kitchen and asked the boys if they would like to help her make cookies. She told them they could take some to their mom when they went to the hospital the next day. They went running and trying to tell Rosa (both at the same time) that Joe was going to adopt them. Joe laughed and said, "I can't believe this has made them so happy." Sidney told him she would've been happy with a dad like him herself. Joe hugged her and told her he wanted to thank her for teaching him to believe in God and to pray. He said, "You taught me to be thankful for everything no matter what my circumstances were. Until you taught me this, every day was just another day to get through. You made me believe that God has a plan for all of us and we only have to be patient enough to let it happen. This is all more wonderful than I ever thought my life could be. Ms. Sidney, from now on, I'm going to pray for you every night and ask God to give you a family. I know now there's nothing like it in the world." Sidney thanked him and told him he deserved all the good things that would ever happen to him. He answered, "So do you, Ms. Sidney. You help everyone else, and you deserve the best." She hugged Joe, with tears in her eyes. Yes, she did want a family and had thought she would have all that with Shade. In the next room, Brandon overheard their conversation. He, too, loved Sidney, and more than anything, he wanted her to be happy. He decided to take it upon himself to check and make absolutely certain she had no living relatives. There could be someone out there her family had neglected to tell her about.

# Chapter 23

# *Searching for a Family*

Brandon began staying late at work and doing computer searches. He was very good at doing things like that. This turned into quite a challenge because Sidney had been left without much information about her family. Things like Social Security numbers and birth certificates had never been given to her. He decided to start at the orphanage and see what they had in her file. There, he actually found a lot of useful information. It had not only her parents' full names and dates of birth and deaths but also their Social Security numbers. He also found the full names of her grandparents on both sides and the dates of their births and deaths. He now had their last address and some good basic information. It was still going to take some time.

One night, while he and Sidney were having dinner, Sidney told him how pleased she was to have him there to eat dinner with. She said, "I've always hated eating alone." Brandon told her he understood what she meant. He hated eating alone too. He added he also hated being alone. That was why he always stayed and worked so late at night. He would much rather be there with her around than at home alone. He told Sidney he knew he might be way out of line telling her this, but he loved her. He always wanted to be near her as much as possible. Sidney became very uneasy and somewhat embarrassed. She assured him that she enjoyed having him around too. Unfortunately, she didn't see how anything could ever come of it. He told her he didn't understand. She said, "It just couldn't work, that's all." He thought she meant because she was rich and he was just her employee. He didn't pursue it any further. From that day on, if Sidney had a strong hunch about a stock, he took every dime he had and invested it. Soon, it began to pay off. He didn't know why he hadn't thought of this before. He figured, when he had at least a million dollars, he would tell her again how he felt.

Meanwhile, he continued his search. It was beginning to seem futile. One day, he decided to send off and get a copy of everybody's birth certificates. He still had a hunch he was missing something. When the birth certificates arrived, he was absolutely correct. After looking them over twice, he noticed on Leander's birth certificate he was listed as the second child of a multiple birth. He had never heard Sidney mention her father having any siblings. Of course, the other child, or children, might have been stillborn. That could explain why she never knew. He decided, maybe it was time to tell Sidney what he had been doing and see if she could shed some light on this whole thing. Maybe she knew something he didn't know. Before he had the opportunity to tell her, he got nervous and couldn't tell her. What if she thought this was an invasion of her privacy? He wanted to marry her someday. He certainly didn't want to blow any chance he might have. He decided to sit on this information for a while. He'd wait and see what he could find out on his own.

When it became time for his vacation, he went to the town where Leander was born. He checked at the hospital to see what they knew about this. They told him it had been so long ago they wouldn't have any records that far back. He asked if they had an archive where they might keep their old records. They said yes but that he'd have to research it himself. They didn't have the time to do it for him. He agreed to do it if they'd point him in the right direction. He looked for several days, and finally, there it was. Sidney's grandmother had given birth to twin boys. One of the twins had been given up for adoption. He made copies of all the information he could find. The most important information came when she named him before giving him up. His name was Alexander Leon Davis. This gave Brandon a way to trace him. It didn't have information about which orphanage he was sent to. He decided to go from one orphanage to the next until he found a record of him. That didn't work because one of the orphanages had burned down about sixteen years after he was born. Brandon knew this had to be the one. Unfortunately, all their records were destroyed in the fire. What if he had been adopted and changed his name? Then, he remembered what Sidney said about how hard it was for Black children to be adopted. He thought about the time this would've taken place and figured the odds were good that he hadn't been adopted. If his name was still the same, there was still a chance he could be found.

The first thing Brandon had to rule out was the chance he was dead. Brandon checked the Social Security death benefits on his computer, and they showed no deaths under the name Alexander Leon Davis born on that date. Next, he sent off for his birth certificate. Sure enough, he was a twin, and it had him listed as being born first. Brandon couldn't help but wonder why he was given up for adoption when they kept the second twin. The idea occurred to him: maybe something was wrong with Alexander. Maybe he had Down syndrome. In those days, it was a common practice to put them in a mental institution, but he was put in an orphanage. Oh well, this speculation wasn't helping him find the man. Everything he tried led him to a dead end. Maybe it wasn't meant for him to find Alexander. You never know; what if he was in prison or a mass murderer? He decided to put it on the shelf for a while and think things through.

As time passed, Brandon was getting richer and richer. It seemed as though Sidney was never wrong when she had one of those hunches. Even though everything seemed to be fine, he saw Sidney sitting by the fishpond, with tears in her eyes. He listened and heard her praying that God would give her a family. She told God she loved the people in her life but she had been without a family for so many years. She longed for the feeling of belonging that most people had. Brandon knew her birthday was approaching and she needed a sense of belonging. He felt her pain and knew she needed someone, to take care of her, instead of her always taking care of everyone else. He went in and dug out the information he had on her uncle. He once again started the search. He checked with the facilities where he might have been placed if he had some sort of disability. He did a thorough search and came up empty. If only he had a Social Security number to go by. He decided this was a case for a private detective. He hired a private investigator and told him all the information he had acquired during his search. It was about a week before he heard back from him. The private investigator had located a man by the same name and birth date in a hospital not far from there. He felt sure this was the right man.

That night, Brandon asked Sidney out to dinner. He told her he had a big surprise for her. Sidney loved surprises and felt excited all evening. Brandon told her not to get too excited. He explained he didn't know if it was a good surprise or a bad one. Now, Sidney felt really confused. When dinner was over, she said, "All right, let's have it. What's the surprise?" Brandon didn't know how to start. He decided to start at the beginning. "Sidney, I know how much it would mean to you if you had a family." Sidney said, "You're not going to propose again, are you?" He said, "No, but I'd like to." He didn't know how to tell her this but straight out. He was hoping it didn't make her mad. He explained he had been searching since Lily was born, to see if by some twist of fate she might have some family she hadn't been aware of. Sidney said, "There wasn't any, right?"

"Quite the contrary," said Brandon. "I've found an uncle you obviously didn't know about." Sidney said, "That's not possible. I know there isn't anyone." Brandon pulled out the birth certificates he had, Leander's and Alexander's birth certificates. He said, "Look these over." Sidney read them and couldn't believe her eyes. She wondered why someone hadn't mentioned this to her. Brandon explained he had discovered the first twin had been placed in an orphanage. She asked, "Why would my grandmother give away one of her children?" Brandon told her he didn't have any answers for that question. Judging from what Sidney told him about her grandmother, he was sure she had her reasons. Sidney said, "I lived in an orphanage, and there is no good-enough reason for doing that to a child." Everyone knew that a Black child had literally no chance of being adopted, especially during the time when her dad was born. Then, Brandon pulled out the private investigator's report, which stated where her uncle was now. She said, "We have to go there and find him." Brandon said, "I don't think that's a good idea tonight." She asked, "Why not?" He expounded what a bad neighborhood it was in. What good would it do to find her uncle if she got shot doing it? It was agreed that they would go the next morning. First, Sidney threw her arms around Brandon, giving him the biggest hug he had ever received. Sidney thanked him for doing such a wonderful thing for her. He said, "Save your thanks until you find out what kind of person your uncle is. You have to remember he never knew a real family during a hard time in history for Black people. He could be bitter and resentful or anything, for that matter."

That night, Sidney thanked God for giving her an uncle she could love. She also thanked him for Brandon being such a good friend to her. She could hardly sleep that night, thinking about what her uncle would be like. She wondered if he would want to know her. Flash kept looking at her like he would like to get some sleep. She rubbed his head and finally fell asleep.

When morning came, Sidney jumped out of bed, so excited she could hardly go through her morning routine. She couldn't decide what to wear. She wanted to impress him but not look gaudy. Then she remembered what Sal had said when he bought her the red dress. She decided she would wear the red dress. She put her hair up since everyone seemed to like it that way. She wore a pair of diamond stud earrings and her mother's locket. When she went downstairs for breakfast, Rosa told her she looked especially lovely. Sidney smiled and said, "Thank you, Rosa. It's a special day today. Has Brandon arrived yet?" Rosa said, "He's in the library, waiting for you." She went to the library and told Brandon to come and eat some breakfast with her. He turned around and said, "Wow, you look great." She couldn't help it; she felt her face begin to flush. She said "Thank you" and turned around so he wouldn't notice. As they ate breakfast, Sidney couldn't stop talking about how excited she was to finally have a family. Sidney said, "We even have something in common." Brandon asked, "What can that be? You don't even know him." Sidney said, "We were both orphans." Brandon again cautioned her not to get her hopes up. He reminded her it might not even be her uncle. As soon as breakfast was over, they left for the hospital, with everyone wishing Sidney good luck.

# RAINBOWS ARE BETTER

When they arrived at the hospital, Sidney just sat there for a minute. Brandon wondered what was wrong. She explained she was trying to think of something to say to him. Brandon said, "Why worry about that? I'm sure something will come to mind after you meet him. The first thing we need to do is make sure he's the right Alexander Leon Davis." They went inside and asked which room Alexander Davis was in. The receptionist had a nurse's aide escort them to his room. When they walked in, Sidney's knees turned to rubber. Brandon saw her and wrapped his arm around her for support. When the nurse introduced them to Alexander, Sidney felt as though she would faint. Alexander was White. Sidney said, "I'm sorry, but we've obliviously made a mistake." Then she explained she was there looking for her uncle. She said, "As you can see, I'm Black, and you're not." She told him she was really sorry to have bothered him. Alexander looked up at her with kind large eyes and said, "So am I, kind of." Sidney said, "You're not Black, anyone can see that." He said, "You don't look very Black, either." Sidney, suddenly feeling incensed, said, "I am Black, I just happen to have lighter skin than most." Alex (which was what everyone called him) said, "You're not as light-skinned as I am." Sidney said, "What makes you think you're Black?" He told her, on his birth certificate, it had listed both his parents as being Black. It also listed him as the firstborn of twins. He continued explaining he didn't know what happened to his twin. He didn't even know if his twin was born alive. Brandon took Sidney aside and told her everything Alexander was telling her was true, "All that information is on your uncle's and your dad's birth certificates." Sidney said, "That can't be true, my father was Black. My father's skin was darker than mine. It's not possible, they're twins." Sidney told Alex they would be back in a few minutes. He told her to take her time he wasn't going anyplace for a while.

Sidney found an obstetrician at the hospital and asked him a few questions. He took her and Brandon to the doctor's lounge. There, he got them a cup of coffee. When he was seated, he said, "Now what's the problem?" Sidney asked him if it was possible for two Black people to have twins, one Black and the other one White. He said, "It's very rare, but it has happened." Sidney asked, "How can

195

that happen?" He told her there were two ways it could occur. First, the mother could've had sex with a Black man and a White man on the same night. The second way is for there to be a White person in their family tree. This has happened on rare occasions, especially if their family tree went back to the time of slavery. White owners, more times than most people would like to believe, either raped or coerced young Black women into having sex with them. If the slaves got pregnant, they usually sold them. That way, no one would ever know what they had done. Sidney said, "My great-great-grandmother was a slave." The doctor, after putting two and two together, asked if she was related to someone who was White. She said, "Yes, I am. It was my grandmother who had the twins." He said, "That would explain why you don't look very Black yourself. I would have guessed you to be French, Indian, or possibly Polynesian." Sidney again felt incensed. She had never thought of herself as anything but Black. Twice that morning, she had that questioned and, even worse, explained. How could all this be happening?

Brandon could tell all these revelations were taking their toll on Sidney. This was one of his worst nightmares coming true. He wished he had not opened this can of worms. He asked Sidney if she would like to go home now. She looked up at him with tears in her eyes and said, "Yes, I would." She thanked the doctor for his help. She asked Brandon if he would mind telling Alex that she wasn't feeling well and she would talk to him later. The doctor told her she could wait there for Brandon. Brandon went to Alex's room and told him they were going home now because Sidney wasn't feeling well. Alex told him he understood everyone treated him that way when they found out about his heritage. Brandon told him how sorry he was for what had happened. Alex said, "Don't worry about it. After all these years, you'd think I'd get used to it." Brandon turned and walked out of the room. Brandon thought to himself, *What difference does all of this make, anyway? They're two lonely people who have wanted a family all their lives. Now that they've found one another, they can't get past this nonsense about color, long enough to be happy?*

Sidney cried all the way home, and Brandon felt awful. He blamed himself for everything. When they got home, he told Sidney how very sorry he was to have put her through all this pain. Sidney hugged him and said, "It's not your fault. I don't even know what I'm crying about." She was too overwhelmed by everything to think clearly. She knew her sense of reality was shattered, and she needed time to deal with it. She asked Brandon how Alex took it when he spoke to him. Brandon told her what Alex said. Sidney said, "I feel so bad for him. I don't want him to think for one minute that I'm upset with him." Brandon asked, "What are you so upset about?" She answered, "I don't really know. I guess I'm upset that a little baby was deserted in an orphanage. That he spent his whole life with no family to love him. He was abandoned for something he had nothing to do with." She was upset that not only did her grandparents give up one of their children but they also never even told her dad he had a brother. She was upset that she had lived most of her life without a family because she didn't know there was anyone out there to even look for. The thing she was most grateful for was Brandon and him caring enough about her to do all this work. That he found the one thing in her life that had been missing. She concluded, before she went to see Alex again, she wanted to get herself together. She wanted him know how happy she was to have found him. Brandon thought to himself, he should have known better than to think she was being insensitive. This woman didn't know how to be anything but caring. Suddenly he felt better about everything.

    He asked Sidney if she was going to be all right. Sidney said, "Yes. I just wish I could understand why my grandparents would give up their child like that." Brandon and Sidney spent the rest of the day together, talking and swimming (because swimming calmed Sidney when she was upset). Brandon told Sidney, in all fairness to her grandparents, she should try looking at things from their point of view. Sidney said, "What possible reason could anyone have to do such a thing?" Brandon said, "I didn't know them, but the first thing I would do is look back at the time frame in which they lived. Add into that equation their financial circumstances." Sidney said, "They always had plenty of money, according to her dad."

    "Okay, so we can rule out the financial thing. Just to play the devil's advocate, maybe they gave up the baby for his own good. In that day and age, would anyone have believed that those babies were twins? Would people have believed that both of the babies belonged to them? Maybe they were embarrassed for anyone to know they had a White ancestor. Maybe they were afraid of people thinking the babies were freaks. Maybe your grandmother was afraid people might think she had an affair with a White man." Brandon felt sure, back then, no one would believe they could have twins, one of whom was Black and the other White. After all, he and Sidney had trouble believing it in this day and age. Maybe they thought that they were doing the best thing for both the boys. Maybe they thought a nice White couple would adopt Alex and give him a better opportunity to have a normal life. He told Sidney she knew more about them than he did, and he asked what she thought about it. They're not here to tell us. Sidney said, "You're right. They would never have made a decision like that, unless they were convinced it was the right thing for everyone." She knew she was being too judgmental of a situation she had no insight into. She knew, when she saw Alex, she couldn't believe her eyes. Even when the doctor explained it to them, she was having trouble believing what her ears were hearing. She felt sorry for her grandparents. She said, "What kind of torment they must have gone through. Not only when they were deciding to give Alex up, but to have lived with such a horrible secret the rest of their lives. It must have torn them apart, never knowing what happened to him." Sidney added, "I do know, if there's any way I can make up for any of Alex's heartaches, I will." Brandon said, "That's my girl, now you're talking. Do you think you can sleep now?" She answered, "Like a baby." He kissed her on the forehead and said, "Good night."

That night, Sidney knew she needed to say her prayers and ask for God's guidance. She had a lot of things she felt she needed forgiveness for. She prayed a very long prayer and asked God many questions she needed answers to. As she slept that night, it was as though God were answering her prayers up close and personal. While she was dreaming, God told her he had a plan for everyone in the world. Her grandparents didn't make their decision without talking to him many times. Although the decision they made might not have been what he wanted, it was still the best solution they could come up with. He told her he never held that kind of decision against anyone, not when they were doing the best they could with what they knew. "If you give the things you do, that much heartfelt prayer and careful consideration before making your choices, I bless you because I know you did all you thought you could. When you're faced with a huge decision to make, I would ask that you do three things before you pray for my help. First, filter all the knowledge you have through your mind and discard anything that doesn't make sense. Secondly, filter the remaining information through your heart, and discard anything that doesn't feel right. Thirdly, filter the remaining information through your soul, because it always knows the right thing to do and will always guide you in the right direction. Too many times, that all-important third step gets ignored. That's when people get into trouble. I'd like you to know how pleased I am that you and your uncle have turned out to be such good people. You, neither one, had much guidance to work with, and I'm sorry about that. Still, you both became good people, and I'm proud of you. I have one suggestion for you. For some reason, you put too much into your uncle being White and you being Black. I have never understood why people are so hung up on their differences. I made all of you, and you're all different in one way or another. If you were all just alike, it wouldn't be much fun now, would it? Your differences are what make you special in your own right. You're not different to make you more or less superior to one another. It hurts me to see you separating yourselves from each other. I never meant it that way. To me, you're all special, and I love every single one of you. To my eyes, you're all beautiful, precious, and wonderful. You're all human, which is the most important thing for you to remember. I put you here to learn to love one another, no matter what your differences might be." Sidney recalled thinking to herself, *Then why are there so many people that are hard to love?* God answered Sidney's question without her asking out loud. "If you were all easy to love, you wouldn't have to challenge yourself to learn the lessons necessary to grow. It's easy to love the lovable-but-hard-to-love someone you don't feel deserves it. It's only when you accomplish loving the unlovable that you're on the right track. When you can love everyone more than yourself and expect nothing in return, you will have achieved perfect love. I know that's a lot to ask, so I only ask you to love one another as you love yourself. I know that it's taken a long time to get you and your uncle together. Sometimes, it takes me a while to work things out for the best. After all, I always have to work around your free will. Right now is the best time for you and your uncle to get to know one another. I want you to make the best of the gift you've been given." When Sidney woke up, she sat straight up in bed, expecting to see God standing right there in front of her. There was no one there, but the dream seemed so real. She couldn't believe it was just a dream. She sat there for what seemed like the longest time, thinking about what God said. If God was willing to forgive and forget, who was she to sit in judgement of anyone? She understood it was her job to make the rest of her uncle's life special. She got out of bed and started getting ready to go to the hospital and set things right.

When Sidney went downstairs to eat breakfast, Rosa told her she looked positively glowing. Sidney said, "Thanks, Rosa." She even felt like she was glowing. Sidney was eating breakfast, when Brandon came in. She asked him if he would like to join her for a bite to eat. He smiled and said, "I thought you would never ask." Rosa, who had never seen this skinny man when he wasn't hungry, brought him a huge plate of food. Brandon asked Sidney if she was planning on going to the hospital after breakfast. She answered, "Most definitely." She felt like she owed her uncle a big apology for her behavior the day before. Brandon asked if he might accompany her to the hospital. "I would love the company, but you don't have go, unless you really want to." Brandon said, "I'd like to go, at least for moral support." It was really more than that, though. He liked Alex and looked forward to seeing him again. He asked her if she knew what she would say. She said, "No, but whatever I say will be said with a lot of love."

When they arrived at the hospital, Sidney began feeling jittery. Brandon (noticing this) asked, "What's wrong?" Sidney said, "What if he doesn't want to see me again?" Brandon responded, "Don't borrow trouble." He could tell Alex was the kind of person who would want very much to see her again. Sidney didn't look too convinced but got out of the car, anyway. She thought to herself, she would never know unless she tried. They walked silently, hand in hand, into the hospital. Brandon gave her hand a gentle squeeze as they walked into Alex's room. He whispered, "It's all right, and I'm right here for you." She walked over to Alex's bed, and he smiled the most wonderful smile she had ever seen. Before she could speak, he said, "I'm so glad you came back." With that statement, she fell into his open arms and began to sob. She tried to explain her behavior the day before. He quieted her by saying "That was yesterday, and this is today. Let's just start over." He hugged her for the longest time. It felt so good to Sidney, she wished it would never end. Finally, he said, "I'm so happy to finally have a family." Sidney anxiously replied, "Me too."

They talked for hours. Sidney explained to him that she was the only family he had left. She told him how she, too, had been raised in an orphanage. They discovered they had both run away at the age of fifteen. Alex explained how he found a job on a cargo ship. He had sailed around the world several times. He had just returned from India and the Far East when he got sick and had to be hospitalized for a ruptured appendix. If it hadn't been for that little emergency, they might never have met. Uncle Alex asked Sidney where she lived. Sidney told him she lived there in New York, not far from where she had lived with her mom and dad before their untimely deaths. He told her, maybe she could have him over sometime. She answered, "That's just what I was going to ask you. I would love to have you stay with me while you recuperate." He answered, "You don't even know me, are you sure?" She hugged him and said, "I have never been more sure of anything in my life." Uncle Alex smiled that wonderful smile of his and said, "I would love to." He wanted her to promise him one thing, though. Sidney asked what he wanted. He told her she had to tell him if things weren't going right and she wanted him to leave. She laughed and said, "I hardly think that will be a problem." But she promised to do whatever he said if it would make him happy.

Brandon asked, "So when do the doctors think you'll be discharged?" Alex answered, "They're talking about letting me out tomorrow." Sidney and Brandon assured him they would be there to pick him up and take him home. He told them that was very kind of them to do. Brandon said, "It isn't that kind of me, it's Sidney's house." Uncle Alex said, "I'm sorry, I thought you were together." Brandon responded, "I wish, but I'm just her employee." Uncle Alex said, "Well, well, Sidney, so you have an employee?" She laughed and said, "I have a few, four, to be exact." Uncle Alex asked her if she was married or anything like that. Sidney said, "Almost once, but the answer is no." She assured him they would talk about all these things when she got him home. She would gladly answer any and all questions he might have. She hugged him and told him she would see him in the morning. Now, she needed to get home. Before she left, she asked him if there was anything she could get him before she left. He said, "No, not really. They take very good care of me."

When Sidney got home, she could hardly contain herself long enough to tell everyone the good news. She told them her uncle would be staying with her for a while. Rosa questioned if he would be able to climb the stairs or if she should prepare the sofa bed in the family room. Sidney decided to prepare the sofa bed in the family room, just in case the stairs were a problem for him. Everyone was happy that Sidney had finally found the family she had always longed for. Sidney and Su Yen went shopping for a few things Sidney felt Uncle Alex might need. Sidney bought him eight pairs of pajamas, a robe, and house shoes. She bought him an electric razor and a regular razor, just in case he preferred one or the other. She bought him several pairs of sweats and even a toothbrush. She got everything she thought would make him comfortable. The only thing that concerned her was the fact that she was only guessing at his sizes. She could only hope that she was right. Su Yen said, "Not worry, if not fit, you take back, exchange, get right size." Sidney replied, "I know you're right, I just want everything to be perfect for him." Su Yen said, "He probably happy having family, like you happy. It be perfect."

That night, Sidney had trouble going to sleep. She got up and said her prayers again. This time, she asked for a good night's sleep so she would be refreshed and ready for the next day. When she got back into bed, she went to sleep immediately and slept like a baby. When she awoke, she was so rested and refreshed, she said a prayer of thanks. She quickly got ready and went downstairs. There, she found Brandon waiting. Rosa brought them both a great breakfast.

## RAINBOWS ARE BETTER

Sidney told Brandon she was so excited, it was hard to remain inside her skin. Brandon responded that, strangely enough, he was pretty excited, too, although he added he wasn't having any skin problems. Sidney laughed, and they finished their breakfast, joking back and forth. Brandon questioned if he should stop coming over for breakfast when Uncle Alex arrived. Sidney said, "No way, after all, you're the one who made all this possible." She added, "By the way, Brandon, thank you for all you've done." He expressed to her all the happiness she was feeling was thanks enough. Then he added, "Unless you want to change your mind and marry me." She looked at him sternly and said, "I thought we had agreed not to discuss that subject anymore." Brandon replied, "You agreed, not me." Sidney didn't want to talk about Brandon's feelings. She just wanted to go pick up Uncle Alex.

When they arrived at the hospital, Uncle Alex was waiting for them. He was already dressed and ready to go. Sidney hugged him and said, "I don't have to ask you if you're ready to go." He told her she needed to ring for the nurse. She would bring a wheelchair to take him out to the car. Sidney asked him if he had any personal belongings. He said, "Nothing but a razor, comb, toothbrush, and a few old clothes." He told her he needed to stop and get a few things on the way to her house. Most of his things were on the ship, and it had already gone out to sea. Sidney told him not to worry. She had taken the liberty of buying him a few things. She told him, if he needed anything else, she would get it later. Uncle Alex wanted to know how much he owed her. She told him it was nothing at all, explaining she wanted him to consider the things she got him, the birthday presents she had never been able to give him.

When they drove up to the front gate, Uncle Alex asked if this was her house. She answered, "Yes, it is. A very nice gentleman who considered himself to be my adopted father left it to me before he died. He and a couple of other wonderful people made sure they made up for all the birthdays and family I had missed. They were so kind to me, and I loved them dearly." When they drove up to the front door, Sidney jumped out to help Uncle Alex. He laughed at her and explained he was able to get around on his own. He told her he had been through much more than this and was still able to get around. He thanked her anyway. They went inside, and Uncle Alex asked Sidney to pinch him to make sure he wasn't dreaming. He told her she had a beautiful home, the most beautiful home he had ever been in. Sidney just smiled and said, "Thanks." Then she asked him if he was able to climb stairs yet. He answered, "Yeah, I can do almost anything I did before the surgery."

"Good," said Sidney. "Would you like to go upstairs and rest for a while before lunch?" He told her that might be a good idea. She took him upstairs to show him his bedroom and his bathroom. She also showed him where his clothes, pajamas, house shoes, and robe were. She told him she was going to leave the intercom on so, if he needed her, she could hear him. Then she left him to get some rest. She left, telling him, she would let him know when it was time for lunch.

When she went downstairs, she said to Brandon, "I wonder where everybody is." Brandon said, "I think they're outside." He heard someone laughing out there just a moment before she asked. Sidney went out back, and there everybody was. They were preparing for a barbecue picnic as a welcome-home party. They had put up banners, balloons, and streamers all over the place. Su Yen said, "I sorry, we not in house to meet Uncle." Sidney retorted, "This is much better, anyway. He's upstairs, resting. He can meet everyone at the party." She thanked them all for being so thoughtful and going to so much trouble to make him feel welcome. Sidney asked what she could do to help. They told her and Brandon to use this time to take care of her business matters. Sidney said, "That's a good idea." With all the commotion lately, she hadn't had much time to check on things.

Brandon challenged her to a race to the house. He won and wanted to know if he was going to get his kiss now. Sidney said, "What are you talking about?" He told her he won, so he wanted his prize. She questioned what that had to do with a kiss. His answer was that's what he wanted his prize to be. Everyone was cheering him on. Joe yelled, "Give him a kiss, Ms. Sidney, it's only fair!" She looked at Brandon and said, "Okay, but just because you won." He took her in his arms and gave her the longest and most passionate kiss she could ever remember getting. It actually made her swoon. Her face flushed a little as she stepped back and looked at him. She couldn't help thinking what she had been missing. At first, she told herself she just couldn't remember how wonderful Shade's kisses were. In her heart, she knew better than that. Sidney and Brandon had just connected on a deeper level than she ever knew existed. She turned and walked into the house, trying not to let him know how she was feeling. It was too late. He, too, had felt all the same passion she did in that kiss. He knew he had just cleared the first hurtle.

When lunch was ready, Sidney went upstairs to tell Uncle Alex. When she got to his room, he was up and ready. She was happy to see him wearing a pair of sweats and the tennis shoes, she gave him. She exclaimed, "Wow! Aren't you looking spiffy?" He hugged her and said, "Thanks, kid, for all the new things." She liked him calling her kid, the same way Sal always did. He told her he felt like it was Christmas or something wonderful. Sidney said, "It is something wonderful. I have my uncle right here in my home." Uncle Alex laughed and said, "I couldn't be happier, either." She asked him if he was hungry. He answered, "Do ducks quack? I'm starving." They walked down the stairs, arm in arm. They were laughing and talking about the bad old days, when getting enough to eat was extremely rare. Sidney assured him he would get enough to eat here. He asked her if she was a good cook. She explained she could cook but she didn't because she had two of the world's best cooks working for her. As they walked to the backyard, Sidney took him past the swimming pool. She told him, if he ever wanted to swim there, he should feel free to do so. He thanked her and said, "Not right now, I smell something wonderful cooking."

When they stepped outside, everyone yelled "Welcome home, Uncle Alex!" He looked around at the balloons, banners, and streamers. Tears began to flood his eyes. Nothing like this had ever happened to him before. He thanked them all for such a warm welcome. Sidney took him around and introduced him to everyone. She was shocked at how quickly he and Rosa took up with each other. They couldn't have made her any happier. It did her heart good to see two people she loved enjoying each other's company so much. What a wonderful time they had that day. They talked, laughed, and had more fun than Sidney ever had before. Her heart was singing. Sidney thought to herself, *So this is what having a family feels like.* She hoped people who had families knew how lucky they are. It was getting late, and she was afraid Uncle Alex was overdoing it a bit. She suggested that they go inside. She took him into the living room and made him all comfy and cozy. The others cleaned up outside. When they finished, they all went into the living room. Brandon sat down at the piano, and everyone started to sing. The children giggled and danced around the room. They continued to party, until Uncle Alex was exhausted. Sidney was afraid she had allowed him to get too worn out. He told her he had always heard laughter was the best medicine. He had never felt so good in his whole life. He admitted Sidney was right. He was feeling a tad bit tired. Everyone told Uncle Alex how glad they were to have him there and wished him a good night. Sidney took him upstairs and told him how happy he had made her life. Things had been wonderful since Brandon had found him. Uncle Alex looked at her and said, "That Brandon is a very special person, isn't he?" Sidney, remembering the kiss earlier, replied, "He certainly is." Sidney kissed Uncle Alex on the cheek and told him to get some rest.

 The next morning, when Sidney was ready to go down for breakfast, Uncle Alex's door was open. He wasn't in his room, though. She thought he was probably downstairs, having breakfast. When she went into the kitchen, he wasn't there either, and her heart sank. She was afraid he might have decided to leave. She asked Rosa if she had seen Uncle Alex. Rosa answered, "Oh sure, he had his breakfast and went outside." Sidney looked out back, and there he was, walking around with Joe. Joe was showing him the grounds and telling him what he had done and planned to do. Sidney asked Rosa how early he got up. Rosa said, "He came downstairs at five thirty, as I was coming in." Sidney asked, "Do you always come in at five thirty in the morning?" Rosa responded, "Oh no. I was worried, him being a man of the sea and all, that he might be up pretty early." Sidney told her that would never have occurred to her. Rosa said, "My uncle was a seaman, and he was always up with the sun." She told Sidney, while she was fixing Uncle Alex's breakfast, he went for a swim. Sidney wondered if he should be doing so much so soon. Rosa said, "He is fine. We'll keep an eye on him. If he starts looking or acting fatigued, we'll suggest that he rest." Sidney hugged Rosa and said, "What would I do without you?"

Right on schedule, Brandon came in ready to eat breakfast. Rosa laughed and said, "I'm ready for you." She had prepared a big breakfast. Brandon asked, "What's the special occasion?" Rosa told him Uncle Alex was a seafaring man, and she knew he would be a big eater. Brandon told her he was really happy Uncle Alex was there. He said, "You know how much I love to eat." Rosa and Sidney both laughed at him, knowing that was, indeed, the truth. Sidney was already vigorously going over the newspaper. Brandon asked, "Is something going on with the stocks?" Sidney answered, "Not yet, but I have a feeling there will be tomorrow." He told her to write down the changes she wanted to make, and he would take care of it right after breakfast.

Just as Sidney finished breakfast, Uncle Alex came in. "Top of the morning to ye" he said with that warm, inviting smile. Sidney smiled and asked him, "How are you feeling?" He replied, "After having the best night's sleep I can ever remember, I feel great." Sidney said, "I'm so glad you liked your bed." She had put a down-filled feather bed on all the beds in the house. She told him she loved them because it felt like someone hugging you to sleep. Uncle Alex said, "I have never slept on a bed that nice before. I absolutely have never slept on anything that soft and relaxing. You're right, though, Sidney, my girl. It is like being hugged all night." He laughed and said, "You gotta like that." Brandon said, "You people and your beds." He didn't understand what could be so special about one bed over another. Uncle Alex said, "Don't knock it till you've tried it." Brandon said, "I'd like to try it, but Sidney won't let me." Sidney blushed the brightest red and said, "That will be quite enough of that kind of talk." Brandon told Uncle Alex, "See what I mean?" Uncle Alex whispered in his ear, "Don't give up, she's showing signs of weakening." Brandon asked him how he could tell. Uncle Alex explained, "The blushing was a dead giveaway, and her leaving the room was another." Brandon put his arm on Uncle Alex's shoulder and said, "Where have you been all this time?" He had needed this kind of advice all along. Uncle Alex told him, "You have to give women some time and space, but not too much, and they'll come around." Brandon went into the library, where Sidney was starting up the computers and getting ready for the day. Brandon said, "Let me take care of the transfers. You should spend the day getting to know your long-lost uncle." Sidney said, "Thanks, Brandon. That's a great idea."

Sidney went outside, where she found Uncle Alex and Joe talking about what kind of tree Joe should plant in his yard. Uncle Alex told Joe to plant a good, sturdy tree so it could hold a tree swing for his kids. Joe said, "They have a swing set already." Uncle Alex said, "Yes, but there's nothing like a tree swing." He thought it made a house feel more like a home. Sidney's heart felt like it was going to break. At least she had known the happiness of having a wonderful home, with a tree swing in the backyard. She couldn't bear to think Uncle Alex had never had a home or knew what it would've been like. She went back into the house and waited for Uncle Alex there. She kept thinking how lucky she was to have had parents, if only for a few years. There were also all the wonderful people she had the good fortune to share her life with.

When Uncle Alex went in, Sidney said, "We have the whole day to ourselves to get to know one another." Uncle Alex asked, "What about your work?" She laughed and said, "Not today. Brandon is taking care of things. He told me you and I need to spend some time together." She told him she wanted to know everything there was to know about him, from his earliest memories. Uncle Alex said, "I don't think you want to know absolutely everything about me. Maybe it would be better if I tell you most of the things about myself." Sidney explained to him she would really like to know every single thing. She reassured him he didn't have to tell her anything he wasn't comfortable telling her. He said, "Actually, there's not that much to tell. All I ever knew was living in the orphanage until I was fifteen, when I ran away. I got a job on a cargo ship and worked there up until now." Sidney knew he couldn't have lived all these years and that was all there was to his life. He told her she should go first and that would help him know what to talk about. He had never talked that much about his life and didn't know where to start. Sidney knew how he felt. She never liked talking about her life, either. She never believed anyone would be interested. She felt embarrassed about most of her life. It took her a long time to understand she didn't choose the things that happened to her when she was young. She thought, for those who hadn't experienced the things she did, her life wouldn't be interesting. She discovered that people really were interested in her life.

Sidney started at her earliest memory and shared everything with him. Sidney told him not only about herself but about her parents, as well, especially about her dad and her grandparents. This was the first time Uncle Alex had heard anything about them. He told her they sounded like very nice people. He wished that he could've met them. Sidney put her loving arms around his neck and said, "I wish you could have too." She knew he and her dad would have been very close. He would've been thrilled to know he had a brother. Uncle Alex said, "Maybe not." He told her, the fact that he was White might have embarrassed him. Sidney said, "I don't know for sure why my grandparents gave you up for adoption. I feel sure they had their reasons. I know my dad would have loved you, no matter what color you are. I also know, if my grandparents could meet you now, they would love you too. As a matter of fact, I'm sure they loved you even when they gave you up for adoption." She continued explaining to him, during that time, they might have been arrested for stealing a White baby. To say nothing of what people would have done to him and to them. Uncle Alex said, "I never thought of it like that, but the way I was treated in that orphanage was no picnic either. If it helped them, I'm glad, and it was worth it."

Sidney said, "I hate people being so racist, including myself." Uncle Alex asked, "Do you have racist feelings toward me?" She said, "No, not now." She had to admit she did at first. When she first saw him, she felt like he had destroyed her idea of who she was. She knew now it had nothing to do with him. Up until the moment she first met him, she didn't even know she could have feelings like that.

Sidney said, "Prejudice is like a thief in the night. Before you even know it's there, it robs you of your rational thinking and compassion." She explained her parents taught her to be proud of herself and her Black heritage. She realized now that respect was a better way to feel. From now on, she would respect her heritage, both Black and White. Uncle Alex asked, "Are you sure I don't make you feel uncomfortable?" She exclaimed, "Absolutely not!" He was a wonderful person, and she couldn't be happier to have found him. She was just trying to explain that sometimes these feelings happened to people even with the best of intentions. When they least expected it, they could have those nasty feelings creep up on them. She thought he was exactly what she needed to truly understand it was not the color of your skin that mattered; it was the content of your heart that did. We should never judge one another by the color of our skin—rather, it should be by the deeds that we do. As a matter of fact; we shouldn't judge one another at all. She felt that was still God's job. After all, skin was just something to cover your body. It had nothing to do with anything. She liked the saying the native Americans always had, "You should never judge another until you've walked a mile in their shoes." It was hard to understand other people, unless you had lived their lives and knew where they were coming from.

Sidney knew now, her whole life, God has been preparing her for the day she would meet Uncle Alex. Even then, she didn't feel she handled it very well. She could only hope he would forgive her and allow her to make it up to him. She wanted to make up not only for her own actions, but for her family's, as well. Uncle Alex was just an innocent baby who came into this world and, through no fault of his own, was cast out. All this occurred just because of the color of his skin.

Uncle Alex hugged Sidney and wept. He told Sidney that was how he had felt when he was a small child. Later on, he decided that was just the way things were. He decided no one was ever going to change their minds and come to get him. After that, he cried and wondered what was wrong with him. He presumed there had to be something wrong with him if his parents didn't even want him. He said, "I went through a lot of stages. First, I blamed my parents, then

# RAINBOWS ARE BETTER

I blamed myself. Finally, I decided, it was probably nobody's fault. I figured it might have been bad circumstances that sent things out of control. I did wonder what happened to my brother when I found out I was a twin. I thought my twin might be in an orphanage too. I knew there was the possibility it had died, either at birth or later on."

Uncle Alex knew, if he were to have any life at all, he had to be able to put the past behind him. He tried to forgive everyone, including himself. For most of his life, he had tried not to think about it, until there was Sidney. Sidney said, "I'm sorry if I've caused any painful memories for you." He said, "That's not it, I had just given up on ever having a family." He was very happy she had found him, because he was definitely lost. He didn't realize how much he needed a family. He knew now that everyone needed that kind of love and acceptance. He told her he had never felt so happy in his life. Sidney agreed she felt the same way. At least she knew she had a family, but it had been so long ago, she had forgotten what it actually felt like.

Sidney asked Uncle Alex if he had any feelings about his family being Black. "Why should I?" asked Uncle Alex, "I'm Black, too, you know. You're a dear, sweet person, so why would that bother me? When I was little, I hated being half-Black and half-White, because that meant neither Blacks nor Whites would adopt me. I had mixed blood, which made me different from everyone else." He had always had trouble understanding what difference that made. He knew, for sure, it made a big difference to other people. There was no hope of him ever being adopted. Sidney understood because she wasn't adoptable either, but that was because she was Black and too old at age eight. They spent hours pouring their hearts out to each other.

Rosa announced lunch was ready. Sidney and Uncle Alex couldn't believe the morning had passed by so quickly. But Uncle Alex admitted he was hungry. While they ate lunch, they discussed what to do with the rest of the day. During lunch, Sidney asked Uncle Alex if there was anything special he always wanted to do as a kid but never had the opportunity to do. Uncle Alex replied, "Yeah, lots of things, but I'm not a kid anymore." Sidney said, "I mean just one thing that you especially wanted to do but couldn't or just didn't." He answered, "It might sound silly, but I always wanted to go to the zoo and amusement park." He knew she said one thing, but he couldn't choose between them. She asked him if he would still like to go to the zoo or the amusement park. They could go to one, one day, and the other, the next day. He knew he wanted to, but he didn't know how soon he would be up for it. Sidney felt silly. Of course, he should wait until the doctor gave him a clean bill of health. She told him, as soon as the doctor said it was okay, they were going to have the greatest time ever.

Sidney said, "When lunch is over, we need to make a list of things you'll need for the rest of your stay here." Uncle Alex told Sidney he had everything he needed to get by and he wouldn't be staying that much longer. Sidney felt her heart sink when she heard those words. She knew that he would be leaving sooner or later. In her heart, she had hoped it would be much, much later, if ever. They finished their meal, and Rosa went in to clear the dishes away. Uncle Alex volunteered to help her. He told Rosa the meal was delicious, the best he'd ever had. He told her she was one great little cook. While they were in the kitchen, Sidney overheard Uncle Alex flirting with Rosa, and she was flirting right back. Sidney suddenly felt much better about things. Uncle Alex and Rosa—if they got together, two of her favorite people would always be right there. For the next few days, Rosa went around the house, smiling and humming all the time. Just as noticeable was the big grin on Uncle Alex's face. Brandon even noticed how giddy the two of them were.

When it was time for Uncle Alex to get his checkup, he didn't seem too thrilled. The doctor checked him over and gave him a clean bill of health. The doctor said he should be able to resume doing anything he had done before the surgery. On their way out to the car, Sidney asked him what was wrong. He answered, "Nothing, nothing at all." Sidney knew better and asked him what it meant for him to be completely well again. He said, "Nothing much. I figure I'll be going back to work now." Sidney asked, "So do you have to leave right away?" Uncle Alex answered, "I have to work to eat. That's the way it is." Sidney explained how she wanted him to live with her more than anything. She had more than enough money for them both to live several lifetimes. She couldn't bear to think of him leaving. He couldn't think of anything he wanted more than to stay. He only knew he couldn't let her take care of him. Sidney knew what he was concerned about, but who cared about the money or if he was working or not? It was her money and their lives. She told him they should take advantage of the money since God had provided it to them. They had already missed having a family for most of their lives. Now that she had found him, she couldn't let him go and be alone again.

Uncle Alex agreed to stay another week so he could think this through. He would make a decision then. Sidney hugged him and smiled. That sounded fair to her. Sidney said, "Don't forget about Rosa while you're thinking it over." Uncle Alex responded, "What about Rosa?" Sidney explained how they all noticed how the two of them had been flirting with each other. Uncle Alex asked Sidney if she thought Rosa was really flirting with him. She answered, "Most definitely." Sidney asked him if he hadn't noticed the way she giggled every time he said something. Her face positively lit up every time he walked in the room. Uncle Alex was afraid he was the only one who felt infatuated. No one had ever been that interested in him before, especially when they knew all about him. He told Sidney she was right about him flirting with Rosa. He thought Rosa was the most wonderful lady (except for Sidney, of course) he had ever met. He knew the first night he met her that he was smitten. When she was singing that night, she stole his heart. He could tell right then she was his kind of woman. It made him happy just to be around her. Sidney said, "Hold that thought while you're deciding if you're going or staying. You can't leave and take Rosa with you. That's out of the question." Sidney needed the kind of happiness Rosa filled the house with. Uncle Alex said, "I don't feel comfortable living at your house. Everyone there has a job doing something, but me, I'd be miserable if I'm not working. All I've ever known is working on a ship." Sidney asked him to let her think about it, and they would talk again.

That night, Sidney prayed to God that he would help her find a way to keep Uncle Alex close to her. She told God she just needed a good idea that would help her find a job Uncle Alex would enjoy. She knew Uncle Alex didn't have much self-confidence and didn't believe he was capable of doing anything new. A few days passed as Sidney waited for an answer to her prayers, but none came, and time was running out. At first, she feared God was trying to tell her it would be best for him to go back to the sea. She was looking for Uncle Alex, when she saw him in the backyard, as usual, playing with Brian and Blake. This was something he had done every day since he arrived. Then, as if a bolt of lightning hit her, Sidney understood. God had been giving her the answer all along. She just hadn't been listening close enough. Maybe he could look after the children's home. He would know more than just about anyone how an orphanage needed to be run. She stopped right there and gave thanks to God, not only for answering her prayer but his patience with her while she took the hint.

When Uncle Alex went in for lunch, Sidney asked to speak to him, in the living room first. She told him about the idea of him being in charge of the children's home. She was eager to hear what he thought. He said, "Let's wait until after lunch." That would give him a chance to think about it. After lunch, Sidney could hardly contain her enthusiasm as she quietly waited for his decision. He looked at her and said, "I can tell you're really excited about this."

"Honestly, I don't know if I'm qualified to do an important job like that." Sidney said, "Who could possibly be better qualified than someone who lived in one and likes kids?" He knew what he wished were different when he was there. Maybe this was his chance to make things better for the children there now. Sidney told him not to make any decision until they went to the home. He could check it out and meet the children. He liked that idea and asked when they could go. Sidney said, "Right now, if you want to." He replied, "There's no time like the present."

Sidney asked Uncle Alex if he knew how to drive a car. He told her no. There wasn't much use for a car at sea. Sidney knew that made sense; he had been at sea since he was fifteen. They would have Joe drive them. Brandon walked in as she was explaining Joe could drive them. He asked, "Drive you where?" Sidney said, "We're going to the children's home so Uncle Alex can take a look at it." Brandon said, "Don't bother Joe. I'll drive you over." He liked going to the

# RAINBOWS ARE BETTER

home, anyway. Uncle Alex said, "You have a deal." Sidney asked for a minute to get ready. Uncle Alex asked Brandon what she was talking about; she looked ready. Brandon said, "She always puts her hair up and wears sweats and tennis shoes to go there." Uncle Alex asked, "Why does she do that?" Brandon laughed and said, "You'll see when we get there." Uncle Alex said, "I'm glad I'm wearing my sweats then." Brandon quipped, "Me too."

Sidney returned, saying, "I'm ready now." Uncle Alex told her she looked so cute like that. He said, "You should always wear your hair up, you look really beautiful that way." Sidney didn't blush for once. It felt good to have her uncle say something so nice to her. She just said "Thank you" and walked proudly to the car. When they arrived, Uncle Alex sat in the car for a moment, just staring at the building. Sidney understood how he felt, because she had felt the same way the first time she went there. She told him to believe her, once he was inside, he would be fine. She held out her petite hand and assured him he would see what she meant. Uncle Alex took her hand and got out of the car. He never imagined going inside one of those places again. Sidney said, "I didn't, either, but my good friend Sal talked me into it before he died. I had to finish building it and then oversee it for him and his wife, Mona. I could never have refused Sal. Not after all he had done for me. I think he knew that was what I needed to do in order to heal. It helped me get past the bad memories I had of an orphanage."

Uncle Alex asked, "Is this the orphanage you were in?" Sidney answered, "Yes and no. Sal built this building and moved the orphanage I lived in to this lovely place. The orphanage I was in was awful. It was located in Harlem. You should have seen it before I had it renovated and gave it to the community. Now it's a recreational facility." Uncle Alex said, "You've been a busy little girl and a very generous one too." Sidney said, "It's all thanks to Angel, Sal, and Mac. They, all three, made everything possible. My life has been blessed by all three of them." Uncle Alex said, "Maybe we should go in and look the place over." He knew, if she had anything to do with it, it couldn't be a bad place.

As they walked through the door, the children spotted Sidney and ran to her. They wrapped their little arms around her and started laughing. One by one, they took turns giving her a hug. Uncle Alex said, "Boy, are they ever glad to see her." Brandon said, "She does more than donate money to this place. She donates her time and love to the children. She even set up a savings account for each child. For every A they get on their report card, she gives them five dollars to deposit into that account. For every B, they get two dollars, and for every C, they get fifty cents. She has a different set of rules for those with learning disabilities. That way, she encourages them all to do the best they can. There's no doubt that she loves these children. I know she'll make a wonderful mother someday, that is, if I can talk her into it." Uncle Alex chuckled and said, "How about me giving you a helping hand?" Brandon said, "All help will be greatly appreciated." He certainly wasn't doing very well on his own. Uncle Alex winked at him and said, "I think you're doing better than you know." Brandon smiled, letting Uncle Alex know he really hoped so.

Sidney told Uncle Alex he should come over and meet the children. The headmistress came into the room. She thought Sidney was there. The children never squealed in such delight unless it was her. Sidney told her she would like for her and the rest of the staff to meet her Uncle Alex. They had a staff meeting in the nursery, where they could keep an eye on the babies. Brandon was reading stories to the rest of the children. Sidney told them, if her Uncle Alex would agree to it, she was going to put him in charge of overseeing the home. He would fill in for her and the duties she performed, to keep the home running smoothly. One of the workers asked, "Does that mean you'll stop coming to see the children?" Sidney said, "No, that won't change, I'll still be here for visitation days. We'll just have one more person coming with us when we all come." Everyone felt better knowing that, because the children loved Sidney so much. They reassured Uncle Alex they would do all they could to help him get started.

Uncle Alex was a good reader of people. He could tell Sidney had done a good job when she hired these people. They all seemed extremely caring and kind. There was one lady he felt strange about.

# RAINBOWS ARE BETTER

He couldn't put his finger on it yet, but he knew he would keep an eye on her. He explained his feeling about her to Sidney. Sidney said, "That's exactly what I need you to do. Does that mean you'll take the job?" Uncle Alex had decided to try it for a while but only if Sidney would agree to fire him if she didn't like the way he was doing things. Sidney said, "Not a chance." If she didn't like the way he was doing something, she would tell him, and they would discuss it. The same was to go for him. If he didn't like something she was doing, he needed only to tell her, and they would discuss that too. Uncle Alex agreed to this arrangement. It was just the way he would have done things. She was his niece, all right. The next few days, Uncle Alex and Sidney spent a lot of time together. She was getting him acquainted with his new job. It worked out well for Uncle Alex. After lunch every day, he and Rosa would go to the home together and play with the children. He continued checking up on the lady he was concerned about. The people at the orphanage adored both of them. The employees at the home told Sidney on one of her visits they thought Uncle Alex and Rosa made a cute couple. Sidney agreed with them because she had thought so from the very beginning.

CHAPTER 24

*Can't Hide from Love*

As time went by, Sidney began to have feelings for Brandon, the kind she didn't think she could have again. Not after Shade died. Like the old saying goes, "Time heals all wounds." One morning, Brandon didn't show up for breakfast and didn't show up for work, either. Sidney knew right away something was wrong. After all, he never missed breakfast. She called him at home, but there was no answer. She was getting very worried. She wondered why he hadn't called like he always did, even if he was only going to be late for breakfast. She started pacing the floor, trying to think where to start looking for him. What if something had happened to him? After all, she knew what happened to everyone else she had loved. The minute she thought that, she knew for the first time she was really in love with him. She had tears come to her eyes. What if she had waited too long to admit he was the one? What if something had happened to him? She would never have the opportunity to tell him how she felt. She picked up a tissue to wipe away the tears, when the phone rang.

She ran to the phone, yelling, "I'll get it." She said, "Hello," and much to her relief, it was Brandon on the other end. She asked him where he was. He explained how sorry he was he hadn't called. He got a call during the night. It was his brother telling him his dad had a heart attack. He went straight to the airport and flew home. He felt he had to be with his dad and his mom. Sidney asked how his dad was doing. He responded, "Not very well. They still don't know if he'll make it." Sidney told him he had done the right thing and not to worry about anything there. She said, "Stay as long as you need to."

When Uncle Alex walked in, he could see how upset she was. He asked her what was wrong. Sidney relayed what Brandon said on the phone. Uncle Alex said, "You really love that guy, don't you?" Sidney looked at him with a shocked look on her face. Uncle Alex said, "Yes, I've noticed how much you care for him. I don't think Brandon knows, though." He asked Sidney if she was going to go be with him. Sidney said, "I don't know if he would want me to." Uncle Alex explained that everyone knew how he felt about her. He felt sure Brandon would love to have her there. Sidney said, "Maybe you're right. I'll ask him first, to be sure."

Sidney tried calling his family's home, and there was no answer. She didn't think to ask what hospital his father was in, so she couldn't call him. She decided to wait. If it was meant to be, he would call her. Sure enough, about an hour later, Brandon called to remind her of some accounts that needed her attention. Sidney summoned up all her courage to ask him if he wanted her to go there and be with him. Brandon was overjoyed at the prospect of having her there. He wondered, did this mean she did care for him on a personal level? She said, "I'll be there as soon as I can." She got the name of the hospital and a phone number she could reach him at. When Brandon hung up, he was smiling ear to ear. His mother asked him what he was so happy about. He told her the woman he loved and was going to marry was coming there to be with him. He was assuming a lot by telling her that, but that was the way he felt. He knew, in his heart, she had to love him. Otherwise, she would never go running to his side like this.

Sidney hurriedly took care of the transfers she wanted to make then went upstairs to pack. Uncle Alex asked her if there was anything he could do to help. She said, "Yes, there is. Would you explain to everyone what has happened to Brandon's dad? Then, if you don't mind, ask Joe if he can drive me to the airport as soon as I'm packed." Uncle Alex said, "Of course," and he would also ride to the airport, with her. She said, "thanks Uncle Alex, you're a sweetheart." She decided to take enough clothes to last a week. In the midst of packing, she called the airport and asked if there was a flight leaving right away. They informed her they were booked solid for at least two or three days. She asked about standby or first class. They told her first class would be the best bet. They could put her on a flight in about two hours. Sidney said, "I'll take it."

Sidney finished her packing and got dressed. Uncle Alex asked her if there was anything he could do while she was gone. She thanked him but couldn't think of anything offhand. Uncle Alex told her not to forget her laptop. She thanked him for reminding her. She didn't think she could get along without her computer. It was only a two-and-a-half-hour flight, but Sidney felt like it was forever. When they arrived, Sidney called a taxi and had him take her to the hospital.

When she arrived, Brandon was in the lobby, waiting for her. She asked, "What are you doing down here?" He answered, "Uncle Alex called me and told me when to expect you." He took her in his arms and gave her another one of those breathtaking kisses until she was weak in the knees. He told her he wanted her to agree to marry him. Sidney replied, "Wouldn't it be better to wait until your father is better before we talk about that?" Brandon said, "No. There's no time like the present." He didn't want to wait and chance something going wrong. He loved her, and he hoped she loved him, so now was as good a time as any. Sidney said, "It's true, I do love you, and I'll marry you as soon as your dad is better." He said, "That may never happen."

Brandon was determined to marry her no matter what. He pulled a small box out of his pocket. He had been carrying an engagement ring in his pocket for several months. He had been waiting for the right time to give it to her, and this was the time. Sidney's eyes nearly popped out of their sockets when she saw the ring. She told Brandon it was the most beautiful ring she had ever seen. She questioned, if he didn't think the diamond was a wee bit large. He explained he wanted her to look at that diamond and know that his love for her was very large. Now, all they needed was to find a justice of the peace and make it legal. Sidney said, "Okay, but I want to have a real wedding when we get home, with our whole family there." Brandon said, "That's a deal, now on to the justice of the peace."

## RAINBOWS ARE BETTER

The justice of the peace informed them they needed a marriage license. In order to get a marriage license, they needed a blood test first. Then, there would be a three-day waiting period. Brandon tried to talk him into skipping all that, but no deal. The justice said, "Don't be in such a big fizz. I'll be happy to perform your ceremony when you have a proper marriage license." When they went back to the hospital, they went to the lab and had a blood test done. They would have their test results in about three or four hours. Brandon wanted to know if they could speed it up. Sidney said, "Three or four hours will be just fine." She looked at Brandon and said, "I'm not going to change my mind. We need time to think about what we're doing and how we're going to do it." Brandon said, "When the lady is right, she's right. Three or four hours will be fine."

Brandon told Sidney he was sorry he hadn't introduced her to his family yet. Sidney said, "They do know about me, don't they?" Brandon said, "Of course, I told them." He told them she was coming and he was going to marry her. Sidney asked, "Did you also tell them I'm biracial?" He answered, "No, that's not an issue, so why should I mention it?" Sidney said, "I think you should have told them so they wouldn't be taken by surprise." Brandon asked, "What do you want me to say? I'm in love with this girl, but she's Black and White. Knowing them, they'd expect you to be Black and White, spotted or striped. I love you, and it doesn't matter to me what anyone else on earth thinks about it. It's nobody's business but our own. If you want to meet my family, I'll introduce you, but personally, I don't care what they think. I know I could never be happy with anyone else." Sidney kissed him and said, "I love you so much. I just thought it might go smoother if you had told them I'm biracial."

Sidney wanted to get this over with. She hoped they would like her one one-hundredth as much as she loved Brandon. When he introduced Sidney to his family, things got very quiet for what felt like forever. Then, his dad took Sidney's hand and said, "I couldn't be happier. Brandon, you certainly have good taste in women." Brandon's mother, on the other hand, was clearly upset, and so were the rest of his family. Brandon's mother wanted to speak to Brandon alone. Brandon said, "No way, Mom." He told her he loved Sidney more than life and nothing she could ever say would change that. If she wanted to say something, she had better be able to say it in front of his fiancée. His mother stormed out of the room, followed by the rest of his family.

Brandon's dad told Sidney and Brandon not to worry; he would straighten everything out with them. He thought they were just confused about what was really important. Before his heart attack, so was he, but now everything was perfectly clear to him. When he had his heart attack, he knew he saw God. He also knew that might sound crazy to them. God told him all that mattered in this world was how much good we did and how much we loved one another. Sidney took his hand in hers, and said, "I don't think you're crazy." She knew, if he said he saw God, he did. She also knew that the greatest thing anyone could do in their lives was to love one another. Brandon's dad thanked her for believing him. He said, "I knew you were a good person the minute I laid eyes on you." Even if he couldn't change the minds of the rest of family, they both had his blessings. More importantly, they had each other. He told them, he was getting very tired and needed to rest. He suggested they go somewhere and spend some time together. He was anxious to get to know his new, soon-to-be daughter-in-law, after his nap. He was just too tired to visit anymore without resting first. Brandon said, "That sounds like a good idea to me." He turned to Sidney and said, "How about some dinner?" Sidney kissed Brandon's dad on the cheek then turned to Brandon and said, "That sounds good to me too."

Brandon took Sidney to a quiet little restaurant where they could spend some time alone. He asked the maître d' if they could be seated in a quiet, secluded booth. The maître d' seated them at the back corner, in a circular booth where you couldn't see them. Brandon thanked him and gave him a nice tip. Sidney asked Brandon if they really needed to be so secluded. Brandon answered, "Yes, we do." He had wanted to spend some private time with her since he first started working for her. Sidney had to laugh. She asked him why he didn't say so. Brandon told her, if she remembered correctly, he did try to tell her. Every time he started to say anything along those lines, she put a stop to it in a hurry. She blushed and admitted she was afraid he was right. In all fairness, though, she genuinely wasn't ready then. Brandon told her he had no way of knowing when or even if she would ever be ready. It wasn't until Uncle Alex assured him she was interested that he had the courage to buy the ring. He said, "I knew when you came here Uncle Alex was right."

Sidney couldn't believe Uncle Alex told him she was interested. Brandon told her Uncle Alex also advised him he should let her know how he felt. Sidney said, "I never told Uncle Alex how I felt about you. Except the time I agreed with him that you were a special young man." Brandon said, "What difference does all that make now? Now, that we're finally together." If Uncle Alex hadn't told him and she hadn't gone there to be with him, Brandon might never have had the courage to ask her to marry him, again. Sidney said, "You're absolutely right. I don't care what it took to get us to this point. I'm just happy to be here." Sidney asked if he thought they should call Uncle Alex and tell him the good news. They'd let him tell the others. Brandon said, "Later, not now." He wrapped her in his arms and kissed her with all the passion in his soul. This was all he wanted to do for now. He thought they had waited long enough for this moment and kissed her again and again.

They both felt as though they were floating on a cloud. They were both experiencing the most peaceful feeling either of them had ever comprehended. It was as if they were, for this moment in time, the only two people on the planet. Sidney felt like her head was reeling and the only thing touching her was Brandon. It felt like the booth and the room had disappeared. There was nothing but time and space, plus the two of them. She knew, without a doubt, this was her soul mate. The one God had always intended for her to be with for the rest of her life. When the waiter went to their table, it was like being shocked back into reality when he spoke. Brandon ordered for both of them. Sidney usually liked ordering for herself. This time, she was glad he took care of it. She couldn't concentrate on food at this point.

To think, this wonderful man had been right there, under her nose, all this time. Yet she was just now realizing how terrific he really was. He was never judgmental, but always kind, thoughtful, considerate, and compassionate. Now, for the first time, she realized he was also handsome, romantic, and very sexy. How could she have been so blind? She thought, no one in their right mind could ask for more than this. She knew he was funny, religious, and open-minded and loved children; what could there be left that could possibly make him any more perfect? Brandon, on the other hand, had no doubt whatsoever that Sidney was the most wonderful person he had ever met. He had known this since the day she hired him. He had loved her from that day to this and knew he always would. She was the kind of person who only got better with time. He felt like the luckiest man alive. Just to be near her like this was sheer heaven.

Sidney and Brandon decided they would get their marriage license after they ate. They could get married when they returned home. They had their dinner then went to City Hall and applied for their license. When they were done, they went back to the hospital. It was there that they called Uncle Alex to share their good news. When he answered the phone, he sounded almost as giddy as they were. Sidney told him Brandon had asked her to marry him and she had accepted. He said, "That's great, I'm getting married too." Sidney was shocked for a moment then asked, "You and Rosa?" He said, "Yeah, me and Rosa, who else?" Sidney told him that was the most wonderful news he could've given her. She assured him she would tell Brandon the good news. They talked for a while and decided, when they got home, they would have a double wedding. Sidney told Uncle Alex how much she loved him and to tell Rosa she loved her too. She promised to call the next day and talk some more about the arrangements. She asked him to tell Joe and Su Yen the good news about all four of them.

They went upstairs to see Brandon's dad before Brandon took Sidney to her hotel room. When they walked in the room, he was wide awake and ready for a nice visit. He told Sidney he wanted her to tell him everything she could about herself. Sidney said, "Why don't you go first and tell me about yourself?" He said, "If I didn't get worn out so easily, I would. Brandon can tell you about me." He knew he didn't have much time, and he really wanted to know about this girl his son was going to marry. Sidney told him a short version of her life story, including how Brandon had found her long-lost uncle. He told Brandon how proud he was to learn what a nice young man he turned out to be. He was also happy he had chosen so well. He told them, if he were a young man, before he got married, of course, he would have wanted to marry Sidney himself. He let Brandon know how lucky he thought he was. Sidney blushed a little and said, "I'm the lucky one."

Brandon's dad said, "We're all lucky to have had this chance to meet before it's too late." Sidney tried to tell him he could get better but he had to try hard and pray a lot. He looked at Sidney and said, "I know my destiny." He only had two things to do before he left this world. He was happy to have had the chance to accomplish these things. He was looking forward to going home and being with his father in heaven. Brandon said, "That's enough of that kind of talk." Brandon explained how much his mom needed him. He smiled and told Brandon his mother would be just fine without him. He was absolutely certain about that. He didn't want to depress Brandon. He just wanted him to understand how happy he was. He didn't want them to be concerned about him. He wanted them both to be happy for him and know what a wonderful place he would be in.

Earlier, Brandon's dad had spoken to Brandon's mother, and she refused to be understanding about their wedding. Someday, maybe she would understand. They would have to be patient with her. Sidney told Brandon's father not to worry; they would be as patient as they needed to be. He took Sidney's hand and said, "I knew I could count on both of you." He told Brandon he should hang on to this one; she was definitely a keeper. He told them he knew they would be happy. He felt sure they would spend the rest of their lives together. He hoped they would have many children. He promised them they could count on him to keep an eye on them from wherever he would be. He told them he would love to visit with them all night but he was very tired and needed to rest. He insisted they should go have some fun. They told him they would be back after he had a good night's rest.

Brandon leaned down to kiss his dad's forehead and said, "I love you, Dad." This was the first time Brandon could remember feeling this close to his father. Sidney was happy to see Brandon make peace with his father. It was such a shame that it took them this long to realize how much they meant to each other. Even so, it was better now than not at all. Sidney and Brandon walked quietly out of the room. Neither one of them said anything, but they both knew this could be the last time to see Brandon's dad alive. Suddenly Brandon turned and went back into the room, just as his father was taking his last breaths on earth. He cradled his father in his arms and comforted him as he passed from this life to the next. Sidney watched and knew the pain Brandon felt. She also knew how much this time Brandon had with his father had meant to him.

Sidney picked up the phone and called the rest of his family to let them know they should come to the hospital. The rest of Mr. Worthington's family couldn't get there in time, but at least he wasn't alone at the end. Brandon looked at Sidney with tears in his eyes and told her he wished he could have known his father like this a long time ago. Sidney said, "Be thankful that you got to know him at all. Some people never do." Brandon knew she was right; it just felt like such a waste. Sidney kissed him and said, "It was a waste, but not a total waste." As Brandon stood there, holding on to Sidney for dear life, they were preparing to take his father to the morgue. He asked if they could wait until the rest of the family arrived. Just as he finished saying that, his family walked through the door.

Brandon's mother asked him not to embarrass her in front of everyone. He should stop acting that way around Sidney. Brandon started to tell her to mind her own business, but Sidney stopped him. She apologized if they were embarrassing her. Brandon told his mother they were leaving and he would see her later. When they left the hospital, he asked Sidney why she stopped him from telling his mother how things were and how they were going to be. Sidney told him his mother had just lost her husband and it was no time to argue. After all, they had promised his father they would be patient with her. Brandon told Sidney he was so thankful to have her there to keep him calm and help him get through this. She hugged him and assured him he would never be alone again. She would always be with him from this day forward, and he would never feel unloved again. Not as long as she could breathe.

That night, when Brandon took Sidney to her hotel room, she asked him if he wanted to spend the night with her. He said, "I thought you wanted to be a virgin on your wedding night." She looked deep into his eyes and said, "We'll say our vows to each other right here and now. It will be our wedding night." She added, "If the vows don't mean anything to us tonight, they wouldn't at a wedding ceremony, either." With that said, they professed their love for each other and vowed to be as one from that day forward. Sidney told Brandon she always believed the family who prayed together stayed together, so could they pray together now. With that, they both knelt and prayed for God to bless their union. As they did, they both experienced a warm energy surrounding them. This energy let them know this union had been blessed by God himself. Then, Brandon took Sidney into his arms and kissed her with all the love and passion in his soul. They both felt a tingling, like electricity, flowing through their bodies. As they stood there, entwined in each other's arms, they genuinely felt they were as one.

Whatever was lacking in their lives before had forever been erased. For the first time, they were truly complete. For the longest time, they stood there in each other's arms, embracing and enjoying this new and wonderful feeling. Finally, Sidney excused herself to get ready for the night of her life. She went into the bedroom and took out a white satin negligee. As she slipped it on and felt it caress her skin, she could hardly wait to feel Brandon's arms around her again. She hurriedly brushed her teeth, brushed her hair, and dabbed a small amount of perfume in all the right places. She turned and walked slowly toward the door, suddenly realizing this was the night that would determine the rest of her life. She reached for the door handle, thinking nothing had ever felt so right before. She opened the door, and Brandon turned around to behold his bride. She absolutely took his breath away. He wondered how such a beautiful woman could actually love him so much.

Sidney wasted no time going to his waiting arms and embracing him with all her body and soul. They spent the rest of the night, loving each other as they had never known possible. In the early hours of the morning, they finally fell asleep in each other's arms. They slept the most blissful sleep known to humankind. Neither one of them had ever imagined this much total happiness to be possible. When they awoke, they were famished and ready for a huge breakfast. Brandon called room service.

When the food arrived, it was like every mouthful had more flavor and nourishment than ever before. It replenished their depleted yet strangely energized bodies. They were both experiencing feelings that were indescribably wonderful. As they finished their meal, they stood up, took one look at each other, and raced each other to the bedroom for round 2. Afterward, they were lying there in a blissful glow. They felt positive there couldn't be a happier couple in all the world. After a brief discussion about who loved who the most, they decided they should get ready for the first day of their new life together.

Brandon suggested maybe they should help make the funeral arrangements. For a moment, that put a damper on the mood, but they were both too happy to let it last. Brandon was happy to know he would have someone who loved him go with him. Brandon needed to go back to his hotel room to change clothes. Sidney told him he should check out and move in with her. He most definitely was anxious to do that. They kissed, and he assured her he would be back shortly.

When Brandon arrived at his hotel room, he quickly gathered his things together. He couldn't wait to return to his beautiful bride. He was about to climb in the shower, when the phone rang. It was his mother. She wanted to know where he had been all night. He informed her that was none of her business. He asked what she wanted. She explained she wanted him to stay with her the rest of the time he would be in town. He said, "I can't do that." She responded, "It's that woman, isn't it?" She asked him if he had spent the night with that shameless hussy. Brandon told his mother he wasn't going to discuss this matter with her. It wasn't any of her business. He told her he and Sidney would be over in a little while to take her to the funeral home. His mom became angry and told

## RAINBOWS ARE BETTER

him she didn't want him to bring his nigger slut into her home. She wasn't about to have Sidney going to the funeral home with them. She added, "After all, that slut is not now nor ever will be a member of our family." Surely his mother couldn't know how much she hurt her son with the horrible, vile, and loathsome language she used about the woman he loved more than life. Brandon felt more furious with his mother than he ever knew possible. He told her, she better never talk about Sidney like that again. He informed her that he and Sidney were married. If Sidney had no business there, neither did he. His mother began to scream at him. How could he do such a horrible thing? Was it his mission in life to embarrass her as much as he possibly could? She screeched he was no son of hers, and she didn't want him at the funeral. She cursed him and said, "I never want to see you again." She added, as far as she was concerned, he was dead too. Brandon slumped into a nearby chair and said, "Mom, you don't mean that." She shrieked, "Yes, I do!" She repeated she never wanted to see or hear from him again. He slammed down the phone, hanging up on her. He wanted to keep from saying anything he might later be sorry for.

Brandon didn't know what to do. He knew one thing for sure: he could never live his life without Sidney. If that meant giving up his family, so be it. He knew his family had never cared for him, anyway. He took his shower and packed his things. Then, he went back to Sidney's hotel room. There, he found Sidney ready and waiting for him. She looked so beautiful standing there in her black silk suit. He didn't understand how his mother could feel the way she did. He didn't know how to break the news to Sidney. The last thing he wanted to do was to hurt her feelings, and he knew it would. Sidney took one look at Brandon and asked what was wrong. He told her he didn't want to stay for the funeral. They should pack up and go home.

Sidney asked him if he told his mother they were married. He said, "Yes, I did. I couldn't help myself." Sidney assured him it would be all right. She told Brandon, if he wanted to go to the funeral alone, she would understand and wait right there for him. Brandon told her it wasn't that simple; his mother had disowned him. She ordered him not to go to the funeral. Sidney took Brandon in her arms and said, "I'm so sorry your mother said that to you." She told him, if she caused this, she was so sorry. She let him know she would understand if he wanted to call the marriage off. Brandon said, "No, definitely not. I couldn't live without you. You're the only thing in life worth living for. I implore you, please promise you will never leave me." Sidney said, "I'll never leave you, unless you want me to." Brandon said, "Good, because I'll never let you go." They knelt in prayer and asked God to be with Brandon's mom and help her understand how much they loved each other and to bring her peace.

They kissed each other passionately and agreed they would go home. Brandon knew there was nothing he could do for his father now. He also knew his father would understand. Sidney asked Brandon if he would like to go to the funeral home early before his mother arrived. That way, he could say his last goodbye to his father. He told her no. He had already said goodbye to his father while he was still living. That was when it actually mattered. He said, "What good would it do now? He's already in heaven, and that body is nothing more than a cold clay body at the funeral home. Sidney told him that was the way she felt too. They packed her things and went to the airport to go home together.

Once they were on the plane, Sidney was encouraged by the change in Brandon's mood. He was much happier and much more relaxed. This change in him made her feel happier too. All the way home, they chatted about the wedding plans and how much they were looking forward to seeing everyone at home. Sidney said, "I think we should tell them we've already exchanged our vows. That way, it won't seem strange when you move in before the wedding." Brandon agreed.

As they were going home, the flight seemed much shorter now that they were together. It was a matter of fact; everything seemed better, easier, happier, and more meaningful now. Sidney told Brandon how she felt. He agreed that everything was better now, and he felt so much happier. Sidney said, "I think that's the way love should be. It should always make you feel better than you've felt before. If it doesn't feel that good, you've probably made a big mistake." With that said, Brandon took Sidney's hand, and she laid her head on his strong but tender shoulder. That was how they spent the rest of the flight.

A few minutes later, their plane landed, and Sidney felt a surge of excitement. She could hardly wait to see Uncle Alex and share all their happy news. Brandon could see the excitement in her eyes. That gave him a sense of excitement too. When they got off the plane, there was Uncle Alex, Rosa, Su Yen, Joe, Brian, Blake, and Lily, all waiting for them. There were hugs and kisses from everyone. This was the most wonderful homecoming they could've wished for. As they picked up the luggage, there was a lot of chatter about the last few days. All the way home, they laughed and discussed the wedding plans.

Suddenly Uncle Alex apologized to Brandon for being so insensitive to his feelings after the recent loss of his father. Brandon preferred everyone being happy about their wedding instead of worrying about his father's death. He told them he and his father had made their peace before he died, and he felt good about that. Sidney could tell, by the expression on Brandon's face, that he didn't want to talk about his dad or his family problems right now. Wanting to spare him any more pain, she said, "For the time being, let's celebrate the good things in life and not worry about anything unpleasant." They all agreed that was a better idea and continued to chat about other things. Brandon gave Sidney a big hug and quietly said, "Thank you."

The days were going quickly now that the wedding plans were underway. They were trying to keep it nice but simple. As wedding plans usually go, it just kept getting bigger and more complex. Sidney and Brandon were making money head over heels in the midst of all this activity. Sidney told Brandon it was a darn good thing they were making so much money. They were all happy to be working on the task at hand. Rosa went around singing all the time. Not that it was unusual for her to sing, it was just all the time now. There was no doubt how happy she was. Finally, the big day was about to arrive. They all felt satisfied, knowing everything had been taken care of.

CHAPTER 25

## *Wedding Bells Will Finally Ring*

The day of the wedding, everyone was scurrying about like chickens with a fox in the henhouse. All, that is, but Sidney. She was sitting quietly in her bedroom, on the window seat overlooking the backyard. She was admiring how beautiful everything looked and giving thanks for such a marvelous day. She couldn't help wishing her parents and friends could be there. She knew they would be there in spirit, but she wished it could be in person. After all, this was a really big day for Uncle Alex, Rosa, Brandon, and herself. She walked over and looked at the white lace gown hanging over the closet door and wondered if it were the kind of dress her mother or Angel would have picked for her. It didn't matter now. In about an hour, she would be wearing that dress and walking down the aisle to publicly marry the man of her dreams. She couldn't shake a feeling of loneliness that swept over her like a shadow. She kept telling herself it was alright to feel this way since the people she loved most in this world, up until now, had passed on. She felt sure this feeling would go away as soon as she saw Brandon again. That very moment, there was a knock at her door.

When she opened it, there stood Uncle Alex. Sidney threw her arms around his neck and hung on for dear life. He said, "I thought you might be feeling this way right about now." With big tears forming in her large brown eyes, she said, "I don't know what's wrong with me. You'd think this would be the happiest day of my life."

Uncle Alex said, "Why don't you come downstairs with me, and we'll have a little uncle-to-niece talk."

Uncle Alex and Sidney went hand in hand out to the fishpond so as not to be disturbed. They sat side by side on the glider overlooking the fishpond. Uncle Alex started by saying "I can't thank you enough for the life you've given me. I've never known anything but loneliness and sadness my whole life, until there was you. I never imagined the kind of happiness I've known since that day you walked through that hospital door. I had no family that I knew of and no one I could call my friend. Oh, I knew a few people I worked with, but I didn't even try to make friends. I didn't think anyone would like me. After all, my own parents gave me away. I felt as though there was something wrong with me. Now, I have a lovely niece and nephew-in-law, who love me. A beautiful lady who also loves me and wants to be my wife. I have the wonderful extended family you gave me, with Joe, Su Yen, and their terrific kids. Now, on top of all that, I'll even have stepchildren and step-grandchildren of my very own. What I'm trying to say here is thank you with all my heart for giving me the gift of living and loving."

Sidney told him it had been her pleasure to give him whatever she could. She told him that he had given her more than she could put into words. Uncle Alex looked shocked by her statement. "What could I possibly have given you?" he inquired. "You already have everything." She told him there were so many things it was hard to know where to start. She said, "I know, because of you, I will forever see the world differently. I'll see it with better understanding, much more clarity, and compassion. You gave me a true sense of belonging and helped me to understand who I really am. While it's true, I've been blessed with people who have loved me and even taken care of me. It's just not the same as having your own family. You've taught me some valuable lessons."

Uncle Alex said, "Now I know you're putting me on. You're just trying to be nice. What could I have taught you?" Sidney said, "You've taught me plenty. The most important things are when you love someone, you should love them unconditionally, without reservations or being judgmental. I was ready to pass judgment on you the first time I saw you because you were White. I didn't want to deal with that. Thanks to Brandon, I thought it through and decided to go back the next day. I think the most important thing I had to learn was the difference between pride and gratitude."

"Okay," said Uncle Alex," you've lost me there." Sidney told him her whole life she had been really proud of her Black heritage. Because of him, she had learned pride was something that separates people. When he came into her life, she realized that being proud of just her Black heritage was no longer an option. She continued by saying "I admire you for having no problems being related to me, even though I'm Black." She knew now she should have been grateful, and she respected all those who made the life she had possible. She said, "I know we should be judged by the content of our heart, not the color of our skin. You brought that home to me in a way no one else ever could. I know because of you, I will never be able to look at the world in the same narrow-minded way again."

Uncle Alex looked at her and said, "Oh boy, I must be awful smart if I taught you all that, without even trying." They both laughed, and Sidney said, "You certainly are smart." Then, she continued by saying "There's more. You also helped me understand the value of money and what it means in life." Uncle Alex said, "Whoa, girl, I know I couldn't have taught you anything about money. I've never had much of that stuff, so I wouldn't know how to teach anyone about it, especially not you. Honey, I think you must have always known about money. You've certainly amassed a fortune in a short amount of time."

Sidney said, "I know I've made a lot of money, and I'm what most people would consider rich. There's so much more to it than that. When I first started making money, I did it for the security I thought it gave me, and it does. When I had a lot of money and I no longer needed to be concerned about financial security, it became a security blanket. It wasn't the money I needed. It was something else I was looking for, but I didn't know what. You taught me what more there was. Of course, the money has made the everyday things in my life easier. I don't have to worry about how I'm going to pay the bills. If I want something, I can buy it. You taught me money is only as good as you make it. You and my dear friend Mac taught me having the money is nice but sharing the money is even better. Money is only as good as the good it can do. The two possessions I have that give me the most pleasure are my little pillow my mother made for me before she died and the bed that Angel gave me when I lived with her. I would have to say Flash is my most prized possession, although I feel like I'm his possession. It's love that has all the real value in life. That's something you can't buy. You only get real love by giving it. The more you give it, the more you have. Giving love has a much-higher dividend return than any investment you could ever make. From now on, I'm going to invest more of my money in helping people. I've got more money than I'll ever need in several lifetimes. I don't need that much. There's a lot of things that need to be done in this world. I know, from Sal, I can't do everything for everybody. However, I can do a lot of good if I try." Uncle Alex said, "And I taught you all that?" Sidney kissed him on the cheek and said, "Yes, you did. You're a wonderful, happy, witty, intelligent, warm, and caring person. The best part is you didn't need money to get that way. When I thought about that, I knew right then money doesn't have nearly the value, people do. I honestly believe I always knew in my heart the lessons you taught me. Still, you helped my mind be aware of what my heart always knew." Uncle Alex hugged Sidney for a long time and then told her he was certain she had always known these things in her heart because she had such a good heart.

Uncle Alex kissed her on the forehead and said, "Now that we've discussed all that heavy stuff, let's get ready to get married, okay?" They walked, arm in arm, back to the house. Sidney went upstairs to fix her hair and makeup. She was looking through her jewelry to find a pair of earrings, when a knock came at her door. When she answered it, it was Su Yen, looking lovely in her soft pink bridesmaid dress. She asked Sidney if she needed help getting dressed. Sidney smiled and said, "I would like that very much." They found a pair of pearl-and-diamond drop earrings. Then came the time to put on the beautiful wedding dress Sidney, Rosa, and Su Yen had picked out. Sidney sat on a footstool so Su Yen could put the wedding veil atop her head. Su Yen said, "You most beautiful bride I ever see." Sidney blushed a little as she walked over to the window seat and sat down to look out. She said, "Thank you, not only for the compliment but for all the hard work you and Joe have done on the preparations for the wedding." Sidney told her it was so beautiful, she could just cry. Su Yen said, "Ms. Sidney, you no cry, you makeup run."

Sidney said, "It's been a while since I've felt this sentimental." She told Su Yen, if she didn't mind, she would like to be alone for a while. Su Yen said, "You not be long, it almost time." Flash jumped up on the window seat, next to Sidney. He somehow knew not to climb on Sidney's dress, but he knew she needed him right now. Sidney said, "Flash, my dear little friend, in a few minutes, we're going to embark on a whole new life. I hope that I do it right." Flash purred and rubbed his head on her hand. It was as if he were trying to tell her everything would be all right. She said, "You're right, Flash, it's not like anything is going to change." She knew she and Brandon were already married. This was just a ceremony to celebrate what had already happened. Sidney kissed his head and said, "My friend, it's time for me to go." She reached up and pulled the sheer curtains back so Flash could lie by the window and watch the whole thing.

Sidney turned and walked out the door and down the stairs. She saw Rosa standing by the back door, holding her bouquet. Rosa was shaking so hard. Sidney was sure she was going to shake the pedals right off the sterling roses that made up her bouquet. Rosa looked radiant in the light-blue lace dress she was wearing. Sidney had no idea how good Rosa would look in blue. It was clearly the right choice. Sidney asked Rosa if she was feeling nervous. Rosa asked, "How did you know?" Sidney answered, "Take a look at your bouquet, and you'll see how I knew." Rosa laughed and said, "I can't stop shaking." Sidney told her how lovely she looked and how happy she was she would soon be her aunt. Rosa had tears come to her eyes. Sidney said, "Oh no, none of that. You'll ruin your makeup, and you look too pretty for that." Rosa said, "You have to stop that, Ms. Sidney, or I'm going to cry for sure."

Sidney said, "Okay." Then she wrapped her arm in Rosa's and said, "Are you ready?"

# RAINBOWS ARE BETTER

"I think so," answered Rosa. With that, they walked out the door and down the aisle together. As they were walking, it dawned on Sidney, by helping Rosa, she had also helped herself. She had been feeling very nervous herself, until she became so concerned about Rosa. Sidney had another revelation. This, too, was something she had always known in her heart but hadn't consciously thought about. If you help someone else who has a problem, your own problems simply melt away. She figured God must alleviate our problems as a reward for helping others. Right before they reached the loves of their lives, Rosa whispered to Sidney, "Thank you for helping me make it down the aisle." Sidney whispered back, "Thanks for letting me hold on to you." They both smiled, and the ceremony began.

The wedding was a huge success. Everyone seemed to have a wonderful time. They danced and partied most of the night. Uncle Alex and Rosa went to the hotel by the airport to spend the night. They left on their honeymoon the next morning. They were going to Hawaii for two weeks then to Mexico for a week so Uncle Alex could meet the rest of Rosa's family. Sidney and Brandon stayed at home that night. They planned to leave the next afternoon. They had a very long honeymoon planned. They were going to spend a week each in Tahiti, Jamaica, Mexico, and then the Cayman Islands.

CHAPTER 26

# *Let the Honeymoons Begin*

Sidney and Brandon planned for a week in Mexico with Uncle Alex and Aunt Rosa. Sidney had arranged for Rosa's children and grandchildren, Su Yen, Joe, and their three children to come down for that week, as well. This was going to be a big surprise for Rosa and Uncle Alex. Sidney had arranged the festivities and put Rosa's family in charge of everything. The first two weeks of the honeymoons were just wonderful, but the best was yet to come.

Everybody arrived in Mexico ahead of Uncle Alex and Aunt Rosa. Sidney sent a limo to pick up Uncle Alex and Aunt Rosa at the airport and take them to the hotel's convention center. Sidney had reserved the center for a party. They were so surprised when they arrived, and everyone was there. Rosa's family had prepared a huge feast to celebrate the wedding of their beloved Rosa and her new husband. There was even a mariachi band. Everyone ate, sang, and danced all night. What a wonderful time they all had. Sidney had never had so much fun in her whole life.

Rosa's brother told Sidney the next night they would have a party in their village, where Rosa grew up. Sidney asked what she could do to help. He didn't think there was anything she needed to do. They would take care of everything. She asked him if she could at least buy the food. He agreed, but the ladies of the village would prepare it. She could go with the women to the marketplace and pay for the food if she really wanted to, but it wasn't necessary. Sidney asked Rosa's sister where and when she wanted to go shopping for

## RAINBOWS ARE BETTER

the food. Rosa's sister would pick Sidney up at 7:00 a.m., and they would go shopping. Sidney smiled, feeling she would be contributing something this way.

Sidney, Su Yen, and Rosa all went to the market with the other women to buy the food. This was a unique experience for Sidney and Su Yen. Rosa, on the other hand, had done this many times before and knew what it was like. Sidney loved the marketplace and watching the women picking the best foods and bargaining for the best deal. This was a far cry from anything Sidney had ever done. When the shopping was complete, they went to the village, where the preparations began. Sidney wasn't allowed to do the cooking. Nonetheless, the sheer joy of just being there and helping out was wonderful. Certainly, she had never had this much fun working before. Everyone was busy but not too busy to sing and socialize with one another. This was a warm and wonderful group of people. Su Yen thought so, too, even though she didn't speak Spanish. Sidney had to translate for her as best she could. Sidney spoke Spanish but not extremely fluently.

Shortly before everything was ready, Sidney, Su Yen, and Rosa headed back to the hotel to get ready. On the way, they stopped to purchase some clothing more appropriate for the occasion. Sidney loved the full skirts and ruffled blouses. They also bought some moccasins. The moccasins were so comfortable, it felt better than going barefoot. They purchased clothing for themselves, the kids, and the guys.

While they were getting ready, Sidney told Brandon what a wonderful time she had that day and all about everything they did. Brandon knew she had a good time because she looked so happy. Brandon and Sidney were ready in plenty of time. They went to Joe and Su Yen's room to see if they needed help with the little ones. Su Yen was happy to see them, because Lily didn't want to get ready. Su Yen knew Lily always liked doing things with Sidney. Sidney and Lily played a game while getting her ready. Lily giggled the whole time she was getting dressed. Su Yen told Sidney she was a lifesaver. For Sidney, it was a pleasure. She asked if the boys needed any help. Brian and Blake were ready and anxious to go. Sidney couldn't get over how cute they looked. They went downstairs, where they all met in the lobby.

Since there were so many of them, Sidney hired a bus for the evening. As they boarded the bus, Uncle Alex stopped and gave Sidney a big hug for all she had done to make this whole trip possible. Sidney kissed him on the cheek and told him it was her pleasure. When they arrived, the festivities began, and these went on into the night. They had such a wonderful time. They learned to do the Mexican hat dance, and they broke the piñatas that were hanging all up and down the street. They ate the most delicious food until they were stuffed. They sang and danced until they could hardly move. They all laughed until their sides hurt. What a wonderful night it had been. Sidney hated to leave. When you're having that much fun, it's hard to stop.

The children were all getting tired, and so was everyone else. Sidney, on the other hand, was wound up like an eight-day clock. Brandon could see how excited she was and decided, rather than go back to their room, he would take her out dancing and maybe a moonlight swim. He was right, and his plan was just what the doctor ordered. The moonlight swim was just the right finishing touch to a perfect day. The next day, they slept late and didn't get up until almost lunchtime, which was totally out of character for Sidney. They went to the hotel restaurant and had a wonderful brunch by a waterfall, in the pool area. Sidney looked at Brandon and told him she hoped he was having as much fun, as she was. She felt as though she was in heaven. They sat there, talking and enjoying the delicious meal that had been sat before them.

Sidney told Brandon Rosa's family was just the kind of family she had only dreamed of having. She had always wanted a really large family. She asked Brandon to promise her they would have a lot of children. She said, "I want our lives to always be as wonderful as this week has been so far." Brandon laughed and said, "I'll be happy to oblige." Then, he told her, if she wanted to hurry through their meal, they could go back to their room and get started. Sidney laughed and said, "Sounds good to me." Brandon said, "I think we should get started right away." Sidney looked deep into his eyes and said, "I'm not hungry anymore, let's go."

Like they say, time flies when you're having fun. Needless to say, the week went by very quickly. The day before they were to leave, Sidney heard on the news a large storm was moving toward the Cayman Islands. It was expected to last for several days. Brandon was busy packing a few things, when Sidney told him about the weather forecast. He said, "The past three weeks have been perfect. I guess that's not too bad." Sidney said, "Do you still want to go there?" He replied, "Not really, but if you want to, it's all right." She quizzed, "Why don't we think of somewhere else we would like to go?"

Sidney asked Brandon where he would like to go. Brandon told her he had never been much of a traveler and didn't know of any good places to go. He paused for a moment and then added there was only one place he had ever thought of going someday. Sidney asked, "Where's that?" He answered, "Tibet." Sidney squealed in delight when he said "Tibet." She told him Tibet had always been a place she wanted to visit. She had never known anyone else who wanted to go with her. Without further ado, Sidney called their travel agent and told her to make the necessary arrangements. By the next day, all the arrangements had been made. That included the guide while they were there.

When they met with Uncle Alex and Aunt Rosa, Sidney told them their new plans. Uncle Alex felt a little uneasy about this turn of events. He asked her if she was sure about going there. She hugged him and reassured him they would have a dependable guide and they would stay in contact with them the whole time. They all went to a farewell party in the village before leaving the next morning. Sidney told them the time she had spent in this magical place would forever be one of her most cherished memories. It was so hard to say goodbye.

The next day, Sidney and Brandon boarded a plane to Los Angeles. On the flight, they read some books about Tibet. Brandon suggested they look on the internet for any information they might find there. Sidney said, "I'm way ahead of you. I picked up a CD, with information and maps of the area." Brandon told her she could check that out while he read about the customs and laws of Tibet. During their stay in Los Angeles, before flying overseas, Sidney bought warm clothing for the trip. She bought everything she could think of, including down-filled parkas and thermal silk underwear. She found cold weather clothing you could wear at Antarctica and still stay warm. She also purchased a global positioning system device, just for good measure. They bought sleeping bags and small pup tents to keep them warm in the coldest weather. She even bought battery-operated socks to keep their feet warm. She shipped their warm weather clothing home. She knew they wouldn't need those where they were going.

Her travel agent faxed her a list of items that would make their trip more pleasurable. Sidney told the travel agent to extend their stay to three weeks so they would have plenty of time. The excitement of the trip was building. That night, they ordered a meal fit for a king. Sidney looked at Brandon and told him this was the last time they would be enjoying modern luxury for a while. He laughed and said, "I can take it, if you can." Sidney said, "Oh, I can take it, all right. You seem to forget where I came from. After living in that horrible orphanage for so many years, this will be a walk in the park." All night, Sidney grew more and more anxious. She kept feeling this was going to be the most important trip of her life. It was as though all the spirits that surrounded her were just as excited about the trip as she was. There was no doubt in her mind this was the right thing to do and the right place to go.

# Chapter 27

## *The Trip to Tibet*

The next day, they boarded the flight that would take them to India. From there, they would take trains, ride horses, and travel by foot to get to Tibet. Sidney had never felt this excited about going anywhere in her life. Brandon was excited, but he could tell his excitement was pale by comparison. When they arrived in India, they were met by their guide. His name was Yuan Jianping, but he told them they could call him Ace. He explained Ace was the nickname his American friend gave him when he was a small child. Sidney and Brandon liked this guy from the moment they met him. He oozed with confidence and was one very funny fellow. He would be their constant companion and best friend on this trip. He kept them laughing the whole time. He taught them about his country, with a wonderful sense of humor. It was hard to believe he had such a strong spirit and good sense of humor, considering he came from such a harsh environment and lifestyle.

At the end of the train ride, they rode in a Hummer vehicle to their next destination. Ace took them to a small town near the base of the Himalayan mountains. This was the town Ace called home when he wasn't guiding people through the mountains. They would start their climb the next morning. This night, they would have good food and a warm place to sleep. The people who lived there were very gracious and friendly.

The next day, they got an early start. Ace wanted to cover as much ground as possible the first day on horseback. He knew, when they got to the high country, Sidney and Brandon would fatigue more easily and it would take longer. Ace kept warning them about the thin air higher up the mountain and how much harder it would be to breathe. Sidney had been in the mountains before and knew he was right. Brandon, on the other hand, had never done anything like this before. He didn't have a clue as to what to expect. He knew, if Ace told them it was so, it was really so.

By nightfall, they had made it two-thirds of the way to their next destination. Sidney was amazed that breathing wasn't more difficult than it was. The air here was the freshest and cleanest air she had ever had the privilege of breathing. The air was cold and brisk, but it was so clean, it felt as though it saturated your lungs with pure oxygen. If anything, she felt more energized by this strange phenomenon. Ace was surprised by her reaction; he knew that was how he felt, but he was accustomed to the thin air. Brandon was a little more tired than usual, but even he wasn't experiencing what Ace knew most outsiders felt. They fixed their evening meal and sat near the campfire, where they discussed their plans for the next day. They went to bed early so they could get an early start the next morning.

The next morning, Sidney was up as dawn was breaking. She felt so invigorated by this wonderful, clean air. She never realized before how polluted the air was everywhere she had been, until now. She thought to herself, *This must be the way God gave us this world—pure, clean, quiet, and spacious.* She felt sure this was what God meant for us to protect when he put us on earth. *We have undeniably made a mess of things*, she told herself. Then she built a fire and prepared breakfast. The marvelous aroma filled the air, waking Brandon and Ace. After breakfast, they continued up the mountain.

When they stopped for lunch, Sidney looked back down the mountain to a large crystal-blue lake. She called Brandon over to see it. With the ice melting and cracking, the lake looked like a large blue sapphire glistening in the sun. Ace told them the name of the lake was Koro Nor. Shortly before nightfall, they could see the beautiful buildings in the distance. With the sun setting behind those buildings, it gave them an eerie glow. It was positively breathtaking. It made you feel, for that moment, you were ascending into heaven.

## RAINBOWS ARE BETTER

Sidney wanted to press on and get there that night. Ace would not hear of it. The mountain terrain was too steep and too tricky to travel without the benefit of full daylight. He promised they would arrive the next day and that would have to be good enough. Sidney acknowledged he was right and apologized for being so impatient. Ace laughed because he knew how she felt. He explained how he had that same feeling every time he saw the sun setting behind the buildings and mountains.

The next morning, Sidney was up at the crack of dawn, filled with excitement and anticipation. At last, she would see this incredible city for herself. As she was building the fire, she wondered why she had always wanted to go to this far-off place. She had always felt it would be important to go there. Oh well, whatever the reason, her dreams were about to come true. She hurried through breakfast. She could hardly eat from all the excitement. Brandon and Ace, on the contrary, were ravenous. Ace said, "The mountain air will do that to you." Sidney packed up while Brandon and Ace finished their breakfast.

When they arrived, Sidney wanted to see everything right then. Brandon and Ace were more inclined to get settled in and cleaned up first. Again, Sidney had to agree with them because they were right. It felt good to get cleaned up. Sidney felt rejuvenated by the fresh, clean mountain water. It was like everything here was energized. It made you feel energized, as well. There was energy in the air that penetrated your being, right to your very core. It felt like a spiritual energy, one Sidney had never encountered before. She had felt God's presence before, but this was like nothing else she had ever known.

If it had not been for the sadness the people felt, this would be the most perfect place on earth. Unfortunately, because of the oppression brought by the Chinese government, the people lived in fear. They could no longer live happy and free. They could no longer enjoy their land and peaceful Buddhist religion. Sidney never thought much about how good we had things in the United States, until she witnessed what happened here. When she listened to the stories of these people, her heart felt like it would break. All these kind people wanted was to live a simple life. She felt powerless to help them. She knew all she could do was pray for them. She would also tell as many people as possible what she had learned here. Maybe if enough people knew what was going on, something could be done. They could be sure she would do all she could until they had their religion, land, and rights restored to them.

She could hardly wait for the second half of their journey. She felt more anxious than ever to meet with the monks at Swarg Ashram, in Dharmshala, India. She felt so sad for them and their people being separated like this. She wanted to see their homeland before meeting with them. She thought seeing Tibet first would give her a better understanding of what they and their people were going through. She was right. There was no other way she could ever have understood what this place felt like. It was important to know what this place meant to the people who lived there.

Sidney and Brandon met an elderly lady who had always lived there. She was the mother of sixteen children, numerous grandchildren, and even great-grandchildren. She spoke a little English and liked talking to them and telling them the history of Tibet. She was old but very alert and articulate. Even at her advanced age, she still worked very hard. These were hearty people, mostly descendants of the Mongolian race. They worked hard and got lots of exercise, walking up and down the mountainside. Sidney believed the fresh air and clean, crystal-clear water had a lot to do with it. They never ate fast foods or things that weren't good for them. The main staple in their diet was an odd concoction called tsamba. It was a mixture of butter and ground barley mixed in hot tea. At first, Sidney didn't like it, but after adding a little sugar (something Sidney brought, at the suggestion of her travel agent), it wasn't bad. Sidney thought this would make a good diet food because it was so filling, and it seemed to continue expanding after she drank it. It made her feel very full. Brandon laughed at her when she told him this. He didn't think the butter and sugar made it a good thing to help one lose weight. Brandon asked her why she cared; she was already thin. Sidney said, "I want to take as much information home with me as I can." She was still anxiously awaiting their journey to India to meet their holy men. Meanwhile, she took as many pictures as she could. She also wrote down notes about every picture she took. She didn't want to forget anything.

When they left Tibet, Sidney and Brandon both had a heavy heart. They were excited to continue their journey. At the same time, they were sad to leave this marvelous place and the extremely kind people. The next few days, they took their time and enjoyed the scenery. They took lots of photos and included Ace in many of them. They had laughed and joked all the way to India. As they approached, Dharmshala, Sidney became more excited and impatient. She asked Ace if he was sure they would be able to meet with a holy man there. Ace laughed and reassured her that everything had been arranged for them to meet with them. When they arrived in Dharmshala, Ace took them to their room and told them to get some rest. He would pick them up for dinner later. All through dinner, Sidney was preoccupied with thoughts of meeting the monks.

Sidney couldn't understand her undeniable enthusiasm to meet with them. She kept telling herself they're just human beings, like everyone else. Oh well, she would find all the answers to these feelings the next day. They ate dinner and conversed about the trip, until it was time to retire for the evening. That night, Brandon held Sidney in his arms and tried to get her to relax. He could tell how excited she was and worried she wouldn't be able to sleep. He was wrong. Sidney fell asleep early, all snuggled in his arms. She slept like a baby.

The next morning, she woke up feeling totally refreshed and revitalized. Needless to say, she was in a hurry to get ready. Brandon laughed at her as she was digging through her things, trying to find just the right thing to wear. He told her, whatever she wore would be fine. She decided that he was right. She would wear something comfortable. She did put her hair up, with loose long curls hanging down, which she often did when getting dressed up for something special. She also wore her mother's locket. Brandon knew this was a very special day for her. When they were ready, they met Ace for breakfast before continuing their journey. When they had finished breakfast, they were on their way. When they arrived at Swarg Ashram, Sidney had a curious feeling she couldn't explain.

The three of them made their way up the walkway to the temple. There, they were greeted by one of the monks. He told them the holy man was waiting to receive them in the garden. When Sidney saw him, she felt she had seen him before. She told herself that wasn't possible. She knew she had never met him or even seen a picture of him. The monk introduced them to the monk they were to meet with. The monk held out his hand to Sidney, telling her he believed his spirit had known her spirit in another life. Sidney was dumbstruck by this statement. Could it be that was why she felt the way she did the moment she first saw him? As they began to talk, Sidney felt very sure there was some kind of connection between this monk and herself. She couldn't believe how comfortable she felt being here with him. During their stay in Dharmshala, this monk spent many hours with them, talking to them and teaching them.

Sidney felt these were the greatest lessons she had learned in her life. It was the same as those from Uncle Alex; it wasn't that he told her anything she didn't already know. It was simply that she hadn't consciously thought about it but she knew it in her heart. He was telling her mind what her heart had always known. Sometimes, these are the greatest lessons we will ever learn. He helped her realize some of the greatest truths in life. One of her personal favorites was how to measure a person's worth. He told her a person should only be measured by the goodness of their hearts and the good deeds they did, for all other things had no meaning. We all need to do the best we can with what we know. Show kindness to all we encounter, and practice understanding. Sidney knew this and thought to herself, *Surely we all know this, so why aren't we practicing what we know?* Unfortunately, not nearly enough people practiced these simple truths. He also taught her it was not necessary or wise to be proud. Pride is a form of arrogance. (Boy, where had she heard all this before?) You should have respect and reverence instead. This is a form of humility. Being humble is what we should all aspire to be. With humility, there is kindness. With pride, we become smug and feel superior, even disdainful toward others.

As she listened and learned from this wise and loving man, she realized that all great truths were simple in nature. It's hard for us to believe things so important could be so simple and easy. We make life a lot harder than it ever needs to be. The most valuable thing the monk taught her was how to meditate. Sidney was no stranger when it came to praying. However, the monk taught her to meditate at a much deeper and more spiritual level than she had ever experienced before. She discovered there was a level of meditating in which your spirit connected to God. It gave you a deeper understanding than you had ever known existed. That is, unless you had gone to that part of your mind and soul before.

One day, while Sidney was meditating, the most unusual thing happened to her. She felt her spirit leave her body and was suspended high above the mountains. She was looking down on her life, which was all laid out beneath her. She could see her life in fragments, like the pieces of a puzzle. When she looked at them, she mentally began putting the pieces together. As the pieces fell into place, she could see not only where she had been and what her life had meant but also where she should go and what her life should mean. She was amazed how clear everything seemed now. How everything in her life, right up to this very moment, had a purpose. Even the bad things had great meaning. Perhaps the bad times had the most meaning because she had learned the most from them. After meditating, she felt happier and more content than she had felt in her whole life. She hurried to the monk to tell him what had happened. When she described what occurred, he didn't seem surprised at all. He took her hand and explained this confirmed what he thought all along. He knew, from the moment they first met, she had a powerful spirit. Sidney told him she knew now it was not enough to just exist; you needed to justify your existence. The monk laughed; if only everyone could feel that way, it would be a much-better world.

Sidney excused herself to go find Brandon and tell him about this miraculous event. Sidney found Brandon in the garden, practicing his tai chi. She went to him and joined his routine. She would tell him later about her revelations. Right now, this felt so good. As they went through the motions, they were in total sync. They moved in perfect unison. There was no doubt, when watching them together like this, they were truly soul mates. Even their breathing was identical. When they completed the exercise, Brandon turned to Sidney and took her in his arms. He told her they should always do their tai chi together. Sidney hugged him and said, "Oh yes, that and much, much more." As they walked back to their room, Sidney told Brandon all about her revelation. He asked if he was present in her puzzle. She assured him he was not only present but also the key to putting her life together. He laughed and said, "Then I don't mind being a bit of a puzzle. As long as it's an important bit."

Too soon, their time in this enchanted place had passed, and it was time to go home. They had taken tons of pictures and videos. Sidney knew these memories would last them a lifetime. She never wanted to forget her time here and the valuable lessons learned. The peace and tranquility of this place were like nothing she had ever experienced before. The total lack of self these monks lived was a shining example for everyone to live by. Sidney knew in her heart, even without pictures and movies, this was one experience she would never forget as long as she lived. The sights, sounds, and memories of this place were forever indelibly etched in her mind and in her soul. As they said goodbye, it was with a heavy heart. The monk could tell how difficult it was for them to leave. He told Sidney and Brandon he looked forward to their return, when they would bring their children with them. Sidney knew he was right; she would return when she had children to bring.

The hardest thing was saying good-bye to Ace. Big tears welled up in Sidney's eyes. She wrapped her arms around him and hung on tightly, as if she were never going to let go. She told him she would write to him often because she never wanted to lose touch with him. Brandon told him, if he were ever in the United States, he could always stay with them while he was there. Sidney said, "I'll go one better, if you ever want to come to the United States, just say the word. I'll arrange a ticket for you. It won't cost you a thing to visit for as long as you want." Ace thanked them both and gave them an address where he picked up his mail. He promised that he would go to the United States someday for a visit. Then he turned and hurried away so they couldn't see how upset he was to say goodbye. Sidney and Brandon went quietly arm in arm to board their plane.

# Chapter 28

## *Time to Visit Denver*

The first leg of their trip home, Sidney and Brandon sat quietly in each other's arms. They were excited to be going home, but they both knew they were leaving part of their hearts behind. Before they reached Los Angeles, Sidney turned to Brandon and asked if he would mind stopping in Denver, Colorado, before going home. He responded, "Whatever you want to do is fine with me, but why Denver?" She said, "In my vision, I saw myself living in Denver and having a very large family." Brandon confessed he liked the sound of that, especially the large-family part.

When they arrived in Los Angeles, they called Uncle Alex to tell him about the change in plans. He expressed how much he was missing them. He said, "Please don't be too much longer." Sidney promised they wouldn't. While waiting on the flight to Denver, Sidney and Brandon were searching the internet for real estate sites. Suddenly, Sidney said, "I think I've found one." They called the real estate broker and set up an appointment to look at the property they were interested in. The real estate broker emailed them pictures of the property. They could look those over, before going the next day. When Sidney saw the pictures, she smiled at Brandon, and said, "this is it." Brandon asked, "are you sure?" She replied, "absolutely." They chatted the rest of the way, about this place, and how Sidney could feel, so certain.

When they arrived in Denver, they were both surprised, by how much they loved this place. When they arrived at the hotel, it was so elegant, and beautiful, but still extremely comfortable. Everything, felt so right. Sidney knew, something wonderful was about to happen here. Brandon was pleased, to see her this happy. The next morning, Sidney was up at dawn preparing to meet with the real estate agent. She called room service, and ordered breakfast. What a breakfast it was. When Brandon smelled the coffee, and food, his eyes popped open, and he sat straight up in bed. When he saw all the food Sidney had ordered, he couldn't believe his eyes. He asked, "What army is coming to breakfast?" She laughed and said, "I thought we would need a good start on the day." They sat down and devoured nearly everything. Brandon said, "I guess I was more ravenous than I knew." Sidney knew her husband better than he knew himself. She kissed him and said, "Now get ready, I'm anxious to get this day started." He knew she was always anxious to do everything. It was like she had to squeeze as much excitement from every day as she possibly could. She loved life and savored every minute of it.

They met with the real estate agent and proceeded to the property. When they arrived, it took their breath away. It was so beautiful, it brought a tear to Sidney's eyes. They got out of the car and walked to the house. Sidney turned to Brandon and whispered, "I want to build our house right over there. This house could be for Su Yen and Joe, don't you think?" Brandon said, "Let's look first. There's no guarantee Joe and Su Yen will want to move here." Sidney stopped in her tracks; this was something she hadn't thought about. What if none of them wanted to move here? The house was so nice, Sidney couldn't believe they wouldn't want to live here. There was such a good feeling about this whole place. It was peaceful and serene. The air was so fresh and clean. Maybe it wasn't as clean as Tibet's, but much cleaner than New York. She couldn't imagine anyone not wanting to live here. She would have to wait and let them decide for themselves.

As they were walking the grounds, Sidney stopped at the graceful, rolling hill she spotted earlier. The energy was so strong here, she turned to Brandon and asked if he could feel the same energy she was feeling. He laughed and said, "Strangely enough, I can." She hugged him and said, "I told you, this was the place. This is where we'll build our home." He wholeheartedly agreed. They drove around and looked over the rest of the property. It covered 275 acres. Even though it was up in the mountains, it was in a relatively flat area. Except for the hill Sidney was so fond of. Brandon turned to the real estate agent and said, "You might have made a sale." They went to the office to get the paperwork started. Sidney told her they would pay cash if the price was right. The price was more than fair. Sidney said, "It's a done deal." Sidney wanted the place to be theirs as soon as the title search was completed.

Sidney took this time to find a Native American medicine man. She wanted him to bless the property and make sure it wasn't an Indian burial ground or anything like that. Luckily, it wasn't. Then, she had a feng shui master fly in to check the grounds for the best place to build their new home. He picked the very same spot Sidney had picked. They checked around for the right construction company to build their home. It would have to be very large. Also, everything had to be environmentally correct. Sidney knew the importance of building an earth-friendly home. They checked with some people who had some pretty incredible homes in the area to see who their architects and builders were. Sidney and Brandon both realized this was going to be a huge undertaking, but when you're building your dream home, it's important to do it right. Within a few days, the transaction was complete. Sidney and Brandon were on their way home, at long last. Sidney knew she could find the right people from home to get things started.

While their plane was landing at the airport, Sidney was squirming in her seat with excitement. She couldn't wait to see her loved ones. Until this very moment, she hadn't realized how much she missed them. Now, however, she couldn't even wait for the plane to land. When they got off the plane, they were all smiling and waving. There was hugging, kissing, and even tears of joy all the way home. How wonderful it was to have all these people to love and to be loved by. For the next several days, they would talk about everything that had happened since last time they were all together.

Uncle Alex said, "I, for one, hope we will never be separated for that long again." Sidney said, "That depends on how you and Rosa feel about moving to Colorado." She told him they had purchased the most beautiful place she had ever seen. She confessed she wanted all of them to move there with her and Brandon. She assured them there was plenty of room for everyone, and then some. She said, "Before you make any decision about moving or not moving, I want all of you to visit the place." Sidney was hoping they couldn't resist it once they saw it. They told Sidney she should rest at home for a while before embarking on another trip. Sidney said, "I'll be ready to go in about a week." Sidney was actually so excited to go back that she could have been ready the next morning. She decided instead to give Brandon a rest. She knew she would take Flash with her the next time. Poor Flash wouldn't get off her lap even for a minute. She stroked his fur and told him, from now on she wouldn't be gone for so long.

The next day, Sidney started early, making all the arrangements for the trip back to Denver. When the arrangements were complete, she started putting all her affairs in order. The week went by in a hurry. That's how it usually is when you're busy. Finally, the day arrived, and off they went. Sidney was so excited, she could hardly wait until they landed. Brandon kept saying, "They may not love this place as much as we do." Sidney said, "Nonsense, of course they will." When they arrived, first they settled into their hotel rooms. Then, they all went to dinner. Sidney explained they would have to wait until morning to see the place because there was no electricity. She needed to call the power and light company to have it turned on. They ate their dinner while discussing what a beautiful place Denver was. This made Sidney feel good because if they liked Denver that much, they should wait until they see her homestead. She thought to herself she needed a name for her new home. She told Brandon later she wanted to think of a name for their new home. He agreed he would be thinking of something. He kissed Sidney and said, "It's so special, we need a perfect name for it."

The next morning, they all met for breakfast and took a limo out to the property. Sidney hoped they would all want to call it home. When they were close enough to see it from the road, Uncle Alex said, "That must be it." Sidney said, "Yes, but how did you know?" He laughed and said, "It looks like paradise to me." Sidney said, "You're right, Uncle Alex, maybe we'll call it Paradise Ranch." They all agreed it was a beautiful place. When they pulled up in front of the house, Sidney said, "This is where Brandon and I will live until our house is finished." Uncle Alex looked shocked. He asked, "Does that mean you won't be living in New York with us anymore?" Sidney replied, "We will off, and on, until our house is completed. Then, I want all of you to move here." She told Su Yen she planned to give her and Joe this house and have a house built for Uncle Alex and Aunt Rosa. All of a sudden, things got very quiet. Sidney's heart sank. Could this mean they didn't want to move and she would once more be without a family? She felt tears welling up in her eyes and fought hard to keep from crying. She didn't want to make anyone feel uncomfortable or guilty if they didn't want to move here.

They all went inside the house, and she showed them around. It was a spacious four-bedroom, three-and-a-half-bath house, with lots of room for a growing family. It was a very elegant house. The rest of the tour, everyone kept saying what a beautiful place this was, but no one said a word about moving there. All the way back to the hotel, Sidney felt so disappointed, she could hardly talk. When they arrived, they went to their respective rooms to prepare for lunch. Sidney fell into Brandon's waiting arms, sobbing as though her heart were completely broken. Brandon hugged her and said, "Don't cry. Give them a chance to think it over. They might need some time to think before coming to a definite decision. Why waste tears over something you're not even sure of?" She sobbed, saying, "I know you're right, but this won't work without them. I could never be happy here without my family to share it with." Brandon said, "In the worst-case scenario, they don't move here, and we'll spend most of our time in New York. We can come here when we need to get away from it all." She looked at him with tear-filled big eyes and said, "Thank you for being my best friend. I know you're right, and I'll try not to worry about it again."

When they all met for lunch, she was true to her word. She never even brought up the subject although she was so tempted. She knew the ball was in their court now. She would have to be patient and wait for their decisions. After lunch, the ladies all went shopping to select some furniture for the new house. Sidney hoped Su Yen would get involved and select the things she would like to have if they moved there. As they shopped, Sidney felt it was working. Su Yen was so happy picking out the furniture for the new house. She thought the things they bought were just right for such an elegant house. When they got back, Joe told Sidney he had been thinking about the house and what kind of flower garden and plants would make it look better. Sidney started smiling and said, "Does that mean you'll move here?" Joe said, "Of course we will. Who else is going to take care of such a big place? You're our family and friend, we'd follow you to the ends of the earth if you wanted us to. Besides, Su Yen, the kids, and I would have to be crazy to turn down such a gracious offer." Sidney hugged them both, and this time, she didn't care if they saw her cry. She loved them both so much and told them so.

Now, was the most important obstacle of all, Uncle Alex and Aunt Rosa. Rosa said nothing as Sidney walked her back to her room. Sidney went inside and gave Uncle Alex a big hug. Still, neither Uncle Alex nor Aunt Rosa said anything. They obliviously weren't ready to say whether or not they would move there. Sidney went back to her room to get ready. They were going out on the town with their group. She told Brandon about her new dilemma. What if Su Yen and Joe moved but not Uncle Alex and Aunt Rosa? Brandon said, "There you go again, borrowing trouble from tomorrow." She smiled and said, "You're right, as usual. Whatever would I do without you?" That night passed with no mention of Uncle Alex moving. Sidney could hardly sleep. The suspense was killing her, and she didn't know how much longer she could wait for them to say something. If Uncle Alex thought it looked like paradise, what could the problem be? The next morning, they all went to the house. The ladies waited at the house for the furniture to be delivered. The guys met with the architect to show him where the new house was to be built.

Brandon turned to Uncle Alex and asked, "So do you think you and Aunt Rosa will be moving here? If so, we could show him where to build your house while he's here." Uncle Alex told Brandon Rosa was having second thoughts because all her children lived in New York. She was torn up about living so far away from them.

Brandon said, "I understand, and this can wait until you decide." They returned to the house to find everything had arrived and was being put in place. Sidney told Su Yen, "We may want to rearrange things when the feng shui master arrives to check things over." Su Yen was very pleased about that. She told Sidney how happy it made her to hear she believed in feng shui. Sidney laughed and said, "I've learned to believe and respect a lot of things on my travels." She told them all she would do everything in her power to make sure they were all happy, healthy, and living in harmony with the earth. Su Yen told Sidney she should make all the changes the feng shui master might suggest so the chi would flow naturally. Sidney laughed and said, "I will, Su Yen. I have a lot of respect for old ways and customs." When the furniture was in place and they had discussed their plans with the contractor, they went back to their hotel rooms to prepare for dinner. Sidney called the feng shui master and asked if he could come to Denver to help the architect design their new home. She told him she also needed his help arranging the furnishings in the home that was already there. He agreed to be there in two days.

When Sidney was ready for dinner, Brandon told her they needed to talk. He pulled her down on his lap and told her he had discovered why Uncle Alex and Aunt Rosa weren't saying anything about moving to Denver. Sidney's eyes grew large as she asked him why. He relayed to her what Uncle Alex told him earlier. She knew something was wrong, but this wasn't so bad. She told Brandon she thought they should offer Rosa's children a place of their own. After all, they had lots of land there and could certainly afford to build a few more houses. Brandon agreed it was a good plan, if Rosa's children would go for it. Sidney said, "At dinner, we'll discuss it with Uncle Alex and Aunt Rosa to see what they think." Su Yen called to say they would like to eat dinner in their room. She wanted her kids to settle down and get to bed early. That was fine with Sidney; it would give her and Brandon some time alone with Uncle Alex and Aunt Rosa. They would discuss this whole thing and work out a solution to everyone's liking.

That evening at dinner, Sidney brought up moving to Denver. She told them she understood why they were hesitant to move.

She could understand them not wanting to live so far away from Rosa's children. Rosa told her she was so glad she understood. She explained it had nothing to do with living there. She wanted to be close to Sidney, but she didn't know what to do. Sidney and Brandon explained their idea of moving Rosa's whole family to Denver, if they wanted to come. They would build each of them a new home and hire them to help Joe keep up the grounds. Sidney told Uncle Alex and Aunt Rosa they could go home and talk it over with Rosa's children. They should take their time and find out what Rosa's children wanted. She even offered to give them their own ten acres of land to go with their new homes. Rosa told them that was too generous and she couldn't let them do that. Sidney told her it was only money and she didn't need the money as much as she needed her family. She told Rosa the money was only worth the good it could do. She told them both that nothing in the world would make her happier than for all of them to be happy. She told Aunt Rosa, if her children didn't want to move there, it would be all right. They would figure out some way of being together. Whatever happened, they would always be family and love one another.

Uncle Alex couldn't wait to get back to New York and hear what Rosa's children would say. It was decided they would leave the next day and talk to them as soon as they got home. Sidney and Brandon thought they would move into the house and have Su Yen, Joe, and the children stay with them, at least until the feng shui master rearranged the house. That way, they could make sure Su Yen would be comfortable with the changes. That would also give the kids a place to play while they waited. Uncle Alex laughed and said, "That's my girl, always thinking about others." Sidney hugged him and said, "I just want everyone to be as happy as I am."

The next morning, Sidney was on the phone, purchasing airline tickets. Then she ordered a ton of playground equipment. It was to be delivered to their new home, for the children. After breakfast, Sidney asked Joe and Su Yen if they would like to spend the rest of the trip in their new home. Su Yen was thrilled. She felt it would be much better for the children than being cooped up in the hotel room. They helped Uncle Alex and Aunt Rosa do their packing, to go home. When they were in the air, Sidney and Brandon scurried back to the hotel to pick up Joe, Su Yen, and the kids. Then, it was out to their new home.

Sidney could hardly wait for the children to see the new playground equipment. When they arrived, the phone company was there to hook up the phones. They hadn't much more than arrived when the truck pulled up with the playground equipment. Sidney wasn't sure who was more excited, the children or Joe. Joe helped the driver unload the truck and started right away to put things together. Brandon had to get in on this. He never knew what fun it could be to assemble toys. The children were cheering them on every step of the way. Even the animals seemed excited with all the commotion. Sidney asked Su Yen if she wanted to go with her to the grocery store while the children were busy. Su Yen agreed this would be a very good time to get things done. Sidney bought everything they would need to have a picnic celebration at their new home. By the time they returned home, the guys had almost all the equipment set up. The children were already trying it out. When Sidney got out of the car, Brain and Blake ran over and gave her lots of hugs and kisses. They kept thanking her for all the new things. Then they hugged Brandon, which brought tears to his eyes. Sidney whispered, "Oh yeah, he's going to be the perfect dad for our children someday."

Time went by quickly, and the feng shui master was about to arrive. Brandon and Joe picked him up at the airport. When they arrived at the house, he remarked the house looked better already just by having people there. He said, "I feel this will be a happy place for everyone." Brandon said, "I believe you're right. I know I am." As the master went through the house, he didn't suggest making very many changes. Sidney had studied feng shui (the belief that the earth has an energy flow, called chi, surrounding it and that if you lived in harmony with that chi, it would bring all good things to you). She wanted to understand feng shui before she purchased the furnishings. He suggested acquiring a fish aquarium and some fish. One red fish and nine black fish would be best placed against the north wall. This would increase the positive flow of chi. He also suggested a few mirrors, plants, and some small crystal balls. He liked the fact that Sidney had placed wind chimes above the entrances. Su Yen was happy about the changes he made. She loved the idea of an aquarium. She knew how much the children would enjoy watching the fish.

Next, the feng shui master met with the architect. Together they decided which direction the house should sit and how it should be designed to create a good chi. The architect thanked the master for teaching him so much about placement and design. Then, the master took Joe around the property, showing him what landscaping would be best to ensure good chi. He told Joe he would create a rough diagram of what he should do and list what he would need. He would give it to him before he went home. Joe was anxious to get started on the grounds. Sidney told the architect and the feng shui master that she wanted them to add four more houses to their plans. She felt certain that Uncle Alex, Aunt Rosa, and Rosa's children would be moving there. Brandon asked, "Are you really sure about that?" She told him she had another vision and it showed them all moving there. She said, "It also showed me a house with twenty bedrooms for all the children that would be living here." Brandon's eyes grew very large. Sidney laughed and said, "You wanted a big family." He said, "You heard the lady, she needs twenty bedrooms and four more houses." They all had a good laugh and set about drawing up the plans for one very large homestead.

# Chapter 29

# *The Family Grows*

The next morning, Sidney took Brandon to the top of the hill that would soon be standing behind their new home. She said, "We need to do our meditating and tai chi here, as long as the weather permits." They enjoyed their meditating, and tai chi routine. Sidney turned to Brandon and said, "I can't wait any longer to tell you." He asked, "Tell me what?" She smiled a smile that rivaled the sun, and she said, "I'm fairly sure we're pregnant." Brandon hugged her and then said, "We are, or you are, because I'm not sure I can give birth." She giggled and hugged him. "Okay, I'll give birth, but you have to go through the whole experience with me." He looked deeply into her soft brown eyes and told her he wouldn't have it any other way. She whispered in his ear, "See, there goes one of those bedrooms. I just hope it's ready in time for the baby to be born." Brandon told her not to worry; he felt sure it would be. If for some reason it couldn't be completed in time, they could go to New York and have the baby there. Sidney said, "You're right, the most important thing is to be with our family when the baby comes." Then, she got a sad look on her face and asked Brandon if he would tell his family about the baby. Brandon told her he'd rather not think about that yet. He only wanted to celebrate right now. Sidney said, "That's all right." She needed time to see a doctor and confirm that she was really pregnant, before telling anyone.

Keeping the baby a secret was not meant to be. The next day, when they met with the architect and the feng shui master, Brandon asked them to hurry as quickly as they could. When the architect asked "What's the big hurry?" Brandon replied he just found out they were having a baby. Sidney looked at him and said, "So much for the big secret." He got a sheepish smile on his face and said, "Whoops!" Sidney asked them not to say anything because they hadn't told their family yet. Sidney decided to send Joe and Su Yen back to New York before Brandon told them too.

Now that everyone had returned to New York, it gave Brandon and Sidney some much-needed time alone. They busied themselves finding the perfect doctors for the blessed event. They knew they would need a family doctor, a gynecologist, and a pediatrician. Sidney wanted the very best doctors she could find. She wasn't the type to leave things to chance. She had always been a careful planner. They even got books on different forms of childbirth. They also rented movies to show them what they could expect. They picked the Bradley method for childbirth, before she went for her first doctor's appointment. The doctor confirmed what Sidney already knew: she was very much pregnant. When the doctor told them the due date, Sidney turned to Brandon and said, "That was your dad's birthday, wasn't it?" He smiled and responded, "Yes, it was, and I know how happy this would have made him." On their way home, Sidney asked Brandon if they could fly to New York the next day to tell Uncle Alex and everyone else the good news. He answered, "Of course we can." As a matter of fact, that was exactly what he had been thinking in the doctor's office. He told Sidney she already knew how excited he was to tell everyone.

When they got home, they made all the arrangements and packed a few things to take with them. They didn't need much because most of their things were still there. The next morning, Sidney was up at the crack of dawn. Brandon was already up and ready. He had prepared her a large breakfast, saying she was eating for two now and he wanted her to stay healthy. She giggled and sat down to this wonderful feast. She was surprised at how good everything tasted. She told Brandon she didn't know he could cook. He laughed and said, "I try to keep that a secret. That way, I don't have to cook unless I want to." They finished breakfast, cleaned up the kitchen, and prepared to leave. Sidney felt like she was going to burst with excitement if they didn't get there soon. She couldn't wait to tell everyone. Brandon said, "You've known for some time now and managed to keep it quiet. Why the big rush now?" She replied, "Yeah, but that was before the doctor confirmed it. Now that it's official, I can't wait." They took a taxi to the house so they could surprise everyone.

They pulled up in front of the house, only to be greeted by everyone. They heard the taxi drive up. They had a family meeting, and Sidney announced their good news. They all hugged, cried, and gave their congratulations to both of them. Sidney and Brandon went upstairs to rest after their trip. While Sidney and Brandon were resting, Su Yen and Rosa prepared a huge meal to celebrate the good news. While they were eating, Rosa said she, too, had an announcement. Her children had talked it over and decided to move to Denver. The timing had been just right for them to move. Their landscaping business hadn't been doing that well. They had been trying to find a way to move out of the neighborhood they lived in. It was no longer safe to live there. There had been a few drive-by shootings, and they feared for their children's safety. They were anxious to move as soon as possible.

That night, Sidney told Brandon she was worried about Rosa's children. She was worried about their safety until they could get their homes built. Brandon told her, if they wanted to move in a hurry, maybe they could put trailers on their land for temporary housing. Sidney thought that was a wonderful idea. She decided to run that by them the next day. Brandon and Sidney told Uncle Alex and Aunt Rosa about their plan and wanted to know what they thought. Aunt Rosa cried and said, "I don't know how to thank you for being so kind to me and my family." Sidney had tears come to her eyes. She told Rosa she didn't want anything bad to happen before the houses could be built. Rosa called her children and asked them to come over for dinner that night. Sidney asked them how they would feel about moving into a trailer on their land until the new homes could be built. They were overjoyed and couldn't wait to move. They would be happy to help with the building and landscaping so things would go faster.

That night, they all sang and danced late into the night. Sidney couldn't wait until they were celebrating like this in their new homes. Later that night, Joe pulled Sidney aside. He asked if it would be too much trouble for him, Su Yen, and the children to move to Denver and live in a trailer like Rosa's kids would. Sidney hugged him and said, "Nothing is too much trouble when it comes to you and your family. I'll get an extra trailer set up next to the house." Joe was overjoyed. That way, he and Su Yen could take care of her during her pregnancy. Sidney told the others Joe and Su Yen would also be moving right away. One of Rosa's sons volunteered to stay in New York to take care of the property there. Joe said, "That's great, and they can stay in our house." Sidney was so pleased that everyone was cooperating to make this move go smoothly. She thanked them all and excused herself for the evening. She was worn out from the trip the day before and celebrating so much. Being pregnant had a few surprises for her. Tiring more easily was just one of them.

The next morning, Sidney and Brandon started getting things set up to move Rosa's children plus Joe and his family to Denver. By that afternoon, they had arranged everything. They called Rosa's children and told them the good news. Joe already knew. He had been underfoot all day. He acted as excited as a child with a new toy. It made Sidney happy just to see how happy he was. Joe rushed to his house to tell Su Yen and start packing. Brandon laughed and said, "I think he's definitely anxious to start their new life in Denver." Sidney hugged Brandon and told him Joe wasn't nearly as happy as she was. They decided that they would fly back to oversee the trailers being set in place and the work being done on their house. They packed all day. The next day, they flew back to Denver. Sidney could hardly wait for everyone to get moved. Brandon suggested they take a look at the trailers before they delivered them and set them in place. After looking at the trailers, Sidney decided they were too small. She preferred to get the larger manufactured homes and set them on the far end of the property. They had Joe and Su Yen's temporary housing set within walking distance of the main house. Brandon looked puzzled. He asked, "Why are you putting them on the far end of the property?" She answered, "That way, when their homes are built, we can use the manufactured homes for other things." He asked, "What other things?" She hugged him and replied, "I don't know yet. I just feel that's what I need to do." That was fine with him; she hadn't been wrong yet. Sidney told Brandon on the way home, "This thing keeps getting bigger and bigger, just like me." They both had a good laugh.

The time was going by quickly, and things were going very smoothly. Su Yen and Joe arrived with their children. Sidney wanted them to go out early and take care of things. She was so tired all the time. She told them they could stay at the house until their place was ready. Brandon took Sidney to the doctor to find out why she was so exhausted all the time. When they saw the doctor, he informed them that was normal. Brandon disagreed and told him so. He told the doctor, up until now, Sidney was always full of energy. This was completely out of character for her. The doctor agreed to set up a few tests to make sure everything was going well. A few days later, the doctor called to let them know everything was all right except for a little anemia. He told her to take two of her pregnancy vitamins a day and prescribed some iron pills. They would keep an eye on her, but she should be fine. A month went by, and Sidney did feel better for a while. Then she began feeling sluggish again. Brandon again insisted she should go see the doctor. She told him it was probably just because she was getting so big. Besides, it was getting warmer outside. Sometimes, heat makes you tired. Brandon didn't buy it and made the appointment. He told Sidney, if the doctor didn't have the right answers this time, they would find a new doctor. Sidney said, "Okay, I'll do whatever you say."

When they went to the doctor, he was surprised by how much she had grown since the last time she was in. He told her he wanted to do an ultrasound. She asked, "Why, is there something wrong?" He told her, "Probably not, but I would normally do one in a couple of months, anyway." He wanted her to go home, rest, and not worry about anything. The next day, she went in for the ultrasound. She still felt apprehensive. The nurse helping her get ready told her not to worry. It was a normal procedure, and it wouldn't hurt her or the baby. The doctor went in and began the procedure. Right away, he started going "Hum, oh yeah." Sidney asked him what he meant by that. He turned to her and Brandon, saying, "It's just like I suspected, only more so." He pointed at the monitor, saying, "See this and this and this?" Brandon asked, "What are we looking at?" The doctor answered, "Your children, all three of them." Sidney squealed. "three of them?" He answered, "Yes, you're going to have triplets. Actually"—he pointed to the screen again—"two of them are identical twins." Brandon got very quiet and pale. After a moment of silence, he asked the doctor if Sidney was going to be all right. The doctor assured them everything looked fine but that, naturally, it would be more difficult than a single birth was.

This certainly explained why she was so tired and growing by leaps and bounds. She would have to slow down and get plenty of rest. Listening to her body would be the best thing she could do for the remainder of her pregnancy. If she felt she needed to rest, she would have to stop everything and take a good rest. They would all need to work closely together if they were going to deliver three happy, healthy babies. Then, he asked them if they would like to know the sex of the babies. Brandon said, "No, that's not necessary." Sidney said, "You can speak for yourself. I want to know." The doctor asked Brandon if he wanted to leave the room while he told Sidney. Brandon said, "No way, if she's going to know, I want to know too." The doctor laughed as he told them they could get ready for a son and two daughters. Sidney began to cry just thinking of how wonderful it would be to hold them in her arms. The doctor thought she was crying because she was overwhelmed at the prospect of having three babies instead of one. She assured him that wasn't it at all. She was just so happy that there were three babies to love instead of only one. The doctor chuckled and said, "We'll see how you feel about that in a few months, when you can hardly waddle." Brandon started laughing. Sidney asked, "What are you laughing about?" He said, "Just the thought of you waddling around the house." She confessed that it would probably be a very funny sight.

Sidney told Brandon they needed to take lots of pictures and movies. She wanted to be able to show the children, when they got older, what she looked like. Brandon asked Sidney if she would like to go out to dinner to celebrate. She replied, "Maybe tomorrow night.

# RAINBOWS ARE BETTER

Right now, I just want to go home and call Uncle Alex and Aunt Rosa with this incredible news flash." He said, "You're right. They're going to be so excited and so shocked." When they arrived home, Sidney was so excited, she could hardly dial the phone number. When Uncle Alex answered the phone, Sidney said, "Have I got some news for you. Are you sitting down?" When she told him about the babies, he started to cry. Sidney asked him if he was all right. He told her he had never been better. He was so overcome with joy; he couldn't control himself. He told Sidney not long ago he had spent his whole life with no family whatsoever. Now he had a niece, a nephew, the prospect of a great-nephew, and two great-nieces. This was more joy than he had ever expected to know. Sidney had tears come to her eyes, as well. This was truly a very special day for both of them.

Little did Sidney know how special this day really was. That night, she and Brandon cuddled on the sofa, watching the evening news on TV As they watched, they saw on the news a woman who was dying of cancer. She had five children. Her husband had been killed a year earlier in an automobile accident. Since she and her husband were both orphans, she had no one to leave her children with. She was pleading for someone to step forward and take all five of her children to raise. She didn't want them to be separated or put in an orphanage. Sidney looked at Brandon and said, "We should adopt those children." Brandon responded, "Need I remind you, we just found out we're having triplets." Sidney told him she knew that but they had enough money to hire whatever help they needed. She knew this was the right thing to do. Brandon knew it too.

Sidney picked up the phone and dialed the television station. She asked how she could contact the woman who had cancer and whom they saw on their news broadcast. A few days later, when they met for the first time, it was amazing how well they got along. They got along well not only with the mother but with the children, as well. The children were so happy, pleasant, and well-behaved. There was no doubt this was meant to be. On the way home, Brandon said, "Wow, what a way to start a marriage, with eight kids." Sidney laughed, and she said, "Maybe we can find four more to make an even dozen." Brandon retorted, "Why not? A few more couldn't hurt." Sidney asked, "Are you sure you're all right with all this?" He kissed her and said, "I really couldn't be happier." Sidney said, "Good, because I thought, when they finish our home, we should ask her and the children if they would like to move into Joe and Su Yen's trailer." Brandon agreed, saying, "That's a good idea. That way, we can take care of her and the children, for the time remaining." Sidney said, "It'll save her money and give them some privacy for whatever time they have left together." Sidney knew that would also give the children a chance to become comfortable being with them. When the time came, it wouldn't be so hard for them to adjust to their new environment.

Unfortunately, the house wasn't complete before Sharon (the children's mother) took a turn for the worse. Sidney and Brandon decided to move her and the children (Susan, Johnny, Amy, Emily, and Randy) in with them so they wouldn't be alone when their mom died. One short month later, Sharon was gone. She had asked to be cremated, as her husband had been. She didn't care what they did with their ashes. Sidney carried out her wishes. She told the children, when the new house was completed, they could plant a tree on top of their ashes. That way, they could sit under the trees and feel close to their mom and their dad. The children liked that idea and looked forward to planting the trees for both of their parents.

The next few months, Sidney was getting very large with child. She knew she needed to hire a couple of nannies to help with all the children. Uncle Alex called Sidney and told her he and Rosa were going to move out there right away. They wanted to help take care of her and all those children. Sidney didn't argue. She needed help right away. She went to the doctor, and he told her the babies were running out of room to grow. He told her she wouldn't be able to carry them full term. He explained, the longer she could carry them, the better chance they would have to survive and be normal. The words *survive* and *normal* struck fear in Sidney's heart. This was something she hadn't even considered. She told the doctor she would do anything he told her to. She pleaded with him to help her deliver three normal, healthy babies. He instructed her to spend most of the remaining months in bed. She looked a little disappointed but agreed to do whatever he suggested. He also suggested she get an adjustable electric bed and place it downstairs. He didn't want her climbing any stairs. She felt her heart sink. Brandon said, "No problem. We'll convert the den into a bedroom and order an electric bed built for two." Sidney hugged Brandon and told him he was the most wonderful husband in the whole world. The doctor had to agree with her; some husbands were not that agreeable. Brandon blushed and said, "Is that all we need to do?" The doctor said, "That's all for now, but even that doesn't ensure she'll be able to carry these babies to term." He feared that she wasn't built to house three babies at once. Not too many women are. The doctor wanted to do another ultrasound as soon as possible. Sidney asked, "How soon?" He told her to ask the nurse on her way out. She would know how soon they could get her in. The nurse told Sidney to go in the next morning.

When they arrived home, Brandon made Sidney lie down on the sofa and rest. She was so tired, she didn't even argue. She was asleep in no time. While she was sleeping, Brandon called and ordered an electric bed to be delivered that very day. Then he had Joe and Rosa's sons help him clean out the den and set up the bedroom before the electric bed arrived. Then he called and ordered two twin-size feather beds, sheets, and blankets. Joe went into town to pick them up. When Sidney woke up, she heard a truck pulling in the driveway. She asked Brandon who that could be. He laughed, and he said, "That must be the bed." She questioned, "Where will we put it?" Brandon said, "In our bedroom. While you were sleeping, I set up the den as our bedroom. I hope you don't mind that I did this without you knowing." She called him over and gave him a big kiss. "Why would I mind someone being so thoughtful?" As they were setting up the bed, Joe came back with the feather beds and linens. Sidney was so astounded. She told Brandon she couldn't believe he had even thought of the feather beds.

Brandon had purchased two twin electric beds. It was on wheels and hooked or unhooked easily from one another. That way, they could wheel her bed into the living room during the day. He didn't think she would want to spend all her time in her room alone. She told him how well he knew her was scary. When Su Yen had finished making up the new beds, Joe wheeled it into the living room. Brandon helped Sidney get in it and see if it would do. Needless to say, she loved it. The children all climbed up on the bed and questioned if she was all right. Susan was worried that Sidney was going to die just like her mom did. Sidney hugged each one of them and assured them she wasn't going to die for a long time if she had anything to do with it. She had Johnny bring her a book, and she read to them until it was time for their cartoons. Meanwhile, Brandon met with the construction supervisor and told him they needed to step up their efforts and finish the house as soon as possible. He told him he didn't care if they had to hire more people, as long as they could just get it done. The man agreed to hire more people and finish it ahead of schedule. He asked Brandon if he would be willing to pay overtime to the workers if they worked extra hours. Brandon told him no but that he would pay them a bonus for every day they finished ahead of schedule. He wanted it finished before the babies arrived, and they would more than likely come early.

The workers were true to their word. The house was completely finished in a month. Sidney was so thrilled to be moved into their new home, and so were the children. It was so big, it was like living in a big hotel. The first thing the children did was remind Sidney about the trees for their parents. Sidney told them to find Joe and he would help them. Joe got everything together for the big event. Brandon wheeled Sidney's bed to the opened window so she could watch. Everybody gathered round, and Uncle Alex said a few kind words as the children poured the ashes in the holes. Then, they all sang songs as they planted the trees. The children seemed very happy and content that night as they looked out the window and viewed their trees before going to bed. It pleased Sidney to see them so happy. Sidney told Brandon that night, if anything happened and she should die first, she wanted him to plant a tree on her ashes too. She felt it would be an honor to help a tree grow. She also wanted it to be planted there on their land so she would always be a part of it. Brandon assured her that he felt the same way and asked her to do the same for him if the situation were reversed. Sidney said, "We should write a will and include that in it." They hugged and agreed that was what they would do the very next morning.

All was going well in their new home, and the other houses were near completion. That was to be short-lived. A week and a half before Sidney's seventh month of pregnancy, she went into labor. They rushed her to the hospital. She had big tears in her eyes because she knew this was too soon for the babies. She asked the doctor if he could stop her labor. He told her he would do everything in his power to help her continue carrying the babies for as long as she could. He also knew it was too early for the babies. Their chances for survival would be greatly reduced at this point in time. They managed to stop her pains completely within an hour of her arrival at the hospital. The doctor insisted that Sidney remain in the hospital for the next few days to make sure they had successfully stopped the labor. By the next morning, Sidney's labor pains had returned. This time, they couldn't stop them. The doctor said, "We'll have to deliver at least one of the babies and try to stop the labor." That was the only way she could continue carrying the other two. She asked him if there was something else they could do. She wanted all the babies to survive and be all right. The doctor said, "We can't, your uterus is too small to carry that many babies." She agreed but only if he felt sure he could save the other two. He made her no promises. He explained that was the only chance any of them had.

They took her into the delivery room, with Brandon at her side. They put her out and delivered the little boy. Brandon couldn't believe how small he was. The doctor worked feverishly to get the pains stopped. They succeeded in stopping the labor, but the doctor didn't know for how long. Brandon asked, "How is my son doing?" The doctor said, "At best, his chances are slim. Every day he lives gives him that much better chance of surviving." He told Brandon to trust that they would do everything in their power to save him. There could be problems, though, even if he did survive. They would discuss that if and when the situation presented itself.

When Sidney was conscious, the first thing she asked was where her baby was and if he was all right. Brandon said, "So far, so good." Sidney wanted to see her baby. Brandon told her he was so small, he wasn't sure they could bring him in. Sidney insisted they allow her to see her son. The doctor allowed the nurses to put the incubator in Sidney's room. They sat it up beside her bed so she could reach him. When Sidney looked at her new born son, she saw something in his eyes she had not seen since the last time she looked into Shade's eyes the day he died. She was going to save her child no matter what it took. She told Brandon to bring her the highest-quality stereo he could find. She wanted it to be set up in her room. She also wanted some CDs of harp music. She had read once about premature babies responding well to harp music. She knew it couldn't hurt. The doctor didn't think this baby had much of a chance. Sidney didn't buy into that. She named him Chance Alexander Worthington. Brandon really liked that name. Upon hearing his son's name, he rushed out to get the things Sidney had requested. He knew, if anyone could save his son, she could. The doctor instructed the nurses to let her handle the baby however she wanted to. He explained that he didn't expect the baby to live anyway. Sidney sang to Chance and massaged him. She would carefully remove him from the incubator and lay him across her chest. She even breastfed him. She played the harp music several times a day. When the doctor found out Sidney was breast-feeding Chance and Chance was able to eat and keep it down, he was amazed. Chance was gaining weight. The doctor still hesitated to get her hopes up. Chance was still very small, and his chances were still extremely slim. Even the doctor had to admit, with each passing day, Chance's chances were improving. Sidney, on the other hand, never doubted her little boy would survive. When she did her meditating each morning, she held him close to her heart so he, too, would receive God's blessing. When Sidney would start having pains, she would meditate to stop the pains, without medication. She wanted to give the girls a better beginning than Chance had. After a week in the hospital, the doctor was ready to let Sidney go home. They would keep Chance in the hospital. Sidney wouldn't hear of it. She told the doctor she had to take Chance home with her. He explained to her she wasn't in any condition to take care of such a fragile little baby. She answered, "That's not a problem. I'll hire nurses to work around-the-clock to help care for him." She didn't trust anyone other than herself to make sure he survived. The doctor had to agree that she had worked miracles with him already. He agreed, saying, "I'll make all the necessary arrangements."

When Sidney arrived home with her tiny bundle of joy, she was greeted by everyone, including Peaches. Peaches instantly bonded with this little baby. When they opened the door, Peaches ran inside and followed the incubator into Sidney's bedroom. She lay down beside it, as if to say "I'll stay right here and keep an eye on him." She would lie quietly on the floor, unless he woke up. When he woke up, she would jump up and stand there. If he cried, she would bark for attention. She only left her post to eat and take a bathroom break. The rest of the time, she stood guard. Sidney asked Brandon to bring Peaches's water bowl in and set it beside Chance's incubator so she wouldn't dehydrate.

At first, the nurses didn't like the idea of the dog being that near the baby. They insisted, if she was going to be allowed in his room, she had to be bathed every day. Brandon said, "No problem, she can shower with me." That was so funny. Peaches actually enjoyed taking a shower. Brandon told her not to get too fond of this arrangement. As soon as the baby was well, things would change. Brandon took his blow-dryer and dried her every morning. She liked this too. The nurses were beginning to get rather fond of this gorgeous animal. They couldn't get over how smart she was. One night, as everyone was sleeping, Peaches started barking, with a real panic in her bark. Brandon ran to the incubator and called for the nurse. The baby had stopped breathing. The nurse blew in his face, which made him gasp for air. He immediately started breathing again. Sidney hugged Peaches and told her what a good girl she was. After that, Peaches gained new respect from the nurses. They now knew she was the best baby monitor ever.

A month after Chance arrived, Sidney went into labor again. This time she knew the babies would be born. They rushed her to the hospital, and within an hour, the girls were born. They both weighed five pounds each. They were perfectly all right even though their birth weight was a little low and they were early. Since Sidney already had around-the-clock nursing at home, they allowed her to go home with the babies the next morning. She named the girls Summer Rose, and Sky Larkyn. Sidney had hoped she could carry them long enough to fully develop. She was overjoyed that she had. When Sidney arrived home with the new babies, Peaches seemed confused. She didn't know what to think with three babies. However, she seemed pleased about it. Peaches acted as though these babies were her responsibility and hers alone. While making a house call a few days later, the doctor was very satisfied to see how well all the babies were doing. He told Sidney he would never have believed Chance could have survived and be as perfectly normal as he was. Chance had managed to surpass the girls in weight.

When the babies were all doing well, Brandon had their pictures taken. Brandon and Sidney were holding the triplets in the picture. He wrote a letter to his mother, inviting her to come to their home to meet her grandchildren. He also enclosed an announcement card, a copy of the picture, and a round-trip airplane ticket to Denver to meet her grandchildren. It was all for naught because they never heard back from her. Brandon was okay with that. He didn't want her to come unless she really wanted to. At least his conscience was clear. She now knew she had these wonderful and beautiful grandchildren.

Sidney went to the doctor for her sixth-week checkup. Rosa and Su Yen accompanied her to the doctor's office to help with all the babies. Sidney laughed and said, "We look like an entourage when we go somewhere." When the doctor examined Sidney, he told her she shouldn't have any more children. Having the triplets had resulted in a prolapsed uterus. He said, "Next time, you might not be so lucky." Sidney said, "I may not give birth again, but I think I'll have many more children." The doctor laughed, thinking to himself she already had a bunch. Sidney told him she was happy she was able to have her three sweet little babies. She told him she would be content to care for them. She knew there would be other babies who needed a new mom and dad. He patted her on the back and said, "I can't think of a better person for the job." He told her the triplets were doing so well, it was amazing.

When she returned home, Brandon asked how things went. Sidney hugged him and said, "I hope you won't be to disappointed when I tell you what the doctor said." He looked worried and asked, "What did the doctor say?" She relayed the whole story to him just the way the doctor had told her. Brandon let out a sigh of relief and told her he was afraid it was going to be something really awful. He laughed and said, "I'm not worried. I know you'll make sure we have more kids than we know what to do with." They both had a good laugh, and that was the last time it was discussed.

About a month later, they went to the doctor's office for the babies' shots. There, they met a lady in the waiting room. She was about the same age as that of Su Yen. She was admiring the babies. She introduced herself to Sidney and to Brandon. Her name was Jody, and Sidney noticed how well the babies took up with her. When the doctor went out to help them with the babies, he spotted Jody laughing and cooing to the babies. When they were in the examination room, the doctor told Sidney, if she was still looking for a nanny, Jody would be the ideal person for the job. He told them he hadn't seen her that happy since before her husband and two children were killed in an automobile accident a year ago. He told them she had no family and had been so lost since their deaths. He didn't know why he hadn't thought of this before. Sidney said she would ask her on their way out if she was interested.

When they were ready to leave, the doctor walked out with them. He told Jody what he had discussed with Sidney and Brandon. He told her he hoped she didn't mind. Jody said, "Not at all. I'd be more than happy to take the job." Sidney told her it would be a big job because she had five more children at home. Jody laughed and said, "You really do need help." Sidney asked, "Would you like to go home with us and meet the other children before making any decisions?" Jody agreed to go, but she knew this job was made in heaven for her.

All the way to the ranch, Jody had the babies cooing. Sidney felt certain Jody was the right person for the job. When they arrived home and went inside, the children came running to see if the babies were all right. Jody said, "I assume this is the rest of the family." Sidney introduced her to the children, and they all, one by one, went to Jody and gave her a hug. Sidney asked Jody when she would be available to start work. Jody said, "Today, if that's not too soon." Sidney told her she would have Joe drive her home to get her things. Sidney said, "That is, if you don't mind living here."

"Mind?" said Jody. "I can't wait." She asked Sidney if Joe could run her back to the doctor's office to get her car. She would then go home and pack what she needed. She could drive herself back when she was done. Sidney told her that would be fine and that she could take her time. While she was gone, just to be on the safe side, Brandon did a background check on her. After all, their children were the most important people in the world to him. He saw no reason to take any chances with their welfare. Fortunately, everything checked out. Sidney thanked him for being so thoughtful and aware of the real world.

# Chapter 30

## *Her Life's Work Begins*

It wasn't long before Sidney began to see the purpose, for buying the manufactured homes. Sidney had finally discovered what her business would be. It was the business of helping people. Sidney knew everything you did in life had a purpose. It was usually greater than the one you thought of in the first place. She would use these homes to help homeless families. These were families who ended up homeless due to hard times. She would not only give them a place to live but also give them job training, training in a field they were interested in. When they were able to get back on their feet and make it on their own, she would take in another family. Before she knew it, she was buying more homes and helping more families. Most of the families were single mothers who couldn't afford a place to live. Some of them were working but couldn't earn enough money to survive. They all had different stories, but the end result was the same. Sidney knew she could make a difference in their lives and was determined to do so. Life was good at Paradise Ranch.

Sidney built a community center so they would have a place for the classes. They took turns babysitting while they got their education. They also used this community center for dinners and social events. Sidney was so happy to see these people working so hard to make a difference in their lives. They not only learned a skill but also found jobs so they could move out. After they were on their own, they came back and helped teach the new people. Sidney helped some of the people start their own small businesses. These people not only helped teach others but also hired them when they were ready to work. This system gave them not only an education but also job experience. This had turned out much better than Sidney had ever hoped. It worked out so well Sidney began setting up these centers all over the country.

## Chapter 31

## *What's in a Color?*

One day, Blake came home from school with a black eye and a bloody mouth. He had been beaten up by some boys after school because he wasn't White. You could see by his demeanor what this did to him emotionally. He couldn't understand why the color of his skin made the boys who beat him up so mad. He was such a sweet little boy; how could anyone be so cruel to him? For that matter, how could anyone be so heartless to another human being? It's not like anyone picks the race they want to be. Even if they could, it shouldn't make a difference. The color of your skin doesn't determine who you are or what you'll be like. Sidney wondered when people would learn that it was what was in your heart that was important. Sidney figured it probably wouldn't matter even if we were all the same shade, of the same color. Those who wanted an excuse to be cruel would find some reason.

That night, Sidney was crying over how confused and heartless some people could be. Sidney knew that someone taught those children hatred like that. It certainly wasn't something they were born with. Brandon hugged her and said, "That's what happens when people make no attempt to understand one another." Sidney said, "Our children could have the same thing happen to them." She told him that not only were their triplets biracial but also that many of the other children living there were of different ethnic backgrounds. Some of them were also multiracial. She asked Brandon if things were ever going to change. She wrapped her arms around Brandon and said, "Promise me our children will be taught to love and care about everyone. I want them to know about and respect all people. Their ethnic heritages, customs, religions, and disabilities should be understood, respected, and learned from." She wanted them to understand and incorporate into their own lives whatever is good about all religions, customs, abilities, or disabilities. That would serve to make their lives better. She wanted them to understand the color of a person's skin should never be an issue.

The next day, Sidney called all the children together to discuss what happened to Blake. She took Blake on her lap and explained to the children what happened to Blake was wrong. The color of a person's skin was not important. Blake asked, "Why did God make people with different-colored skin in the first place?" Sidney looked at him with loving eyes and answered him. She said, "Because rainbows are better." Blake and the other children didn't understand. What did rainbows have to do with getting beaten up or the color of a person's skin? Sidney went on, saying, "When God makes a rainbow, it wouldn't be very pretty or interesting if it were all one color. When God gave us rainbows, as a promise, he wanted it to be very special. God knew, when making a rainbow, it's better to use all colors. That's what makes a rainbow beautiful. It's easy to see God loves colors. All you have to do is look at rainbows or flowers. He made them lots of different colors. When he made people, he must have thought the same thing. Color makes us look different, therefore more interesting and beautiful to look at. When I look at all of you, I see a beautiful rainbow of people. Always remember, when you see people of different color or anything that makes them different that rainbows are better. From now on, we'll call our ranch Rainbow Ranch. Here, we'll always celebrate the beauty of rainbows and the differences of our fellow man or woman, whichever the case may be." The children clapped their hands and yelled, "Yeah!" They liked the idea of living at the Rainbow Ranch. The children seemed satisfied with her explanation. She said, "You should feel sorry for the children who have been so mean. It's clear they haven't been taught how to love others and appreciate the gift of everyone being different." With that, the children ran outside to play. She was so happy to watch them and know they weren't filled with such horrible hatred.

Sidney decided to build a private school right there on her property. Then, the children could go to school and be safe, safe from prejudice and harm. She knew she couldn't always protect them, but at least she could give them a head start. She would see to it they were taught much more than the three Rs. She wanted them to be well-rounded individuals. They would learn not only the basics but also the arts, sports, and other cultures. The children would also be taught the everyday skills of living. Things like keeping a checkbook, cooking, buying insurance, working on cars, woodworking, gardening, and running a household, plus many other things. Of course, she left it to each family to decide if their children would go to this school or to public school. When the children were older, they could help decide for themselves if they would rather go to a public school.

Sidney hired only the best teachers. She wanted to make sure the children would be in a loving and learning environment. Their moms also helped with the duties of teaching. This was good for lots of reasons, mainly so they could keep an eye on things and make sure the children were being treated with love, kindness, and respect. The children were doing so well and learning so fast; it was amazing.

Sidney decided it wasn't enough to give people homes and jobs. Some people were living in the streets because of mental illness, physical illness, or drug addiction. She sat up health clinics and asked nurses and doctors to take turns donating their time to help these people. She hired the best drug-addiction therapist to visit the clinics and train the people volunteering to help. She spoke to drug companies and got huge discounts on the medicine needed to treat these people. Sidney and Brandon spent a lot of time and money traveling from city, to city. They helped set up clinics wherever they could. You would think by that time their funds would have been seriously depleted. Quite the contrary was true. Don't forget Sidney had outside help from her dad and from Sal when making her decisions on her stocks. With that kind of help, how could she help but make money?

By Sidney's thirty-fifth birthday, she had gone from a millionaire to a billionaire. Her family had grown, and they now had twenty-two children. At her birthday party, they had a lot to celebrate. She hugged Uncle Alex as she looked around the room. She whispered to him softly, "The love in this room is more precious and valuable than all the money I possess." Uncle Alex laughed, and he said, "Now that's a whole lot of precious because that's a whole lot of dough. All kidding aside, I'm truly amazed at how much money you've amassed. Considering how much money you've spent on other people, it's amazing." She confessed, "It's really astonishing even to me. It seems the more I give, the more I make." It was like God had determined there would always be enough money to continue his work. God knew she would never value money more than loving and helping others. That had to be why he kept giving her more.

Sidney told Uncle Alex she had learned a lot of valuable lessons while earning so much money. The one lesson she felt to be the most valuable was money can only make you as happy as the people you make happy with it. Another one was all good deeds had their own rewards. Sidney went for a stroll in the garden. She looked at the garden and admired what a wonderful work of art Joe and the feng shui master had created. It was breathtakingly beautiful, especially in the moonlight. The air smelled brisk, fresh, and clean, with the subtle aroma of fragrant flowers. When she took in a deep breath, she felt it restore her very soul. As she looked up at the bright stars that filled the clear, dark sky, it occurred to her that everything that had happened to her, good or bad, had happened to bring her to this place in her life. She started whirling around and around, with her arms outstretched, repeating over and over, "Thank you, God! Thank you, God!"

As we leave Sidney alone in the garden, we know she will always do well. We also leave her with the knowledge that our race doesn't matter, or our religion or disabilities, not even our gender. The only true things that matter are our love for one another and a strong belief in something greater than ourselves. May we all live in love and the service of others, no matter who we are.

## RAINBOWS ARE BETTER

As I leave you, my most fervent prayer will be that we all understand our skin is nothing, more or less, than a protective cover around our bodies. The color doesn't matter any more than the color of our hair or the color of our eyes does. God made us all. He made each one of us special, unique, precious, and interesting. Even a deformity makes us fascinating and extraordinary. Having a disability only means we have exceptional abilities to overcome these disabilities. We can all learn from that. If only we can all look at one another as the genuine work of art that each of us is. In the words of Sidney Marie Davis-Worthington, may we never forget "rainbows are better."

# About the Author

Author Carol Lowe was born and raised in the middle of the United States and has always worked to support people of all walks of life to achieve their goals to be their best and happiest selves. She is an amazing mom, with strong family ties. She has three children of her own, as well as many friends of those three children, who have claimed her as their mom too. According to D. Madrigal, "Author Carol Marie is the oldest sister of five who all adore and love her. She has always made each one of us feel as if we were her favorite, but the truth is I am her favorite. I have always told everyone that my sister Carol was the kindest person you will ever meet and I still stand by this statement. She is not only educated and walks with an abundance of common sense but opens her heart to any and all who are in need." Meanwhile, J. Sanders says, "Carol Marie Lowe: three words that equal a beautiful soul."